DOHA 12

A NOVEL

BY LANCE CHARNES

WOMBAT GROUP MEDIA — ANAHEIM, CALIFORNIA

Wombat Group Media
Post Office Box 17190
Anaheim, CA 92817
http://www.wombatgroup.com/

First Printing December 2012
Second Printing October 2016
Third Printing November 2017

ISBN 978-0-9886903-0-1

Cover design by Damonza.

This is a work of fiction. Names, characters, businesses, places, events and incidents are either the products of the author's imagination or used in a fictitious manner. Any resemblance to actual persons, living or dead, or actual events is purely coincidental.

No animals were harmed in the writing of this novel.

Printed in the United States of America

FOR BETTY

WHO PUT UP WITH ALL THIS

Other Books by Lance Charnes

South
The Collection
Stealing Ghosts

For bonus chapters from *Doha 12*, reading group questions and an interview with the author, check out
http://www.wombatgroup.com/doha12/doha12-bonus-material/

DOHA 12

CAST OF CHARACTERS

The "Doha 12"

Jake Eldar: *bookstore manager, Brooklyn*
- Rinnah Eldar: *Jake's wife*
- Eve (Chava) Eldar: *their daughter*
- Gene Eldar: *NYPD inspector; Jake's uncle*

Miriam Schaffer: *legal secretary, Philadelphia*

Nathan Brown: *advertising, East Islip, NY*
Frank Demetrio: *estate lawyer, Burbank, CA*
Andre Dujardin: *architect, Paris*
Erika Grusst: *chemistry professor, Hamburg*
Stuart Kaminsky: *corporate security consultant, Paramus, NJ*
Jules Krosner: *shipping agent, Marseille*
Carlo Massarani: *Maserati executive, Modena*
Oren Nussberger: *IMF, Arlington, VA*
Elia Sabatello: *stockbroker, Milan*
Albert Schoonhaven: *engineer, Rotterdam*

Mossad

Refael Gur (aka Ephraim): *team leader*
Gur's team:
- Amzi Bar'el
- Natan Ettinger
- Kelila Haberman (aka Elena, Sandrine)
- David Holmeyer
- Sasha Panikovsky

Chaim Orgad: *chief of Komemiute; Gur's boss*

Hezbollah

Fadi Alayan (aka Jabbar): *direct-action team leader*
Alayan's team:
- Kassim Haddad: *2nd in command*
- Sohrab Alikhani
- Ziyad al-Amin
- Rafiq Herzallah
- Gabir Raad

Adad al-Shami (aka Majid): *bombmaster, Detroit*
Fayiz Jenyat: *al-Shami's assistant*
Mahir Hashim: *shahid (suicide bomber)*
Haroun Sahabi: *shahid*

Note: A printable cast list is available at
http://www.wombatgroup.com/doha12/doha-12-bonus-material/

ONE

Jake heaved the wheeled metal cart into the Religion section, rolled out his shoulders, then started reshelving the books the morning's customers had left strewn all over the café and lounge. He smiled at the great cosmic joke this section told—Christian Inspiration across from Eastern Religions, Buddhism and Hinduism next to Islam. Nothing burning and nobody dying. Try *that* in the real world.

He didn't have to pull shelf duty—he was the manager, he could get one of the kids to do it—but it let him have some contact with the books as something other than entries on a spreadsheet. Even after six years of ten- or twelve-hour days, he still loved the smell of new books, crisp paper and glue promising new ideas or new worlds.

His phone chirped. He pressed the switch on his headset. "Yeah?"

"Jake, um, could you come down here?" Gwyneth sounded jumpier than usual. "Some kinda scary guys wanna talk to you."

"Sure." Jake sighed, wrestled the overloaded cart out of the aisle, parked it next to the endcap. What set off Gwyneth this time? To her, "scary" meant someone wearing a tie.

He spotted them the moment the escalator brought him within sight of the register counter. Two men, dark suits, safe ties, short hair, watchful eyes. Cops, he figured. What did they want? Gwyneth cowered behind her register a few feet to the right of the cops, wrapping herself tight in her black knit cardigan, as if waiting for the men to bite her.

Jake closed with the men, gave each of them a scan. One fair-

1

haired white, one semi-dark Latino, clean-shaven, thirties, serious. "You looking for me?"

The white one returned the examination. "Jacob Eldar?"

"Yeah."

The cop pulled a flat leather folder from his inside coat pocket, let it fall open. "Special Agent Johanssen, FBI. This is Special Agent Medina. There someplace we can talk?"

"Uh, sure, come on." Jake led them upstairs to the edge of the mostly-empty café. Why would the FBI want to talk to him? Subversive books? Sure, like those would make the buy list.

They sat at a red laminate two-top next to the windows overlooking the street, Jake on one side, both the agents crowded around the other. Kelli, the new girl on coffee duty, took one look at the three of them and skittered to the café's far end to wipe down tables.

Medina started before Jake could think of anything to say. "Do you still hold dual citizenship, Mr. Eldar? American and Israeli?"

"Yeah."

"Are you in contact with anyone in Israel? Other than your parents."

Something scurried around Jake's gut. The FBI knew about his parents? "Couple friends, an army buddy. Why?"

"Have you been approached by anyone with the Israeli government, or, say, an Israeli company?"

He hadn't had any contact with the Israeli government since he'd dragged Rinnah here to get away from the place. He hoped he never would. "No, nobody. What's this about?"

Johanssen leaned his forearms on the table. "Read the paper, Mr. Eldar?"

"Yeah."

"You see about that terrorist guy got killed in Qatar couple weeks back?"

"I saw it happened. Didn't spend a lot of time on it."

"Well." Johanssen tapped the table with two fingers. "Someone using your passport and your name may have been involved. You lend your passport to anyone, Mr. Eldar?"

Jake glanced between the two agents, wondering when they'd break out laughing and the guy with the video camera would pop out from behind the espresso machine. "Are you serious? Why would I do that?"

Medina pulled a paper from inside his coat, unfolded it, smoothed it on the middle of the table. "Do you know this man?"

A man in his forties stared back at him from the grainy, blown-up passport photo. Triangular face, broken nose, straight black hair, moustache, sober glasses. Darkish skin; he could be any kind of Mediterranean, even Latino. "Never saw him before."

"According to Qatari Immigration, that's Jacob Eldar of 475 18th Street, Brooklyn."

Shit. Jake looked into the fixed dark eyes in the photo. His name, his address. But why him? What else did this guy take? "Who is he really?"

Johanssen shrugged. "Don't know. Smart money's on Mossad right now. You know, the Israeli CIA."

"I know who they are." And wished he didn't, but the Feds didn't need to know about that. "Can't help you. Sorry."

The two agents exchanged *are you done?* glances. Medina flashed Jake a polite smile, snapped a business card down on the table. "Thank you for your time, Mr. Eldar. If you think of anything, please call." They stood; so did Jake.

He shook hands with them both. "Buy some coffee while you're here. We need the business."

Jake drifted back downstairs to the customer service desk while the agents confused Kelli with their orders. He slumped on the stool, stared at the company screen saver bouncing across the computer monitor. *Mossad used my name? Why?* It couldn't be random; Mossad didn't do random.

Payback?

He braced his elbows on the green laminate desktop, lowered his face into his hands.

Mossad did payback.

TWO

12 SEPTEMBER
TEL AVIV, ISRAEL

Refael Gur's morning coffee hadn't yet kicked in when he got the call to report to the chief's office. This, he didn't need. He needed to dedicate his first day back at Mossad headquarters to his expense vouchers and the mission report. The accountants probably already flagged him late with his receipts.

He threaded his way through the narrow hallways, returning nods, ignoring the whispers as he passed. *Komemiute* was a small operation; it didn't take an intelligence analyst to figure out who'd done the Doha job. At least he was finally rid of that damn moustache.

Chaim Orgad glanced up from the paper he was signing when Gur knocked on his doorframe. "Raffi." He pointed to the chrome-framed chair in front of his desk. Gur didn't have to be told to close the door behind him.

Orgad tossed the morning's *Yediot Aharonot* in Gur's lap. Gur already knew what the front-page headline said; the same as every other newspaper in Israel that morning. He skimmed the story to see if this bunch knew anything more than *Haaretz.*

> DOHA, Qatar — The Qatari National Police revealed today that Masoud Talhami, who was discovered dead of an apparent heroin overdose in his luxury hotel room on August 30, may have been killed by an Israeli assassination squad.
>   Talhami, 53, a ranking member of Hezbollah's military committee, was

one of the instigators of the second
Palestinian intifada…

"I've seen it."

"Good. So?"

"So what? We knew they'd figure it out. I told you this would be a repeat of Dubai. I guess the P.M. didn't care?"

"Perhaps. We'd get blamed even if the bastard cooked himself, so perhaps the P.M. decided it was worth being rid of him." Orgad slapped closed a folder, flapped it into his plastic out box. "What did they find? What do they have on you?"

Gur shrugged. "Lots of video, I'm sure. We took out the camera covering Talhami's door, but it's not even worth trying to get them all. It's not like when you were in the field anymore." It was hard to picture this gray-fringed, paunchy, bald old man as a trained killer, but Gur knew better. Menachem Begin hadn't looked much like an assassin, either. "Nothing physical in the hotel. We didn't stay there except for the couple of hours around the job, and I made sure the team kept their gloves on. The Qataris will eventually find the rooms we stayed in, but the maids will have taken care of anything we left behind there. So, probably nothing."

Orgad nodded, folded his hands over the faded windowpane-plaid shirt stretched across his belly. "At least you didn't look into the cameras, like those idiots in Dubai." He pointed to the newspaper. "Still, there you are on the front page. I have a meeting with the Director at ten. He'll want to know why we can't manage a simple job without becoming media stars. What do I tell him?"

"Tell him we can't do this shit anymore." Gur twirled the newspaper back onto Orgad's desk blotter. "1972 was a long time ago. There's too damn many cameras now. There's biometrics in the passports. There's watch lists. You can't use cash anymore. It's over, Chaim. Let's just build ourselves some more drones and kill these bastards from a thousand miles away, like the Americans."

Orgad frowned as he, eyed Gur across the cheap laminate desk. Gur avoided him by roving his gaze around this monk's cell of an office. The only wall decorations were the official photos of the President and Prime Minister. In this line of work, you didn't accumulate a lot of pictures of yourself with your co-workers, far

5

less with the high and mighty.

Finally, Orgad stopped nodding. "Those are the words of a tired man."

Gur flashed back two weeks: the nighttime view of Doha from the twelfth floor. That miserable prostitute-addict they'd dredged out of the guest-worker slums at the southwest end of the city, a jumble of skin-wrapped bones dead on the bed from an overdose of pure Afghan heroin. That bastard Talhami, drugged and stuffed full of vodka before he followed the whore to hell. His team watching the scene unfold, surrounded by the beige luxury of yet another high-end hotel in yet another city he'd never wanted to see. *This is how I serve my country.* Would the man whose name he'd used—Jaakov Eldar—be proud of what they'd done?

"Raffi?"

"I can't stop being tired," he sighed. "We do this—" Gur pointed toward the paper "—over and over, and it doesn't help. We're not winning the war. We can't kill our way to victory." He knew he shouldn't say these things to his boss, but he didn't care anymore. He'd be happy to sit a desk for the next ten years until he retired. Maybe he could try to build another life if he wasn't always a visitor to his own homeland.

Orgad nodded some more, then folded his arms on the desktop. "Well. You need a rest. Things always look dark after a nasty job. Tsach Voydievsky just left for embassy duty in Brazil, so the Director needs an interim day chief in the Watch Center. I'll give him your name. With your face all over the news, you'll have to stay home anyway."

Whatever *home* was. "Thanks. We should keep an eye on those people whose names we used, just in case. We've put them in harm's way, it's the least we can do."

"In case Hezbollah decides to go after them? You know that's not how they play the game. Stay out of nightclubs and cafes for a couple of weeks, wait for the bombing, then we move on, yes?"

Gur tried not to grimace. They had an obligation to those people. "Yes, of course." He stood, turned to the door, then stopped. "When did you know it was time to get out of the field?"

"When I almost shot my wife sneaking into the bedroom with breakfast for me on my birthday. But you?" Orgad squinted at Gur, as if looking into his skull. "I think you're close. We'll talk in a few days. *Shalom*, Raffi."

THREE

13 SEPTEMBER
HARET HRAIK, SOUTH BEIRUT, LEBANON

Fadi Alayan stood on the seventh-floor balcony with his face turned to the buttery afternoon sun. Happy traffic sounds pinged off the apartment-block canyon to bless his ears. Car and truck horns, engines revving, squawks from tires spinning too suddenly or stopping too fast. Arabic rap, Lebanese pop, Nelly Furtado. An ambulance siren, the neighbors' television turned too loud.

Noise was a good thing, a happy thing. After the 2006 war with the Zionists, this area lay destroyed, the streets piled with concrete rubble and torn-apart cars. You could hear from a block away the women crying in the night for the innocent dead. Among those dead were his wife and parents. He could still see the ruins of their bodies when his mind went to the wrong places.

Now the martyrs were buried, the apartments rebuilt and the markets open again. Kids played in the alleys and went to school. Alayan watched the people stream by on the sidewalks below his balcony. His pride stood tall inside him; in his own little way, he'd helped bring this area back to life.

Him, and the Party of God. Hezbollah.

"Fadi." Alayan glanced over his shoulder to Kassim, who stood in the open sliding door. He looked himself again: carefully dressed, hair neatly cut, the dark circles gone from around his large eyes. The last job had been hard on them all. "Rafiq finally showed up. They're all here."

Alayan nodded, took one last look at the street parade, then followed his lieutenant into the white-walled apartment. He detoured to the kitchen, grabbed a bottle of Raya water from the humming refrigerator, then straddled the wood-frame chair at the

8

little living room's center. Two overused blue sofas met in the opposite corner. Two of his team sprawled on the sofa to his right; three, including Kassim, filled the one to his left, under the yellow-and-green martyr poster Ziyad had taped up the day before. Masoud Talhami gazed back at him out of the poster, clean and sober and serious in a dark business suit and *kaffiyeh*. The stupid son of a whore.

"All right," Alayan started. "You men are doing okay? You're rested?" He looked from face to face. Each nodded in his turn. Kassim lit one of his wretched Byblos cigarettes. Rafiq, as usual, looked like he'd just rolled out of bed. "Are you getting any sleep, Rafiq?"

"Trying not to, *sidi*."

Alayan shook his head, bemused. "Well, stay out of the clubs tonight. Get your lives in order. Shave. We have work, and we're going to be gone a while."

His team woke up, sat up straighter, watched with sharper eyes. He could hear the speculation whir in their brains.

He nodded toward the poster. "The Qataris are certain the Zionists killed Talhami. The Mossad. So far they've released the names of twelve people on the country team, and they're still digging. Knowing it's Mossad, eight to sixteen's the usual number."

"I knew it," Ziyad said. "Who else, except maybe the Americans?"

Alayan took a swig of water, thought about how to say this next part. "*Sayyid* Nasrallah pledged our revenge for this on al-Manar. The Council has decided we're the ones to deliver it."

Now all of them leaned forward, elbows or forearms on their knees, eyes locked on his face. Gabir smiled like a hungry dog, dark head bobbing over his tight green, long-sleeved t-shirt. "We finally get to drive a bomb into the Dizengoff mall?"

"No." Gabir frowned; Alayan knew he'd pout now. "No, we're not doing anything like that. That's just what the Jews expect, and that's not what the Council wants this time." He folded his arms on top of the chair's back. "Think about the Mossad for a moment."

"Bastards," muttered Ziyad.

"Maybe. But think of their reputation. Why does the world

think they're the best intelligence service?"

"Because fucking Spielberg made that movie about them," Sohrab snarled.

"Yes, but why? Because they've got balls the size of melons. They tracked down Black September after Munich and wiped them out. They went at it for twenty years. They went all over Europe to do it. Even when they failed, like they did in Norway, they got through it with sheer balls.

"How many Hamas men have they killed? How many of our people have they martyred? I can't keep track. They do it, and everybody knows they do it, and they still almost never get caught. Yes, Ziyad, they're bastards, but, think about it." Alayan watched the team's faces harden. "I'm not praising them, don't think that. But look at what they did to Talhami. He didn't just die. He died a drunken heroin addict in bed with a Western whore. The Mossad didn't just kill him, they destroyed his reputation. They used his own weaknesses against him. That's what they do best."

Ziyad and Sohrab looked away, not so willing to be indignant now. *Good.* Alayan needed these men to think, not just be mad. Anger would make them sloppy, and he couldn't afford that, not this time.

"How would we have done a job like that? We'd get righteous and pledge our lives to Allah and blast the face off a hotel and kill dozens of people. All the Western news programs would show video of bloody women and dead babies and talk about 'terrorists' and 'murderers.'" He watched Kassim nod; they'd talked about this before. "We probably wouldn't even kill the man we're trying for. That's what the Jews expect. They expect us to be stupid."

Ziyad's eyes crinkled as if he would cry. "How can you say these things about our martyrs, *sidi?*"

"Because it's true. Yes, we revere them, we pray to Allah to take them into his heart and reward them in Paradise, but we're *not winning the war.* So we're going to use Mossad's rules." He drained his water bottle and set it on the tiled floor beside the chair leg, waiting for the puzzlement to settle on the men's faces. "The Mossad country team used American and European passports belonging to real people in those countries. They've been doing that for years. They did the same thing in the Dubai job, with

Mabhouh. In that one, most of the people lived in Palestine. This time, they all live in other countries." Alayan paused, let them think. "We're going to find them and kill them."

Gasps. Wide eyes.

"Wait, wait, wait." Rafiq leaned forward, held up his hand to signal *stop*. "They're not Mossad. They weren't in the Gulf. Why are we wasting our time?"

"Because it's what the Zionists would do if they were us." He stood, rotated his bad left shoulder, then stepped around the chair. "What do we want to do? Kill Mossad agents? Who would care besides the Zionists? We want to send a message to the rest of the world. 'Mossad is killing your people too. *They* brought this on you. *They're* the real terrorists.'"

Alayan did another face check; five pairs of eyes stared back. Kassim and Sohrab seemed to be getting the point. He focused on Gabir. If the dullest one of them understood, they all would. "Remember, the Jews used to ask before they used other people's passports. If these people let Mossad use their identities, they're part of the same gang. If they didn't, then they're innocent victims of Mossad's murderers. Look at the reaction after Dubai. Australia almost recalled their ambassador. The British started saying things *we* usually do. Now imagine if their citizens die because of something those Mossad bastards did." He let them imagine. Even Gabir nodded now. "Rafiq, if it makes you feel any better, they're all Zionists, just living outside Palestine."

He watched them absorb the terms of this new mission. He'd prepared them for this over the past eighteen months; their surprise didn't last long. It wasn't time yet for them to know the rest of the Council's orders. With any luck, that time may not come.

Sohrab, the slightest and youngest-looking of them, awash in a too-large blue track suit, put on the most evil smile. "When do we start?" His heavy Persian accent made his Arabic sound mumbled, even when he spoke up.

"We pick up our documents tomorrow. Once we enter Europe, we'll travel on European passports. Gabir, how's your French these days?"

"*Tres bon.*"

"Good. You'll be French Moroccan again. If you weren't so

11

dark, we could do something else with you." A couple of the others chuckled. Kassim ruffled Gabir's shaggy black hair. "We'll fly into different airports at different times and meet in Amsterdam in four days. We'll make contact in the usual way. Save your questions until tomorrow. Now go get ready."

FOUR

Miriam had just returned to her desk when her intercom buzzed. "Ms. Schaffer? Could you come here for a moment, please?"

"Yes, sir." She took a deep breath, straightened her charcoal suit skirt, gathered her notepad and pen, then stepped into her boss' office.

The high-backed leather chair put a great halo of black around Clark Dickinson's blond, white bread-handsome head. He twisted a heavy silver pen in his hands. "Close the door, please."

Now what have I done? Miriam shut the door silently, then turned and stood at attention. The office could double for a squash court; it always made her feel small, no matter how hard she tried to ignore everything but the big, modern tropical-hardwood desk.

"Carla at Reception tells me those were FBI agents who came to see you. Is that true?"

Miriam made a note to strangle Carla the next time they were alone together. "Yes, sir."

"Is there something I should know about?"

All the firm's partners thought they needed to know everything about everybody; Dickinson was no different. "It's all a mistake, sir. The people who killed that terrorist in the Middle East a couple weeks ago used other people's names. Mine was one of them."

Dickinson swiveled left and right, over and over. His eyes never stopped examining her. "Why would they use your name?"

"I don't know, sir. I'm wondering the same thing, myself."

"Is it because you're from Israel?"

"It could be." That would explain a lot. But why her? The

13

woman who'd used her name was maybe in her mid-thirties like Miriam, but looked nothing like her. *How do things like this happen? Hadn't she paid enough already?*

"I see. And you knew nothing about this."

She recognized the accusation in his voice. Miriam knew Mossad used to ask permission to borrow people's identities; her stepfather had let them do that once. But they'd never given her the opportunity to tell them *no*. "No, sir, I didn't. It's a surprise to me, too."

Dickinson flexed his shoulders. He probably thought it made him look tougher, but to Miriam it just made him look like a squirming little boy. "Is this going to become a problem, Ms. Schaffer?"

A problem? "Well… no, sir, I can't think why it would."

"Really." Dickinson tossed his pen onto the open case file in front of him. "This firm has a number of important clients from the Gulf region, you know that, right?"

"Yes, sir, I know that." It also had a few Jewish clients, but she knew he wouldn't go into that.

"So now some of your people killed one of theirs, and used your name to do it. You can't see how that could be a problem?"

She almost blurted, "*My* people?" but swallowed it. Then she nearly led with, "That man was a terrorist!" but cut that off, too. She had no comeback that wouldn't result in "you're fired."

"Sheikh Saleh has already mentioned your attitude to me. This could upset him further."

That weasel Saleh probably funneled his zakat *straight to Hamas.* "Sir, I'm perfectly polite to the Sheikh, just like I am with every other client. Mr. Henshaw never had any issues with my work or my attitude, and I haven't changed a thing."

Dickinson put on his you-poor-dear smile. "Miriam, Saleh's a sheikh. He expects more than 'perfectly polite.' And I have different standards than Henshaw did. I can't allow your feelings about Moslems to harm this firm or its clients. Understand?"

"With Arabs, not Moslems." She wanted to grab the words and stuff them back into her mouth the moment they escaped, but too late. Then the regret turned to contempt. He simply had no idea. What would this Main Line rich boy do if he had to sit through a rocket attack, like she had? Piss his two-thousand-dollar suit?

Calm down, she reminded herself. *You need the job.* "Yes, sir." She just couldn't fawn over that toad Saleh the way her boss did, no matter how many billable hours the man was worth.

"All right, then. As good as you are at your job, you're just a secretary and secretaries *are* replaceable. For now, please take your nameplate down. The Sheikh will be visiting tomorrow, and I don't want to have to explain any of this to him. Is that clear?"

Miriam squared her shoulders and jaw. She knew it made her look taller. "Is there anything else, sir?"

"That's all."

She turned a crisp about-face and marched from the office. She could still do that after all these years, even in heels. She tried very hard not to slam the door on her way out.

FIVE

23 SEPTEMBER
ROTTERDAM, THE NETHERLANDS

Albert Schoonhaven pedaled carefully down the red asphalt bike path along Prins Alexanderlaan. He'd been overheated in the pub, but now the damp evening chill clawed through his trouser legs and down his neck. He took one hand off the handlebars to pull his rough wool coat collar tighter around his throat.

He knew he'd had too much to drink. Everyone was having such a good time, though, with plenty of fun at his expense. Pieter had bought a bright yellow water gun for him and waved it at everyone at the pub. "For your next secret mission!" he crowed.

It had been that way for two weeks, ever since the Qataris announced the names of the people who killed that Arab. Albert had awakened one day to find his name in the *Algameen Dagblad*. He hadn't even thought about the Mossad in the twelve years since he'd left Israel, and now he was linked to some spy adventure. How crazy the world was.

The humming streetlights wore amber mist halos and flashed off the windshields of the oncoming cars. Apartment-block windows glowed softly on the other side of the tram line to his right; offices sat dark on his left, with the occasional lit house or flat in between. Even at night, everything was very Dutch—clean and orderly and a little cold.

He rolled past the blocky brick-and-concrete De Nieuwe Unie building—the glass lobby dark and still—and braked at the intersection with Kralingseweg. He obediently waited for the green light, got a wobbly start in the crosswalk. He passed the Schenkel tram station, bumped over the tracks. Almost home.

Traffic was just a rumor off the main street. Not many people

16

were out at this hour. Albert noticed a man crossing the little bridge over a night-black fragment of the Hollandse Ijssel, just past the bus shelter. The man moved slowly, as if he had no place to go. Albert registered blue jeans and a gray pullover with a hood that shadowed the man's face.

They passed each other at the bridge's end.

Albert Schoonhaven didn't notice the man turn. He never heard the shot that killed him.

Alayan watched the Jew tumble backward off his bicycle, bounce off the bike path and roll against the curb. The bike glanced off the bridge railing, clattered onto its side. He tucked the still-warm pistol under his sweatshirt. He always took the first kill of every mission to show the men he could do the work, not just plan it.

He glanced toward the tram station's car park. A couple dozen meters away, Sohrab held up their compact black video camera and smiled. All on tape.

Just as we'd planned, Alayan thought. He quickly dragged the body onto the grass next to the bridge, tugged out the man's wallet, then rolled him into the canal. Gabir jogged out of the nearby bus shelter, grabbed the bike, dropped it over the railing. Two minutes later, they headed north on Prins Alexanderlaan toward the A20 and, eventually, Amsterdam.

Perfect. Alayan leaned back into his seat and sighed. *Eleven to go.*

SIX

"Well, look who's here! It's James Bond!"

Jake shook his head in exasperation. If he'd had a buck for every time he'd heard that over the past three weeks... "Hello to you too, Gene." He stepped back to allow room for the screen door, then walked into his uncle's beefy arms.

"Hey, kid, don't let it get to you." Gene Eldar pounded Jake's back, then held him out at arm's length. "Glad you could make it way out here in the country."

"Like we'd miss Petey's birthday." He held out the present wrapped in shiny blue paper. "Where's the monster grandson, anyway?"

"Out back, with all the other little monsters." Gene took the box, let Jake through the door, then threw his arms open again. "Rinnah! Come here, beautiful!" He buried Jake's wife in a hug, traded loud cheek-kisses with her. "You're way too good for this nut. Ready to run away with me?"

Rinnah pulled back and aimed a deadly eyebrow at him. "Monica says you can go now?"

Gene turned her loose and clapped a hand to his heart. "The way you do me, it's good you're gorgeous." His white dress shirt threatened to split across his back when he leaned over the little girl hanging back at the step's edge, all pink dress and wild black curly hair, a Princess Jasmine doll clutched to her chest. "There's my Chava! Look at you! Say, will you marry me? Your mama won't take me."

Eve smiled and stuck an index finger in her mouth. "No. I'm gonna marry Petey."

18

Gene let her hug his neck, then told her, "Your future husband is out back, go get him." Eve burst past and charged down the hall. "Come on in, you two. Chava's grown, what, a foot since last month?"

"It's Eve," Jake said, "and yeah, we can't keep clothes on her."

Jake knew his uncle's two-story Colonial wasn't large by neighborhood standards, but compared to the apartment in Brooklyn, it was a palace. Cream-colored walls covered with framed photos, crown molding, wall-to-wall carpet, rooms the size of nightclubs; was this even the same city?

Short-haired men wearing loose, untucked shirts or light windbreakers overflowed the house. Bulges that weren't cell phones appeared at waistbands and the smalls of backs. Cop parties. Jake never knew whether to believe he was incredibly safe or one drink away from a firefight.

Gene ushered them into the crowded family room overlooking the back yard. "What can I get you to drink?"

Rinnah broke away from admiring the grassy back yard. "Wine?"

"Out back, with the women."

She uncorked one of her neon-white smiles. "I'll talk to Monica about that trip to Tahiti you keep promising to me." Rinnah gave Jake a quick kiss, then sauntered through the milling cops out the open patio slider.

Gene said, "Love that accent of hers."

"I can get her to swear at you in Hebrew, like she does to me. That oughtta really turn you on."

Gene snorted and shook his head. "Beer?"

"Sure."

Bottles in hand, they pulled up a corner of the kitchen counter overlooking the yard. A swarm of little kids charged around like multicolored locusts, laughing and squealing and falling down.

"Never thought I'd see an INTERPOL Red Notice on any nephew of mine," Gene said. "Seriously, kid, how you doing?"

Jake shrugged. "Okay. Crank calls have petered out. Since that jumper on the D line, I'm old news, reporters aren't ambushing me outside the apartment anymore. Now it's just little stuff, people calling me 'James Bond.'"

Gene held up his hands, a silent *what can you do?*

Jake shook his head. "There's a regular at the store, Mrs. Daumberg, sweet old gal, comes by every day. She's volunteered to babysit Eve if I have to go off and kill bad guys again."

A shaved-bald hulk slid by, draped in an aloha shirt that fit like a tarp. He slapped Jake hard on the bicep. "Hey, Jake, good going with that terrorist fuck."

"Yeah, thanks." Jake sighed. "See that, Gene? That's my life now."

"Could be worse. Your name could be Talhami." Gene angled his stoutness closer to his nephew. "You, um, haven't had any trouble? No guys hanging around who shouldn't be, anything like that?"

"Nooo. Why?"

Gene held up his hand. "Nothing. Just wondering."

"Bullshit. What?"

Jake watched with a tinge of alarm as his uncle began to look uncomfortable. Gene ran his thick fingers through his wavy gray hair. "Okay, look. Shit like this brings out the crazies, you know? The religious fanatics, the bush-league holy warriors, the skinheads, the Trilateral Commission cranks, all the wingnuts."

The beer soured in Jake's mouth. "What are you saying?"

"I'm saying whoever did this hung a sign around your neck. I don't want to see some wanna-be Johnny Jihad or some cut-rate Nazi take a crack at you."

"You seriously think anyone'll bother?"

"Look, kid, I'm a Jew, I worry, it's in my DNA. Just keep an eye out, that's all."

"I live in Brooklyn. You think I don't pay attention when I go outside?"

They fell silent, nursed their beers and thoughts. Jake watched the kids run around outside, Eve in the middle of the pack. He could handle whatever came his way, but what if someone went after his wife or daughter? The shadow of that thought ran a shiver up his neck.

"I hope this is serious man talk, because the women are arguing about wallpaper."

Jake turned, looped an arm around Rinnah and pulled her

against his hip. She fit well with him; she always had. Her touch made him feel warm and safe again. He cranked up a reassuring smile. "You gave up wallpaper for us?"

"Just shop talk," Gene said. He waved his beer bottle toward her wine glass. "Refill?"

"No, thank you." She put down her glass, swiped the bottle from Jake's hand and took a long pull. "Police talk or book talk? I hope police talk. Bookstore gossip is really boring."

"Oh, thanks," Jake groused. Rinnah popped up and kissed his chin. Eight years together, and her kisses still lit him up. The wind had scattered her dark-brown pixie-cut hair, and her olive skin glowed. Was it from the wine or the early-autumn tang in the air? Maybe it was just from being someplace green and spacious and quiet. He wished he could give her quiet. It was never quiet in the city, and green came in pots on windowsills.

"Actually—" Gene pushed a new beer in Jake's direction "—I was telling my favorite nephew here we're hiring analysts in the Intel Division again. I can talk to the deputy there, put in a word."

Jake snorted. "So it's true—you've started talking to yourself."

"Hey, sometimes it's the only person I can have an intelligent conversation with." Gene stood so he could look squarely at both of them. "Seriously, your background, you'd be perfect. Starts at seventy, you know our benefits are bulletproof."

Almost half again what he earned at the bookstore, plus benefits only the executives got. But it would mean plunging back into the swamp he'd climbed out of over ten years before and sworn never to go near again.

He glanced down to see Rinnah's huge, dark eyes watching him. He knew what she was thinking. Larger apartment. Save something for Eve's college. Go out for something nicer than cheap Thai every once in a while. Another round of the same discussion.

"NYPD's family," Gene said. "We take care of each other. Protect each other. Know what I'm saying, kid?"

"Yeah. I'll think about it."

Family. That's what they'd said in the army, too. They'd lied.

SEVEN

Al-Shami was already connected to the computer in his home's spare bedroom when the Skype call came in. "Majid?"

"Yes. Altair."

Codewords exchanged, al-Shami's handler asked, "Are you well? Any problems?"

"No problems. The weather here is miserable and this city is worse than you can imagine."

"So everything's normal. *Jayed.*" Even on the muddy voice-over-IP connection, al-Shami could hear the man in Lebanon sigh. "The Council is activating *Muhunnad* for 17 Muharram."

It took al-Shami a few moments to convert the Islamic date to something useful. The 23rd of December. First day of Hanukkah. "Target?"

"*Yasir.*"

Al-Shami let out a whistle. Finally, they were serious this time.

"Are your *shuhada* ready?"

"Yes, of course." For months, waiting for the Council to make up its mind. He leaned back into his black armless office chair, swiveled, stared at a mental checklist. He had nearly everything he needed—a vehicle, electronics, detonators, a payload. He had work ahead of him to assemble everything for this particular target, but that's why the Party paid him.

Yasir. The Party had finally decided to stop sparing the nation that made the Zionist terror possible. The Americans would experience the 1983 Beirut Marine barracks attack all over again. But this time, it would happen in a place they couldn't ignore.

"Right. I'll get started."

EIGHT

16 OCTOBER
BEVERLY, NEW JERSEY

Miriam brushed a few tattered leaves from the lawn, sat, wrapped her arms around her knees. She turned her face to the sun for a few moments, took what warmth she could from the pale blob fighting the chill and losing. Only a murmur of voices a few rows of markers away broke the ringing silence.

Fifteen times she'd come here, once a month. She'd seen the place from summer humidity through autumn's flaming trees to the still of blanketed snow, spring rain and green, back to summer and fall. Now another winter snapped at autumn's heels. The first winter was cold and dark and empty, a perfect mirror for her moods. What would this one be like?

She brushed the grass over the grave with her fingertips. Cool, a little damp, but still springy for a few more weeks, until the first snow. Then she traced the engraved cross on the headstone with her eyes and read the inscription. It was a ritual; she knew the words by heart.

WILLIAM
JAMES
SCHAFFER
GYSGT
US MARINE CORPS
JUL 18 1974
JUL 20 2010
SILVER STAR
PURPLE HEART
OPERATION

23

IRAQI FREEDOM
OPERATION
ENDURING FREEDOM

"Hi, darling," she said. "It's getting cold early. Most of the leaves are down by now. Last month they were just turning color. Remember how pretty they were?"

She waited to hear his voice. When she'd first started these visits—back when the grass over his grave was just rectangles of fresh sod—she could hear him so clearly, talking back. But his voice had slowly faded and now it was gone, just like that. Just like one day he was gone.

"You'll love this. The Mossad used my name in some assassination plot over in the Gulf. I guess they had a female agent, and she was me for a while. Can you believe it? So now I'm wanted by INTERPOL, or at least my name is. I think the woman's prettier than I am. The FBI came to talk to me—that was exciting." She'd like to hear Bill chuckle at the situation, but imagining was all she could do.

"Dickinson's still being an ass, as usual. He wanted me to take down my nameplate so that damn sheikh wouldn't be upset by my name, since I used it to kill some terrorist. Well, I didn't. Honestly, I forgot. Well, that pompous Arab jerk comes strolling in with his entourage, and he takes one look at my nameplate and says, 'I hope you're not going to kill me, too, Mrs. Schaffer.' Ha ha ha, everybody had a big laugh. So I said, 'Not as long as you have an appointment, sir.' And they laughed." She pulled up a few blades of grass and hurled them away from her. "He complained to Dickinson, who read me out, so now I'm on some kind of probation. I'm really getting to hate that place."

No answer. She didn't expect one, but an answer would've been nice.

"Listen to me, complaining. That's what you get for marrying a Jewish girl." In the first few months, this was when Miriam would start to cry. She ran out of tears sometime last winter. In a lot of ways, she'd run out of feelings, too. She could go two or three weeks without noticing she hadn't laughed at anything. True, she wasn't sad so often anymore, but neither was she happy. Angry, she could still do.

"Look, there's this guy at the gym. Really nice, a couple years older than you. His wife died of leukemia last year. We've talked a few times." She swallowed. "Well, he's asked me out. On a date." She stroked the grass covering her husband and started to feel like a traitor. "I want to go, Bill. I'm lonely. All my friends are married and have kids and I'm tired of them being nice to poor Miriam the widow lady. I want someone to talk to. Someone who'll talk back. Someone who can hold me."

Miriam stared at the skeletal trees a few yards away, slate gray against a sky the blue of skim milk. She had to admit to herself the Mossad thing had made her feel more alive than she had for a year. A little scared, yes, but also a little excited. Someone had noticed her. She'd been something other than the grieving widow to someone.

An unexpected flash of anger hit. *You left me, damn you.* "I'm not asking for permission. I just want to tell you what I'm doing and why." She swallowed the little burst of flame before it grew too hot. He wasn't the one to blame. "I hit my 'pause' button when you died, and I think it's time to press 'play' again, don't you? I'm tired of feeling like I belong down there with you instead of up here, living."

She stood, brushed the grass and leaf bits from the seat of her jeans. She took a round, white pebble from her pocket and placed it on the marker. "I'll always love you, darling. Always. And I'll still visit. But I want to live now." She kissed her fingertips, pressed them to the marble, then slowly paced away.

25

NINE

Orgad looked up from the paper Gur had handed him. "Three of them?"

"In the past month."

"Hm. A robbery in Rotterdam, a fall down stairs in Hamburg, and a mugging in Paris." Orgad carefully laid the paper on his desk. "Not exactly uncommon events."

Gur had expected this reaction. If he'd been on the other side of the desk, he might say the same thing. "We used twelve names. Ten were on the Qatari list. Massarani and Nussberger aren't ours. Now three of them are dead in a little less than a month. What are the odds?"

"To live as an Israeli is to beat the odds every day." Orgad folded his hands on his belly. "The Watch Center belongs to the Director. Why are you telling me this?"

"I trust you."

"Ah. So, what do you propose?"

"Have Kaisarut tell the *Police Nationale* and the *Carabinieri*. If the pattern holds, they'll go to Marseille next, then Italy. They can say we've noticed a pattern, or we're hearing chatter, or whatever they think they can sell. Someone needs to look out for the other nine."

Orgad pooched out his lips, pushed the summary around the blotter with his finger. "We call the French and the Italians and tell them their citizens whose identities we borrowed are now being killed by—who? Hezbollah?" He held out a hand, palm up. "Do we have proof? No. We have a hunch. But we have very good hunches, trust us." He dropped his hand to the desk. "The French just

26

cancelled a cultural exchange program the P.M.'s wife was sponsoring. The Italians recalled their ambassador. All this, and we haven't admitted we're behind Doha. So imagine if we do." Orgad shook his head. "Raffi, what are you doing to me here?"

Gur rubbed the throbbing in his right temple. "We should tip them off somehow. We could work the *Mishteret* connection, do a cop-to-cop warning. But there's something else we need to think about."

"That is?"

"If someone's working the list, they're going to run out of Europeans pretty soon. You know what happens then."

"Then they move on to America."

"And you're worried about the Italians?"

Orgad sighed, shook his head as if it was swollen and painful. "Thank you for ruining my day. But there's no proof. It's three people in three different countries, victims of street crime or accidents. Tragic, but not a pattern yet. I need more, you know that."

Gur set his elbows on his knees, rubbed his eyes. "Yes, I know that."

Orgad nodded slowly for a few moments, taking all this in. Then he cleared his throat. "No warnings. One loudmouthed cop in Milan can turn this into a total disaster for us. Keep an eye on the situation, let me know what happens."

Gur didn't know why he'd expected anything different. Above all else, the Institute looked after itself. "All right. For everybody's sake, I hope I'm wrong."

"That would be good."

TEN

Eve giggled and belted out, "*Jia yow! Jia yow!*"

"Shh!" Jake shifted under Eve's weight on his thigh. "You don't have to yell."

"Kai-lan did."

"Yeah, well, her neighbors don't mind. Okay, click on the next one."

Eve strained against his arm holding her against his chest. Her four-month-old, pink Dora the Explorer pajamas were already too small. She wrapped her little hand around the laptop's mouse and clicked on the picture of anime-eyed Kai-lan tugging a cart. "*La!*"

"That's too easy," Eve said. When she crinkled her nose, she looked just like her mother.

Rinnah appeared at Jake's right shoulder, in sweat pants and an olive sleep shirt. "No more Chinese tonight. Time for bed, *ahrnavon*. Say goodnight to Daddy."

"*Ai ya*, Mommy!"

"It's time. No whining." Rinnah made a face at Jake, switched to Hebrew. "You *could* teach her Hebrew, you know."

He answered in Hebrew, "At least she can use this." He poked the fidgeting little girl on both sides of her waist, returned to English. "Sleepy time, Bunny."

Eve threw her arms around Jake's neck and peeped, "*Bao-bao!*"

He did as he was told and hugged her back. Every time he held his daughter, he understood the old phrase "bundle of joy."

"Night-night, Daddy."

"Night-night. Love you." He kissed her forehead, helped her slide off his leg. She snatched Princess Jasmine off her perch on the desk and shuffled to Rinnah's side. The only two people in the world he'd gladly die for padded from the little living room hand-in-hand.

With Eve gone, Jake could hear the rain flit against the curtained window in front of him. He closed the Nick Jr. tab on his Web browser and brought up www.interpol.int. At the top of the index page splashed the headline "INTERPOL issues Red Notices to assist in identification of 12 Qatar murder suspects."

Jake clicked on "See all photos and Red Notices." Twelve faces appeared in three columns, some partly obscured by the holographic overprinting some nations stamped on their passport photos. He scrolled to the third row and clicked on the triangular-faced man whose picture the FBI had shown him over a month before. A new window opened.

```
WANTED
Alias ELDAR, Alias Jacob
Present family name: ALIAS ELDAR
Forename: ALIAS JACOB
Sex: MALE
Date of birth: (unknown)
Nationality: USA
```

Jake let out a long, pained breath. Even with the wrong picture, seeing his name on an international wanted poster made him vaguely ill. Who decided to steal his name? Who set up the credit card in his name? That had taken hours on the phone with Visa to get shut down. How long did this asshole pretend to be Jake? How many places was his address floating around?

He closed "his" Red Notice, opened the document he'd started a couple weeks before, and scrolled down to the fourth row, second picture. The second of the two women. This one was sort of but not quite pretty, with good cheekbones and a graceful neck. She was blond in the picture, but it didn't look like her real color; her skin was a shade darker than Rinnah's, and her eyebrows were brown. He clicked on the photo.

```
WANTED
Alias SCHAFFER, Alias Miriam
```

He started another tab, Google this time, typed "Miriam Schaffer" in the box, hit the search button. Forty-six hundred hits. *Shit.* He quickly scanned the excerpts, dismissing the wanted-list repostings or interviews with the Qataris or recountings of the hit on the terrorist. On the third page, he found what he was looking for: "Cherry Hill Woman to Qatar: 'It's Not Me'" on the Philadelphia *Inquirer's* website.

> Miriam Schaffer, suspected of being an Israeli spy, is blond and wanted for murder.
> Miriam Schaffer from Cherry Hill is neither. "It's not me," she wants everyone to know.
> Schaffer, 35, a secretary for downtown Philadelphia law firm Canby Matheson & Phelps, says she was just as surprised as anyone when she discovered she was connected with the murder of Hezbollah terrorist Masoud Talhami in Qatar on Aug. 30…

Jake brought up his document and started taking notes.

"Is that your new Internet girlfriend?" Rinnah wrapped an arm around his neck and rested her chin on top of his head. "I think you don't like blondes."

Busted. He sighed, let his shoulders sag. He hadn't wanted to let Rinnah know he was doing this; it might upset her. "I don't. She's one of the others."

"You mean, like you? With your name stolen?"

"Uh-huh. I'm trying to find them, see who they are, see if we have anything in common. I've nailed down eight of the eleven I've looked at so far."

Rinnah didn't say anything for longer than he liked. He wondered if she was reading his notes—name, city, profession, any biographical info he could find. Between Facebook, LinkedIn, newspaper articles, blogs and all the other electronic footprints people had left behind, he'd put together a scary amount of data on each of them. He had actual photos of five so far.

"Why?"

"Like I said, I want to see who they are. Near as I can figure, we all have some connection with Israel. Maybe that's how the Mossad picked us—they already have our data." He started closing the windows on his screen. "I'm sorry, I'll stop. It's a little weird, I know."

"No, it's okay." She stroked his chest through his undershirt. "Is all this going to make you crazy?"

"No." Jake took her hand, kissed it. "It's fine. Don't worry."

Rinnah pressed her cheek against his hair. "*Yakiri?* Are you still thinking about Gene's offer?"

The interest in her voice made him squirm. "I guess. I just never thought I'd get back into that world. I was so glad to get out."

"It won't be the same world." She swung around and straddled him, trailed her fingers through his hair. "It'll be gangsters, not Palestinian teenagers. Real bad guys for you to find. It isn't *Yahmam*. No one shoots at you."

She'd lost her sweats since she'd collected Eve for bed. The warmth of her legs burned through his thin warm-up pants. He stroked her bare thigh, grew hard at the thought of everything she wasn't wearing under her sleep shirt. "I know. You really think I should do it?"

Rinnah kissed the corner of his mouth. "I think a change is good for you. The bookstore was someplace to work when we came here, not a career, not your life. I see you do this—" she gestured over her shoulder at the laptop "—and I think this is what you should do. You're good at it, and you can help people. You always want to do that."

He ran his fingers under the hem of her shirt, caressed her bare hip and rear. "I don't know. I know the bookstore was supposed to be temporary, but I really like the place. I can help people there, I can make them happy—"

"But think about the future. Our future. Eve's. I just want us to all be happy."

"I want that, too."

"I know." She kissed his lips, tenderly, for a wonderfully long time. When she pulled back, she glanced down for a moment, unsure, then looked deep into his eyes. "If you're going to decide, a good time would be now." Rinnah showed him her left hand, the one not caressing his chest. It held a white plastic wand.

Jake didn't have to look for the little blue plus sign to know what it said. The huge smile that spread from Rinnah's lips to her eyes told him all he needed to know. "You're..."

"Yes! We're going to have another baby!" She wrapped her arms around his neck and kissed him again, hard.

He held her tight against him, rocked them both. *Another baby!* They'd talked about it since Eve was a toddler, and now it had finally happened. A brother (he hoped) or sister for Eve, the second child they'd always wanted.

Another baby. They hadn't been trying to get pregnant, but they hadn't been *not* trying. As each year passed, it seemed ever less a possibility, that they'd had their chance. But now...

Another baby? They were just getting by now. Clothes and diapers and baby food. The pediatrician on speed dial. Shots, colic, earaches. Even with Rinnah's job at the hospital, it would cost a fortune.

She pulled back, brushed hair off his forehead. "You are happy?"

"Can't you tell? Yeah, I'm, jeez, this is great." He felt the way he had when that mortar round had gone off a few yards behind him—dazed, deaf, happy to be alive, unsure what just happened. "How long have you known?"

"For certain? Ten minutes maybe. I'm a few days late, I thought I should check." She laughed, scrunched her nose. "I'm numb a little, I think I don't believe it yet."

Jake squeezed her to him again. "God, I love you," he murmured.

"*Ani ohevet otkha.*"

They'd make it work. He didn't have a choice, now; he'd have to take his uncle's offer. It couldn't be too bad, could it? Maybe this time he really could help people.

Rinnah's body flowed against his. Her heat, the beat of her heart, her breath on his cheek, the smell of her hair enveloped him. He wanted to press this moment into his mental scrapbook so he could hold onto it forever, as he had with all those other moments with her.

But when he closed his eyes, he felt like he'd just stepped off the roof of a skyscraper.

ELEVEN

Kassim and Alayan turned a corner off the Via Castellaro into the Piazza Grande and jerked to a stop simultaneously. Alayan let out a low whistle. "Spectacular."

A vast thunderhead of a building thoroughly dominated the piazza. Modena's Duomo was not so much taller than the ocher stone buildings surrounding it, but the cathedral dared everyone to look at anything else. Marble blocks in hundreds of shades of gray made up its arches and gables and turrets, arctic white to dove gray to the near-blush of a china-doll face. From a nearby corner loomed the massive hundred-meter-tall campanile, the Ghirlandina, punctured at steady intervals by arched and columned windows.

The Christians seemed to have a knack for the grand gesture, Kassim mused. He'd seen the Ayasofya in Istanbul—a former Christian basilica—the Imm Ridh in Mashhad, the Jama Masjid in Delhi. They were close to the same idea. But so many mosques were low and sprawling—practical, perhaps, but hardly the embodiment of Allah's work on Earth. Not like Cologne's cathedral, or St. Paul's or Winchester in England, or the Duomo in Milan.

"Kassim? Are you still here?"

He broke out of his thoughts and smiled at his friend. "Sorry. I was just thinking. How does a little market town like this end up with something like that?"

"They're everywhere in Italy," Alayan said. "Let's look closer."

They drifted clockwise around the cathedral, pausing to peer at the bas reliefs of saints and biblical scenes, the stone lions and

34

elaborate Corinthian capitals. "Thank you for letting the men take the day off," Kassim said. "We miss so many of the holidays. At least we can celebrate Eid this year."

Alayan arched his eyebrows. "I didn't think I had a choice. You were pretty insistent. I've never known you to be so worked up over a religious festival."

"It's not about the festival."

"I know. Maybe you'll tell me what it's really about."

Kassim paused to light a cigarette and measure Alayan's mood. Though his face was lighthearted, his eyes were weary, and the fatigue showed in his voice from time to time. Little wonder. Five days in Rotterdam, eight in Hamburg for the German woman Grusst, then those eleven endless days in Paris before they'd finally caught Dujardin in the open. After that, they'd made Jules Krosner disappear from Marseilles after seven eighteen-hour days of surveillance. The gas explosion that killed Elia Sabatello in Milan had taken another seven days to engineer. The only rest any of them had had was on the train between cities.

"You're driving the men hard. We've been at it nonstop. They're tired, and so are you."

"That's nothing new." Alayan shrugged. "We always work hard in the field."

"But not like this. We need to be careful, Fadi. Careful takes time. Mossad took twenty years to finish with Black September, remember? It's not like we're on a deadline or schedule."

Alayan paced to the front of the church, pointed up. "Look at that rose window."

Kassim's scalp prickled, not from the chill. "We're not, are we?" No answer. "Fadi?"

"They call this Romanesque. It came before Gothic, very straight, plain forms, but look how they go together."

Alarms pulsed in the back of Kassim's brain. "Answer me!"

"Speed makes us think harder. The gas explosion in Milan, that just came up, but it worked, didn't it?"

"That's not the point. We're going too fast, we'll make mistakes, like when Ziyad ran into the police in Milan. You keep saying we can't afford mistakes. Fadi, what—"

Alayan finally spun to frown at him. "We need to do it quickly, that's all. We can do it. We… we can do it." His voice had turned anxious, as if trying to convince himself.

The bottom fell out of Kassim's stomach. "What have you done? What did you promise them?" Alayan spent far too much visible effort to keep his eyes trained on the carved marble procession over the cathedral doors. "You've been pushing the men every day since we left. Why, Fadi? Why are we in such a hurry?"

The few tourists were far enough away to be only a rustle of sound. Kassim and Alayan were alone, and a good thing it was. Kassim stared at his friend, his mind stacking up a nasty pile of bad possibilities, his chest constricting as the pile grew higher. "Please tell me I'm wrong," he pleaded. "Please tell me we don't have to work a miracle."

Alayan took a deep breath, heaved it out in something resembling a sob. "Hanukkah."

"What about Hanukkah?"

"The Council expects us to be done in time to announce our victory on the first day of Hanukkah." He kept rubbing his hands together slowly, as if washing them in a ritual. "Our present to the Jews for their festival of light."

The pile of bad outcomes collapsed in Kassim's gut. "And when is that?"

"The 23rd of December."

No. No. Not so soon. We can't do it, no…

"You know, the prayers they say during Hanukkah thank God for delivering the strong into the hands of the weak and the wicked into the hands of the righteous. It's perfect if you think about it, really. We ought to have a prayer like that. So we—"

"A month and a half?" Kassim didn't even try to keep his voice from cracking. "Seven more in a *month and a half?* Are you insane? Why did you agree to that? We can't possibly work that fast! We'll make mistakes, we'll get caught or killed!"

"It's settled. We don't have a choice."

The words' meaning took a few moments to reach Kassim, like hearing an echo. "We don't have…"

"If we don't finish, they'll do it the old-fashioned way, with car bombs. They're moving people into place right now. If all twelve targets aren't dead by the 22nd, on the 23rd the bombs will hit Jews in all five countries. Dozens, maybe hundreds will die, and it'll set the cause back a decade. I tried to tell the Council, but they wouldn't listen."

"Wait. You told us they wanted us to do the job the way we'd planned."

"I convinced them they wanted that. I told them we don't have to act like animals. But we're an experiment, and you know how much patience they have for experiments."

Kassim closed his eyes and offered up a silent prayer. *Allah, the great, the merciful, please protect and deliver us from the stupidity of our leaders.* "What happens... to us?"

No answer for an eon. Then, "You know how they feel about failure."

TWELVE

8 NOVEMBER
MODENA

Carlo Massarani thanked the Virgin for her kindness as he slipped his emerald-green Maserati Quattroporte into a rare open parking spot across from the Teatro Communale. He didn't know how much farther he could drive. He quieted the engine's throaty purr and flopped back against the glovelike Poltrona Frau leather seat. Another riff of pain spiked from his upper chest and sprinted up the side of his thick neck, the third in twenty minutes. *Merda*, it hurt. No matter how he shifted his bulk in the seat, he couldn't drop the boulder from his chest.

He fumbled for the switch to roll down his window. The cool air didn't stop the sweat rolling down his forehead. His lunch had begun to eat him.

The next shock of pain ripped through his upper chest and down his left arm, a searing flame of agony lodged deep in his heart. He battled for a breath, but couldn't get air past the growing balloon of fire inside him. He tried to call for help, but only a gurgle escaped his throat. His hand flapped on its own against the center armrest to his right.

Massarani's vision shrank to the size of a saucer, then a button, then was gone forever.

Sohrab forced himself to walk normally, not stiffen or rush as he drew near the beautiful green car drawn up on the curb. He wanted to appreciate the flowing, almost feminine curves, but his mind clamped onto the mission to the exclusion of all else. He fingered the syringe in his jacket pocket.

He reached the driver's door. The window was down. The target had made this so easy; all he'd have to do is reach in, inject the scoline into the man, and the overdose of muscle relaxant would stop the target's heart. Fat as Massarani was, nobody would think twice about him having a heart attack.

Sohrab glanced into the car, then stared. The target slumped in his seat, collapsed against the door, his face an unhealthy purple. This beached whale looked at best like a distant relative of the younger, thinner man in the passport photo.

Sohrab checked both ends of the street, saw no one, then probed the man's throat for a pulse. Nothing. He felt a spike of wariness, stepped back, scanned the area again. An old woman in black hobbled down the sidewalk two blocks away. No one in the windows or the parked cars.

He approached the Maserati again, checked the target's body. No blood, no wounds, skin still warm. *No, this is too good.* He pressed his radio's transmit button. "*Sidi?* He's dead."

Alayan's voice came back a moment later. "Good work. Come back."

"No, you don't understand. I didn't touch him. He's dead. It looks like... well, like he had a stroke or his heart gave out."

"Truly? You didn't do it?"

"No, *sidi*. Allah took his soul before I could."

Long silence. Finally, Alayan chuckled. "Well, Allah *is* great, then. Come back, we're done here. Six down, six to go."

THIRTEEN

In a Hollywood movie, the Mossad Watch Center would be full of dark glass and steel and dramatic lighting and high-tech toys. Gur had been to the watch centers of many of the world's intelligence agencies and had never seen anything like that, even in America. The Institute would never spend money on that kind of foolishness, anyway.

No, his Watch Center—after less than two months, it was already his—was a middling-sized room with small beige half-height cubicles lining the two long walls, a third set running down the middle. Various news programs played on four flat-screen televisions hung on the walls. His cubicle squatted at the end of the room nearest the main entry.

Gur leaned back in his chair and watched his analysts pore over their message traffic. He could get used to this. Regular hours, his own desk, sleeping in his own bed every night. The luxury of being himself, not having to remember a cover identity. No tension every time he saw a policeman or had to hand over identification. No running routes, no checking for tails. No one trying to kill him. Was this what "normal" felt like? If so, he rather liked it.

Where was Kelila? She usually came by the Watch Center to visit him every morning around this time. She was late. His heart drooped in a way that told him just how much he'd come to look forward to seeing her.

They'd met two years before, when she first transferred from the Paris embassy into *Komemiute*. Ever since they'd been training, preparing for a mission, working a mission, or debriefing, and as she worked for Gur, he'd been careful not to notice too much how

40

attractive she was. Perhaps not classically pretty, but strong and proud and healthy in a way that made men look twice or more.

Now they were on restricted duty, they could be friends. More than that, perhaps? She was ten years younger than Gur; a potential problem. She had a nine-year-old daughter by a soldier who died in Lebanon. She was young enough to want more children. Was he ready to be a father again?

He laughed at himself. *You should go on a date with her first, maybe?*

"What's so funny, Raffi?"

Gur startled from his thoughts and smiled up at Kelila. "You're late. I thought you'd run off with Amzi."

She made a face and held out a paper cup. "Please, I just ate. This is for you."

He took the cup, blew away the steam, had a sip. For all its faults, the canteen could brew decent tea. "Thanks. Late for breakfast, isn't it?"

She brushed a drift of hair from her cheek. That ridiculous blond bleach from Qatar had finally disappeared, revealing a natural rich bronze that reminded Gur of his wife Varda in her younger years. Kelila's short-sleeved cream blouse set off shapely arms as golden as the jewelry glittering from her neck, wrists and ears. She'd worn a skirt again today, thank God. "My old boss wants me back. He spent seventeen shekels on me." Kelila leaned a bare elbow atop Gur's half-height cubicle wall, smiled, raised an eyebrow. "So, how are you going to top that?"

His throat tightened a notch. He'd gone on two dates in the three years since Varda died, and both had been utter disasters. He liked Kelila too much to risk that. If he didn't risk it, though, someone else would claim her. He stalled. "What did you tell him?"

"I didn't say 'no.'" Her smile drained away. "It's hard being a single mom and doing what we do." She looked away, set her chin. "Hoping Hasia will never find out what I really do."

The killing, she meant. He understood much too well. "Um, we should talk about it. Maybe... at dinner?"

Kelila's smile crept out of hiding. "Really?"

"If you can stand to be seen in public with an old man."

She gave him a you-silly-man look. "You're not old."

41

At that moment, he didn't feel so old, either.

"Sir? I have something here." One of the analysts, Yegorov, raised his hand.

Gur sighed, then rocked out of his worn-shiny chair and motioned to Kelila. "Come see my exciting new life."

The analyst enlarged a website on his right-hand flat-screen monitor. "This just hit on one of the profiles you asked for, sir." Gur had to concentrate to cut through the young man's heavily Russian-accented Hebrew. As one of three open-source analysts in the Center, he monitored the world's news, public statements, press conferences and so on for useful intelligence. Open Source nearly always discovered developing situations long before the people who played in the classified sandbox.

Yegorov pointed to the *Gazzetta di Modena* website as filtered through Google Translate.

> Maserati executive dies of heart attack
> An executive for Maserati was found dead in his car yesterday in the center of Modena.
> Massarani Charles, 49, could be dead for a heart attack, according to a police spokesman. It was found by a British tourist at the Municipal Theatre at 13:30.
> Maserati Massarani worked for 26 years, most recently as sales manager for the Middle East....

"Fuck!" Gur spat. Carlo Massarani. On the list, but not a name they'd used. A true innocent.

"What is it?" Kelila asked. "Who is he?"

"He's no one." Gur rubbed his eyes. "That's the problem."

Orgad stared at the folder on the desk blotter in front of him for what seemed like years before he looked up at Gur. "The P.M. wants to deal with this. Get in front of it. Actually, he said something like, 'Go get those Hezbollah sons of dogs before they kill anyone else.'"

"'Get in front of it'?" Gur had taken punches that stunned him less. "The rest of the names are in America. He wants us to go after these guys in *America?* That's insane!"

Orgad drooped into his chair, crossed his hands over his gut. "As I told the man. 'Can you imagine if we're caught?' I told him. But you know how he is. If he could call down the plagues of Egypt on our enemies, he would. He'd stand up on Mount Hebron in a robe and staff." He waved away the vision. "You know what the man says to me? 'Don't get caught, then.'"

"Right." Gur dug the heel of his hand into the headache developing behind his right ear. "This is crazy. Why not tell the FBI what's happening and let them handle it? It's their job."

"Raffi, let me tell you how things are right now. On Tuesday our ambassador in Washington spent ninety minutes with their Secretary of State being dressed down like a recruit in training. Why? Because we used American passports for you and your team. Of course, the ambassador denied everything. Now six of our resident assets are being expelled. Six, Raffi, they cleaned out our entire station in the embassy." Orgad leaned forward, thumped his spread fingers on the desk blotter. "So you think we can tell their FBI a Hezbollah direct-action team is going to start killing American citizens because we used their names? *That's* crazy."

"So you're starting an operation inside the U.S. *without telling them?* Our closest ally? If they find out, it won't be just the liaison station we lose." Gur squeezed his eyes shut. This was a worse decision than the hit on Talhami. The damage this could do... "Who are you sending?"

"You, of course."

Kusemek! Back in the field again? So soon? He'd settled into being a normal person. He enjoyed living in his homeland. He liked the Watch Center. But he couldn't tell Orgad any of that; he was supposed to be a professional. "My face is still out there," he said instead.

"It's out of my hands. The P.M. chose you himself. He said, 'Send the guy who did Talhami, make him clean up his mess.'"

"I never wanted the Talhami job to begin with! I told you it'd turn to shit, and it did. Now you're sending me to America into a carpet-bombing of shit?" Gur wished there was enough room in this little office to pace off the sense of doom building up inside him. "What exactly do you expect me to do over there, anyway?"

"Find the Hezbollah team and neutralize it. Seriously, a heart attack? *We* do that sort of thing. These men are too good to let them live. If you can save the people on the list, then do it, but that's secondary."

"We don't even know who we're looking for! Kelila's been looking for missing Hezbollah squads and hasn't found any. Who's my target?"

Orgad shrugged. "Find the people on the list and the terrorists will be someplace near. It's all going to be 'operational requirement.' Find them and eliminate them. You have the Director's support. Understand?"

"As much as I understand any of this."

"Then think of this." Orgad tapped the blotter again. "Let's assume Hezbollah is behind this. Assume they're killing the people on the Qataris' list. Yes? That's your theory?"

Gur nodded.

"Suppose they succeed. Then that bastard Nasrallah announces to the world that the all-powerful Party of God has killed twelve Zionist agents and got away with it. Can we deny they're ours? No. We'd have to explain how we know. The host countries may know better, but they'll be angry we caused their citizens to die. Or they won't know better, and they'll be angry we have people living under non-official cover inside their boundaries. And by 'angry,' I mean more than cancelling museum exhibits. I mean recalling ambassadors, cutting trade, U.N. resolutions. Perhaps now it's clearer to you?"

Gur heaved out a sigh that took a part of his soul with it. The Institute had done some truly stupid things in the past, but this plan was idiotic even by those standards. He could—should—resign in protest, but then someone else would go. His people would have to deal with a leader they didn't know or trust, someone who'd turn this into even more of a disaster. "When?"

"Tomorrow. Take a small team, no more than six of you total. Keep a small footprint. We don't have time to work up fresh covers

44

for you, so you'll go in with your police credentials. We'll fly you direct to New York City, private aircraft. Okay?"

"No, not okay. But I suppose we don't have a choice." Orgad arched an eyebrow. "Right. After this is over, if I survive it, I'll want a permanent transfer. I'm done with this."

Orgad just nodded as if he'd expected that.

❖

Kelila slouched in Gur's Watch Center chair, fiddling with her cell phone. She glanced up with sad eyes as he plodded into the room. "Where are we going?"

"America." He collapsed on the guest chair, ran his fingers through his hair. "Tomorrow. I'm sorry. You didn't have to stay this late, I'd have called."

She nodded. "Will this end it?"

"Does anything we do ever end it?"

"No, I guess not." Kelila punched a button on her keypad, closed the phone. "I'll call my mother, see if she can take Hasia for a while. Sir?"

Gur winced. Now they were on a mission, he was "sir" again. "Yes?"

"Would you mind a lot if I tell my old boss I'd like to go back when this is done?"

He patted her forearm, rested his fingertips on the warm, tanned skin of her wrist. "No. Maybe you should. Before this—" he waved his free hand toward the door "—ruins your life."

She glanced at his hand on her wrist and smiled. "I guess no dinner tonight."

Damn it. When would he get another chance? Was he foolish to even think about Kelila? "No time, now. I'm sorry. I wish I'd asked earlier."

"So do I."

You do?

Kelila stood, brushed down the front of her rust-red skirt. "Has all this ruined *your* life?" She echoed Gur's gesture toward the door.

He dropped his gaze to his hands. "Pack for cold weather. I'll see you in the morning."

FOURTEEN

Alayan settled on an English-language pop-music radio station to break the silence. He repeated words the announcers said, trying to knock down his accent. He'd considered a couple of Spanish stations—he'd taught himself the language since he'd started travelling on a Spanish passport—but knew he'd never be able to pass as a native speaker in a city full of Mexicans. Generic "foreigner" was the best he could hope for.

Four days ago, he'd been in an Italian factory town. Now he crossed a great desert an ocean away. The change always gave him mental whiplash when he allowed himself to think about it.

He pushed his palms hard against the big rental sedan's steering wheel. Over two hours on a motorway—Interstate 10, according to the red-white-and-blue signs—that ran so straight for so long he wondered if he could doze off and wake up still on the road. Driving this distance from Beirut would have put him in Turkey, but here he'd barely crossed into California, only a third of the way to his destination.

The scale of this country was something he couldn't fully understand. He was used to the eastern Mediterranean's tiny nations, or the slightly larger ones of Europe. He'd been to New York City before, but as crowded and overbuilt as that place was, it was still a manageable physical size. But this, *this* was unimaginably huge, and so undeveloped.

Still, some parts reminded him of home: the dusty, low-rise towns full of stucco walls and tile roofs, the groves of palms, the jagged brown mountains floating on the horizon. The big four-wheel-drive vehicles that blew past him in the left lane were

46

familiar, too. All the rich people drove them back home, huge battering rams to get them safely through roadblocks or kidnap attempts. He wondered why the Americans needed them. Surely that sort of thing didn't happen here, too?

Alayan hadn't been in this country since before the 2001 attacks, and despite all he'd heard from other Party members, he'd worried whether the team would get through security. But despite all the money the Americans had spent, all the controversy and argument, entry was still easy enough. European passports, European names, enough of the right languages to get them by, and the immigration officers waved them through—even dark-faced Gabir with his false Moroccan surname. They hadn't even needed visas. In the meantime, the Americans still believed more machines and guards would keep them safe. Fools.

The others were on the ground by now, in Los Angeles, San Diego and Las Vegas. Alayan had flown into Phoenix, where Kassim had bought the weapons now hiding under the spare tire in the car's trunk. Kassim's experience proved their research had been correct; it was absurdly easy to buy guns in this state of Arizona, which appeared to still be the Wild West. He'd sent an email to Alayan: "It's like a Bekaa Valley bazaar here."

He passed a green sign that said, "Los Angeles 215." Miles, not kilometers. Three hours, perhaps more if the traffic in Los Angeles was as bad as everyone said.

As the miles unspooled behind him, Alayan thought about the upcoming action.

Now they were in America. For people who went on so much about freedom, the Americans had so many police, and they were so powerful. The team would have to fly from Los Angeles to the next target in Washington; another exposure to airline security. Ziyad would insist on praying no matter what. That would draw the wrong kind of attention.

But they had an advantage: Americans had no idea about personal security. In the old days, it could take weeks for a skilled team to work out the patterns of a target's life. Following, photographing, long hours in parked cars or dark hotel rooms watching the target come and go.

Now all Alayan had to do was follow a Twitter feed.

By the time he reached the suburb of Los Angeles called Burbank, he'd have a good working knowledge of the rhythms of Frank Demetrio's life. The 33-year-old estate lawyer worked in a tall, black office building on the outer edge of what appeared to be the central part of this Burbank place. On Wednesdays and Fridays, he joined friends at one of the bars and restaurants surrounding the large shopping mall that, as far as Alayan could tell, was the town's actual center. Alayan even had pictures of Demetrio from the man's Facebook page—far more and far better than agents could get under normal field conditions.

He'd sent the team the link to a post Demetrio made to the page on the eleventh of September: "Hoo-YAH! Mossad kicks terrorist ass AGAIN!"

We'll see.

The team would be in Burbank Sunday night. Demetrio would be dead by Wednesday.

FIFTEEN

13 NOVEMBER
TETERBORO, NEW JERSEY

Gur staggered down the ladder to the hangar's polished concrete floor. Fresh air was a fine thing, even if it was cold and smelled of jet fuel. The chill cut through the muzziness blanketing his brain. Fourteen hours in the Gulfstream business jet was like being packed in a particularly plush coffin and shaken regularly.

He buttoned up his slate-gray overcoat to his throat and scanned the area. Their vehicles—a cypress green Nissan Pathfinder and a dark blue Chevrolet Suburban—waited at the far side of the metal hangar. Between him and them hunched an anonymous gray Ford sedan, retiring almost to the point of embarrassment.

A man—fair skin, rimless glasses, styled blond hair—pushed off the car's side and strolled in Gur's direction, his hands in the pockets of his khaki overcoat. Gur knew he could be from one of only two places; he'd know which one the moment the man opened his mouth. If the man spoke English, they might as well get back on the plane and fly home.

The man stopped three paces away. "Ephraim?"

"You are...?" Gur replied in English.

The man watched Amzi lumber down the Gulfstream's ladder, then turned his attention back to Gur. "They made us fly over on El Al." Hebrew. Not the FBI.

"You're from the embassy?" Gur asked in Hebrew.

"Until Thursday, when they're kicking us out. Brian Doron. I used to be the station chief until you pulled that stunt in Doha." He snapped a nod toward the cowering Ford and turned back in its direction. Gur followed. When they reached the car, Doron

49

pivoted, folded his arms and scowled at Gur. "Police credentials? The Institute is getting lazy."

"That's all we had time for. It's true, your whole section's being expelled?"

"Yes. This was a good job. My wife loves D.C. My son loves his school. They're not speaking to me right now, thanks to you *Komemiute* idiots. You just had to use American passports, didn't you?"

Gur sighed. "It wasn't my decision. Talk to the man in the Director's office. If it helps at all, I told them it'd go bad."

"It doesn't." Doron let a long breath hiss out as he massaged his neck. "At least you got the son-of-a-bitch."

"I'm sorry." Apologizing to the boss for making mistakes wasn't hard anymore; apologizing to a fellow combatant whose life he'd screwed up was. Just another victim of Doha.

Doron nodded. He pulled a stiff manila envelope, folded lengthwise, from his inside coat pocket and handed it to Gur. "You and your team are registered at a TSA conference downtown. That's officially why you're here. These are your badges. They get you into the workshops and the trade show, but not the lunches. Don't bother to go, it's just a cover."

"Nothing good to see?"

"No. They're discovering things we knew fifteen years ago, except they do them half as well and spend five times as much doing it. And that, 'Inspector', is all you're going to get from the embassy. We have to wind up our work and brief in our replacements." Doron shot a hateful look at the Gulfstream. "They also have to fly El Al."

"Honestly? I'd rather have the movies and the flight attendants."

"I'll bet. I also put in the secure number for the *katsa* in the U.N. delegation. I've no idea if he's been briefed. I doubt it."

Gur stuffed the envelope into his coat pocket. "How many others know about us?"

"You mean, know who you are? Just me. I don't plan to tell my relief. My assistant made your arrangements, but she thinks you're really police. Don't be surprised if the law enforcement attaché calls up and wants to have drinks. You people are on your own. Keep it that way."

That's how things usually were. Gur didn't hold it against Doron or the embassy; in their place, he'd want to ignore this operation too. "Thank you for this. We'll take it from here. Again, I'm sorry you have to leave."

Doron frowned into Gur's eyes for a silent moment, then pivoted on his heel, circled to the driver's door and climbed in. The Ford lumbered from view with hardly a sound.

"He wasn't very happy," Kelila remarked.

Gur turned and smiled at her. Her cheeks flushed in the cold; he squashed the impulse to warm them with his hands. "Our last physical contact with the government. We've ruined his life. Come on, let's get to work."

SIXTEEN

16 NOVEMBER
BURBANK, CALIFORNIA

Demetrio's tweet at 5:03 PM told Alayan—and everyone else in the world who could bring themselves to care—where to go: "`elephant bar @ orng grove c u there.`"

The Zionist made this so easy. Alayan and the team had done everything so fast: less than three days of surveillance, and they'd first driven inside this parking structure two hours ago. So many loose ends, unfilled holes. But it had to work. They had to make up the time lost in Europe. Kassim waited for them in Washington D.C., guns and rooms ready for their next exploit.

"Why don't we just blow up his car and get it over with?" Gabir grumped.

Alayan sighed, shook his head. "How many targets do we have in America?"

"I don't know. Four? Five?"

"Six. How many of those would you like to hit?"

"All of them."

"Of course. And how many do you think we'll get to if we start setting off bombs all around this country?" Gabir scowled, turned his face toward the side window. "We can't announce what we're doing until it's done, or we'll never get to finish. We have to make each job look like something normal, like Americans killing each other. They do that so much—I'd be afraid to live here."

"So we hide in shadows and shoot people in the back. We're warriors, *sidi*, this isn't our way."

"It's Mossad's way. If we act like them, we'll succeed like them." Alayan plucked his phone from the dashboard, selected Sohrab, pushed the button that made the phone chirp like a

52

cricket. "Status."

"Clear."

He selected Rafiq. "Status."

Rafiq's easy voice came accompanied by a jitter of crowd noises, televisions, laughter. "Still here," he said in English.

Still? Alayan chirped Ziyad. "Status."

"Waiting."

"Hold." He placed the phone back in the cupholder, pushed both hands against the steering wheel to work the stiffness from his shoulders. His entire body was wound tighter than the stitching on the leather seats.

Alayan's phone bleeped. "Heading out," Rafiq announced.

Finally. Alayan selected the three others, pressed the button. "Stand by." He nudged Gabir. "Get the camera ready."

This was the worst part: the target moving, walking into the trap, so close to success, but so many things could still go wrong. The seconds take hours to pass. Alayan rolled down his window, both to get a better view and to let some fresh air chase the body-sweat funk out of the car. Still warm outside, just like home at this time of year.

Sohrab's voice from the phone. "In the stairwell."

Gabir silently slipped through his door to set up the video camera. Each of the men had taped one of the European actions; Gabir's video had come out best, so he got to shoot their first job in America.

The rapid-fire clack of a woman's footsteps echoed from Alayan's right. *Damn it!* He leaned over the passenger seat, hissed, "Gabir, get back in here!"

Sohrab. "Out of the stairwell, on your level."

Gabir slammed into the seat, pulled the door closed. Alayan could hear a man's steps on concrete behind him. Demetrio? He chirped Rafiq. "Slow him down. Someone's coming."

This damned flashy car was as conspicuous as an elephant. When he'd replaced the sedan he'd rented in Phoenix, he'd wanted another boring, forgettable American four-door. The rental agency instead upgraded him to a wine-red Jaguar. He knew better than to object; that would be suspicious. There hadn't been time to get rid of it. *No time.* He'd said that a lot lately.

Lights flashed on the bronze Lexus four-wheel-drive across the aisle from their car. Alayan whispered "Get down!" to Gabir, pulled the newspaper from the back seat, opened it on the steering wheel. Gabir slid down the passenger seat until his head sank below window level.

Just in time. The woman strode into view, immersed in thumbing her cell phone. Alayan didn't dare even rustle the paper, she seemed so close. She was a Western kind of pretty, with long blond hair down her back, a tight white shirt unbuttoned far enough to show her cleavage, and a tighter yellow skirt that exposed her legs from the knees down. Alayan was used to such costumes on Beiruti Christian women—even many of the Sunnis—so it didn't shock him, although since he'd never liked blondes, it didn't do much else for him either. He knew people who'd be scandalized by her "undress." Ziyad, for one.

The woman opened her car door but didn't get in. She slung her big, black handbag inside, then stood fiddling with her phone. Faint male voices drifted in from outside, behind and to Alayan's left. Rafiq and Demetrio?

Gabir slipped his pistol from his waistband, nudged Alayan, nodded toward the woman. Alayan clamped his hand hard on Gabir's forearm.

Now the woman was talking. Loudly. "Hi! You home yet? Yeah, just got off. You up for it tonight?"

She looked at the Jaguar, bounced her eyebrows. Then she looked straight at Alayan.

She smiled, a lot of blazing white teeth. An invitation?

Khara! His heart jumped sideways at the speed of sound. He automatically waved back, hoped he didn't look too stunned. *She saw me! Will she remember?*

His phone chirped. "*Sidi!*" Ziyad, waiting in the white panel van parked next to Demetrio's BMW. "What's happening?"

The woman slid into her car, phone still clamped to her ear. Her skirt rode high up her thigh. She looked back at Alayan, smiled again. The door thumped shut. Brake lights, engine starting, back-up lights. A few moments later, the Lexus and the woman were gone.

Alayan sagged back into his seat, let out a huge breath. Of all the times to flirt... He selected Sohrab. "Go! We're clear!"

Gabir bolted from the car to set up the camera again. A few seconds later, Sohrab sauntered into view from the next aisle over, heading for the van. The male voices took on a goodbye-nice-to-meet-you tone. Alayan's heart crept back to its rightful place. The plan could still work. The woman wouldn't remember anything. No problem.

Demetrio ambled into the aisle. Dark blond hair, shirt sleeves rolled to his elbows, black suit coat slung over one shoulder. He aimed a black key fob; the BMW flashed and yelped.

Ziyad's shoulder peeked out from behind the driver's side of the van. *Get back!* Alayan wanted to yell. *Not yet!*

The target strolled to the driver's door. Ziyad ghosted along the van's back doors in full view now, pistol out and ready. Baggy white t-shirt, oversized blue jeans, baseball cap worn backwards; he could almost pass as a Hispanic gang member.

Demetrio paused, bent to look closer at the BMW's black flank just behind the driver's door. He licked the tip of his middle finger, rubbed at the offending spot.

Just get in! "Ziyad, hold—"

Too late.

Ziyad was supposed to shoot the man in his car to lessen the noise and mess, steal it, dump it in East Los Angeles, let the gangs take the blame for now. But when Ziyad pivoted around the van's back end, Demetrio was still fussing with the car's paint. The two stared at each other for a moment.

Demetrio dropped his focus from Ziyad's face to the gun.

Ziyad rushed the target, jammed the pistol's muzzle against the man's chest. A muted *fump* echoed around the concrete, a car door slammed too hard rather than a gunshot. Blood splattered the wall and pillar. Demetrio toppled from sight.

While the others cleaned up, Alayan carefully folded the newspaper and let his breathing settle down. The plan had worked. Things went wrong, but they'd recovered. *Praise Allah.* He started his car, left the parking garage slowly and carefully, kept just below the speed limit, signaled when he turned.

By 11PM, he was on an American Airlines flight to Dulles International Airport.

SEVENTEEN

18 NOVEMBER
SECAUCUS, NEW JERSEY

Gur heard the door open and close behind him for the fifth time. He turned to find everyone standing in a loose group near the little round table by the mini-kitchen, watching him. Amzi and Sasha looked bleary; they must have been out drinking last night.

"All right," he started, not moving from the window. "Demetrio was killed on Wednesday. He's the one in Los Angeles." The others shook their heads, mumbled curses. Too late in the wrong place. "So clearly, the Hezbollah team isn't starting here and working west the way we would, they're doing the opposite."

"Fucking Arabs do everything backwards," Amzi muttered.

Smart Arabs, Gur thought. They went for the most remote and unlikely target first. Their team leader had to be eliminated, and soon—or the Institute needed to recruit him. "Hezbollah has two options. They can come straight here, or they can go to Washington and finish the man Nussberger. We can't afford to commit to either option, so we have to cover both."

"How do we do that?" David asked.

With six people? Good question. "David, Natan, take the train to Washington, rent cars, keep watch on Nussberger. Don't make contact, report in regularly. The rest of us? We know where the four targets here live and work. One person to a target, keep on them, watch for shadows. Sasha, see if you can track down Kaminsky. If anyone sees anything, report it immediately. Any questions?"

Sasha asked, "Do we have a picture of Kaminsky yet?"

"Not yet," Kelila said. "I keep asking, but it never comes."

56

David raised his hand. "What if we see Hezbollah? Do we engage?"

Gur considered this possibility—probability?—and the men he'd assigned the task. David had the face of a Raphaelite saint and could put a bullet through a one-shekel coin at three hundred meters. Natan looked soft as a suburban office drone and excelled at close-in work; by the time the target realized the clear blue eyes were empty, he'd be dead. "Do what you can without attracting too much attention. Don't get into situations you can't get out of. We can't afford to lose you. Understand?"

David said, "Yes, sir." Natan nodded.

"Excellent." Gur checked his watch. They were later than the time suggested. "Get going. Hezbollah's driving this bus. Let's take the wheels off before it runs over us."

EIGHTEEN

18 NOVEMBER
BROOKLYN

Jake balanced the plate holding his formerly frozen individual supreme pizza on a stack of books to one side of his laptop. He conjured up Google and started a search for "Qatar +Hezbollah +Mossad."

He'd gone underground with his homework since Rinnah had caught him a month ago, waiting until she was in bed or out of the apartment. She'd said she didn't mind, but he didn't want to push it. Media interest in the Doha story had slackened in the past few weeks, so the Mississippi-sized flood of news in September had withered into a drainage-ditch trickle.

He sorted his hits by date, newest on top. Jake pulled a slice of pizza from the plate, but before he could finish his first bite, his eyes locked on the fourth result: "Burbank Man Killed in Carjacking," from that day's Los Angeles *Times*.

> A Burbank man was killed yesterday in the aftermath of what Los Angeles Police Department detectives are calling a carjacking turned deadly.
>
> Frank Demetrio, 33, was discovered by drivers at 6 a.m. yesterday in the open trunk of his 2009 BMW M3. The car, which had been stripped of its wheels, seats, and electronics, had been left in an industrial area on South Mission Road near the 6th Street bridge...

Jake considered this for a moment. What were the odds that out of six billion people, one on a list of twelve would suddenly show up dead? Pretty long, he figured.

He started at the top of his notes, Googled each name in turn, looked for new activity, especially activity ending in death. Three names down, a Dutch website showed him what he'd hoped he wouldn't see.

Albert Schoonhaven, 41, killed in a street robbery in Rotterdam on September 23rd.

Two out of twelve? Jake's pizza started attacking his stomach.

More appeared. Erika Grusst, a professor in Germany. Andre Dujardin in France. Elia Sabatello and Carlo Massarani in Italy. All dead.

Six dead. Out of twelve. Suddenly, he was freezing cold.

He hauled out his cellphone, stabbed his uncle's number. While he listened to ringing, he tried to figure out what to say so he wouldn't sound nuts. "Gene? It's Jake."

"Hey, kid, how you doing? Rinnah spent your first paycheck yet?"

"Yeah, she's crazy excited. We're going out to buy me some suits this weekend. Say, can you do me a favor? Look up some names?"

Gene laughed. "You on the job already? Christ, kid, we're not paying you yet."

"Just... humor me. Frank Aaron Demetrio from Burbank, California." He listed the other five. "They're all dead, in the past couple months."

Gene repeated the names under his breath. "What's this about?"

"They were all on the list. The INTERPOL list." He hesitated. "The one I'm on."

Gene breathed into the phone for a few seconds. "I'll call it in. Don't tell Rinnah."

"I wouldn't dare."

NINETEEN

20 NOVEMBER
CHERRY HILL, NEW JERSEY

"In Israel today, a rocket barrage on the embattled southern town of Sderot killed two civilians and raised tensions between the Israeli military and Hamas..."

Miriam tried to switch away from CNN, but it was too late. The pictures pinned her to the sofa. A dusty little town, too much sunlight, a crater. A body covered by a shocking yellow tarp; Magen David Adom in their red vests hauling burned people on stretchers. Women crying. Men holding their heads.

She was ten years old again.

Huddled in her mother's arms, both of them curled into a tight ball in a half-buried concrete culvert pipe piled with sandbags, sixteen other people pressed together all around them. The hiccup of suppressed crying filled the gaps between the muffled *thwumps* of rockets gouging holes in the earth outside. The fourth time in two weeks; no one had slept since the last attack three nights before. She'd hardly been able to eat. Her stomach clutched from both fear and hunger.

"Mama," she whimpered, "where's Papa?"

"He's safe, Miri." Shopworn confidence in her mother's voice.

The fifth explosion crashed nearby. Eighteen people in the concrete tube shrank into each other as one.

Smoke spiced with the tang of roasted lemons snaked into the shelter. A rocket must have come down in the orchard, just steps away. People nearest the opening started to cough. Gas? Did Hezbollah use gas? Should she breathe? Would they all die there?

Where's papa? "Mama? Mama!"

"Shh, Miri." Her mother's hands smoothed her hair, caressed

her cheek. "Be brave, my darling. Don't let them know you're scared. They can't win if you're not scared. Remember."

Grown-up Miriam resurfaced in her living room clutching a pillow, tears on her cheeks. Bastet the Abyssinian nosed around her ankles. She remembered. *Don't let them know you're scared.* She'd lived that since she was ten, since she'd learned anger felt better than fear. Except for the moments when she was ten years old again, it still worked today.

TWENTY

Al-Shami worked the edge of a 4mm iron plate on his bench grinder. A rooster-tail of sparks arched onto the concrete floor, bounced, and died. The heavy-duty noise suppressors over his ears allowed through only a distant whine. Even if the tool's shriek escaped outside, no one important would hear it. Only people who had no interest in reporting anything to the police ventured into this industrial ghost town.

He shut down the grinder, sprayed water on the iron's fresh edge, and climbed into the open, gutted back of the white panel van behind him. Without bothering to remove his goggles or earmuffs, he carefully slid the plate into to back of a set of modular aluminum shelves fastened to the passenger side of the cargo space. It fit, finally. Four bolt holes and some paint, and the last piece of this part of the puzzle would be ready.

The plate was just thick enough to focus the energy of a C4 charge outward through the van's thin sheet-metal body. That and shaping the charges into hemispheres would ensure the van would explode out rather than up when detonated, creating its own shrapnel. He appreciated the efficiency.

Al-Shami stepped from the van, dropped the plate on his workbench, then paced to the nearest door as he lit a cigarette. Outside, the breeze rustled the head-high weeds in what used to be a parking lot for the abandoned spark-plug factory that was al-Shami's workshop. The hair on his bare forearms began to prickle as the sweat dried and chilled. He'd never been so cold for so long as he had in this place; he'd be glad to leave it behind. But it had been useful in its own bleak way. More Arabs lived in the greater

Detroit area than anywhere else in America, and because of the economy and the general hopelessness of the place, many of those people were poor, desperate, and angry. Excellent raw material.

He pinched the end of his cigarette and dropped it into a coffee can next to the door, returned to the long work table in the room's middle, and picked up a five-inch diameter aluminum tube with one open end. The domed top sat on its flat end next to the saw he'd used to separate the two. The half-kilo block of white claylike plastique was still firmly in place against the tube's inside wall, even after all the handling.

This was the cattle prod. It would get the herd moving. The van was a slaughterhouse on wheels. It would cut the herd down by the dozens, hundreds if everything worked according to plan. He'd used this combination in Baghdad with great success. It would work just as well in New York City.

TWENTY-ONE

The worn orange seats and scratched windows on the Metro car hadn't changed a bit in the ten years since Rafiq's previous life as a George Washington University student. But he had.

Morning commuters on autopilot packed this 7:30 train. Rafiq stood near the rear of the car; in the middle, Oren Nussberger read his folded Washington *Post*, screened by all the bodies between them. Fiftyish, receding hairline, a head like an inverted egg, gray raincoat draped over his anonymous blue suit. The Qatari list featured his picture; unlike the others, his real name was attached. This one had actually been there. Alayan was convinced the man was Mossad; Rafiq had yet to decide.

Rafiq scanned his fellow riders, both to look for threats and to remind himself what Americans looked like. Especially the women. So many good-looking women in this city, as if they'd won a beauty contest to get in. He'd learned growing up outside Sour that girls found him attractive, and American women were no different. Back then he'd got rid of his accent as soon as he arrived in Washington. He could be just a regular Joe if that's what the lady wanted, or he could turn the accent back on and be the charming, exotic foreigner.

A blonde huddled in the seat next to the door, gray business suit and gym shoes, reading a vampire book. Lovely legs, good chest, pretty fine-boned face. He watched her, remembered some of the blondes from school. The fair-haired ones seemed to like darker men. He didn't complain.

As if his gaze had weight, she looked up from her novel, found him, raised her plucked eyebrows. He gave her what the girls always called his "aw, shucks" smile. She returned it, favored him with a lingering once-over, then returned to her reading.

Damn, he thought. A few minutes and he might have her phone number. He sighed. If he went on a date, Alayan would go crazy.

Then it dawned on him these people would call him a terrorist. He didn't feel like a terrorist—whatever that felt like—but it didn't matter.

He flashed back to his senior year at GWU, when the airliners crashed into New York and the Pentagon. Having a last name like "Herzallah" and being even vaguely Arab became a mark of evil. His friends—people he'd partied with—started giving him wary looks. Exotic didn't work for the women anymore, either. Washington became an armed camp. The irony was, he'd been as shocked and hurt as the Americans. Killing thousands of innocent people had nothing to do with Islam or the Arab world. That's what the Zionists had done for years in his country. That was why he fought them now.

Nussberger clamped the newspaper under his arm. The man's shoulders slumped with premature seriousness. The passport photo hadn't shown how deep-set Nussberger's eyes were behind the thick-rimmed glasses; his brows were like grey cliffs looming over a pair of dark waterholes.

Was this truly a Zionist spy?

Alayan picked up on the first ring. "Yes?"

Rafiq lounged against the rough cast-concrete wall of GWU's Funger Hall overlooking 22nd and G streets. "He's at work."

"And?"

"No stops. Not for coffee, or cleaning, or breakfast, straight from home to work." Too straight. A trained operative would have checked for tails, doubled back or taken sudden detours. Nussberger just plodded on his way. No Mossad man would be so oblivious. "Lots of people everywhere he went. There's no way we can take him anyplace along his route."

Alayan didn't answer for a moment. "Well, good planning on

his part. Come back now. I need you to be the electricity man. We should look inside his home."

Rafiq flipped closed his phone, tapped the case against his palm. If Nussberger wasn't an agent but really was in Qatar, that would mean neither he nor his name had anything to do with Talhami. Was Alayan wrong about Nussberger?

He took a last look around at the familiar buildings. A knot of students chattered by, both boys and girls. He felt a pang as he watched them pass. That had been him not so long ago.

These few blocks held lots of good memories. Fun, friends, women, challenging studies, interesting talk. Things were so much simpler then—no false identities, no watching for surveillance, no midnight operations, no killing. If that younger version of himself had known what was in store, he might never have gone home.

TWENTY-TWO

23 NOVEMBER
ARLINGTON

At well past midnight the outside world was dark and silent. Inside Nussberger's townhouse, only the sports program on the television broke the stillness.

Seven hours hiding in a closet with Sohrab had left Alayan's joints feeling brittle as old wood. His hands, sweating in the latex gloves he'd worn for hours, felt pasty and bloated. But it was almost over.

The light blazing in the kitchen doorway burned Alayan's eyes, but also picked out the rumpled white dress shirt on the boneless sack of Nussberger slumped snoring in one corner of the sofa. One leg sprawled along the cushions, the other spilled off onto the floor. An empty liquor bottle idled on the low table in front of him. *Perfect.*

Rafiq had discovered the signs when he and Alayan had broken into Nussberger's home: a wife recently left, a son grown and moved away, a lonely old man. The scenario wrote itself.

While Sohrab charged the syringe in the kitchen, Alayan watched from the doorway as Nussberger slept. The injection would surely wake the man—but not for long. Alayan smiled at the irony of using scoline, one of Mossad's favorite drugs, against one of their own people.

They shushed across the beige carpet to the sofa. Alayan hovered his hands over Nussberger's shoulders, ready to catch him when he awoke. Sohrab knelt by the man's foot on the floor, aimed, and slipped the needle through the dark sock into the vein running up the man's vulnerable inside ankle.

Nussberger muttered, jerked. His eyes cracked open, failed to focus, slewed toward Alayan's face above him. "Wha— ?"

Alayan didn't want to do anything to leave an unexplained bruise. "Is all okay, yes?" he said in English, softly as if to a child who'd just burst out of a bad dream. He patted the man's shoulder. Sixty seconds before the muscle relaxer took effect; keep him calm. "We help, yes?"

The man's head rolled on invisible gimbals, his face turned first toward Alayan, then to Sohrab's shadowy figure holding Nussberger's ankles, then to the television. He tried to sit up, but couldn't make his arms coordinate. Alayan felt a tinge of uneasiness; how did scoline and alcohol mix? The drug shouldn't be working this fast. His mind rushed to the "overdose" scenario: Nussberger dead of a "heart attack" within a few minutes, too fast for him to metabolize the drug. There'd be some left over in his blood, a sure sign he'd been killed if anyone looked. *Slow down,* Alayan thought. *Don't die yet. That's not the plan.*

The man struggled again to sit up, slurred out some soft sounds of dismay. Alayan gently helped him up, rested a hand on the man's shoulder, hoping it would calm him. Nussberger peered into Alayan's face. "Doris?" Alayan could smell liquor on the man's words. "Who're—?"

"A *saheb,*" Alayan said. He patted the man's shoulder. "A friend."

Sohrab sat back on his heels. The man's legs weren't moving anymore. A few moments later, neither were his arms. Then his head lolled back against the flowered cushion.

"Quickly," Alayan whispered to Sohrab in Arabic. "Let's get him to the stairs. We have to get him on the rope before the scoline wears off and he can fight back."

No one would suspect a thing.

TWENTY-THREE

24 NOVEMBER
ARLINGTON

Something was wrong. David rubbed the crud from his eyes with his thumb knuckles and checked his watch. *Four in the fucking morning.* The lights inside Nussberger's townhouse hadn't changed in the past ten hours. Everyone turned lights on and off as they went through their own home; it was reflex.

He tapped his earphone. "Something smells," he told Natan in the other car. "I'm going in."

"Shit. Wait a minute."

They rang the doorbell twice, just to check. They'd play drunk if the old man answered, but everything remained still inside. The front-door lock was easy enough to pick. Four steps into the townhouse, they found Nussberger.

"Goddamnit," Natan muttered. "Not even one of our covers."

The man hung in the stairwell from white cotton clothesline, face purple-black, hands limp at his sides. He smelled of alcohol and piss. On a step near his feet, David found two framed photos of a plain middle-aged woman and a teenaged boy, resting atop a single sheet of white paper. "My beloved Doris and Michael," the note began.

David sighed and trudged down the steps. *Poor bastard.* Either this was an incredible coincidence—which he didn't believe for a moment—or this Hezbollah team was scary good. He and Natan had followed Nussberger for the past three days and had seen nothing, no tails. Those Hezbollah assholes pulled this off while he and Natan watched from their cars outside. "How'd they get out?"

"This way." At the back of the townhouse, Natan pushed open the sliding balcony door with one gloved finger and peeked outside.

"Three meters down to the pavement, maybe. Can't see the door from the street."

David sagged back against the wall facing the doorway into the kitchen. Natan had it right: *God damn it. Right under our noses.* "I want to meet these guys."

Natan closed the sliding door, stuffed his hands in his pockets. As usual, his face was blank. "I want to kill these guys."

TWENTY-FOUR

25 NOVEMBER
NEWARK, NEW JERSEY

Alayan moved with the crowd through the glass doors leading from the train platform. When their eyes met, Kassim pushed off the corridor's marble wall and raised his hand. Alayan's mood brightened; he smiled in return. They embraced just out of the stream of travelers, thumped each other's backs. Another safe journey. "I'm glad you made it, Fadi."

"It wasn't a bad trip," Alayan said. They walked side-by-side down the corridor, following the exit signs. "I've read so many bad things about Amtrak, but it was rather nice."

"Good." Kassim held out a bag of popcorn. "Want some?"

"Thanks." Alayan scooped a handful, nibbled on it one-handed. Too salty, but fresh. He glanced at Kassim, noted the troubled twist of his friend's mouth, the heavy eyes. After over dozen years together, he knew the signs. *What's wrong?*

The corridor led them to the low, wide shopping arcade tunneled beneath the railroad tracks, tan marble and bright lights and a thick bustle of early-evening travelers. Alayan had expected more suits and fewer families; perhaps the Friday after their Thanksgiving festival was also a holiday. The casual winter clothes he and Kassim wore blended in well.

"It's good to be back in the same city with you," Alayan said. "You keep me grounded, you always have. I need that."

"Someone has to look out for you." Kassim paused, pursed his lips. "You sent Gabir and Ziyad up here before you finished Nussberger. Are you sure that was a good idea?"

Alayan bit back a flash of annoyance. He didn't expect or need second-guessing from Kassim; enough other people were happy to

71

do that. "I didn't need them anymore. Why?"

"What if something had gone wrong? What if the police came? You'd only have Rafiq for backup. That was a big risk, Fadi. We have to be more careful."

They approached an African Amtrak policeman pacing down the concourse toward them, eyeing the crowd. Out of reflex, Alayan fell silent and avoided looking at the man. He and Kassim weren't the only brown-skinned men in the station, but they might be the only ones speaking Arabic. The policeman's eyes skidded over them as he passed, then he was gone.

Alayan let out his held breath and peered at Kassim. "Well, everything worked out. We have to stay on schedule. Are they complaining?"

"They're nervous, all of them are. They see the corners we're cutting." Kassim took a deep breath. "You need to tell them. They deserve to know."

"No. I don't want them distracted, and I don't want them worrying about this."

"You've never kept secrets from us before, not like this."

"How do you know?" He'd kept secrets when he'd had to, such as shielding them from the Council's pressure. It was his job to deal with those fools, not the team's.

"Because I know you."

"Yes, I suppose you do." Since university. Kassim was the last person alive to have known him *before*. Alayan wiped his popcorn hand on his jeans leg, touched Kassim's sleeve. "Perhaps you should be leading this operation. You're more careful than I am."

"No, Fadi. You have… a strategy. I just make it work. You know how to make these actions look right. I haven't watched as many American crime shows on television as you. I wouldn't know where to start."

"Stop it, I know better. But thank you."

A flash of color attracted Alayan's eye: a fuchsia snowsuit on a cute little brown-haired girl. Alayan watched her waddle past holding her young mother's hand. He could never pass up looking at children, no matter how much it hurt. Always the sore that never quite heals.

They pushed through into the station's main waiting area, an

Art Deco temple to transportation with elaborate metalwork surrounding the doors, a thirty-foot-high vaulted blue ceiling, towering windows and massive wooden benches. Alayan stopped, took in the hall, and smiled. He'd once dreamed of building spaces like this, back when he had dreams of creating and not destroying, before he'd traded away his soul.

They stepped into the outside chill. Alayan asked, "What's your plan for us here?"

Kassim waited until they were in the car park off a windy Market Street before he answered Alayan's question. "We start with the two closest targets, Eldar in Brooklyn and Brown on Long Island. Surveil each on alternating days so we don't stand out in the neighborhoods, follow the family members too so we know their schedules as well as the targets'. Then switch to the other two, Kaminsky in Paramus and Schaffer in Cherry Hill. There's the van." He pointed, shifted their direction. "Once we have their patterns down, we plan all four actions and execute on four consecutive days. We leave Schaffer for last, then fly out of Philadelphia immediately after."

A good plan. Too bad. "That'll take a lot of time. Remember Hanukkah?"

"Yes, I remember. If we get caught, we'll miss the deadline, too."

Alayan stared straight ahead. He hated turning down good advice, but he hated even more the thought of the disaster breaking the deadline would bring. "We'll split into two teams of three and track Eldar and Brown at the same time. Quick surveillance, just enough to get their schedules, then hit them fast, move to the next two. Three, maybe four days for each set of two."

Kassim flung his hands in the air. "Do you *want* this to fail? We're rushing everything. How long before our luck runs out?"

Alayan worked very hard to keep his eyes away from Kassim's view. "We finished Demetrio in three days," he shot back. "We can do this."

"That donkey practically shot himself!" Kassim's voice steadily rose in pitch and volume—a bad sign. "Do you really think the rest are self-involved morons like him? That they'll make this easy for us?"

"It doesn't matter if they do. We can do this. No one suspects. Only four left, Kassim. Four more and we've won." Alayan stopped, tugged at Kassim's arm to turn him around. Of all the team's members, he needed Kassim's support and understanding the most. If Kassim didn't believe, none of them would. "Just imagine the reaction when *Sayyid* Nasrallah announces what we've done. The West won't be able to pretend we're just a pack of stupid animals anymore. We'll show we can match the Zionists with weapons *and* brains."

Kassim let out a heavy sigh. "I hope you're right, Fadi. But we need to survive long enough to see that happen."

"We will." He had to believe. They all did. Alayan squeezed Kassim's shoulder gently. "We start tomorrow with Eldar and Brown. Only four more to go."

TWENTY-FIVE

28 NOVEMBER
BROOKLYN

Jake trailed Trina as she wrestled the book cart to a stop. "Okay, where are we now?"

Trina—wildflower-blue eyes, blond cornrows, Laura Ashley over blue tights—peered at the sign. "Fiction and Literature."

"What goes here?"

"Everything that doesn't belong someplace else."

"Right. Now check what's in the cart."

She walked her forefinger along the book spines, matching each to the notes in her other hand. The new replacing the old. Jake saw himself in her place six years ago, his first stumbling steps learning this business. If she stayed with it, she'd eventually know everything about this place, be able to shelve in her sleep the way he could. He envied her the journey.

"Charles Dickens? Candace Bushnell? Stephen King?"

"That's right."

Trina wrinkled her cheerleader's nose in confusion. "Seriously? All in the same place?"

Someone dropped a book on the café floor a few yards away. Hardbound on linoleum sounded like a large-caliber pistol shot. Jake found himself backed against a shelf unit that had been a couple feet away a moment before. *Calm down. You won't hear the one that gets you.*

Trina held her knuckles to her mouth, stared at him. "Um, Mr. Eldar, are you okay?"

He nodded too quickly, held up his hand. "Yeah, fine. Just keep going. It seems weird, I know. It's your first week, you'll learn." *Mr. Eldar? Am I that old?*

75

He turned to find Gene in his usual suit and black overcoat, leaning against the Romance shelf unit, checking out Trina's calves. "Jesus, Gene, you startled me. What are you doing here?"

His uncle shrugged. "I was around, thought I'd stop by, get you to comp me some coffee. You take shield here, right?"

"No. Put your badge away and buy your own damn coffee, you make enough money. We need the business." Jake grabbed Gene's elbow and steered him to the café. He dropped his volume a few clicks. "And bullshit you were around. You never come over here. What's up?"

"Actually, I had to go to the courthouse, so never say never." He'd pulled back his volume, too. "Anyway, I had my guys look at..." They stopped at the café register behind two men in suits. Gene trailed off, then half-turned to look around the store. "Gonna miss all this?"

Jake ran a quick check of the men: white, yuppie, clean-cut, good shoes. No threat. One had his cup, the other waited. Not the time or place to talk about dead people.

He turned to look out over the shelves and signs—*his* shelves and signs. *Two days left.* "Yeah. This is a great job, Gene. The pay's crap and I work a lot of hours, but... when a writer shows me something new, and I get someone to buy his book, and she comes back all lit up because she loved it, too, well..." He glanced at Gene, who wore a borderline-blank expression, as if Jake was speaking Mandarin. "You can't buy that feeling."

"Can't raise two kids on it, either."

"Yeah, so Rinnah keeps telling me. Get your coffee. I'll be downstairs in greeting cards."

When his uncle tapped his shoulder a couple minutes later, Jake spun and grabbed his hand. "Fuck! Don't do that!"

Gene frowned. "Lay off the caffeine, kid."

Jake let his uncle go, pressed his back against the nearest shelves, dug the heels of his hands into the sides of his head. "It's not caffeine. It's ten days knowing I'm on a list that's getting shorter. It's like every guy on the street with a dark tan and five o'clock shadow is going to shoot me. You know how many guys there are like that out there?"

Gene sighed, laid his free paw on Jake's shoulder. "Hey. Calm down. If I thought anything was coming for you, there'd be a uniform on your door, bet on it."

Just then, an NYPD babysitter didn't sound so bad. "Have you found out anything?"

Gene watched him for a moment, then shook his head. "Like I was saying upstairs, I had my guys look at those names. You heard about the one down in D.C., right?"

"Oh, yeah." Jake had set up Google News alerts for each of the surviving Doha 12, as he'd come to think of them. "They're saying suicide. That look straight?"

Gene nodded. "So far. Guy was going through a not-so-friendly divorce. Got drunk, left a note, hung himself. No sign of forced entry, no sign anyone else was there, no witnesses. And that picture on the Red Notice? That was him. He had meetings with the Qatari Central Bank about the same time that Talhami shit cashed out."

"So he wasn't part of it." Jake checked the window for snipers, then paced a tight circle around his uncle. "This is nuts. I'm taking different routes to work every day. On the subway, I stand where the cameras can see, or next to transit cops. I stole Rinnah's mailbox key so she can't get to the mail first. I go to a place, I know where the back door is. Everything we used to do in Tel Aviv. I never wanted Eve to live like this. Ten days. How much longer?"

"Stop pacing, willya?" Gene grabbed Jake's arm. He stepped close, looked up into Jake's eyes. "You're scared. Weird shit going down, another kid on the way, I get it."

Jake shook his arm free. "I'm not scared for me. Whatever they throw at me, I can take. But what if they go for Rinnah? Or Eve? What then? It's not like I'm in the army anymore, I've got them to worry about now. I don't need protection, they do. You get that?"

Gene seized Jake's shoulder, squeezed hard. "Yeah. Listen. My guys are on this. They hooked up with the locals in the other cities, read the M.E. reports. Know what they got?"

The question held its own answer. Jake's insides sagged. "Nothing. They got nothing."

"They got nothing." He released Jake, shook his head. "There's only three no-shit crimes out of the eight. Nothing common between them."

"Except we're all on the same fucking list."

Gene held up a placating hand. "Yeah, except that." He shrugged. "Don't know what to tell you, kid. We spent time on this. International calls, INTERPOL, the whole shot. I almost wish we'd found something. Then we'd know what's going on, we could do something."

This wasn't what Jake had wanted to hear. Task forces, FBI, warrants; that's what he'd wanted. He leaned his elbows on one of the greeting-card shelves, wiped his fingers over his hair as he watched people come and go, gauging the threat from each. "Do I need a gun here?"

"Oh, Christ, kid, no. Not with Chava in the house, no." Gene stepped beside Jake, wrapped an arm around his shoulders. "Besides, you don't want to get caught carrying. If I think you need one, I'll lend you one of mine." Gene's eyes probed him. "How's Rinnah?"

Jake blew out a sharp breath. "First day of morning sickness. Man, was she cranky." He broke away from his uncle, folded his arms hard, tried to take the frustration out of his voice. "I can't keep this from her much longer, Gene. She's asking why I'm in guard-dog mode. Couple nights back, we went out for Chinese. Know how I always like to sit by the windows, watch the people?" Gene nodded. "This time, I dragged her as far into the back as I could. She looked at me like I'm nuts." He held out an open hand. "Am I? Tell me I'm nuts. Please."

Gene looked out the window at the street vendor's fake designer handbags, weighing his words. "Look, I know you're worried about this. I asked my guys to keep an eye on the other three, just in case. I've mentioned it to a buddy in JTTF. I wish I knew what else to do."

Again, not what Jake wanted to hear. At least Gene hadn't called him nuts. "Yeah. Thanks, Gene, thanks for looking. I... just worry. I'm a Jew, it's in my DNA, right?"

Gene snorted. "Yeah, I've heard that. Hey, on the first, come in a little early, I'll introduce you to the Commissioner before the Intel standup, okay?"

"Sure."

"It'll be fine, kid. You'll love the job, really. Hell, you're already doing the damn job."

"Yeah, sure."

"Good." Gene slapped Jake's bicep, then pointed toward Jake with the first two fingers of his coffee hand. "Fucking ease off, will you? You're gonna pop something. And for Christ's sake, don't tell Rinnah. She's pregnant, she doesn't need the stress. You gotta talk to someone, talk to me, okay?"

"Yeah, I get it. I remember someone telling me to be careful. Looked a lot like you."

"I know, I know. Anything weird starts happening, tell me, I'll put a unit on you. Until then, take it down a few notches. You're too young to vapor-lock yet. See you, kid."

Jake watched his uncle shamble away and wished he could have Gene's confidence in the reliability of the system. But the system had never screwed Gene the way it had Jake.

He wouldn't cancel the news alerts anytime soon.

TWENTY-SIX

28 NOVEMBER
BROOKLYN

The knock on the door broke Rinnah from her attempts to puzzle together dinner from the bits and pieces in the refrigerator. She checked her watch. *Six already?* "Coming!"

She padded barefoot to the door, peeked through the spyhole. A man wearing a hardhat, black-blue sweatshirt and a yellow safety vest stood just far enough away that she could see the clipboard he had propped on his belt buckle. "Who is it?"

"Con Ed, ma'am. I need to ask you a couple of questions."

The hardhat was the familiar sky blue. He looked harmless enough. Rinnah flipped the deadbolt and cracked the door until the chain stopped it, framing the man in the gap.

Caramel skin, a strong chin, short, thick black hair, lush eyelashes—*why do men get such good lashes, anyway?*—and eyes that made her think of melted chocolate. She paused before she spoke, not wanting to spoil the Harlequin moment. "Um, how can I help you?"

"Sorry to bother you so late." He ducked his head to read from his clipboard, gazed at her through those eyelashes. "One of your neighbors reported his lights flickering and running dim. I need to know if this is happening in the whole building or just his unit. Is this Jacob Eldar's apartment?"

"Yes. He's my husband."

"Lucky man." He smiled. *Oh, wow.* "Is he home? Can I talk to him?"

Flirting? Not that she minded. She loved Jake—despite how edgy and preoccupied he'd been lately—but it was nice to be noticed by someone else, especially now she'd started to puff up.

80

She slipped the chain, opened the door wider. "I haven't noticed anything."

"No flickering, no dimming, no humming?"

"No, nothing."

"Okay. Are you at home during the day? The problem was reported late this morning."

"No, I work."

"I can see that. In an office, it looks like."

"Yes. They lock me to a desk with chains. No handsome prince ever rescues me, like in the books."

He smiled again. "That's a shame. The prince doesn't know what he's missing."

Rinnah regretted not wearing a skirt. This might be her last chance to show off her legs before they turned into tree trunks. Little arms wrapped around Rinnah's hips from behind; she looked down to see Eve peeking around her at the workman.

His eyes got bigger and softer, which she wouldn't have believed possible. He bent over a few degrees. "Who's this? What's your name?"

Eve giggled. "Eve."

"Hello, Eve." He straightened and returned his attention to Rinnah. "She's beautiful. She looks like her mom."

Did he do this with all the women he met? Probably. But it was just what she'd needed. "Anything else I can do for you?" If he could flirt, so could she.

He lofted his eyebrows. "Sure. Has your husband mentioned the lights? Maybe not, he must work days, too."

"No, he hasn't said anything."

"All right." He twitched his nose like a rabbit for Eve, who giggled and hid behind Rinnah. "Can I get your name for the report?" He hovered his ballpoint over the papers on his clipboard.

"Rinnah." She spelled it. He tapped the paper after the last letter.

"Thank you, Rinnah Eldar. Again, sorry to bother you so late." He smiled again.

Rinnah smiled back. She couldn't help it. "No problem. Good luck fixing the lights."

"Thanks." He waggled his fingers at Eve. "Bye, Eve."

"Bye-bye."

It wasn't until she closed the door that Rinnah realized how much information she'd given the Con Ed guy. She didn't even get his name, or look at his ID, even though he had one half-hidden behind his vest. *You idiot*, she chided herself on her way back to the kitchen.

But she wouldn't mind so much paying the electric bill anymore.

❖

Rafiq slid into the driver's seat of the white van, parked half a block down from number 475. "He's not home, but his wife is. Her name's Rinnah." *And she's lovely*, he didn't say.

Alayan tapped on his laptop's keys. "Did it go well? Did you have to use the identification?"

"No, she didn't ask."

"Good." Alayan poked around with the touchpad for a minute. He nodded, then swiveled the laptop so Rafiq could see the screen. "Is this her?"

Rinnah smiled out at him from a Flickr page, her face in bright sunlight, all of lower Manhattan stretched out behind her. Eve's cheek pressed against her ear. Rafiq recognized the view from the Empire State Building's observation deck; he'd been there a lifetime ago. "Yes, that's her. That's not a very good picture—she's prettier than that. The little girl is Eve."

Alayan turned the screen back to face him. "You can marry her after we eliminate her husband." He tapped the touchpad a few more times, then showed Rafiq another picture. "This is the husband."

A man with curly black-brown hair looked straight into the camera. He had a long, slender face with sharp features, a straight nose, strong chin, dark eyes. He smiled with nearly-closed lips, as if he held in a joke. Eve perched on his lap, his arms wrapped around her, her smile showing off a missing front tooth.

"There are several Jacob Eldars, but only one Rinnah." Alayan pivoted the laptop back to himself. "Good, now we know who we're looking for. We'll follow him tomorrow, get an idea of his schedule." He patted Rafiq's shoulder. "Good work."

Rafiq felt gnawing in his guts. Guilt? "Um, *sidi?* We're only after him, right? Not the woman, not the little girl. Right?"

Alayan gave him a smile as wintry as the evening. "Of course. Only the man."

TWENTY-SEVEN

30 NOVEMBER
MIDTOWN MANHATTAN

Flashing lights, a music bassline strong enough to stop a heart, shouting, bodies everywhere. Sohrab's head was full to exploding. Nothing like this existed in Tehran anymore, hardly anything like it in Beirut. If the *Basiji* back home ever found anything like this place, everyone here would be beaten bloody. And that was just the men.

The women? He couldn't imagine what would happen to them. The nearly naked ones dancing on the three stages, rubbing themselves on the men for tips, the spotlights and colored neon strips painting bizarre glows on their bodies. Or the slightly less naked ones hauling trays of alcohol through the crowd. Or even—this had taken some effort to absorb—the women in the *audience*, watching the dancers, even *tipping* the dancers. Beatings? Prison? Torture? Death?

How was he supposed to keep track of Brown in this brothel?

He wasn't a prude. He enjoyed the sight of an attractive woman's body, in the proper place. But this was just... obscene. Overwhelming. And so blatantly commercial; money everywhere, and he didn't doubt that with enough money, a man (or a woman, but he had to stop thinking about that) could get anything—*anything*—he wanted here.

Sohrab flinched when a hand landed on his shoulder. Then he heard Kassim's voice in his ear. "Alayan says to go ahead." He paused. "This one's actually pretty. Brown has taste."

"American women do this to themselves?" Sohrab said, stunned.

"Just concentrate on Brown. The fire door is next to the toilets.

84

I disabled the alarm. We'll pick you up on 52nd Street." Kassim faded into the murk and the crowd.

At least they weren't the only non-white men here. White, black, brown, yellow, suits and jeans, ties and hoodies, united by their grazing eyes and a willingness to pay $20 to see bored semi-naked women pretend to perform for them. No one had paid the least bit of attention to him except the predatory cocktail waitresses and the *jendeh* hustling lap dances.

When a hipless Slavic blonde replaced the curvy redhead Kassim had complimented, Brown lurched out of his padded metal chair, grabbed his black-leather briefcase and started his upstream swim toward the toilets. Sohrab sighed in relief. *Finally.* He waited a few seconds, then abandoned his chair and edged through the spectators, keeping one eye on Brown's progress across the tiger-striped carpet toward the last piss the man would ever take.

Sohrab clutched the stiletto's grip in his coat pocket. This wouldn't be one of Alayan's elaborate charades. Nathan Brown usually went straight from his Long Island home to the train to his office, then back again, always surrounded by people. Tonight he'd delayed returning to his wife and children for... *this.* Kassim's idea was simple: a robbery in the toilet. Simple was good.

But Kassim had missed the middle-aged Latin bathroom attendant standing by the sinks, handing out paper towels and breath mints for tips. *Madar Ghahbeh!* Sohrab stalked past the man, pretended to piss at a urinal near Brown. *Now what? I can't kill him here!*

After a moment, he knew what to do. Sohrab flushed, hurried out into the short, dark hallway outside the toilets, pressed his back against the black wall next to the hinge side of the men's room door. He tucked his stiletto behind his leg, ready.

Brown stepped through the door a few tense seconds later. Sohrab grabbed the man's loose tie, yanked him farther into the shadows, then plunged the stiletto between the man's ribs into his heart. Brown's eyes bolted wide open; he let out a muffled "oof." His briefcase thumped to the floor. "What?" he gasped. "Who?"

But he was already dead. Sohrab felt no heartbeat through the knife's shaft. A moment later, Brown's brain also died. He sagged into Sohrab's waiting arms.

Quickly. Sohrab sat him against the wall, carefully drew out his knife, wiped it on the carpet. The thin blade made a tiny, self-sealing wound; only a dribble of dark red on his shirt showed Brown hadn't passed out from drink. Sohrab patted the pockets in the man's gray suit, looking for a wallet.

"Hey you! You!" A man built like a safe stared down at Sohrab from the hallway's end. All in black, the club's logo on his polo shirt. A bouncer. *An!* "What are you doing?"

Take the bouncer? He was out of reach, and too many people were nearby. *Run?* The fire-escape door lay perhaps two meters away. *Can I make it?*

The bouncer marched forward, eyes narrowing, hands flexing.

Run.

Sohrab crashed through the fire escape door and charged two steps at a time up the concrete stairs leading to street level. Before he was halfway up, the door slammed open again. The bouncer yelled, "Stop, goddamnit!"

He saw me! Sohrab reached the top of the stairs, sprinted down a grubby, half-lit service hallway smelling of cigarettes and wilted produce. Heavy breathing and thudding footsteps loomed behind him.

Even with a knife, Sohrab didn't like his chances going hand-to-hand against a man who had eight or ten centimeters and a good fifteen kilos on him. He couldn't risk getting that close.

He yanked his collapsible baton from his pocket, swiveled and swung the black stainless steel rod in a vicious arc behind him. The baton snicked to its full length an instant before it crashed into the bouncer's extended right arm. The scream of pain almost drowned out the sound of bones cracking.

Sohrab stood aside to let the man's momentum take him a few steps farther. The bouncer turned, red-faced, a leather blackjack in his left hand. He swatted at Sohrab, who stumbled back a step, feeling the breeze from the close miss.

The bouncer charged. Sohrab tried to sidestep, but a meaty fist caught him in the center of his chest and bounced him off the stained plaster wall. He lurched under the man's next swing, slammed the baton forehand into the side of the bouncer's skull. The man tumbled against the wall, then slid onto the worn tile floor.

Sohrab peered down at the unconscious man with a twinge of irritation, rubbed the dull ache where the man had hit him. "Why?" he panted to the bouncer in Farsi, not expecting an answer. "Now I have to kill you." He snapped the baton into the man's throat, then dashed for the door. He caught himself just in time. Sohrab collapsed the baton back to carrying size, straightened his leather bomber jacket, took a couple deep breaths, then pushed through into the night.

Brown was finished. Eldar tomorrow.

TWENTY-EIGHT

1 DECEMBER
BROOKLYN

"Chava, where's your backpack?"

"In my room."

Rinnah stifled a groan. She was already running late; she didn't need this, too. "Go get it. *Now.* We have to go."

"Mommeee..."

"Now!"

Eve flounced through an about-face, arms windmilling, and stomped away. "I don't wanna go to school! It's boooring..."

Alayan hunched in the driver's seat of the van, his arms folded over the wheel. He could just see Eldar's building three doors west, number 475: brick, three floors, three tall windows across, blue front door. Holes opened in the files of parked cars lining each side of the street as people emerged from their homes to go to work.

He checked his watch. 7:05. The woman was late. He texted Gabir and Ziyad: *Hold in place.*

Each chirped back. No words; the connection sound was their acknowledgement. Every day, they learned something new, became just a bit more efficient. They'd taken Brown in three days, now Eldar in four. This could work.

Come on, woman. We have a schedule.

Four doors west of number 475, Kelila warmed her hands on a

paper cup of Starbucks tea. She'd cranked the sedan's passenger-side mirror so she could watch the front of Eldar's building. No action yet. She used the little joystick on the dash to sweep the mirror back and forth, searching for lurkers. No one was foolish enough to stand around in the cold.

"Anything?" Raffi's voice buzzed in her ear. He was out there somewhere, patrolling.

"All quiet."

If Hezbollah was still tailing Eldar, they'd have to pick him up at his home. It was too much to hope she'd see them setting up. Still, she and Raffi—*Mr. Gur, you're on a mission*—had to try. She might have spotted a tail when they followed him yesterday morning, but the guy broke off before she could confirm it. Good-looking, Arab coloring, maybe her age, in a gray suit. If he showed up again, she'd recognize him.

Jake appeared in the mouth of the hallway, dressed and freshly shaved. "What's wrong?"

Rinnah growled. "Eve doesn't want to go to school today, so we're late, of course." She took a calming breath. "You're ready early. Making a good impression on your first day?"

"No, Gene said he'd introduce me to the Commissioner if I came in a little early. I don't know what today'll be like. I'll call if I'm running late."

"Okay." Rinnah never got tired of looking at Jake, even though he wasn't classically handsome. He had great eyes. Everyone called him "nice-looking," which Rinnah thought was much too little praise. "That suit looks so good on you."

"Thanks. This hot babe helped me pick it out." He smiled, closed the distance to her in two strides, wrapped an arm around her waist.

"Anyone I know?" She ran her fingertips over the smooth cotton of his sapphire-blue dress shirt. If she wasn't late for work and Eve wasn't tramping around, she'd love to take Jake right here, in the hall. She guessed from his reaction he wouldn't mind. She'd been non-stop randy for the past six weeks, just like when she was pregnant the first time. Stocking up for when she got huge and sex became too uncomfortable.

Eve trudged around the corner, dragging her pink Hello Kitty backpack behind her and a rain cloud over her head. Rinnah sighed and kissed Jake. "Time to go. See you tonight."

"Love you." His face suddenly grew serious. "Hey. Be careful out there, okay?"

He'd said this for a couple weeks now. What had gotten into him? She made a face. "Always. I love you." She broke away, glared down at Eve. "Pick up your pack, young lady. Say goodbye to Daddy."

"Bye-bye, Daddy," she grumped.

The woman finally appeared at 7:09. Black hip-length winter coat, dark green scarf, black slacks. The little girl holding her hand was pink from the top of her cap to the hem of her parka, where blue jeans took over. Alayan remembered the photos; such a cute child. If Samirah had lived, what would their children have looked like? The thought stabbed deep, as it always did.

Eldar would leave in about fifty minutes. Alayan decided to wait five minutes, then give Gabir the "go" signal. In the meantime, he watched the mother and child trundle west, away from him. He mourned what should have been.

"The wife and daughter just left," Kelila told Gur through the radio.

Gur was within steps of the corner of Prospect Park West and 18th. He'd circled the block clockwise, looking for men loitering or watching Eldar's building. So far, nothing. He hoped his worn and slightly snug track suit made him look like a lazy jogger and not a burglar-to-be.

He stopped after turning the corner, placed both hands on a barren tree next to the tan-brick McFadden Brothers American Legion post, pretended to stretch his hamstrings as he scanned the parked cars on both sides of the street. They appeared empty. He couldn't see into the two nearby tradesmen's vans, both white; he'd have to check them as he passed.

Gur decided to stretch for another minute or so. It actually felt good. He hadn't had the will to work out since Doha. He should ask Kelila if he could join her on her morning run. Exercise was always easier with company.

❖

Jake shrugged on his coat, shouldered his black leather carry bag with his laptop, then left the apartment. When he turned to lock the door, he kicked something. Eve's backpack.

That little turkey. Sometime during her six years, she'd perfected passive-aggressive behavior. He sighed, bent to sweep the pint-sized bag off the floor. What would she be like when she was a teenager?

He pulled out his phone to call Rinnah; with any luck, he could catch her before she turned around to come back. The screen stayed stubbornly dark. He'd forgotten to charge it last night. *Damn.* If he hurried, he might be able to catch up to them.

Jake thumped down the stairs to find Mrs. Sahakian standing at the door of her apartment in her faded yellow housedress, leaning on her aluminum cane. Her round face frowned at a thoroughly wrecked wooden chair. When she heard him, she swapped the frown for a look of relief. "Oh, Jake, good morning."

"Morning, Mrs. Sahakian." Often he'd stop to chat with the old widow, but today he needed to get going.

"Please can you help me? This chair, she must go to rubbish. They take rubbish today."

Jake stopped, hand on the front doorknob, and tried not to make any frustrated noises. "Um, sorry, really, I have to try to catch Rinnah. Eve forgot her school things."

"Is okay, you go out back door, by rubbish, yes?"

She had a point, and she was using her basset-hound eyes on him. Jake owed her; sometimes she'd watch Eve for an hour or so, sing old Armenian folk songs to her. "Okay, no problem." He grabbed the remains of the surprisingly heavy chair and charged down the hall to the back door, waving and smiling at the cloud of blessings and thanks she sent after him. He'd already planned his detour through the service alley to 17th.

❖

Rinnah set the quickest pace Eve's short little legs could handle, enough to set her daughter complaining, "Mommy, you're going too fast!"

After the fifth or sixth repeat, Rinnah glared down at Eve. "This is what we have to do when you don't get ready like a good…" She blinked, looked hard at her daughter's back, then jerked to a halt. "Chava, where is your backpack?"

Eve found a spot on the sidewalk to talk to. "At home."

"But… you had it when we left!" She muttered a few Hebrew curses—ones she hoped Eve didn't understand—then tore her phone out of her purse to call Jake. Ringing. *Answer!*

"Hi, this is Jake, leave your name and number, I'll call you back."

She groaned and punched the "disconnect" button. He'd left his mobile off again, or didn't recharge it. If only they had a traditional phone for times like this. Rinnah fixed her position: 8th Avenue, almost exactly halfway to school. Do without the backpack? No, it had Eve's workbooks and her alphabet and arithmetic homework.

She turned, grabbed Eve's hand, started marching back toward 18th.

"Where are we going, Mommy?"

"Back home, to get your bag. No computer for you tonight! You've been a bad girl."

"Mommeee…"

❖

Alayan texted Gabir and Ziyad. *Go.*
Two chirps replied.

❖

Gabir and Ziyad emerged from the dark walkway between the Jew's building and the one next door. They checked out the back of the property: a concrete pad, fence on one side, large wooden shed attached to the back of the building on the other, a tall tree screening the fire escape.

Gabir managed to pull the ladder down without making much noise. As he mounted the first rung, Ziyad clapped his arm. "Allah be with you."

"Stay awake," Gabir replied, more gruffly than he'd meant. Ziyad would watch to make sure nothing trapped them from behind.

Even though he weighed over ninety kilos, his feet made only light rustling sounds on his way up. The metal slats on the second-floor platform were pocked with rust and peeling brown paint that crunched softly under him.

Gabir knelt between the left two windows, back to the wall. The cheap vinyl duffel slung over his shoulder crackled against the brick. He checked his exposure. If the tree still had leaves, he'd be invisible to the building across from this one; as it was, the scrim of gray branches and twigs obscured but didn't block the view. Gabir peeked through the metal slats underfoot, spied Ziyad standing guard next to the ladder, nervously scanning the area.

A white curtain shrouded the outermost window. He examined the frame; a thumblatch on top, two securing pins near the bottom. Too hard to get through quietly. He risked a glance through the center window's open curtain. The same locking hardware as before. Beyond, a bedroom; no one in view. Gabir checked his watch; thirty-five minutes before the Jew left the flat. *Breathe. There's time.*

He slipped past, stopped at the third window's edge, peered in. An empty hallway, a strip of carpet down the center, stairs to the right, apartment door to the left, weak morning glow in the window at the other end. This one had a simple rotating latch. Gabir pulled from his coat pocket a thin sheet of tin the size and shape of a playing card and went to work.

❖

The white panel van slumbering in front of number 493 advertised a plumber's shop, radio dispatched, results guaranteed. The frost on the windshield told Gur the vehicle had been there overnight. The front seats were cluttered with everything except people.

The unmarked second white van, its recent film of road grime spotted by bygone rain, stood two doors down and across the street. Gur strolled past a couple cars, leaned out just far enough to check the front.

A man sat hunched over the wheel, gazing out the windshield.

Gur stepped back two paces to see the rear license plate. He fished his phone and wallet from his pocket, pulled a slip of paper from between his credit cards. It held a series of ten-digit numbers. He selected the second one that began with "545," subtracted three from each digit, thumbed the result into his phone.

Three rings. "Hey, Greg here."

"Hello," Gur said in English. "This is Ephraim."

Pause. "Yeah?"

"I need information on a vehicle. New York five one zero eight six Oscar Echo."

"Hold on."

Gur leaned against the building side of a tree, watching the van sit quietly in its space while Greg—the *sayan* who happened to be an NYPD patrol sergeant—ran its plate. Mossad leaned heavily on its *sayanim*, the civilians who helped it around the world. It was the only way an organization with a mere 1200 members could maintain a global reach.

"Okay. A 2009 Chevy Express cargo van, registered to Hertz Commercial Rentals. Need an address?"

"No, thank you. Who is the driver?"

"That'll take a while. You need it?"

Do I? Gur didn't want to compromise this *sayan* on a hunch, but he didn't want to let a possible lead slip away. "A citizen rang you. There is a suspicious vehicle on 18th Street in Brooklyn, west of Prospect Park West, a white Chevrolet van. No sirens." He disconnected.

❖

Jake didn't see Rinnah on 17th Street. He figured she must have already dropped Eve at school, so he humped it all the way to P.S. 10's 7th Avenue entrance. A young receptionist in the front office said she'd be glad to get Eve's bag to her.

Chore finished, Jake charged off to the Prospect Park subway station.

❖

Gabir eased the flat's front door closed. Picking the locks while wearing gloves took a few seconds more than usual, but doing it quietly took even longer. Still, no alarms, human or electronic. He drew his pistol, a .32 caliber semiautomatic that almost disappeared in his hand. It felt like a cheap toy, but Alayan said it could be the sort of thing a criminal might carry.

He searched the flat in less than 90 seconds. The Jew was gone. But it was too early for that. Where was he? Maybe he'd gone out for a minute.

Gabir wouldn't ruin this job by rushing. He'd show Alayan he could be trusted to handle the sophisticated work, that he wasn't just some thug who broke necks. He was a warrior, and he was going to prove it.

He'd wait.

❖

Alayan kept a death grip on his phone and didn't take his eyes off the front door of number 475. Gabir had checked in just before he entered the building almost ten minutes before, then nothing. What was he doing in there?

This had to go as planned. Last night's action against Brown may yet become a disaster; a simple operation had turned into double-murder, and now they'd have to be careful where Sohrab appeared in public. He could be on a security camera. They might need to make him grow a beard, dye his hair, shave his head. Complications they didn't need.

Bright blue spiked through his concentration. He glanced at the side-view mirror.

95

Flashing blue lights. Police.

The African policeman watched Alayan sit on the curb while his white partner searched the van. Other than their skin color, the two men were nearly identical: big, broad shoulders, black turtlenecks, dark blue uniforms and parkas, peaked caps.

Alayan did what he could to ignore the building three doors down. He didn't dare look its way. His phone lodged in the breast pocket of his flannel shirt, turned off. *What's happening down there? Is it done? Where's Gabir?*

"You're not here working, now, are you, Mr. Alvarez?" The African cop loomed over him, black-gloved hands wrapped around the buckle of his gun belt.

He'd given them the passport and Spanish identity papers. Any other police force on Earth outside Spain, he wouldn't have worried, but the NYPD was legendary. His heart had seized when they radioed his name to their station, asking about warrants. What if they got him mixed up with someone else?

What if the white cop found the gun under the driver's seat?

"No, *señor*," Alayan answered, remembering to lisp. "I help my cousin today. We move the furniture today. I visit, on holiday."

What if the cops hear the gunshot? He'd planned for Gabir and Ziyad to have at least five minutes to get away. But the police were right *here*, in walking distance. Gabir could never get out of the apartment, and Ziyad was too dedicated to flee. It could all come apart in a minute.

He peeked at his watch. Ten minutes since he'd turned off his phone.

Kelila pressed the transmit button on her radio. "The wife and child are back."

The wife looked frazzled. The little girl's face twisted like a wrung-out washcloth. Kelila recognized her expression: meltdown. She knew this scene so well.

"Back? Why?"

"I don't know. No sign of Eldar yet." She checked the rearview mirror, saw the flashing blue lights behind the white van. "What's happening back there?"

"Just checking a hunch."

❖

Rinnah felt the steam spouting out her ears by the time she tromped up the stairs to the apartment. Her daughter had whined nonstop all the way back, dragging her feet like a cat on a leash. Rinnah finally gave the girl a swat on the behind, which sparked off dry crying on Eve's part and a spiraling sense of guilt and failure on her own. *I'm turning into my parents*, she brooded. *Chava is just like I was, and now I'm just like them.*

"I don't see your backpack, Chava," she said when the apartment door came into view. "Where is it really?"

"I left it there, Mommy!" Each of Eve's words came out as a sob. "Really I did."

Damn it! She'd be so late for work. Jake must have taken it inside when he left. "We'll have to look for it, then."

❖

Gabir was ready. He'd filled the small duffel with things a burglar might take—some of the woman's jewelry, an iPod, CDs, a nice man's watch. For Jews, these people didn't have much that was valuable. He left the bag on the bed in the rear bedroom, unlatched and cracked open the window leading to the fire escape.

Keys scraped in the front door lock. Eldar must have returned. Gabir moved to the bedroom door and flipped off the pistol's safety.

❖

The white policeman finished with the van, joined his partner, shrugged. The African pulled a cell phone from his jacket pocket. "Give me your cousin's number."

Alayan recited Rafiq's phone number. He hoped Rafiq

97

remembered the plan.

Rafiq. Kassim. Had they found Kaminsky yet?

Forget Kaminsky, he scolded himself. *Worry about Eldar. Where's Gabir?*

"Hello, Mr. Hernandez? This is Officer Jardine of the NYPD. I have someone here who claims to be your cousin... yes, that's right, Federico Alvarez... nothing, sir, we're responding to a citizen's complaint about a suspicious vehicle... 18th and Prospect Park West... I see. Thank you for your time, sir." The policemen stabbed his phone with his thumb and gave Alayan a you-dumb-bastard look. "Your cousin says you're on the wrong street and you're an hour early. You're supposed to be at 505 16th."

Alayan hung his head in mock shame, and also to hide the scraps of relief he felt break out on his face. Rafiq had remembered the cover story. "*Lo siento, señor.*"

The white policeman handed Alayan his Spanish driver's license. "Best get moving."

"*Si, si*, I will." Once Eldar was dead.

❖

Gabir expected anything but a woman's voice. "Look in your room, Chava, quickly."

Or a child's. "Yes, Mommy."

A sharp dose of something like panic drilled his heart. *Now what? Leave?* No time; she was walking his way. *Hide? Where?* There wasn't that much to the flat—even the closets were tiny. *Face her down?* He didn't wear a mask; the whole idea was to let people see a black face run away from the scene, and with the dark makeup his face was certainly black.

Where's Eldar? Gabir swore to himself. *Why did this have to happen now?*

The woman stopped in the doorway, stared at him. Her mouth gapped, a silent "oh."

When Eldar returned, she'd warn him. She might call the police. She was in the way and had to go. He raised the gun, aimed at her forehead, and pulled the trigger.

❖

The police were less than thirty seconds gone when Alayan's phone bleeped. He flinched, then mashed down the button. "Yes?"

"The woman came back," Gabir's voice reported. "I eliminated her. I'm waiting—"

"You *what?*" *No no no no, you idiot...*

"I eliminated her. The man isn't here. How long should I wait for him, *sidi?*"

"Get out! Get out now! Someone will report the gunshot, the police are right here! Go, now!" Eldar wasn't there, so Gabir killed the woman instead? Why?

"Um, yes, *sidi.*" Gabir's voice had a tiny shake in it. "What do I do with the child?"

"The *what?*"

"The child, *sidi.* She's here, too. She hasn't seen me yet."

Damn damn damn... Her picture flashed in his mind. Adorable. *We have to draw the line somewhere.* "Leave her, get out! I'll get you on 17ᵗʰ Street. Get out, damn you, now!"

TWENTY-NINE

1 DECEMBER
BROOKLYN

Jake tried to picture her face. The image wouldn't focus, as if dirty fingers had smudged his mind's eye. *Rinnah...*

The strip lights in the Kings County Hospital pediatric ER waiting area ought to have been bright, but instead seemed on half-power. Sounds were muffled, far away, despite the crowd of new victims and their companions, doctors and nurses, cleaners, clerks, and cops.

He stared at the NYPD officer who'd driven him here. The uniform leaned a shoulder against the cream corridor wall, vending-machine coffee cup in hand, chatting with a hospital cop. How could he be so calm? Why wasn't he looking for the bastard who did this? NYPD glanced back at Jake, gave him a pitying shake of his head, turned away.

A hard, gray emptiness packed Jake's brain, blotting out all feeling except the biting cold and the whirlpool in his stomach that splashed bile into his throat. He closed his eyes, dropped his head between his knees. He wanted to cry, but couldn't. He wanted to get mad, but couldn't.

The fat woman next to him left; another big presence replaced her, rocking his plastic chair. The newcomer was quiet for a few moments. "How you doing, kid?"

Jake willed himself upright, pried open his eyes. Gene's black wool overcoat spread open, revealing his dark blue double-breasted suit. An NYPD shield in a leather holder hung from the coat's breast pocket. The sparkle was gone from his uncle's eyes.

"I..." Jake couldn't make his mouth connect with his brain. He worked his jaw a few times before he forced out, "I should feel something. Why can't I feel anything?"

"You're in shock." Gene patted Jake's thigh. "Shock's a good place to be right now, believe me. Pretty soon you'll feel plenty."

Jake heard the words but didn't process them. He returned his attention to the corridor wall. "I want Eve."

"Soon, kid, they—"

"I want my daughter!" He didn't think he had that much volume left in him. Several people in the waiting area turned to look.

"Jake." Gene grabbed his bicep. "The doctors are taking care of her. You can see her soon."

"Doctors? Why? What happened to her? Is she hurt?"

"No, no, nothing like that. Look. EMS had a hard time getting her away from Rinnah. She was hysterical. I talked to the nurse. They gave her something to calm her down, they're checking her for injuries, they're cleaning her up. She'll be fine."

"Cleaning her up? What does that mean?"

Gene took a deep breath, pushed his fingers through his hair. "There was a lot of blood."

"Blood? You said she wasn't hurt! Why was she bleeding? How—"

"Kid. It wasn't her blood."

Jake's stomach heaved. He clamped a shaking hand over his mouth and looked away, fought the visions that tore at his mind. *Not her blood. Rinnah's...* "I need to see her."

"You can see Chava pretty soon, they'll come—"

"No. Rinnah."

"No." Gene shook his big, square head, his face grim. "You don't."

Jake grabbed his overcoat lapel, tried to shake him. "I have to see her! I want... I need..."

Gene enveloped Jake's hand in both of his. "No, kid, you don't. Not the way she is now. First of all, she's maybe still at the scene, you don't want to go there."

The scene. Their home—the place they'd shared, lived in, loved in—was a just another crime scene now. "Still? Why?"

"CSU has to process the scene, then the M.E. has to look her over in place before they take her to the morgue. It takes time, it's not like on TV." He squeezed Jake's hand. "You'll get her back, I promise."

"Don't I have to... identify her or something?"

"No, I already did. I went there before I came here. That's how I know you don't want to see her now. Let the M.E. clean her up. Then you can see her." Gene gently released Jake's hand, laid his arm across Jake's shoulders. "I put the word out—this is a family thing. The guys at the Seven-Two are all over this, and the borough Homicide Squad's involved. We're going to get the son-of-a-bitch who did this, and it won't go easy for him, you understand?"

Jake nodded. It wouldn't bring Rinnah back; nothing could. *She's innocent, damn it!* She'd done nothing to deserve this. He'd enjoy killing the bastard who took her away from him and Eve. There, another feeling—anger.

"Monica and I want you two to stay with us, for as long as you—"

"No, I can't, I don't want to put you—"

"Kid, just shut up, alright? You're in no condition to think right now. We have lots of room, and Chava's going to need a woman's touch for a while. We're glad to have you. In fact, if you don't come stay, I'll be insulted, you don't want that. All right?"

"Okay." Jake tried to take a deep breath, but still couldn't. The emptiness weighed heavy on his lungs.

"Mr. Eldar?"

Both Gene and Jake answered together. "Yeah?"

A female doctor—petite, Asian eyes and flat planes in her face—stood in front of them in green scrubs and a white coat, clipboard in her hand. "Jacob Eldar?"

Jake raised his hand. "That's me."

"Want to come back and see your daughter?"

The men followed her through a double swinging door, past busy exam rooms and bustling staff. They pushed into one of the rooms. Eve was laid out on a stainless-steel examination table, draped in an oversized white paper gown. Jake leaped to the table, gathered her up, crushed her limp body to his chest, started gently rocking her. "Eve! Bunny! Thank God! It's okay, Daddy's here, and Uncle Gene. You're safe."

No response. He pulled back a few inches. Eve's eyes swiveled his way, still red from crying, but didn't focus.

"You're okay now. It's gonna be okay." Jake brushed some damp hair from her forehead, rocked some more, just as he had when she woke up crying as a baby. He caressed her little round, soft cheek. She pressed against his palm, but stayed silent. Fear started to chip through Jake's gray void. "Eve? Bunny?"

Eve slowly wrapped her arms around his neck and held on with what little strength she had. Her chin trembled. She was so quiet, not even a whisper or a sob.

He glanced back to the doctor. "Is she okay? Is she hurt?"

"Not physically."

"What does that mean?"

The doctor motioned to the door with her clipboard. Gene reached for Eve, but Jake hunched over her and held her tighter. His uncle wrapped an arm around his shoulders. "Kid, it's okay. I'll hold her. Talk to the doctor."

Gene pulled Eve from Jake's unwilling arms, gave his nephew a gentle push. Jake drifted back to the door, his eyes riveted to his daughter. Her face. She had Rinnah's face.

At the door, the doctor—her ID badge said "Evelyn Kwan"— touched his sleeve. "Mr. Eldar... your daughter's had a terrible experience. The little ones deal with that differently than we do. It's hard to predict how they'll react." Jake half-listened, watching Eve nestle like a cub in Gene's bear-like arms. "She's in shock. We gave her a strong sedative; she should be asleep pretty soon. We won't know what she'll do until she does it. I'd like you to bring her back tomorrow to see one of our pediatric psychologists." Jake barely noticed the pause until she said, "Mr. Eldar?"

"Yeah, whatever." He watched Gene sway from side to side, his arms a cradle. Eve's eyes drooped closed; the hand gripping Gene's lapel slid to her chest. "What do I do? How do I help her?"

Dr. Kwan touched his sleeve again. "Just love her. Be with her. She'll probably be clingy, but let her cling. She's going to be different for a while. So will you, I imagine. Help her feel safe. It's the best medicine for you both."

Safe. What was that? Would either of them ever feel safe again?

In the restroom, Jake pushed water into his eyes to wash away the nervous sweat and the hopelessness. A thought burned through the void. *Rinnah's face. I have to see Rinnah's face.*

A series of pointed fingers sent him out the Emergency Department's back doors into the cold, across Winthrop, to the brick-and-glass NYC Medical Examiner's Brooklyn headquarters. He saw only the patch of ground in front of him; everything else was a smear. He could hear Rinnah's voice, sounds without words, echoing to him from a long way off. Through the glass doors, to the reception desk. "I need to identify a... my wife."

A young, round-faced investigator appeared, fast-talking, Puerto Rican accent, his collar and tie too tight. "Sir, an Inspector Eldar already ID'ed your wife at the scene. He's related?"

"I need to see her."

"Sir, she just came in. The M.E. hasn't gotten to her yet. If you could wait—"

"I need to see her."

"If you give me a few minutes, I can bring you a photo—"

Tears poured down Jake's neck. His voice broke. "No photo. Her. Now."

Hurried phone calls, hushed voices, pitying glances. Rinnah images flickered in Jake's head. Rinnah splashing on the beach in Tel Aviv, Rinnah beckoning to him from his bed at the university, Rinnah anxiously showing her visa to the Immigration guy at JFK for the first time. In every one, her face was smudged, shaded. Jake palmed away the tears, tried to clear his eyes. He had to see her face. *I'm coming, honey, soon...*

"Sir?" The investigator was back, anxious. Jake didn't want to stop the film running in his head. "Give me ten minutes, okay? You can see her, just ten minutes."

Jake paced, but the images took over his world. Small moments. Rinnah hanging curtains at that first crappy apartment, in her bra and briefs because of the heat. Her first nighttime walk through Times Square, wonder in her eyes. Shopping for their first furniture together. Rinnah holding Eve moments after she was born. This morning: "I love you."

The investigator led Jake through buzzing security doors and down a corridor. Alcohol and disinfectant attacked his nose. The tunnel vision worked for Jake—he could see linoleum and white paint, but not the sheet-draped shapes on the gurneys. Until they stopped.

"Sir, are you sure you want to do this?"

It's not real 'til you see her. "I have to. I have to." When did his voice get so shaky?

Does she know I'm here?

I'm here, honey, I've come for you...

The investigator sighed, nodded, then carefully peeled the sheet away from her face.

Pale, still. Livid puckered skin around a single neat, round hole in her forehead. Her face was wet; they'd clearly tried to wash off the blood, but it had gathered in the crevices around her closed eyes, in her ears, her hairline. A water droplet heavy with red residue hung at the corner of her eye, then slid down her temple into her hair; a tear of blood.

My love. He reached out, but couldn't bear to touch her. *My wife. Eve's mother.*

Gone. And our baby too...

The Rinnah movie jammed, burned through. Jake's mind, overfull with the void, tried to claw back the images. They wouldn't come. The picture before him was all he could see now. He felt things breaking inside him, his world tearing in two.

A wounded-animal howl echoed off the corridor walls.

It was the sound of his heart shattering.

105

THIRTY

A New York City television station carried the story on its midday news. Alayan recognized 18th Street, Eldar's building, even the policeman who'd searched the van. Police cars filled the road. *All that for a woman?* His anger and frustration turned to dread when the police spokesman said, "We consider the victim part of the NYPD family, and a crime committed against any part of our family is committed against all of us."

She was in the *police?* Alayan stepped through all 143 photos in the woman's Flickr portfolio and didn't find one of her in uniform. Was she a detective? Someone in their crime lab? No matter; they wouldn't stop looking for who killed her. An NYPD jihad. *Why now? Only three targets left...*

Gabir slumped in the chunky green armchair facing the window. Alayan had berated that donkey on the way back from Brooklyn until he lost his fire and nearly his voice. All he could see now was the back of Gabir's head, silhouetted against the midday haze; he couldn't tell whether Gabir was still awake. He didn't really care.

A single knock on the door, a pause, another single knock.

Alayan started. He swept his pistol off the desktop and moved noiselessly to the door. He cupped his gun hand around the peephole, then peeled back the painters' tape covering the glass eyepiece. Kassim and Rafiq stood outside.

Alayan murmured "We have a problem" as he let them slip into the room. He glanced down the corridor to check for watchers.

"You mean in addition to Kaminsky's house being empty?" Kassim replied.

"What do you mean, 'empty'?"

"Just that. Nobody lives there." Kassim sat on the end of the bed closest to the door, whipped off his woolen scarf, rubbed his upper arms. "Rafiq played electric man and checked. There's no furniture."

Damn it! Alayan hit the wall next to the bathroom door with the heel of his hand. "How can that be? That's the address on his passport. Our friends in the Beirut police confirmed it."

"That's where his passport was sent when he got it." Rafiq stood in front of the muted television, watching the flickering pictures. "Americans don't have to change the address when they move until they renew the passport."

Alayan said, "Not a problem. We follow him from his work to his new home."

"He's travelling for his company. I called to check. They wouldn't say where he was or when he'd be back." Rafiq gave Alayan a grim smile. "More Americans who understand security."

Alayan stifled the urge to kick the bathroom door. Could anything else go wrong today?

Kassim asked, "Is Eldar eliminated?"

"No. He wasn't in the flat, but the wife was. Gabir shot her."

Rafiq's eyes went huge. "What?" He rounded on Gabir, who had pushed himself out of the chair. "You did *what?*"

"I had to," Gabir said. "She saw me."

"You idiot!" Rafiq rushed Gabir, grabbed him by the throat and rammed him into the wall next to the window. "Stupid son of a whore!"

Kassim and Alayan waded into the cursing, struggling men. Alayan ripped Gabir away from Rafiq, shouted "Enough!" and flung the larger man toward the closest bed. Rafiq shrugged out of Kassim's arms and stalked to the window, raising his hands in an "I'm done" gesture.

After a few moments of glares and tense breathing, Alayan snapped, "We have enough problems without the two of you fighting like jealous women. Yes, Gabir failed. I know you fancied her, Rafiq, but we could live with the woman's death if Eldar was eliminated. But he wasn't—he's still alive and he's going to be harder to reach now."

"You don't understand, *sidi*." The desolate look in Rafiq's eyes told Alayan the man was hurt more than he wanted to show. Why? Was Rafiq getting too soft for this? "Yes, she was pretty and nice. Killing her was totally unnecessary. But that's not the big problem."

Alayan caught Kassim's eye, saw the deepening gloom there. "All right, tell us."

"Fine. You kill a black man in this country and no one notices. You kill a white man, everybody says, 'oh, what a tragedy,' then they go about their business. But kill a young, pretty white woman—" he thrust an angry finger toward Gabir, who grimaced "—like that *bokhesh* did, and it'll be on the news for days, weeks maybe. *Especially* when she's a mother. The police go crazy looking for the killer, they get so much pressure from the news and the politicians. That dog—" he shook his finger again at Gabir "—just put us in the middle of what they call a 'shitstorm' here." He used the English word.

"But she saw me," Gabir repeated, stubborn and angry.

"Then knock her on the head and tie her up. She'd tell them some big, stupid black man hit her, and you know what? Everybody would be glad it didn't turn out worse. Burglary's hardly even a real crime here anymore, there are so many." Rafiq's eyes turned hard and black. "You better not have shot that beautiful little girl."

"No. She didn't see me."

Clouds of dread gathered and grew dark around Alayan's head as Rafiq ranted on. Back home, the murder of a woman would barely rate a mention in the papers unless she was related to someone important. Rafiq had spent four years living with these people, learning how they think and act, and now they all knew they had yet another complication on top of the rest.

Time to take control again. "That's enough. All that aside, Eldar's been warned. He'll be more careful, he may even get police protection." He glared at Gabir and Rafiq in turn. "I need you men to think. We need to get to Eldar. You've both watched him, now make something of it. Gabir, go to your room."

Gabir shot one more venomous look at Rafiq, mumbled, "Yes, *sidi*," and stomped out the door.

The three remaining men watched each other, their breathing

the only definite sound in the room. Finally, Alayan said, "There's something else. The police searched me and the van during the operation."

Kassim moaned and dragged his hands through his hair.

"They can place me and the van on that street when everything happened."

Kassim swore and stomped to the window. "Where's the van now?"

"Down the street, at the Hampton Inn. It needs to go back to where it came from, and we need another one, from another company. I need you two to take care of that."

"That's easy," Kassim answered. "How in hell do we take *you* back?"

Alayan's own frustration echoed in his friend's voice. "Ziyad's working on one of the backup passports for me. He said he'll be done tonight. One more thing. We need the police to think they've solved the woman's case."

"Are you going to give them Gabir?" Rafiq grumbled.

"No. I've been doing some research. There's an African street gang called the Slope Mafia on the other side of the motorway from Eldar's flat. Kassim, take Gabir there tonight, find one of these Slope Mafia people, kill him, put Gabir's weapon on him and leave the things he took from the flat. Understand?"

Kassim stared back at him, eyebrows raised, eyes blank. "Are you insane?"

"You have a better plan?"

"Yes. Get Gabir out of the country, now, before a witness shows up or someone recognizes him." Kassim's words were bit off at the ends, driven home like nails.

"You're the one who's always complaining we don't have enough people. Now you want to just send one away?"

"At least it's sure to work, not like this charade you—"

"Hey, hey, hey!" Rafiq stood between them, hands outstretched, waving them down. "You two can't fight, understand? You fight, and we're all dead. Okay?" He looked from Alayan to Kassim, who turned away, nodded, took a deep breath. After a moment, Rafiq said, "It's not guaranteed, but this might almost work. Nobody will care about a dead gangster. The only people who can clear him are other gangsters. Who'll listen, right?"

"Kassim?" Alayan said to his friend's back.

Kassim shook his head and sighed. "All right, fine, we'll find a gang." He glanced back, face rigid. "But you're still insane."

THIRTY-ONE

1 DECEMBER
SECAUCUS

Gur and his five agents clustered around the hotel room's wood-topped, two-person round table, examining the screen of Kelila's secure laptop.

"We found the van in the Hampton Inn car park by the Newark airport, around three," David reported. "Good hunch, sir. Around three-forty, two men came out and got in the van."

It was almost more than a hunch, Gur thought. He and Kelila had followed the white van for miles until the driver bolted, veered away from the entrance to the New Jersey Turnpike at the very last moment and disappeared into the industrial port area. *So close...*

David clicked to a telephoto shot of the white van and two men in winter coats, the shorter one's head half-turned to his taller companion. Dark curly hair almost in ringlets, a Roman nose, a Mediterranean complexion.

"Anyone?" Gur asked the group. They shook their heads. No one recognized the man.

David advanced to the next picture. Now the taller man turned full-face to the shorter one. Good-looking, light-skinned, short black hair.

Kelila bent, examined the picture. "I saw him when we were tailing Eldar on Tuesday. He was in a suit. When Eldar crossed Court Street to go to the store, this one turned north and walked off."

"Are you sure?" Gur asked, already knowing the answer. Kelila didn't speak out unless she was sure of what she was saying.

She glanced up at him, still grumpy from the morning's failure. "Yes, I'm sure."

"Right." If only they had enough people, they could've kept watch on Eldar's place properly. But they didn't, and Eldar's wife was dead because of it. Another dead innocent; a family torn apart. He knew what Eldar was going through right now, and that knowledge made him feel weak and useless. He sighed, put those thoughts away for later.

He turned back to David. "What happened then?"

"They took the van to Hertz, where they dropped it off and took the train to the airport. Natan tailed them. They got off and got right back on going the other way. They took a shuttle to the Enterprise rental office, where they rented a Ford Econoline cargo van with New Jersey registration plates. We followed them back to the airport Renaissance."

These Arabs had done this before. Amateurs would hold onto the other van, or rent another at the same place or one next door. "Did they make you?"

"If they did, they didn't act like it."

"Natan, how close did you get to them in the train?"

Natan stuffed his hands in the pockets of his suede bomber jacket and shrugged. "In the next train car, so they didn't see me."

Good tradecraft, but not helpful. "Did you hear anything?"

"No. They were quiet at the bus stop. Alert, but no talking."

Gur leaned back, laced his fingers on top of his head and forced a breath between his lips. "Right. There's at least three of them then, probably more."

"More," Amzi said. "They did Brown last night and Eldar's wife this morning. Even we're not that good. They have two teams going."

"Good point. So six or eight, perhaps more, and we've seen three. Kelila, any help from Research?"

Kelila stood straighter, going into briefing mode. "I talked to the desk officer when we got back here. Six known Hezbollah militiamen flew out of Beirut on 10th October. Each of them headed for a different country, but we lost track of them there. The analyst thinks they switched to European passports when they touched down, then flew to Amsterdam. Our guys are checking security footage at the airports now."

"No identities?"

"Not yet, but we're leaning on our Hezbollah sources."

"Excellent." Gur stifled another sigh; the Watch Center had begun to look like paradise. "Kelila, send the pictures of these two over to Research and see what they can come up with. Also, see if they can pull the passport photo for Mr. Alvarez."

"Yes, sir."

"Amzi, Sasha, go to the Renaissance. One of you watches the van, the other checks out the lobby and restaurants. Switch off, stay on post for four hours. David, Natan, you're next, four hours. Kelila and I will relieve you. We watch that van until it moves, then we follow it. Understand?" Everyone nodded. Gur pointed to Amzi and Sasha. "You two, dress warm. It's supposed to start snowing tonight. The last thing we need is a pair of frozen Jews."

"We Russians don't freeze, boss," Sasha said, straight-faced. "Just you sabra pussies."

A couple of the others chuckled. Amzi flicked the back of Sasha's blond head. Gur snorted. "Get to work, people."

They filtered from Gur's room one by one until only Kelila was left behind. She perched on the edge of her chair, lips pressed flat, pounding her laptop's keys as if they were bugs needing to be squashed.

Gur read her face: frustration, helpless anger. He leaned forward, tried to catch her eye. "Kelila." The keyboard's clicks didn't slow. "You're taking the letters off the keys."

She slapped her palms on the tabletop. "We should've done something. We let her down." Kelila threw a half-pleading, half-accusing look at Gur. "We're supposed to protect people like them, but we didn't and now that little girl doesn't have a mother anymore. I think of Hasia without me, and it just makes me…" She rushed out a hard breath. "I feel like I should've tried harder. Like it's our fault. *My* fault."

Gur understood all too well. Rinnah Eldar was yet another name to add to the long list of people he'd failed to save. He rocked out of his chair, eased behind her, gently laid a hand on each of her shoulders. "Yes, we let her down. No, it's not our fault." He began to knead the tension out of her shoulders. She dropped her hands to her lap and rocked with each stroke. "Remember who did this. Hold onto that, you'll need it later."

"It was easier running agents in France with the DCRI on my butt."

"I warned you about that when you first came to us." Kelila smiled with only one corner of her mouth. Gur slid his hands up until his thumbs brushed the sides of her neck. The softness of her skin melted through his hands. "I know how you feel. It's miserable. It helps to have someone to talk to, someone who understands. I'm happy to listen."

She twisted to look up at him. "I hate whining. You know that."

He gave her shoulders a squeeze. "It's not whining. Either you let it out, or it chews its way out. It's better to let it out, believe me."

She turned away and sighed. "Just keep doing what you're doing. It feels great."

How many times had he done this for Varda? She'd come home from the Ministry tired and frustrated, and he'd help her wind down—when he'd been home, which hadn't been often enough. The feel of Kelila's strong shoulders relaxing under his fingertips and her warmth flowing from beneath her blouse awakened a jumble of old memories and newer feelings.

Kelila let her head roll back until her hair just brushed the front of his heavy twill shirt. The silence lingered. *Comfortable*, Gur thought. *Natural. I've missed this so.* But what had he missed—the physical contact? Well, yes. The gentle weight of her hair against his stomach stirred a reaction he hoped she wouldn't notice, or she wouldn't mind if she did. But more than that, he'd missed *being*, sharing quiet time, companionship. Comfort. Had she missed it too?

Her breathing became deep and content. It would be so easy to bend down and kiss her, to run his hands over the rise of her breasts. She'd let him know in the Watch Center she'd welcome that. But so many traps lurked along that road; falling in one would cost him not just her, but *this*. *Being*. Was it worth the risk? Really?

Gur sighed. "Just be glad you can feel this way. It means you're still human. There's still hope for you."

"You think?"

"Yes."

She slipped a warm hand over his, looked up at him, smiled. "Thank you, Raffi. And if you can say things like that, there's hope for you, too."

He squeezed her hand, and she squeezed back. "From your lips to God's ears."

THIRTY-TWO

1 DECEMBER
NEWARK

Two hours after he'd left, Kassim charged back through Alayan's door. "We're leaving."

"Excuse me?"

Kassim grabbed the suitcase off the wardrobe floor, tossed it on the bed. "We were followed to the airport." Alayan stood rooted by the door, absorbing this latest disaster. Kassim watched him for a moment, then spread his hands. "Fadi? Did you hear me?"

"Yes. Yes." Alayan shook off the momentary shock and strode to the bed. They'd been so careful; how did the police find them? "Who was it?"

"It doesn't matter. It was time to go this morning, this just confirms it. We're done here. Let's go south, eliminate Schaffer and get out of this country."

"And leave Eldar and Kaminsky? Fail to finish the mission? You remember what happens then, don't you?"

Kassim closed the distance between them and clapped his hands on Alayan's shoulders. "Think. We've eliminated nine of the twelve in two and a half months. Kaminsky's disappeared, and Eldar's life is destroyed. If the Council wants to start throwing bombs around after all that, there's no satisfying them. Being dead or in prison won't stop them, either."

Alayan looked away. They were so close to success. Kaminsky couldn't stay away forever. Eldar would come out of hiding eventually. *But how long is that?* Alayan asked himself. *Before the start of Hanukkah? Before the Party sets off its bombs?* The sense of Kassim's words finally seeped into his better judgment. "You still have to clean up from this morning."

116

"Yes, yes, I know, I will. But we need you to get out of here first."

"What about the others?"

"They're already packing. I told them you'd ordered it." He tried on a smile. "You're not going to make me a liar, are you?"

It felt like a defeat, running away like this. But Alayan realized Kassim had a point—staying would be foolish and could lead them to disaster. *Be smart, listen to Kassim,* he told himself. Mossad would move on, live to fight again tomorrow. And so would he.

THIRTY-THREE

Al-Shami finished wiring the light bulb and ducked between the twin banks of gray-painted metal shelves, straight out the van's open back doors. He straightened and made a leisurely circuit of the vehicle, examining his work.

The Eastside Electric logo on the back doors and each side of the cargo box came from a real Upper East Side firm he'd found on the Internet, phone numbers and all. Weathering had taken some time, since he'd needed the van to look used but not wrecked; a bit of gravel scour at the rear edge of each wheel well, a crease in the right front fender, bare metal on a windshield-wiper arm, scrapes in the white paint, scratches on the chrome grille. He was especially happy with the New York commercial plates. He'd found them in a junkyard in Buffalo on a mangled van much like this one, hammered them flat, repainted them so they'd look weathered but undamaged. He'd even had a contact print replica registration stickers for them. Perfect.

He stopped when he reached the rear doors once again. Al-Shami slid his cell phone from his back pocket and thumbed in a number. He punched "dial." One ring. The light bulb on the floor behind the seats glowed white.

Satisfied, he put away his phone. The van's electronics were complete. The cheap pre-paid cellphone he'd bought in a Buffalo Wal-Mart was now a detonator. He'd learned in Iraq that no matter how dedicated the *shahid*, there was a huge gulf between the theory of sacrificing one's life for the cause and actually pushing the button. If the driver of this bomb-on-wheels lost his will at the last moment, al-Shami could call a single phone number to set off the explosives.

The van was ready. The wheeled aluminum oxygen tank was ready. The parcel in the businesslike brown cardboard box was done. The *shuhada* were nearly ready. All al-Shami needed was the final go-ahead from the Council. Then the 650-mile drive to New York City, and an appointment in Manhattan.

THIRTY-FOUR

Jake wasn't even trying to go to sleep anymore. Every time he started sliding off the edge of consciousness, what slithered out of the back of his brain jolted him awake. The eerie quiet didn't help; he was too used to the white noise of home, the traffic, the old building's groans, the thumps of his neighbors. Music outside, TVs inside. Rinnah softly buzzing next to him.

The empty grayness inside him slowly retreated, making room for the hurt and fear and sorrow and anger that kept him alert and open-eyed in his uncle's darkened guest bedroom. And the guilt. He should've told her what was happening. He should've been there. Any other day, he would've been there. He was supposed to protect Rinnah, and he'd failed her catastrophically. The image of the hole in her forehead stayed burned into the movie screen of his mind.

He'd failed Eve, too. The walls of his heart cracked as he stroked her hair. She'd lasted perhaps two minutes in the other bed before she crawled into his. Now she was a tight coil of girl burrowed into his chest. The pills Dr. Kwan prescribed were supposed to drop Eve like a rock into a deep, dreamless sleep, but her broken whimpers and twitching feet disproved that theory.

When the clock plowed past two-thirty, Jake gave up. He carefully slid out of bed, tucked up Eve, and stumbled to the little desk where he'd placed his laptop. Maybe he could read himself to sleep.

The shockingly-bright computer screen lit half the room in pale blue. He let his eyes adjust, then opened a browser. The Feeds tab listed half a dozen publishing blogs he followed. He stabbed the top one with his mouse pointer and started to read.

The text bounced off his eyes and landed on the floor without making the tiniest impression. Instead of dozing off, his brain started listing all the things he needed to do. He hadn't yet told Rinnah's parents, or his own. He needed to make arrangements. That's how it came into his mind: "make arrangements," code for the details of morticians and caskets and graves. How do people do that? The worst day in their lives, and they're expected to make decisions about things they've tried to never think about. He needed to talk to Rabbi Teitelman; she'd know what to do.

Which reminded him he hadn't prayed for Rinnah yet. He was very out of practice with praying. Why would God listen to him now? But if He existed, He could look after Rinnah. This was all Jake could do for her now, so he should at least try. Maybe later Jake could ask God just what the hell He was thinking, letting this happen.

He noticed the "Doha 12" folder's name showed in bold, meaning it held new feeds. He clicked on it, found the Google News feed for Nathan Brown also in bold. Jake hesitated, then clicked. After reading it he stared at the screen, hands covering his mouth.

Jake knew who killed Rinnah.

THIRTY-FIVE

2 DECEMBER
STATEN ISLAND

Jake hunched over Gene's and Monica's dining table, chin on his hands, staring at his phone. He'd done enough damage with it already this morning; could he stand to do more?

He rubbed at the caffeine headache he'd developed after finishing off most of a pot of coffee since five A.M., when he started calling Israel. He'd told his parents first; it went just as badly as he'd expected. He got a lot of "You should've stayed here" and "you went there to be safer?" He'd hoped maybe this once they wouldn't bust his chops. It was too much to hope for.

Rinnah's parents were even worse, but in a completely different way. They were far more gracious than they should have been, considering the news he brought them. They worried about Jake and Eve, sympathized, asked "Are you okay?" a million times. In the end, their concern made him feel more worthless than his parents' barbs.

He'd cornered Gene in the kitchen when his uncle came out at six and showed him the article about Nathan Brown, how the East Islip father of two was one of the victims of a double-murder at FlashDancers. Surly and sleep-deprived, Jake had demanded, "How many more of us get to die before you guys take this seriously?"

Gene frowned at the screen and ran his fingers through his hair. "Okay, you got a point, kid. This is getting too weird. I'll hit JTTF with it this morning, hard. That okay?"

The Joint Terrorism Task Force people lived for this kind of puzzle. If anyone would break it open, they would. "Yeah. Thanks, Gene."

"Go back to bed, kid. Take care of Chava."

The clock on the mantelpiece read eight thirty. Monica was giving Eve a bath. Jake spun his phone with his fingers, watched the snow trickle down outside. Lack of sleep and blankness instead of a future left him feeling half-dead. Concentration became an exotic mental exercise. Every time he looked at Eve, his heart turned to sand.

Only two of the other Doha 12 were still alive. Should he warn them? What if he was wrong? He'd look and sound like a nut. Would he believe this story if some stranger called to tell it to him?

But what if he was right?

❖

Miriam picked up her phone on the third ring. "Mr. Dickinson's office, may I help you?"

"Are you Miriam Schaffer?"

"Yes, I am. May I help you?"

The man on the other end of the line took a deep, hesitant breath. "My name is Jake Eldar. I live in Brooklyn. You don't know me, but we have something in common."

She pulled the receiver away from her head, checked the earpiece to see if anything was crawling out. Who was this person? Was one of her friends trying to set her up with someone? "Um... what would that be, Mr. Eldar?"

"We're both on the INTERPOL list, from the thing in Qatar. And neither of us had anything to do with it."

Something went still and watchful inside her. Was this a joke? Yet another crank call? She brought up her computer's web browser and looked up the INTERPOL Red Notice page. A moment later, there he was. "I'll assume this picture isn't yours, Mr. Eldar."

"No, just like the one for you isn't you." He took another deep breath. "Look, I'm sorry to call you like this, but I need to tell you something. It's going to sound pretty weird, but, well, please just go with it, okay?"

Now an alarm blasted inside her. She'd dealt with so many freaks and idiots after the list came out. What kind of gibberish would this one come up with? Aliens had chosen them to mate? They were tools of the Antichrist? The Masons were behind that

LANCE CHARNES

terrorist's death? "Really, I don't want to get involved in whatever—"

"Someone's trying to kill us."

Miriam shook her head hard to confirm she was awake. "I beg your pardon?"

"Look. Go over the twelve names on the list. All the Europeans are dead except for Krosner, who's missing. Demetrio, Brown and Nussberger are dead, too. All between the 23rd of September and this past Wednesday. And yesterday... yesterday, someone killed my wife."

She couldn't stop the gasp that jumped from her mouth. This, she hadn't expected. But it couldn't be true, could it? "Um, excuse me, but wouldn't this be all over the news? I haven't heard anything about this, not at all, and I keep up with the news."

"Nobody's put it together yet. All the killings were done differently. My uncle's an inspector in the NYPD, he's going to talk to the terrorism people about it, but I think you and Kaminsky need to know so you can be careful. That's why I'm calling."

"Who's Kaminsky?"

"Another one of us. He lives in Paramus, works in Midtown."

While this Eldar person gabbled on, Miriam searched for the name "Oren Nussberger." A brief news article: he'd hung himself on Thanksgiving. "Nussberger committed suicide," she said, more confident this supposed Eldar person was just another crazy.

"Uh-huh, sure. Demetrio, Brown, Schoonhaven and Dujardin were murdered. The rest had accidents. Look it up. Please, I know it's hard to—"

"Could you give me a moment?" she asked just before she punched the "hold" button.

Think. Is he serious? Another kook? Eldar sounded frazzled, but if his wife had been killed the day before, he had a right to be. She searched for "Eldar +Brooklyn +murder" and clicked through to a New York TV station website. A pretty dark-haired woman in a sundress smiled out from a photo. Rinnah Eldar, 34, shot in the head by a burglar yesterday morning. *God, and pregnant, too.*

Her finger took a long time to reach the "hold" button again. "How did you get my number, Mr. Eldar?"

"The story in the *Inquirer* from a few weeks back said where you work. That's kinda the point—if I can find you, so can they."

"They who?"

"If I had to bet, I'd say Hezbollah. It's their guy we supposedly killed."

Now she knew this guy was a kook. "You're wrong, Mr. Eldar. I have some experience with those—" she almost said *bastards*, but remembered herself "—people, and they couldn't do anything like what you're suggesting. I don't know what you want, but I'm not—"

"All I want is for you to be careful, that's all, I—"

"Goodbye, Mr. Eldar—"

"Look, please, I know it sounds crazy, just look it up—"

"Goodbye. Please don't call me again." She hung up with more force than she needed but not enough to get her point across.

Hezbollah. Really! Those cockroaches who'd attacked her home, killed her father? Eldar's story sounded like a spy movie, and that just wasn't something the damned Arabs were capable of. She'd gotten a lot of crank phone calls after the Qataris released her name—that's why she'd agreed to the newspaper story—but nothing this bizarre.

Rinnah Eldar still smiled on the screen. If this really was his wife, then Miriam would try to be charitable and figure he was distraught, not thinking straight. But she certainly hoped she'd never hear from Mr. Eldar again.

125

THIRTY-SIX

3 DECEMBER
STATEN ISLAND

Jake stopped rolling the tire-sized ball of snow and hunched to look into Eve's eyes. "What do you think, Bunny? Bigger?"

Eve pondered the snowman's bottom end, then peeked across the street at the competing snowman the Rodgers' three grandsons were scraping together on their front lawn. After a moment, she shrugged.

He stifled a sigh. Why wouldn't she talk? Jake screwed on a smile he didn't feel, hoped it wouldn't look too fake. "How 'bout a little bigger, then? We want a good snowman for Uncle Gene and Aunt Monica, right?" Eve nodded. "Okay, help me push."

Jake had tried to keep Eve busy for the past two days, tried to make her feel safe and to keep himself from thinking—reading, watching DVDs, baking cookies. Now this. As they heaved the globe another six feet up the incline toward the house, he glimpsed the white-and-blue car behind them. Officially, the 122nd Precinct couldn't post a guard on the house; unofficially, a patrol unit lurked at the curb whenever it wasn't on a call. Jake couldn't decide if this was a comfort or yet another shadow over his head and Eve's.

Jake knelt next to Eve. His jeans were already cold and wet from the knees down. "Big enough? You want it big like Uncle Gene?" He curved his arms around an imaginary belly. The ghost of a smile flitted over Eve's lips, gone in a moment, but the best sight Jake had seen in the past couple of days. "Okay. Pack on some more snow."

He watched Eve's pink mittens plump out the snowman-to-be and saw another winter seven years gone. Rinnah hadn't been in snow since her parents took her to Mount Hermon when she was thirteen. On the first Saturday morning they'd awakened to a white-cloaked New York City, Jake had taken Rinnah to Central Park. They rode a horse-drawn carriage and rented plastic saucers to slide down a gentle slope. And they'd built a snowman.

Eve looked just like her mother. Their faces melted together—Eve, then Rinnah, then Eve again—until Jake had to look away, choke down the sob fighting up his throat. *I'm sorry* ran in a loop through his head. Who was he apologizing to? Rinnah? Eve? Himself? Did it matter?

Car doors slammed. Jake twisted, noticed the dark-blue Crown Victoria nosed up behind the patrol car. Two men in dark overcoats and gloves slogged through the snowplow's leavings to get to the shoveled front walk.

Eve flung herself to his side, trying to disappear into the bulk of his parka. He sucked in a halting breath, wrapped his arms around her. "It's okay, Bunny. They're policemen." Brooklyn Homicide Squad. Detective DeAngelo, in the lead, had questioned Jake the evening Rinnah was killed; Jake couldn't remember the black partner's name.

DeAngelo nodded to him as the pair marched to the front door. *What do they want?* He heard Gene's voice but couldn't make out the words. If they had news, they'd tell him, right?

Jake turned back to Eve. "Hey, let's fatten this guy up, okay?"

They padded out the snowman half-heartedly, each of them watching the front doorstep and each other. When the two detectives reappeared, Eve scrambled behind Jake again, panic all over her face. Jake squatted in the snow until Gene shouldered his way past the Homicide Squad men and beckoned to him. "Hey, kid, got a minute?"

Jake couldn't read Gene's expression. *Good thing or bad?* Eve's hands grabbed at the hem of his parka when he stood. He pulled off a glove, bent, cupped her cheek in his hand. "I'm just going over there with Uncle Gene. You can watch me, okay? I'll be right there. Jasmine'll keep you company." He slid the doll from his coat pocket, pressed her into Eve's hands, kissed the top of his daughter's head through her hood, then backed away until he stood next to Gene. Eve never took her eyes off him. "What's up?" he asked Gene.

DeAngelo edged into Jake's field of vision, glanced at Eve, then hunched in closer. "We think we got the fuck who did your wife," he said, keeping his voice low.

Stunned, Jake staggered back a step. "Already? Who? What, an Arab guy? When?"

"Not an Arab guy." DeAngelo closed the gap. "A dead guy."

THIRTY-SEVEN

4 DECEMBER
CHERRY HILL

Morning mist blurred the flat planes of Schaffer's apartment block across the street. Frost shimmered beneath the milk-blue streetlights and the lobby doors' lightwash. Gur leaned forward slightly, peered up through the windshield's top edge. The dawn bleached the sky a pale lavender. No sign of Hezbollah.

"Why'd we wait so long to talk like this?" Kelila asked.

He shifted to face her once again. Kelila curled up in the Pathfinder's passenger seat, wrapped in her camel wool coat and a contented smile, as close as if they sat in bed. Isolated in the dark, they'd talked nonstop for three hours about surprisingly personal things—love and loss, dead spouses, raising children alone, delayed dreams, joy and sorrow. For the first time since Varda's murder, he could speak plainly with a woman who understood him, a feeling as soothing as a swim in warm, calm water.

"I don't know. I'm glad we did."

"So am I." Kelila watched him with soft, hooded eyes, then leaned forward and took Gur's face in her hands. She kissed him, briefly but tenderly.

The kiss burned its way to the soles of his feet. His body wanted more, but he squashed the impulse. *Not in the field.* Crazy schedules, no privacy, tired all the time. The team would know, they'd analyze everything he said to her, everything she did, see favoritism or abuse in the smallest look or word. It wouldn't be fair to her, to him, anyone. *If only we were home, where we belong.*

"Our shift isn't over," he mumbled. "We'll miss the Arabs." *Of all the things to say...*

"I know." Smiling, she leaned back in her seat. "I'll behave."

They sat in a charged silence as dawn's muted colors dripped onto the trees and buildings around them. Gur started the engine and ran the heater for a few minutes. Nothing stirred—no white van, no Arabs, no watchers. Just him and this attractive, interesting woman he dearly wanted to pursue, if not for the job.

"Do you think she knows?" Kelila asked once he stopped the engine.

He didn't want to talk about this. He wanted to return to the dark intimacy of an hour before. He ached to kiss Kelila again, but if he started he wouldn't stop. "I don't know how she could. There's been nothing in the news. How would she know?"

She shrugged. "Maybe we should warn her, give her a chance."

"How do we do that? We can't risk the contact."

"I know." She sighed. "I'd hate to be in her place, left out like a staked goat."

"We need to draw out the dogs. It's the only way we'll put them down."

Kelila frowned out the windshield. "I just hope they don't put her down first."

THIRTY-EIGHT

4 DECEMBER
CHERRY HILL

Miriam hefted the two-pound hand weight. How far could she throw this and hit a target? It weighed about twice as much as the hand grenades she'd carried in the *Magav*, and she could heave those a good twenty-five or thirty meters at the range. This thing, not nearly so far. Then again, the dumbbell didn't explode; no fragmentation to worry about.

She'd never realized how many weapons she could find in this mirrored, enameled, echoing, thumping gym. She'd never needed to—until Friday.

Miriam had looked up the names on the INTERPOL list, and they were dead, just like Eldar had said. She was still processing that. It would've been so easy to forget him and his warning if he'd been wrong, but he'd been right, and she'd started seeing things in shadows.

One of the few other gym inmates paced by, both hands pulling his towel tight against the back of his neck. Miriam didn't recognize him; her muscles snapped alert. She sidestepped to the rack of chromed iron bars for the universal machine, gripped a heavy four-foot pull-down bar, ready to come out swinging. The man veered away, shaking his head.

Don't be silly. You think the terrorists are playing racquetball?

She'd caught herself thinking in Hebrew over the past couple of days, a sure sign she was on edge. When she'd stepped into the One Commerce Square courtyard Friday evening, she could have sworn a man followed her to her car. Once she was behind her locked front door that evening, she felt unmentionably stupid for believing such a thing; at the time, though, she actually got nervous, fingering the pepper-spray canister in her purse as she stormed through the melting snow. Yesterday, she'd thought some men in a white van followed her home from the Shop Rite. But that couldn't be... could it?

Paranoia was wearing her out. Miriam needed to turn off her brain.

She dropped to the floor and clicked off push-ups, real ones like she'd learned in the *Magav*, not the girly ones other women did. While she pumped, she eyed the exits. Fire flowed into her biceps. The pain felt good, necessary. She urged it on by dipping lower, rising faster.

Miriam finished thirty, flipped onto her rear and flexed out her gimpy knee. Her poly warmup pants made faint scraping noises as they dragged over her spandex knee brace.

Was Eldar crazy?

Was she?

Just because you're paranoid doesn't mean someone isn't out to get you.

She didn't hurt enough yet; she could still think. Thirty minutes on the elliptical would fix that.

She'd take the pull-down bar with her. Just in case.

THIRTY-NINE

4 DECEMBER
STATEN ISLAND

Jake pounded out an ambitious pace on Gene's dormant treadmill. He felt flabby and lazy. He and Rinnah used to run and play tennis together, but once Eve came along, parenthood had cut into workout time, and sleeping time, and all other kinds of time. Now his time with Rinnah was done. Just the thought threatened to squeeze his windpipe shut.

He glanced to the other end of the finished basement, where Monica read Milne's *Winnie the Pooh* to Eve. Gene's house was littered with kid books for the grandchildren, but Jake had to mount a major search to find one that didn't feature a dead or missing parent. Eve huddled against Monica's substantial figure on the couch, Jasmine clutched to her chest, her eyes locked on Jake. It was the farthest she'd been from him since yesterday's Homicide Squad visit.

Gene clanked his beer bottle against the treadmill console. "You wanted to talk, kid, so talk."

Jake faced his uncle, who slumped on a barstool like a bear. "You know this gangbanger thing is bullshit." He kept his voice low so Eve couldn't hear over the treadmill's rumble.

"Maybe it is, maybe it isn't."

"Oh, come on." Jake slowed the treadmill a couple clicks so he could talk and breathe at the same time. "This LaVon whatever was a hard case, right? Drugs, armed robbery, ADW, all that? He's got all of Sunset Park to play in, and he comes up twenty blocks to rob *my* apartment? You believe that?"

Gene took a swig from his bottle, looked past Jake to Eve, waved a sad paw at her, then returned to Jake. "I believe it more than I do some terrorist killed Rinnah, then capped this guy and planted the gun and the swag on him. Know what that sounds like?"

It sounded nuts, Jake knew. He ran a few paces, trying to scrape his words together. "How about the guy who stabbed Brown? They catch him yet? Same guy maybe?"

"Nope. Witnesses say that one's a skinny Hispanic guy, used a knife and some kind of pipe or club. Your neighbors saw a big black dude coming out your window. LaVon Delaine's a big black dude. Was. Plus he had the piece that fired the slug CSU found in your apartment, and he had your stuff. Plus he was a total shitbag." He leaned back, pushed his fingers through his hair. "So maybe you can see why Seven-Two and the Homicide Squad like him for this."

Jake could, even though his gut told him they were wrong. "He didn't do it, Gene. It's too easy, it doesn't make any sense. He's—"

Gene held up a hand. "Kid. They're not closing it out yet. The Commissioner wants it closed yesterday, but Seven-Two'll keep it going another couple days as a personal favor to me. Check it all out, make sure it's solid. That's the best they can do, okay?"

No, it wasn't. They'd spend the time confirming what they already believed. But what could he do? What proof did he have?

He looked toward Eve again. She stared back at him, anguish in her dark eyes. He saw Rinnah's face pleading for an explanation. He couldn't bear to see that look, but it was hard to turn away. He deserved it. He'd failed Rinnah and Eve in the most fundamental possible way.

If he left things the way they were, Miriam Schaffer would die and he'd have failed her, too. The phone call had been a disaster. She obviously figured him for some kind of nut. He'd been afraid to check his computer this morning, dreaded seeing the Google News alert with her name in boldface. It wasn't; today, she was still alive. But tomorrow?

Jake cranked the treadmill back to a fast walk. "I gotta go to Philly tomorrow."

Gene scowled. "Philly?"

"I gotta talk to Schaffer, face-to-face. Make her believe she's in danger. It was stupid to do it on the phone, I—"

"You need to stay here with Chava. She needs you."

"Keep it down. I know. I can't just let Schaffer die. I can't live with that, not if I can still help her see what's going on. I should've told Rinnah, but I didn't and now she's dead."

Gene lumbered off the stool and grabbed Jake's arm. "It's not your fault, kid. There's nothing you could've done, except maybe die with her if you were there. Schaffer isn't your problem, Chava is. You can't just leave her, not now."

Jake shook off his uncle's hand, glanced back at Eve. Her stare still burned holes through his soul. "Once is enough, Gene. I owe it to Rinnah. I gotta save somebody."

FORTY

"Sir? She's here."

Jake followed the receptionist's nod to see Miriam Schaffer, hands folded at her lap, standing at the entrance to a blue-carpeted corridor that led to the law firm's inner sanctum.

The news photo of her at her husband's funeral didn't do her justice. In her businesslike black pumps she was a good head taller than Rinnah, only a couple inches shorter than Jake. Her pearl-blue long-sleeved blouse and slim slate-blue skirt showcased a well-kept figure. If Rinnah's hair had been dark walnut, Miriam's was rosewood, pulled back tight in a no-nonsense bun. But what he noticed most as he closed the distance between them was her posture—erect, shoulders square, chest out, chin up, like she was on parade. Jake felt like he was reporting to the principal's office; he was glad he'd worn a suit and had a fresh haircut.

"Miriam Schaffer?"

"Yes. And you are...?"

He held out his right hand. "Jake Eldar."

Her rust-brown eyes turned to rock. "Why doesn't this surprise me?"

Jake dropped his hand. He sensed he had maybe ten seconds to keep this from being a wasted trip. "Look, I'm sorry about the call. I wasn't really thinking straight. I was still pretty messed up from... what happened to my wife. I probably sounded pretty scattered. I came here because I want you to see I'm not crazy. And I still think you're in danger."

He watched her eyes turn from granite to marble to hardwood. She drew in a long, deep breath. "Mr. Eldar, do you have any idea

136

what my weekend was like after talking to you?"

"Probably like my past three weeks. Look, is there someplace we can talk for a few minutes? I just want you to know what's going on. That's all."

She worked her jaw for a moment, as if chewing over her decision. "Follow me."

❖

She'd expected a madman with wild hair and shabby clothes, clutching plastic bags stuffed with newspapers. He wasn't anything like that. Tall—Bill's height, an honest six feet—good shoulders, sharp suit, conservative haircut. Not handsome, but nice-looking. Pretty eyes, big and warm. The eyes finally clinched it: calm, tired, sad, but steady.

Miriam led him a short way down the corridor to one of the firm's meeting rooms, all the while wondering whether her irritation and paranoia really needed booster shots. She ushered him through a glass door set into the glass wall and pointed to the nearest of the eight black chairs around the lozenge-shaped table. He stole a look out the room-wide windows. First-time visitors always stopped for the view. "Wow. Bet that's great when it's clear out."

"Yes. I can almost see home from here."

He pulled a stack of papers from his leather portfolio. "First, I'm sorry about your husband. I know now what that's like."

"Thank you." She settled into a chair across from his, sweeping her skirt straight as she sat. "I'm sorry about your wife. It must be a terrible time for you. I know how you must feel."

"Thanks."

"The news stories say you have a daughter?"

He nodded. "Eve. She's six. She's... taking it pretty hard. She was there when it happened."

"Oh, my God." She hadn't meant to flinch, but did anyway. "Was she hurt?"

"Not physically." He ducked his head, sat still for a moment, holding his papers. Then he looked up, flashed the saddest smile she'd seen since looking in the mirror sixteen months before.

"You've probably already looked up the names I told you on the phone, but in case you didn't, I printed some things about them." He extended the sheaf toward her.

She waved away the papers. "Yes, I did my homework. I don't doubt they're dead, but I have a hard time believing Hezbollah has something to do with it. What does your uncle the policeman say?"

He sighed. "He's passed it to the Joint Terrorism Task Force. That's FBI and NYPD together, looking for terrorists. He thinks... well, let's just say he's not convinced."

She could see why. Nine people, one missing, eight unpleasant but very different deaths, plus Eldar's wife. Nothing to link them but entries on a list. The more it nagged at her, the more she realized it would take too much coincidence to explain. But if it wasn't coincidence... that was a step her brain wasn't willing to take, not yet.

He pulled another chunk of paper from his portfolio, leaned forward, passed it to her. "You said you've had experience with Hezbollah. In Israel?" She nodded. "You're right, lately they've been in love with car bombs and missiles, but they didn't always operate that way. They have a long history of targeted assassination. That top one, Gholam Oveissi, is a great example. He was one of the Shah's generals and he became active in the Iranian exile movement after '79. They tracked him to Paris and shot him and his brother out in broad daylight on the street."

She skimmed the material. She appreciated the care this Eldar person had put into his work—fresh, crisp sheets, edges aligned, neatly stapled. Not what she'd expect from a crazy person. "This says Islamic Jihad, not Hezbollah."

"That's the name they went by then. There's some others in there. The Mykonos one is interesting. In '92, Hezbollah killed four Iranian Kurdish dissidents in a Greek restaurant in Berlin. Look at that report there—it was a pretty slick operation for them. The point is, they've done stuff like this before, just not recently. God knows they've got the resources to do it now."

Miriam flipped through the dense, thickly footnoted report from the Iran Human Rights Documentation Center and started to feel queasy. The Hezbollah she grew up hating was a pack of rabid dogs. These were sophisticated operations, almost like... well, some of Mossad's.

Her hands worked on automatic, making neat piles of the papers while she sorted out her thoughts. It was getting uncomfortably hard to ignore Eldar's story. "What am I supposed to do about this, Mr. Eldar?"

"Please, it's Jake. Be careful. Stay alert. When you're out, stick around other people. Keep your doors locked. Do you drive or take the train?"

"I drove today, but the lot's just a block away."

"Good. Check your car before you get in. You know, the kind of things we used to do in Israel." He slid a manila folder from his portfolio, held it in both hands, hesitated, then bobbed his head once. "It was incredibly easy for me to find you. These guys are part of the Lebanese government, which means they're in bed with the Lebanese police. Anything INTERPOL has, they have." He pushed the folder across the table. "But even without that, we're our own worst enemies."

"What's this?"

"A dossier, on you. I built it yesterday."

A dossier? Was Eldar really some kind of crazy stalker? Miriam swallowed, gingerly opened the file's front flap, expecting spy pictures taken through her blinds. Instead, she found her life in black and white. Work history, address history, club memberships, her car, which major stores she shopped in.

"That's forty-nine bucks on the web," he explained. "It comes from one of those data aggregators. By the way, if you want your own data, you have to pay for it. The credit agencies are regulated, but these guys aren't."

Her stomach started to churn. All this, in one place? "They just let you buy it?"

"All I needed was a major credit card. Didn't even have to talk to anyone." He gestured to the file. "You want to see what I found for free, keep going."

The *Inquirer* article. The *Courier-Post* story about Bill's death, and the funeral photo. A picture of her from a friend's Facebook page. Her notary license. A small-claims court judgment from that car wreck five years ago. Bit by bit, he'd scooped up far too many details of her life in America. She absently neatened the stack of papers, closed the file, but couldn't stop staring at it. "Who are you?"

"Just a bookstore manager. Sorry, I was until Thursday. Now I work for NYPD."

She looked up. "Bookstore managers don't do things like this."

"This one does." They watched each other watch each other. "I used to be an intelligence analyst in the army. You never forget how to ride a bicycle, or build a file."

"The American army?"

"No, Israeli."

"*Tzahal?*"

He nodded. "I was in Target Field Intel for four years. So I know about these guys, too."

This was so wrong. She'd been so sure he was just another kook, but he was serious and he seemed to know what he was talking about. A tremor of fear slithered up her spine. She didn't realize she'd pressed her fingertips to her lips until she tried to speak. "You really think they're trying to kill us?"

"I hope not. But if they are, you need to protect yourself."

He folded his arms on the table; his sad eyes grew sadder. Not just sad, but weary. Had he slept since Thursday? After Bill died, how long was it before she had a full night's sleep?

"I knew all this before Rinnah…" He looked away, then back to her. "I never told her. I thought it'd scare her. I wish I had. She might have been more careful, she might still be…" He turned his face away again, swallowed. "Sorry."

"It's okay." She turned her hands loose on restacking the papers while she tried to digest everything he'd said. The man on Friday? The white van at the supermarket? Were they real? Were they… *them?*

He took the loose papers from her but pushed the folder away. "Keep that. You should know what the web's saying about you." He stowed his research material in his portfolio, stood, buttoned his suit coat. "I'll leave you alone now. Be safe. Please."

She rose, carefully arranged the chair in its place. Dark thoughts raced through her mind, obscuring the certainty she'd had just minutes before. "How long do you think this will last?"

"Until someone catches them, or we're all dead."

"That's awfully grim."

"Yeah. So's being a target." He held out his right hand. "Miriam, thanks for listening."

This time, she took his hand. "Thank you for being so persistent, Jake."

FORTY-ONE

A cold, gray day had become a drizzling twilight by the time Miriam pushed through her building's heavy glass doors to face the going-home tangle of Market Street. In a few minutes, she'd be part of the logjam. She hated driving to work, but she'd started late this morning and missed her train. She belted her raincoat, turned up the collar against the saw-toothed wind and joined the scurrying crowd on the sidewalk.

She checked over her shoulder as she trotted across 21st Street on the yellow light. No one waved an RPG at her, but she knew she'd never spot a lurker in the mob.

As she marched head-down across Market, she shifted her pepper spray from her purse to her coat pocket. She'd thought all afternoon about what Eldar had told her. This was America, and she was an American now. Hezbollah didn't kill random people in America. Or did they?

David keyed the radio. "Got her?"

Amzi's voice squawked back, "Yeah. Tan raincoat, southwest corner."

"Breaking off." David stepped up on the southeast corner of Market and 21st. He glimpsed Amzi's broad back in a green field jacket ten meters down 21st Street. David turned left at a steel-and-glass shoebox of a vacant office building and hurried east.

"Say again?"

Sohrab's voice gargled through Kassim's phone. "She's coming."

Time for work. Kassim started the van's engine, turned up the heater. He checked the rear-view mirror. "Ready?"

Ziyad rolled up his prayer rug. He'd finished his fourth prayer of the day just moments before. "Yes, I'm ready."

The foot traffic on 21st thinned dramatically only half a block off Market. The *clack-clack* of Miriam's heels on cement sounded like someone hammering a large nail. At least she'd get more exercise walking this fast.

She glanced over her shoulder. Across the street a big man hurried through the drizzle, hands jammed in the pockets of a green field jacket, the brim of his Phillies baseball cap shrouding his downturned face. He didn't seem to notice her, just headed the same way.

The handful of people behind her also appeared to be wrapped in their own affairs. A little of her tension drained away. She was just short of the corner of Ludlow; the parking lot's entrance was maybe fifty feet away.

"Almost there. Fifteen, twenty meters."

Kassim checked the right side-view mirror again. The woman's dark-green Honda Prelude slept two parking stalls behind the van, facing the side of a splotched-brick building. A sticker on the bumper read, "My Husband is a U.S. Marine."

❖

Schaffer appeared in the Suburban's side-view mirror as she entered the car park. Gur pressed the transmit button on his radio. "Schaffer's at the driveway. Where's the attendant?"

"Shuffling cars," Kelila answered.

"Van," Natan said. "Seven or eight meters east of her car."

Gur twisted hard in his seat to look. "That's the target. Stand by. How many in the van?"

"One."

One? That's not right. "The others are here somewhere. Wait for them."

"One by the west end," Natan said.

"We can terminate them?" Amzi asked.

"It would be nice to get one alive, but don't risk yourselves."

Miriam dug her keys from her purse. She noted the white van idling near her car.

A white van. Near her car.

She paused a moment, her scalp tingling. She twisted to look behind her. The man in the green field jacket stood near the parking lot entrance, staring at the sign. Following her? If not, why was he just standing there?

She turned back to the van. The white van. She'd have to walk by it to reach her car. *Don't be silly,* she scolded herself. Half a dozen white vans had passed her on Market Street just a few minutes before. *Get in the car. You're safe in the car.*

Kassim said over his shoulder, "Wait for my word. She's almost here."

Ziyad squatted next to the back doors, his hand already on the latch. His lips were moving. A prayer for going into action?

The plan was simple for one of Fadi's productions. Ziyad drags the woman into the van. Kassim drives away from the car park while Ziyad strangles her, then tears her clothes to make the police think someone tried and failed to rape her. They take her purse and jewelry, go to the river, dump her body. If she somehow escapes, Fadi, Gabir and Sohrab are waiting at her apartment block to try the same ploy. One way or another, they'd finish her tonight.

That was the plan.

"Today is Ashura," Ziyad said. "We should be mourning

Hussein. We should be fasting."

"We have work to do," Kassim told him. "Remember him in your heart. Be careful."

Ziyad glanced back at him, gave him a small smile. "How hard is it to kill a woman?"

The target circled around the back of the van.

"Go!"

❖

The Honda beeped when Miriam tweaked the alarm. The van's driver hadn't even looked at her when she passed. However, the man in the green coat still trailed behind her, maybe fifty feet back. Miriam's heart bashed at her ribs. *Get in the car!*

She felt rather than heard the van's back door open. Before she could turn, a man's gloved hand clamped across her mouth, and an arm vise-gripped her neck. The man yanked her back, almost off her feet.

No!

She mule-kicked, buried the back of her heel in the man's shin, heard him swear in Arabic. She tried to raise her leg high enough to jackhammer his knee, but her skirt was too tight. *Damn it!* She jerked to her left, then right, elbows flailing, trying to break his grip, but he ratcheted down his arm on her throat, making her choke as she screamed into his palm. Leather and old sweat from his glove filled her nostrils. She drove an elbow into his ribs, but his layers of clothing and the awkward angle robbed the blow of its strength. Her right hand dove into her coat pocket, groped for the little metal canister, found it, lost it, grabbed it again.

The man dragged her back a step. She tried to snap her head back into his face, but his grip was too strong. She knocked the side of her right foot against the inside of his, then stomped down as hard as she could with her heel, spiked the arch of his foot. Then again. And again.

He choked out a scream.

❖

145

Natan saw the struggle, drew his pistol. "It's started," he told the radio.

He stepped out from behind the brick wall, wound up to dash across the alley, climb the meter-tall retaining wall and vault the iron railing, then take down the man in the black hooded sweatshirt who'd grabbed the woman.

An instant later he was on his back, clutching his collarbone, gasping against the pain.

A young man loomed over him. Persian features, short black coat, blue jeans, a collapsible black metal baton in his hand. "Good night," he said in English. Then he brought down the baton again.

Kassim could hear the struggle—the woman's strangled cries, then Ziyad's wail—saw Sohrab knock down a man who'd appeared from nowhere, noticed the man and woman edging through the parked cars about twenty meters away. Police?

He took his pistol from the console and focused his mind on action.

Miriam fumbled with the pepper-spray's flip-top safety cap.

The man jerked her backwards another step. The van appeared in the corner of her eye. One more good yank and she'd be inside.

The cap popped open. Miriam closed her eyes, held her breath, snapped the canister to her shoulder, then sprayed wildly behind her. The man screamed full-out. His hand slipped from her mouth.

She shrieked as loudly as she could with the man's arm still blocking her windpipe, then blinked open her eyes.

Jake Eldar skidded to a halt in front of her.

What?

His fist grazed past her hair and connected with something just behind her, a wet *crunch* loud in her ear. The arm fell away from her throat.

Jake shoved her behind him. She spun in time to see him wrench a pistol away from a dark, bloody-faced man in a black hoodie, punch his jaw, then kick him in the groin. Her attacker doubled over, coughing, grabbing his injuries with both hands. He stumbled aside but stayed on his feet.

"Put him down!" she barked at Jake. "Get that bastard!"

❖

Eldar? Here? How?

Kassim, stunned, watched through the van's back door as Eldar tore the pistol out of Ziyad's hand and kicked him viciously between his legs.

The plan was unraveling in front of him.

Kassim bolted from his seat and charged toward the open door. *Time to finish this.*

❖

"Move in!" Gur shouted into the radio. "Move in!"

"That's Eldar!" Amzi's voice bellowed from Gur's radio. "He's got a gun!"

Gur tumbled from the Suburban, raised his binoculars. He couldn't see past the van.

Amzi couldn't be right. There was no reason Eldar should be here. But what if he was? And with a gun?

What will he do when he sees us?

❖

It hadn't been hard for Jake to find Miriam's car. He'd lurked in the nearby alley, running down his phone's charge talking to a still-silent Eve, until the van pulled into position.

The few seconds it took to reach Miriam lasted for hours.

Miriam yelled, "Jake! In the van!"

He looked up in time to see a man in a heavy coat just inside the van's rear doors, raising a pistol.

Jake's training came back all at once. He snapped up the gun he'd taken from Miriam's attacker, fired twice into the center of mass. The man inside the van collapsed backward.

Miriam's attacker bellowed in Arabic as he crashed his shoulder into Jake's side. Jake staggered back two steps into the open van door, blasted out a lungful of air.

A bullet *thunked* through the van's wide-open door, just inches from Jake's head.

"Jake! Another one! He followed me!"

❖

Harah, Amzi thought. *Great place for a firefight.*

Eldar had a gun, fired twice, the shots echoing sharp and hard off the brick walls. *Shooting at who? Is he in on it? Put 'em both down, get it sorted later.*

Amzi jinked to his right, took cover behind a car. The van's open back door shuddered. He aimed, fired, scrambled to the next car, fired again.

❖

The Arab's attack took Jake off-guard. But the man fumbled a follow-up punch, his fist glancing off Jake's ribs. Jake was too revved to feel it. He smashed the pistol butt down on the Arab's head, once, twice, three times, shoved him away, then whipped the barrel across the man's face. Jake staggered back a step to get his footing. Miriam appeared up next to him, aimed a small metal canister and shot of stream of pepper spray into the man's eyes and mouth. The Arab screamed and tumbled into the back of the van.

Another bullet winged off the door latch. Jake pushed Miriam behind an SUV for cover, dropped flat, peered beyond the rear tire. A big guy in a green coat a few yards away, pistol aimed across the hood of a car. Jake saw a flash.

How many are there?

Green Coat circled the car's nose and scrambled for the next. Too slow.

He made a big target.

❖

"Amzi's down!" Kelila's voice on the radio, high and fast. Gur watched her burst out from between the parked cars, weapon ready, head snapping back and forth.

"Who got him?" Gur demanded.

"Couldn't see."

Gur crouched behind a car at the lot's eastern end, tried to figure out what was happening. Where was Schaffer? What the hell was Eldar doing here?

❖

Jake watched Green Coat go down, checked for the next threat. Nothing obvious. He lunged upright, pistol sweeping the lot.

"Come on!" he shouted, holding out his hand. "Let's get out of here!"

She didn't hesitate.

By the time they reached the driveway ten yards away, they were running at full speed.

❖

Gur saw them pelt around a corner as if all the bulls in Pamplona were after them. The man was definitely Eldar, and definitely armed.

The drizzle roared into rain. Someone in a black bomber jacket popped up from behind a car near the van, dashed through the murk to the driver's door, leaped in, screeched away.

Kelila stepped forward, pumped shot after shot into the windshield. The driver swerved the van's punctured nose at her. An unfamiliar panic shot through Gur. He sprung to his feet, screamed "No!" and ran toward her.

The van was right on top of her. She stood her ground, fired a round low, into the grille.

"Move!" Gur roared. "Get out!"

At the last moment, Kelila threw herself onto the hood of the silver sedan behind her, then rolled off out of sight. The van jerked away, picking up speed.

Gur put three shots through the driver's side of the windshield in a tight group. Blood spattered the side window. He dived into a pickup truck's bed just as the van whooshed past, a sliver away. It jolted out the driveway and blasted down Ludlow, disappearing into the now-pouring rain.

David dashed into the lot, pistol at ready, as Gur stood up. "Sir! What happened?"

"Get the car!" Gur jumped to the asphalt. "Pick up Natan and Amzi! Now! Go!" He splashed toward the last place he'd seen Kelila, mashing down the radio button as he ran. "Sasha, do you see them?"

"Yes, they turned left at 20th. I'm on them."

Let Sasha go? Bring him back? "Stay with them. Don't go back to the hotel until you hear from me, understand?"

"Okay, boss."

Distant, whining sirens closed in. *Good God, what a disaster.* A firefight in downtown Philadelphia, two men down, the Arabs escaped. Schaffer and Eldar on the run.

Kelila leaned back against the sedan that had saved her life, breathing hard, wet hair plastered to her face. "Are you okay?" he asked, out of breath.

She nodded. "We need to get out of here."

"Yes, we do." The Suburban heaved to a halt next to Amzi's still form. Gur's reactions collided: relief that Kelila was unhurt, anger that Amzi was flat and bleeding. "Pick up your casings. We've got to clean up this mess."

FORTY-TWO

5 DECEMBER
PHILADELPHIA

They sprinted down Van Pelt—an oversized alley hemmed in by red brick—until Miriam yelled, "Hold on! Stop!"

Jake twisted to look behind him. "What? Are you hurt?"

"I can't run in these heels!"

He buttoned his raincoat against the enthusiastic rain while he waited for her to catch up.

Miriam palmed the streams of melting mascara and blush from her face, craned to look over her shoulder. "I don't see anyone behind us."

"Come on, let's get out of this."

They squelched down Sansom Street until they found a broad overhang in front of the tan-brick-and-gray-marble Weinstein Geriatric Center. There they huddled against the locked front door, catching their breath, dripping on their shoes. The rain pounded the street in front of them. The gun in Jake's pocket weighed down the right side of his coat. He zeroed in on every passing car, searching for anyone too interested in them, hoping to see them first.

"You okay?" Jake finally asked. He couldn't push the shake from his voice.

"Yes. My neck hurts." She frowned at him. "I thought you were going home."

He studied the iron railing in front of them. "I was worried about you, so I waited. Then the van showed up."

If he'd gone home, Miriam would be dead. He'd shot two men for a woman he didn't know. Jake took stock of her face: blinking too fast, jaw working, eyes focused a mile away.

151

More silence. Then she whispered, "Thank you."

"Yeah." The adrenaline was nearly gone from Jake's system, replaced by rising fear and the awful realization he was a killer... again. The more he thought about it, the sicker he felt. He hadn't planned any of this. He could've died back there, left Eve alone. Was Miriam worth it?

Was it just about her? The asshole who attacked Miriam—did he shoot Rinnah? Did the big bruiser by the car? Had he struck back? Did it matter?

"Are you okay?"

He nodded, too quickly. "Fine. They didn't touch me."

"Jake." She grabbed his coat sleeve, turned him to face her. "You just shot two men. Are you okay?"

She had to remind him? He tried to think of something brave to say, but eventually went with "No."

"At least you're honest." Miriam let go of his sleeve, smoothed out the creases with a shaking hand. She shouldered deeper into her coat. "So what's the next part of your plan?"

"What plan?"

"Don't say that!" she snapped. "I need to know there's a plan, it's the way I am."

A shadow of something flitted through her eyes before she could hide it—fear. For an instant, she looked vulnerable. Then her eyes hardened again. She looked away, lifted her chin, squared her shoulders. Back on parade.

Jake sighed. "Sorry." Long pause. "I'm a little out of practice with this kind of thing."

"So am I."

He waited for her to explain. "What did you do for your national service?"

"*Magav.*"

"*Border Police?*"

She turned her head fractionally. "Is that a problem?"

"Noooo. Explains how you kicked the shit out of that guy."

"Not well enough." She heaved out a sigh. "I should've taken him down."

They watched the rain settle from a deluge into a steady shower. Jake's mind kept running the action over and over. Rifle fire at long range was a lot different from a pistol up close and personal. Bile sloshed in the back of his throat, but he didn't dare throw up in front of Miriam. "The cops are probably there by now."

"Probably."

"I need to turn myself in."

Miriam looked his way. "Are you sure you want to do that?" Her voice was gentler than he'd expected from someone as tough as she seemed to be.

"There were witnesses. Someone'll put my picture on TV. I'd better go in under my own power." He tried to give her a brave smile. "You can walk away if you want."

She shook her head. Her eyes were softer than at any time since he'd met her, leather instead of wood. Her lips weren't pressed flat anymore, either. "I'll go with you. It's the least I can do. I can tell them what happened, that you only did what you had to."

"Thanks." The condors circled Jake's gut again. He took a deep breath, swallowed the rock in his throat, and fought to smother the mental picture of Eve visiting him in jail. "Walk you to your car?"

FORTY-THREE

Alayan's bowels clutched when the van's shattered, nearly opaque windscreen glinted in the headlights, framed by the dark bulk of the Whitman Bridge looming over the ragged dirt lot on Philadelphia's seaport. Rafiq guided their van through a careful arc, stopped when their lights picked out two figures huddled in the front seats. Alayan was out of the vehicle before it stopped.

Ziyad tumbled out the van's passenger-side door, limped toward Alayan. The harsh bluish lights turned the blood on his face gray. "*Sidi*, I—"

"Where is he?"

Ziyad bowed his head, turned and pushed open the cargo door. Alayan drifted to the opening, looked down. A primeval sound escaped his throat.

Kassim lay on his back in a pool of congealed blood, arms at his side, head lolled to his left. Thankfully, someone had closed his eyes. Blood caked the chest of his heavy sweater. Alayan could smell it—sharp, metallic, slightly sweet.

He crouched in the doorway, reached out, hesitated, then brushed the matted hair off Kassim's face. He ignored Sohrab's grunt as he lurched out of the driver's seat. He ignored Ziyad's babbling next to him. He ignored the press of eyes staring at his back.

You're not supposed to die, he silently told Kassim. *I need your help. I need your friendship. I need you to tell me when I'm wrong. What do I do now?*

Someone appeared to his left, put his hand on Alayan's shoulder—Rafiq, looking graver than ever before. "I'm sorry, *sidi*," he whispered. "He was a good man."

Alayan nodded, turned back to Kassim, bowed his head. *I'll cry for you, my friend,* he thought as his tears splashed at the blood pool's edge. *There's no one else left to cry for.*

"Get him out of there," Rafiq told the others. "Break out the windshield. Bullet holes make the police curious. Unlock all the doors and leave the keys in it. Throw the license plates in the water." Quiet. Then, "Get moving. We can't stay here."

Rafiq returned to the van, gripped Alayan's arm, tugged gently. "Come on, *sidi.* Let the men work."

Alayan let himself be led away from Kassim's body. He recalled the years they'd known each other, the good times. All gone. Alayan's past was finally gone, too; Kassim was the last person who'd known him the way he was before he took up this new calling.

"What... what do we do with him?" Rafiq asked.

"We have to bury him," Alayan croaked. "Properly. Say prayers."

"We'll have to find a mosque."

"Yes." A sudden swell of anger surged through him. "Who did this?"

"I don't know, *sidi.*" Rafiq stopped, turned toward the crowd surrounding the van. "Ziyad? Who shot him?"

"The Jew Eldar. He did it."

Alayan wrenched his arm from Rafiq's grasp, swung on Ziyad. "Eldar? What are you talking about?"

"It was Eldar, *sidi,* truly, he was there..."

Sorrow and rage collided in Alayan's brain, threw off sparks. He charged Ziyad, caught him by the throat, slammed him against the van's side. "That's impossible! Don't lie, you worm! Who did this really? Why didn't you protect him? Why'd you let him die?"

"It's true, *sidi!* It's true! It was Eldar, he was there, I swear before Allah..."

Two pairs of arms dragged Alayan off Ziyad, hauled him out of reach, held him fast when he tried to break away. He wanted to hurt something, someone, he didn't care who or what. Someone was going to pay. "Why was he there?" he demanded.

"I don't know, but he was, he was." Ziyad slid down the door into a crouch, hugged himself, began to cry. "The woman put chemicals in my eyes, and he did this to my face and shot Kassim. We barely got away from the police—"

"The *police?* You saw the police there?"

"Yes! Yes. They shot at us." Ziyad rocked back and forth, sobbing, his shoulders shaking. "I'm sorry, *sidi*, I'm sorry, Eldar and the woman escaped—"

"Kassim died and the woman's still alive?" Alayan roared. "He died for *nothing?*"

Rafiq grabbed both of Alayan's arms and shook him once, hard. "Stop it!" he hissed. "This isn't helping!" He pointed to the second van. "Go sit down. We'll leave in a couple minutes."

Alayan looked up into Rafiq's eyes. There was nothing lazy about them now. Where did this new attitude come from? No matter; Alayan was too gutted to fight it.

He stumbled to the second van, crawled into the passenger seat and let sorrow's deadness wash over him. Tonight he'd let Rafiq take the burden. Alayan had to remember the dead, everyone who'd left him behind. Especially Kassim.

And tomorrow, he'd plan his revenge.

FORTY-FOUR

5 DECEMBER
EAST PARKSIDE, PHILADELPHIA

"No, I need this now!" Gur yelled into his secure cell phone. "I have two men down! I need a *sayan* who's a doctor in the Philadelphia area."

He could hear the duty officer in Tel Aviv do a double-take. "In America?"

"Yes, in America. Now, damn it!"

They'd shuttled from one major highway to another, not going anywhere, just moving. He had no idea where they were. Philadelphia's suburbs had turned into a blanket of lights, the traffic around them only shapes marked by headlights and tail lights.

The Suburban reeked of blood, wet wool, and anger. Gur checked Kelila: intent on her driving, grim-faced, jaw set. Behind him, Natan lay flat on the bench seat, wheezing, eyes closed, a dressing pressed to his bloody forehead. Behind him, David bent over a hidden Amzi. David looked up at Gur, shook his head. *Kusemek!*

"Raffi?"

Of all the voices he'd expected to hear on the phone, Orgad's wasn't among them. "Chaim? What are you doing in the office? It's past one there."

"We're all working late. What happened? Why do you need a doctor?"

"Just give me a name. We're driving in circles on the highway so we're not a static target."

"Fine. Philip Strassberger, 215-383-1095. Use the name Solomon." Gur copied the number and code name on a fast-food

157

napkin, thrust it toward David. "What happened?"

The last thing Gur wanted right now was to spit out a status report. "First, there really is a hit team. We engaged them in downtown Philadelphia while they were trying to snatch one of the covers. We think two of them are down, but Natan is injured and Amzi's dead."

"Damn!" The scrambled signal turned Orgad's huffing into the wheeze of a hospital ventilator. "Police?"

David called out, "University of Pennsylvania Medical Center, on Spruce Street." Kelila punched the destination into the GPS unit they'd Velcroed to the dashboard.

"No police. We cleaned up and got out before they arrived."

"Are you still in contact?"

"Sasha's following them. I need an airplane to take Natan and Amzi home and at least two replacements, more if possible. Anatoly and—"

"No, Raffi, no more people. You're a sideshow now."

Gur considered that for a moment as they plunged down a long, dark offramp. "*What?* We're in contact with a Hezbollah hit team, in *America*, and we're a..." He glanced at the team; two pairs of eyes stared back. He wouldn't repeat the word. "What's happened?"

"The German Federal Police shut down a Hezbollah cell this morning. In Hamburg, of course. They were preparing two car bombs, and by 'preparing,' I mean they had everything they needed, just not assembled."

Gur closed his eyes. "Erika Grusst." The German cover for Sara Tuchman on the Doha surveillance team.

"Exactly. This is the start of the real revenge campaign, Raffi. We're sending people out the door every hour. And you think we can send you replacements?"

"But—"

"Get by with what you have. We're good at that; we've done it for thousands of years. I'll arrange an airplane for Natan and Amzi. Damned shame. Now, I have work. Good night."

Gur stared at his phone's glowing screen until it turned itself off. The silence in the Suburban festered. He looked outside and realized they were going back the way they'd come, along a highway that cut through a blue-black slot lined with trees. Driving through the dark was an apt metaphor just then.

His phone rang. Sasha. "Sorry, boss, I lost them in traffic."

"Of course you did," Gur sighed. "It's that kind of night."

FORTY-FIVE

"So where's this white van now, Mr. Eldar?"

"I don't know."

"We didn't find any bodies, Mr. Eldar."

"They were there when we escaped."

"No blood, either. These kidnappers, did they bleed?"

"It started raining hard. Maybe that washed it away."

And on it went, five hours in a six-by-eight interview room with an endless line of Philadelphia detectives. Jake gave them the gun, his fingerprints, a DNA swab, and a gunshot residue test. In between cop tag-teams, he worried about Eve and the hours since he'd last talked to her on the phone. He also wondered what the cops were doing to Miriam. He and Miriam had decided on their way back to the parking lot to not mention Hezbollah or anything else that might complicate matters. Was she still following that plan?

Finally he asked for his phone call. He'd so very much wanted to avoid doing this. "Hello, Gene? It's Jake. Yeah, I'm still in Philly. Um, look, I've got a problem…"

An hour later, the cops cut him loose. They talked about charging him with possession of an unregistered weapon and discharging a firearm within the city limits, but finally told him it wasn't worth the effort. "Don't leave the country," they warned him as if they meant it, but he could hear the heads shaking as he staggered out of the detectives' offices into an over-lit corridor that supposedly would take him outside.

Jake's brain ached as much as his empty stomach. He didn't know whether to be relieved or disappointed. He'd shot two men

160

and got away with it, at least for now. The cops thought he was crazy. As tired, wrung-out and raw as he was, he couldn't blame them.

"Jake?"

He lurched out of his daze and found Miriam parked in a plastic chair near the office door. Her empty shoes were lined up precisely under her chair, her legs outstretched, ankles crossed. With the impression Jake had formed of her, seeing her in her stocking feet was almost like seeing her naked. "Hi. You're still here."

"Of course." She slipped her feet into her pumps, rocked out of the chair and rolled back her shoulders. Her freshly-arranged hair bun contrasted with the circles under her eyes. "I wanted to make sure you're all right. They let you go?"

"Yeah. No evidence anything happened." He plodded in her direction while he massaged the back of his head. "You have an accent. You didn't this afternoon."

"It comes back when I'm tired or upset."

"Hm. How were the police with you?"

"I'm sure they think I'm insane, but not enough to lock up. What will you do now?"

He shrugged. His planning horizon had shrunk to less than five minutes. "Don't know. Get a cab to the station, I guess. Go home, take care of Eve."

Miriam checked her watch. "The last train to New York left twenty minutes ago." She looked down the hall away from Jake, sighed, then turned back to him. "You saved my life. The least I can do is offer you a sofa to sleep on. It's not much—"

"No, really, I don't want to put you out. I'll get a room downtown here, it's—"

"Jake." Her voice took on a hint of steel. "You risked your life for me. I feel obligated." Jake opened his mouth to object, but she shot up her hand like a traffic cop signaling *stop*. "No, don't. I take my obligations seriously. Besides, those people might still be out there, and we have a better chance together than apart. Okay?"

This was like arguing with Gene. "Yes, ma'am."

"Good. Are you hungry?"

"Starving."

She almost smiled. "So am I. There's an IHOP a few blocks from my office, they're open until two. Let's get away from this place."

❖

The waitress brought their drinks—decaf for Jake, hot tea for Miriam—and bustled away before they could say "thank you." Miriam hid the lemon slice behind the plate holding the little plastic cream cups.

The bright lights on the antiseptic white laminate and blond wood and multicolored upholstery made Jake's eyes buzz and his headache shimmy. It felt like a hangover, minus the drunk beforehand.

They hadn't said much in the cab going to Miriam's car or in her car on their way here. Sitting in the dark was a form of decompression. Now faced with the pitiless light, they exchanged sighs and glum smiles, like at the end of a sub-par blind date.

"You don't have an accent," Miriam finally said. "Why is that?"

"I was born here. Not *here* here, Long Island, a place called West Hempstead. Heard of it?"

She shook her head.

"Nobody else has, either."

"When did you go to Israel?"

"'87. I was ten, my sister was twelve. Mom and Dad got sick of Reagan and decided we were going to move to Israel. Next thing I know, we're in Haifa. Welcome to fifth grade, huh?"

Miriam cradled her tea mug in both hands. "Are they still there?"

"Ohhh, yeah. It took Mom and Dad about two years to figure out that the 'plucky little Israel' they'd read about for years had turned into the neighborhood bully. They couldn't admit they'd made a mistake, even with the *intifada* and Likud running the place."

"But you left."

"Yeah. Long story."

"We have time."

"Well, okay. I was in the army, then out of the army. Went to college, met Rinnah, married Rinnah. People were blowing up buses and cafes. We decided we couldn't deal with walking out the door in the morning and not knowing if we'd ever come home. Plus we wanted kids, and I wanted my kids to be American. So we moved back here."

"Rinnah was a sabra?"

"Yeah. We thought she might have trouble adjusting. But with all the Jews and Arabs in New York, it was like being in Tel Aviv, except the buses and restaurants won't kill you. Usually." The corners of her mouth turned up at the idea. "How about you?"

The waitress delivered their food in a hit-and-run: pancakes and sausage for him, a chicken Caesar salad for her. Miriam didn't answer until after her second forkful. "I grew up on a kibbutz."

"Yeah?"

She nodded. "In the north, near Netu'a. My parents were old-time socialists, and our kibbutz followed some of the old ways. We grew lemons and avocados. One of the first things I remember, I was maybe five, going with the other children to see our parents working in the orchards. That was their idea of a field trip."

He couldn't see her as a farm girl. He couldn't see her as a little girl at all; little girls laugh and play and skip and make a mess, like Eve. Miriam was too grown-up to her core. "What happened?"

"I hated it." She stabbed her salad. "Especially when I got older. I hated working in the orchards. My father died in a rocket attack, and my mother married another man. I didn't like him, and I don't think he liked me. I didn't want to end up like the older girls, marrying a *kibbutznik* boy and sacking avocados while I'm six months pregnant. So the day after I turned eighteen, I got a ride to Ma'alot and enlisted."

"Why the Border Police?"

"I wanted to fight. It was 1994, women weren't allowed in combat in the Army yet. The recruiter said, 'I can get you a nice clerical job in Zefat, you can visit your family on weekends,' and I said, 'I want to get as far from here as I can, what do you have?' He had the Border Police. I spent three years in Gaza."

"Wow. Tough duty. So how'd you end up here?"

"I met a man."

"Your husband?"

"Yes." This time, she did smile, very small, almost bashful. "Have you ever seen a Marine in his dress uniform?"

"The blue coat and white cap? Yeah, they're sharp."

"They're beautiful. The first time I saw Bill, that's what he wore. He was an Embassy guard. I went to a party there with my boss, and there he was. We got married a year later and we came here."

Jake smiled. "That's great. Love at first sight." He watched her eat for a few moments. When the blocks of ice behind her face melted, she was an attractive woman in the same Mediterranean way as Rinnah, with the setting desert sun glowing in her skin.

"Is that how it was with you and Rinnah?"

"Pretty much. We met at school, Tel Aviv University. Took us two years to get married, though."

"You didn't have the Marines hurrying you along."

"No, we didn't." He finished his last mouthful of pancakes, washed it down with coffee, and leaned back in the booth. "So with your husband in the Marines, you must've moved around a lot."

"No. He went into the Reserves and joined the State Police. We stayed in Cherry Hill the whole time. He went to Iraq and came back. Then he went to Afghanistan... and he didn't come back." She dropped her gaze to the remains of her salad, pushed around some lettuce.

It had been so nice to watch Miriam thaw that he wished he hadn't asked the question. "What are you going to do now?"

She glanced up over a forkful of greens, a slice of her previous wariness creeping back into her eyes. "You mean, after what happened today?"

"Yeah."

Miriam chewed with more care than necessary before she answered. "I don't know. I can't just lock myself in my apartment. What are you going to do?"

"I don't know, either. Go home, take care of Eve. Try to keep going, I guess. Watch out for white vans. You got kids?" She shook her head, a sad shake she seemed to have used before. "Got anyone you can be with? Family? Friends?"

"I'll be fine." She rearranged her salad scraps with her fork. "They won't give up, you know."

164

He hoped she was wrong, but knew she wasn't. "I know. It's how they've gotten where they are now."

"Yes. Our kibbutz was only two kilometers from the border. These thugs were always crossing over, shooting people, or shooting rockets at us from the other side. Once we found a mine in one of our orchards. The army would keep chasing them and killing them and shell them whenever they mortared us, but they kept at it."

"They were on their own ground then. It's different here."

"Is it, Jake?" Miriam's eyes grew heavy and serious. "Is it really?"

FORTY-SIX

6 DECEMBER
CHERRY HILL

"Sorry about this morning." Jake turned to watch tree-filled suburbia slip by the car window, hoping to cover the flush he felt seeping into his cheeks. "That was a hell of a dream."

"You really thought I was Rinnah?" Miriam asked, concentrating on traffic. Her accent was gone again.

"Yeah. I saw her, like I see you now." Miriam had wakened him on the sofa. In his dream—vision? hallucination?—Rinnah called his name, standing there fresh from the shower, naked, a white towel wrapped around her hair. He'd wanted her so badly he was sure the pain of it woke him. "Did I... say anything?"

"Yes, you did. It's okay, I understand."

"Sorry." Now his cheeks were smoldering. Jake let the fire die down before he went on. "Where are we going?"

"To the train station. You said we should stay around people, right? So why not a train?"

Gabir jinked the van to the left so he could see around an SUV to the green Honda they were following. "Why do these people need such damn big cars?" he grumbled.

"To go with their damn big houses?" Sohrab said. He knelt between the two front bucket seats, one elbow on Ziyad's seat back. "Rafiq would know."

Gabir's face turned even darker. "Yeah, Rafiq." He hunched deeper into his black quilted parka. "I say we just drive past and shoot them now. I'm sick of sneaking around."

166

"We can't be sure we'd kill them," Sohrab said. "We'll wait until they stop."

"That's not what the boss wants," Ziyad said. "He said, 'follow them.'"

Gabir laughed. "He's not here. You want to wrestle with that woman again? Or maybe it's my turn this time."

Ziyad watched the neat houses and lawns stream by, struggling to stay silent. That Zionist *labwa* was so unlike the soft, pliant women back home. The things he'd felt while her firm, muscular body writhed against his shamed him. Was that why he hadn't mastered her? Last night he'd prayed for strength, for clarity, and for forgiveness. He hoped Allah listened.

Kelila drove the Pathfinder three vehicles behind the white van. She pictured Raffi waiting at the airport for the plane that would take Amzi and Natan home. She'd volunteered to do it, but he'd insisted, said it was his responsibility. She'd have reached out to him if the others weren't watching. He looked so alone, so tired. But something else lurked behind this, a low smolder in his eyes she'd seen a few times before. He was angry. His mood had infected the two men with her.

"Let's just run these assholes off the road and finish them here," Sasha growled. His Russian accent made his Hebrew sound even more aggressive than his words.

"No, it's too public," Kelila said. "Remember, officially we're not here."

"Fuck that. These animals killed Amzi and knocked the hell out of Natan. Let's get rid of them. David, you ready?"

David shrugged. "Always am."

"No!" Kelila said. "We follow the boss' orders. Just stick with the plan, okay?"

"Yes, Mother," Sasha grumbled.

No seats were left on the train, of course; there rarely were.

Miriam didn't mind standing for the half-hour trip into Philadelphia. She'd learned how to stand for long stretches in various guard posts ringing the Gaza. She and Jake joined the line of commuters in the aisle as the New Jersey Transit train slid away from the bare-bones Cherry Hill station.

"Is it always this crowded?" Jake asked.

"It's a little light today. It always is around the holidays."

She watched Jake take in what she'd grown so used to seeing. Blue bench seats, strip lights, aluminum overhead luggage racks half-full with briefcases and laptop bags, gray walls, dirty windows. Rustling newspapers, laptop keys clicking, murmured phone conversations.

Jake said, "You look nice."

Really? She'd worn a plain black pantsuit, simple pale-green blouse and flat shoes, clothes that would let her move fast if she had to. "Um, thanks." Jake looked rumpled and tired, his day-old shadow and now-limp shirt collar spoiling the effect of his crisp haircut.

"Can I borrow your phone? I need to call Eve. I ran mine down yesterday while I was waiting for you."

"Okay." Miriam fished her phone from her purse and handed it to Jake. He thumbed in a number. When he said, "Hi, Monica, it's Jake," Miriam tuned out and watched for anyone who seemed out of place. She realized that by looking around and even sometimes making eye contact, she was the suspicious one. Some things you just don't do on a commuter train.

Sohrab peeked through the doorway connecting the two train cars. He could just see the back of Eldar's head; the Schaffer woman must be in front of him. Another man and woman stood behind them and the aisle was packed in front, so they weren't going anywhere. Good.

They hadn't counted on a policeman being parked in front of the Cherry Hill station. They'd have to take the two Jews in the confusion of the Philadelphia station at the other end.

He checked out the other passengers. Business people in suits, mostly white, absorbed in their reading or their phones. No one paid attention to three casually-dressed men who clearly didn't belong. His father—a lieutenant colonel in the Revolutionary Guard Corps—had told him many times that when the war between Iran and America finally started, it would be this inattention that would bring the Americans down.

He turned to Gabir and murmured, "Keep Ziyad behind you. If the woman sees him, she'll recognize him." Gabir nodded, accepting the direction without question. Sohrab stood a little straighter. He should have taken over for Kassim yesterday, not Rafiq. After all, he'd be an IRGC officer after he gained more experience with Hezbollah. When he led the men to kill the two Jews today, Alayan would have to value him more than that Westernized mongrel Rafiq.

❖

Kelila wrapped both hands around a stainless-steel pole near the middle door of the second train car. While she braced against the train's sway, she examined her fellow riders.

She noticed three men at the car's front, warmly dressed in casual work clothes. That alone was unusual. Stranger still, all three were darker than most everyone else on the train.

Then the smallest of the three turned to look behind him. Their eyes met, then locked. Surprise washed over his face. A flash lit up her brain.

Yesterday, in the car park. He was the one who'd almost run her down with the van.

❖

"She's been frantic ever since you left," Monica scolded Jake. "All she does is cry."

But once Monica handed Eve the phone, only an occasional sniffle broke the silence no matter what Jake said. Not even "I love you, Bunny" could coax a word from her.

Jake disconnected, knuckled his eyes clear, then returned the phone to Miriam. Once again, a lead brick of guilt weighed down his insides. He should be with his daughter, he told himself, not some woman he barely knew.

"How is she?" Miriam asked, eyebrows raised.

He shook his head. "She's not talking. Hasn't since Thursday. I want to help her, but I don't know what to say." He buried his fists in his coat pockets. A good father *would* know. What did that say about him? "Anyway, thanks. That's long distance. I'll pay you for the call."

"Don't you dare." She slipped her phone into her purse. "Jake, little girls are tougher than you think. I know—I was one once."

"Maybe it's you *kibbutznik* girls who're so tough. You know, rifle practice when you're five, all that."

"I didn't touch a rifle until I was eight, but that's not the point. Maybe Eve sees how sad you are. Maybe if you show her it's possible to be sad and strong at the same time, she'll think it's safe to open up." Her fingertips brushed his sleeve. "Just a thought, from a former little girl."

This, he hadn't expected. He thought some genuine concern edged into her eyes, which had finally changed from softwood to brown cashmere, matching her hair. "Thanks."

A male face from a classical painting, halfway down the train car: soft, almost feminine features, a long straight nose, searching eyes. *I've seen him before*, Jake thought, but couldn't quite decide where. Then a wild, random notion smacked into him. "Miriam, you get the web on your phone?" She nodded. "Bring up the INTERPOL site, okay?"

She frowned, but unearthed her phone again and fiddled with the screen for a few seconds. "Okay. What do you need?"

"The Doha pictures." She poked at the screen some more, then turned the phone so he could see. He moved in close enough to smell her shampoo (nice, more feminine than he'd expected), scanned the tiny pictures, then pressed one in the third row. A passport photo filled the screen. It was the man on the train. *What the...?* "Look toward the center of the car," he whispered. "By the right-hand door. The guy in the green jacket with short dark-blond hair. See him?"

She nodded, then glanced at the photo. He heard the sharp breath.

"Same guy?"

"Yes." She turned to face him, their noses less than six inches apart. "Does that mean...?"

He plucked the phone from her hand, found another picture, held it up for Miriam. "This gal stopped me on my way to work last week to ask directions. Real friendly, said she was from Greece, on vacation." A glum Elena from Athens stared back at them, blond in the photo but otherwise unchanged. He knew he'd seen her someplace before. He scrolled down to the text block. *Alias Schaffer, alias Miriam.* "She was you in Doha. It's gotta be Mossad."

Miriam felt a flutter in her chest. *Mossad, here? Following us? Why? Is that even possible?* Of course it was possible; they could go anywhere. *What do they want?*

"If they're here on the train," Miriam whispered, her voice straining its leashes, "is Hezbollah here too?"

Sohrab turned away instantly, but he knew it was too late. She'd seen him. The woman from the car park, the one who'd shot at him. Police? FBI? How had she found them?

How many others were on this train? At the station?

His heart threw itself against his ribs; all the hair on his body tingled with the adrenaline storm. *Police. Armed. They know we're here.* He smiled to himself. *That just makes it better.*

He edged back against Gabir. "Tell Ziyad," he whispered. "Surround them, get in close, fire at zero range. Use their bodies to muffle the shots. Then split up and meet at the woman's office building." Gabir nodded. "By the doors. There's a woman wearing a tan coat and a white cap. She's police—she was at the action yesterday. Keep the crowd between us and her."

"We could just kill her," Gabir mumbled.

"David, Sasha? They're here."

David's voice came back into Kelila's ear instantly.

"Hezbollah?"

"Yes, three of them." Kelila gave them a quick description. She wished she knew the station's layout; she never liked walking into a situation blind. "Form a triangle around the covers. Wait for the hostiles to come to us. Take them out quietly." *And don't get caught.*

❖

They both watched for anyone they recognized from yesterday's attack, but couldn't see anything beyond their car. Jake's mainspring wound so tight he was sure it would snap. Miriam's eyes turned back into rock and her lips vanished under pressure.

"You don't have to come with me," Miriam murmured. "I'll be okay once I get a taxi."

"Bullshit. You're stuck with me. We're going straight to the cops."

"What're they going to do?" She leaned in closer. "That didn't work very well last night, did it? The police have to believe me before they'll protect me. These people will wait until we come out, or they'll come back tomorrow."

"So you're going to *work?* Really?"

Miriam crossed her arms hard, frowned. "What else can I do? Hide? Where? If they're on this train, they know where I live. What do you want from me, Jake? What should I do?"

Jake realized he had no idea. He should know, he ought to have a plan, but he was blank. "I don't know. But I'm going to keep you alive long enough to figure it out."

She gave him a tight but grateful smile. "Thanks. We'll be safe enough in a cab until we can work out a plan. We should come in on Track 1, right by the 29th Street exit. The taxis are usually on the other side, but that exit's closed for a couple weeks."

"Whatever." Maybe nobody would kill them between the stairs and the doors.

The windows darkened when the train rumbled into Philadelphia's 30th Street Station. The car filled with people standing, putting on their coats, gathering their bags. Miriam and Jake lost sight of the Mossad man in the scrum.

"Ready?" he whispered when the train jerked to a halt.

She looped her purse strap over her head and one shoulder, let out some slack so the purse rested against her right hip, then slipped her hand in up to her wrist. He wondered what she had in there. More pepper spray? Hand grenades? Rocket launcher? "Ready."

Jake thought he should say something encouraging, even though the condor in his stomach had dived off its perch again. "I've got your back."

Miriam nodded, perhaps a little too quickly.

The doors ground open.

FORTY-SEVEN

6 DECEMBER
PHILADELPHIA

The platform filled like a river valley after a dam blowout. Jake and Miriam were swept along by dozens of people streaming through the perpetual gloom toward the stairway to the station's main level. Jake watched behind them, but all he saw were the blank faces of legions of undead commuters. The rasp of shuffling feet filled his ears.

The silver sign hanging from the concrete ceiling just before the stairs caught Jake's eye. He elbowed Miriam's arm, pointed up. She stopped and swore in Hebrew.

"Where's Track Nine?" he asked, afraid he already knew the answer.

"The other end of the station, by 30th Street. The side that's closed."

They took the stairs two steps at a time. Jake used his temporary height advantage to check the crowd behind them. He spied a Persian face and black leather several steps back. The young man looked straight at him. "Might be one behind us," Jake reported.

"Mossad or Hezbollah?"

"Hezbollah, I think."

The stairway spilled them into a massive Art Deco hall of honey-colored marble the size of a football field, busy with a couple hundred commuters. A coffered ceiling hung a hundred feet overhead, while tall, narrow multi-paned windows stretched from the doorway tops to the geometric frieze. The instant they left the stairwell, Jake and Miriam broke from the pack and headed for the middle of the dove-gray, marble-tiled floor.

Miriam pivoted to scan their surroundings. Jake edged next to her. "Got him? Bomber jacket?"

"Yes. I'm looking for his friends."

All the moving bodies created too much visual clutter. Jake couldn't see any obvious candidates. "Let's move. If they're here, they'll follow us."

"Right." Miriam nodded down the concourse. "That way." She quick-stepped east. Jake traced the line of lit Christmas wreaths on the walls to the hall's opposite end. A perfectly conical 30-foot Christmas tree towered perhaps fifty yards away beyond the Amtrak information counter, its lights and ornaments packed so tight that hardly any greenery was visible. The 29th Street doors lay a very long 25 yards past that.

"We should've driven," Jake grumbled.

Kelila surfaced just in time to see Schaffer and Eldar march down the huge hall. The Persian boy trailed them by no more than five meters. She didn't want to spook him, so she paused at the top of the stairway to figure out the layout.

Five facing pairs of numbered stairways lay at ten-meter intervals down the length of the concourse, odd numbers to the north, even to the south. She stood on Stairway 10. A marble half-wall flanked by massive carved wooden benches surrounded each stairwell. The 30th Street exit was at the west end to her left, the exit doors blocked by yellow "caution" tape. An Amtrak information booth topped by a black flip sign lay between Stairways 7 and 8. Two long red-and-blue banners announced "Food Court" on the south wall behind her.

Kelila slipped in behind the Persian, buttoned her coat, pulled on her gloves. Her heart pumped with the familiar rush of imminent action. She spotted the other two hostiles flanking Schaffer and Eldar, then David and Sasha gliding along the hall's outside edges. A blizzard of civilians blew through the little procession. Taking down the hostiles here would be like doing it on a busy city street—no chance for cover or anonymity, no good way to escape. *Damn.* She tapped her earpiece. "See them?"

"Got 'em," David said. "Big guy on the north side. The one on this side, his face went through a blender." He cut toward the center.

"No, stay out there. Take them when they go outside. It's too crowded in here."

The formation pulled even with Stairways 7 and 8. The hostiles gradually drew closer to Schaffer and Eldar.

Sasha's voice on the radio: "Gun."

❖

"Miriam? The guy from yesterday. Behind us, on our right."

"How close?"

"Too close."

Miriam glanced to her right. The man who'd attacked her the day before stared back through bright red eyes set into livid bruises. A taped nose finished the ugly picture. A flash of light on blue steel swung out from under his coat. Behind him, the Mossad man from the train bulled through the travelers milling between two benches, something shiny in his hand.

Someone screamed, "He's got a gun!"

Suddenly the hall was a wild stampede of shrieking people scattering like BBs poured from a box, luggage flying, trash cans clanging. A stocky man in a sport coat blindsided Miriam. She hit the floor hard on her shoulder, rolled and sprawled as her purse spewed its contents.

A shot.

The Mossad man's feet skittered out from under him. He fell like a toppled smokestack onto the arc of blood that spurted out his back. His head bounced off the floor.

Oh God. Oh God. The same thing she'd always thought at the start of every firefight. Then the adrenaline hit. Everything she saw turned extra sharp. She could hear the mice in the basement.

Jake skidded on his knees next to her. "Are you okay?"

Another shot. Behind her, an ash-blond man rolled behind a massive dark-wood bench, took aim, tracking a target from his right to his left. More gunshots clattered off the marble. Policemen charged for cover behind a station map, shooting on the fly.

These bastards weren't going to kill her the way they'd killed her father and her husband. Not if she got to them first. "Help me get my stuff!"

"Are you nuts?" Jake squawked. "Leave it!"

Miriam flipped onto her stomach and elbow-crawled toward the puddle of her purse gear a few feet away. Jake, cursing, caught up and batted stray bits her way. She didn't care about her makeup or aspirin or Kleenex; she wanted her wallet and phone. And her gun.

The Arab with the broken face knelt inside Stairway 8 just a few yards away, near a fallen commuter. He and the blond man exchanged fire over her head. She grabbed her phone and stuffed it into her coat pocket. "Get my wallet!" she yelled, pointing to the black leather bundle in front of Jake. She scrabbled a few feet further, swept up her blued Walther PPK/S.

"Miriam, what the fuck?"

She had a shot. She could see the Arab's hip, poking out from behind the marble railing. She stretched out flat, flipped off the safety, aimed. Her breathing churned like a dishwasher. The front sight wobbled. She fired. The Arab's leg jerked out of sight. A hit?

Jake swooped by and clutched her arm. "Come on! This way!"

Kelila drew her Beretta at the first gunshot, threw herself toward the nearest benches for cover. The Persian boy was already dashing for the south wall, a pistol in his hands. She couldn't see the big Arab or her team. She dodged from bench to bench past the screaming, sniveling, huddling bodies of commuters and tourists, trying to figure out who was shooting at whom.

Behind the second bench she found blood smeared across the floor. At the end of it she found David, grimacing with pain and anger amid half a dozen prone, trembling civilians. Kelila squatted next to him, pulled his coat away from his chest. Blood welled through his shirt from a hole low on the left side of his rib cage. *Goddamnit! Goddamnit!* She grabbed a child's abandoned blue blanket and pressed it hard against the wound. "Can you walk?"

He mumbled "Not far" through gritted teeth.

Shit! Nothing she could do about it. No backup, no way to get him out. She peeked over the bench's back to catch a glimpse of Schaffer and Eldar disappearing into a side corridor past the nearby glass-faced Cosi café. The big Arab was just seconds behind. *Stay with the covers*, she told herself. *They need help.* "Sorry," she told David, "Do what you can. I have to go." Then she launched into a sprint, staying low, pumping hard.

❖

Jake yelled, "Where's this go?"

"Market Street." Miriam dodged a fallen table and the woman sheltering behind it.

"You! Stop! Police!" An Amtrak cop popped up next to the closed Ben & Jerry's stand at the corridor's end. He aimed straight at Miriam. Before either of them could react, Jake heard a *slam* behind him. The cop collapsed into a puddle of midnight blue.

Glancing back, Jake spotted the big dark-skinned Arab stampeding toward him like an angry buffalo. The weapon he pointed at Jake looked like a tank gun.

Jake spied an opening and bellowed "Go right!" He clamped a struggling Miriam in his arms, hauled her off her feet, and dragged her along in his lunge to shelter.

He landed hard on his back in a narrow hallway lined with food counters. The bright colors and neon signs seemed obscenely cheerful for a shooting gallery. Miriam, heavy on top of him, thrashed in his arms. "Let go! I've got a shot!"

A flash of movement at the other end of the hall. The Persian kid, pistol in both hands.

Jake rolled them both against the chrome cold case of Delilah's Southern Cuisine just as the Persian shot at them. His bullet screamed off the marble floor. Miriam fired back twice, the pistol so close to Jake's head his left ear went dead. The kid disappeared.

The buffalo lurched into the mouth of the hall, just a few feet from Jake and Miriam. He grinned and raised his pistol.

Kelila rounded the corner into the food court to find the big Arab next to Dunkin' Donuts, aiming into a side passage. She charged, firing at a run. Her second shot slapped into his right shoulder as he turned to face her, knocking him back a step.

She sidestepped and rolled for cover behind a huge, fake terra-cotta flower pot just as the big Arab let off a shot. The reverb off the marble sounded like artillery. His second round crackled through the plastic above her head. Kelila jerked upright, fired twice, the *pop* of her .22 almost lost in the racket. Then another weapon sounded. Heavy running feet. She peeked over the pot's rim as the big Arab thumped past the ice cream stand.

Kelila hesitated only a moment before she jumped into a flat run toward the corridor's far end. She yelled into her earpiece, "Sasha! Take the covers, I've got a hostile!"

"I'm going after him!" Miriam blurted, her voice too fast, her face too hard.

"And get yourself killed?" Jake panted. "The only way. You're going to die today. Is if I kill you myself. Mossad's got him. We keep moving."

Jake peeked around the corner, tried to sort out who was shooting where, but the echoes of the bystanders' screams and the high-pitched whine in his left ear didn't help. The smell of donuts briefly overwhelmed the stink of gunpowder and fear. He grabbed Miriam's arm and towed her across yards of frighteningly exposed floor to the substantial tile-and-wood shelter of the Saxby's Coffee kiosk.

Two shots behind them—one big, one small—shattering glass, a scream. Who won that one, the buffalo or Elena from Athens? Didn't matter. Miriam breathed fast and hard next to him, her eyes and gun swiveling like a radar dish searching for a bogie. "How many rounds you got?"

She hesitated. "Four."

Shit. "Stay here."

Sprinting the twenty feet to the fallen policeman felt like crossing Central Park naked. Jake hunkered down, noted the cop was still breathing, eased the blocky Glock 22 from the man's hand. More gunfire screamed down the hallway behind him, but no one had shot him yet; so far, so good. Then another streak across the park. He was surprised to still be alive when he threw himself down next to Miriam. "Pretzels."

"What?"

Jake led Miriam in a scramble over a pile of prone, mewling commuters—the longest five yards of his life—to the open wood-and-white cube of Auntie Anne's Pretzels.

The blond plainclothes cop who had dogged Sohrab all the way down the hall was out of sight now, praise Allah. Sohrab crouched at the concourse's east end behind a black stone pedestal holding a huge sculpture of an angel carrying a dead man. From there, he could stop anyone going in or out the 29th Street doors.

The targets were behind the stairwell by the tree. Sohrab didn't have a good angle on them, but he could see the top of the woman's head. He fired, sprayed chips from the top of the marble half-wall, caused them both to drop out of sight. *Damn!*

He heard scrabbling to his right. Three travelers scurried out the farthest set of doors, their faces bright with terror. Closer in lay the woman cop he'd shot a few moments before. A teenaged blond girl lay crying on the floor no more than a couple meters behind Sohrab, rolled in a knot, her shoulders shuddering.

Where was Gabir? Where was Ziyad? Who were these people with the woman in the tan coat? He tried to tune out the crying and moaning so he could hear something useful, but the station was full of frightened people and bounced sound like a men's toilet.

Come out. Let's finish this.

Jake prairie-dogged over the back of the bench lining the Stairway 4 rail, then hunched down next to Miriam, his back to the Christmas tree looming just a couple dozen feet away. He tried but failed to catch his breath. "I think he's at the statue. We can circle around. Two more benches. Then the wall around the last stairwell. Have shelter almost all the way. To the doors."

"No!" She breathed hard, her eyes burning bright. "I'm going to get that bastard!"

Oh, God, she's Rambo. He clamped a hand on her shoulder. "Miriam. We're not SWAT. SWAT's coming. Let them take care of him. Our job is to survive."

She yanked her shoulder away. "If we leave, he'll get away! He'll come back after us. Look what they're doing! These people aren't going to stop!"

Another *crack*, more splinters, way too close. Jake levered up from his crouch, fired a round at the pedestal, dropped down again. "I have a little girl. I'm not dying today."

"You're scared? Is that it?"

"Of course I'm fucking scared, you idiot! People are trying to kill us! What, you're not?" Miriam jerked her face away. "We die, they win. I'm *not* going to watch you get yourself killed. Understand?" She clamped her teeth so hard, her jaw shivered. Jake grabbed her chin and forced her to look at him. "Understand?"

She gave him the death-ray stare. "Yes."

"Good. Now follow me. And if you even look like you're going after him, so help me I'll put a round through your leg. Got it?" *Holy shit, where did that come from?*

Miriam snorted, "Yes, *sir*."

Bent double, they scrambled behind the stairwell's back wall, stopped at the end. Jake dashed the few feet to the next bench as a bullet smashed through the Faber convenience store window beside him. He took cover behind the bench's wooden end cap, aimed, then beckoned Miriam as he fired at a flash of movement by the pedestal. She rolled behind him, shouldered him from his position, aimed double-handed at the statue. Jake was in motion even before he heard the sharp *snap* of her Walther, pulling off a baseball slide to steal the last bench. In a moment, she was next to him.

Another very long ten feet to the low marble wall surrounding Stairway 2. Maybe twenty feet beyond that to the doors. From where they were, they didn't have a good angle on the guy by the statue. Jake noticed the bawling blond girl balled up on the floor near the pedestal. *Get out of here, kid! Go, now!*

"I'll go first," Jake said. Miriam nodded. "Watch out for that girl."

Sasha had picked up the little Arab down by the Amtrak booth and played cat-and-mouse with him most of the way down the huge station concourse. From behind the big Christmas tree he could see the little shit by the towering pedestal fifteen meters or so away, his black bomber jacket blending with the granite. Sasha didn't have a solution on him from behind the tree and there was nothing but open floor on either side.

Eldar and Schaffer hopscotched the benches to Sasha's right like a couple of pros, heading for the doors. Who were these people, anyway? They'd had some kind of training.

"Sasha," Kelila's voice buzzed in his ear. "Where are you?"

"Behind the tree. Where are you?"

"Just outside, chasing the big one. Do you see Eldar and Schaffer?"

"Right here." *Great, no backup.* Eldar sprinted across the gap between the bench and the stair surround while the woman laid down measured covering fire. Not bad for civilians. "They're trying to escape. The little one's got the doors covered."

"Get out as soon as you can."

Sorry, honey. He'd keep this joker busy so the covers could get out.

Sohrab crouched facing the doors, his back squeezed against the pedestal's cold stone. The blond girl glanced at him, wrapped her arms over her head and cried louder.

The plan had turned to shit. The Jews were much harder to kill than any of them had expected. Even now they were spread out in a way that made it impossible for him to keep track of them both at the same time. He was alone. His shoulder wound had reopened, an aching souvenir from the day before. Sirens sounded outside— lots of sirens. He glanced at his watch; four and a half minutes since the first shot. It seemed like an hour.

He swung around the side of the granite block away from the two Jews. A shadow of movement caught his eye. A man lay prone next to the decorated tree, aiming a pistol. *An!*

Sohrab ducked back behind the pedestal just as the man fired. A sharp tug on his pants leg; a ragged tear appeared on the cuff of his jeans. Sohrab slammed his back against the stone.

Time to go. But how?

The stairway led to a train platform. He could go down there, disappear into the darkness, follow the tracks out. The police would be busy with the terminal and all the people in it.

But the Jews would kill him before he made it to the stairs.

He stared at the sniveling teenager, so close. Black tights, a denim skirt, striped top, pigtails. Almost a child.

Perfect.

❖

Jake set himself up to cover Miriam. He was about to wave her to him when a figure leaped onto the blond girl. A moment later, she was on her knees screaming, a black-clad arm across her throat, a gun in her ear, a thin Persian face half obscured behind her head.

Goddamnit!

The Persian wrestled her to her feet, pivoting her so she faced Jake, then Miriam, then Jake again. He shoved her forward one step, then two, heading for the stairs.

Jake heard a clatter of hard-soled shoes, then Miriam flung herself onto the bench against the half-wall. He wiped the nervous sweat from his eyes on his sleeve, aimed, watched the man shuffle closer. The only chance was a head shot, and that was a slim chance—too small a target, too much movement.

A male figure slid into the edge of Jake's peripheral vision. Nondescript sturdy clothes, ash blond. Wrong hair color for Hezbollah. He stepped past the Christmas tree, angled toward the Persian and the girl, gun raised and ready.

The Persian noticed the blond man too, swung hard to present the girl's orange-and-white striped shirt to him. For a moment, the Persian's head was clear.

Take the shot.

I'll hit her. I can't take that chance.

Take the shot!

He adjusted his grip on the policeman's gun, sighted, squeezed just enough to feel the trigger-mounted safety move. *Do it do it do it no no no what if I kill her I can't I can't...*

The Persian swung back, showing Jake the girl's mascara-streaked face, not yet done with its baby fat. He edged down the first step, pressed his butt against the brass handrail. Jake twisted to keep a line on the two of them.

Gunman and hostage reached the first landing, started down the second flight. They faded into the murk under the overhang.

Jake grunted "shit!" and slapped his hand against the top of the wall. That poor girl. It had been years since he'd seen that kind of terror in a human face. And he'd let the asshole get away. He had the shot. He could've done it.

He slowly stood, took his first deep breath for what seemed like hours, and looked toward Miriam. She also stood, face grim, shoulders sagging. Was she thinking the same thing?

The blond man approached the top of the stairs. He gestured abruptly toward the door. "You. Get out. Go." He had a Russian accent. *Russian? What the hell?*

"Who *are* you?" Miriam demanded.

The man said "Go!" again. "Safe for now. Go to police." He then wrapped both hands around the butt of his pistol and carefully descended the stairs without a look back.

Jake popped the magazine from his gun, dropped it into the stairwell followed by the chambered round, then set the now-harmless weapon on the marble wall. He turned toward Miriam. "Put that thing away. We're outta here."

FORTY-EIGHT

6 DECEMBER
PHILADELPHIA

Every inch of Miriam trembled. While gallons of adrenaline saturated her system, she was Superwoman, bulletproof, invincible. But her adrenaline had run down a storm drain, leaving her full of watery Jell-O, borderline sick to her stomach. Train-station floor crud covered her black suit. Her bad knee throbbed. She couldn't stop shivering.

A herd of other crying, hugging, shell-shocked escapees from the station milled around the PECO Tower patio across the Schuylkill from the station. What appeared to be the Philadelphia Police Department's entire vehicle fleet was strewn haphazardly everywhere she looked, blocking Market Street, surrounding the station, light bars blazing. A police helicopter and three news choppers darted back and forth a few hundred feet overhead.

Jake stood at the Salvation Army mobile kitchen's counter across the street. Thank God he'd kept his head in the station. He'd saved her from herself. She'd have gone toe-to-toe with those Arab bastards, run straight at their guns. And would've died.

Don't let him know you're scared.

He shuffled in her direction, juggling two steaming Styrofoam cups and a bottle of water. He handed her a cup—coffee, black— sat beside her on the granite half-wall, cracked open the water, wet a paper napkin, then dabbed at her cheek.

She knocked his hand away. "What are you doing?"

"There's blood." *Blood?* He leaned in, gently wiped with the napkin. "Hold still." She felt his fingers warm on her skin, then a tiny pull. "Splinter. All gone."

She pulled away from him, wrapped both hands around her

185

coffee, let its steam rise into her face. "I'm not helpless, you know. I can take care of myself."

Jake leaned his elbows on his knees, blew on his coffee, took a sip. His hands shook. "I know you're not helpless. Neither was Rinnah. Damned if I'm gonna let you get killed, too." He watched her for a moment. "You okay?"

"I'm fine." She wondered if she sounded as fake as she felt. "We need to get out of here."

"The cops are—"

"We need to get out of here!" She stopped to rein herself in. "We need to go someplace safe. There could be more of those people, right here."

"We're surrounded by half the cops in Pennsylvania."

"Yes, and a lot of good that did us in there. We need to find someplace safe."

Jake let out a boulder of a sigh and stared into the crowd of refugees. "Okay, I have an idea. How do we get back to your car?"

"Not on the train." She held the cup against her right cheek, then her left, as she fished transit schedules from the swirling mess in her head. The coffee didn't warm her either inside or out. "There's a bus, the 406, that leaves from 10th and Market."

Jake nodded, stood and held out his hand. "Let's go."

Miriam ignored his hand and stood. Her knee collapsed under her, jolting her coffee out onto Jake's coat. Jake caught her under her arms on her way down and held her upright. Miriam was very aware of him, the warmth of his body, the strength in his hands holding her. How long since a man had been this close to her? *Stop it.* She figured out how to put a little weight on her bad leg and stood straight. "Sorry."

"No problem." A flush of pink stole into his cheeks. "Sure you're okay?"

Miriam nodded. "I hurt my knee. It'll be okay if I can get some ice on it." She pulled away from him to test her theory. She could stand, but walking would be a chore. "I can't make it all the way to 10th, but I can get to the trolley station down there on 22nd."

"Long as the cops don't stop us." He crooked his arm for her.

She considered his offer. She hated being dependent; she didn't want him to think she was weak. But her knee really, really hurt.

Miriam drew in a deep breath and took his arm.

❖

"No one's following us," Miriam said.

A small blessing. Jake looked down from the Honda's rear window to the back seat. A pair of huge, golden eyes glared out at him through the blue plastic pet carrier's wire-mesh door. As they'd prepared to abandon Miriam's apartment, Miriam dispatched him to put the cat in her cage. Bastet apparently held a grudge. Her triangular head, oversized ears and grim expression reminded Jake of Egyptian tomb carvings. He wondered if she was sizing him up for Anubis.

He turned to face forward again, stole a glance at Miriam. She'd changed clothes—into another suit, this one the color of fresh asphalt. Did she ever wear anything casual? That flash of softness or vulnerability he'd seen outside the station was gone, too; her eyes were back to something resembling mahogany. Only the ice pack strapped to her left knee spoiled the Wonder Woman image.

"Do you want to try calling your uncle again?" she asked.

"Yeah." He'd gone straight to voicemail when he'd called from the apartment. He pulled the phone from the Honda's center console, thumbed in the number. Gene's voice interrupted the fourth ring. "Yeah?"

This wasn't a call Jake had been looking forward to. He felt like a little kid calling Daddy for help. "Hey, it's me."

Silence. Then, "Where the fuck are you? And what the hell's going on down there? We got Grand Central and Penn Station on lockdown."

"It was them. They tried again. We got out, but..."

"Jesus, kid, you okay? You sound like shit, you know?"

"Thanks, Gene. I feel like it, too. We're both okay. A little banged up, but we're alive."

Bastet yowled. Miriam stage-whispered, "Hush, you."

"What was that?"

"A cat."

"Still with that Schaffer broad?"

187

"Yeah." Jake hesitated, then decided to lay it all out. "There was somebody else in the station, too. Looks like the Mossad team from Qatar is here."

"What? Are you nuts? They wouldn't send hitters over here. They're not that stupid."

"Well, I guess this time they are. I recognized them from the INTERPOL pictures. Look, we need to come in. These guys started a firefight in a crowded train station at rush hour to get to us. I don't think they're going to give up."

Bastet yowled again. Miriam reached behind her, pushed her fingers through the mesh door and wiggled them. "I know, sweetie. Be good." The cat rubbed her face on Miriam's fingers, purring like a diesel engine. Jake watched, fascinated; this was the first tenderness he'd seen Miriam show another creature. Maybe there was still a heart in there somewhere.

"Twice in twelve hours?" Gene fell uncharacteristically silent for a moment. "You're right. We talking safe house here? That what you're looking for?"

"Yeah. We'll talk to whoever, tell them what we know, but we need to disappear until this gets sorted out." He watched some trees smear past. "We had our own little gunfight with one of the Hezbollah guys. Philly PD's going to be looking for us once they see the security tapes." *Maybe now they'll believe us.*

Gene snorted. "Screw Intel, kid, I'm putting you in for ESU. Okay, I'll go talk to JTTF right now, see if they'll buy off on it. I'll call you in an hour. This number good?"

"Yeah, it's Miriam's phone. How's Eve?"

"Scared sick and missing her daddy. How do you think?"

Shit. "We'll be there as fast as we can. Tell her I'm coming. Thanks, Gene."

"Don't shoot anyone for the next hour."

Miriam asked, "What did he say?"

"Don't worry. He'll come up with something."

A couple miles went by before she replied. "Can he really keep us safe? Keep them away from us?"

Can he? "Sure. It's NYPD, they do this all the time." He hoped he was right. He'd bet both their lives on it.

FORTY-NINE

6 DECEMBER
CHERRY HILL

The motel bathroom smelled of blood, sweat and soap. Alayan took one look at the scene, pivoted, and slammed the heel of his hand into the opposite wall so hard it left a dent.

An hour ago, Alayan had helped bury Kassim. He and Rafiq had found a sympathetic imam at a storefront mosque in a ragged fringe of Philadelphia. Having died a martyr, Kassim should have met the angels wearing the clothes in which he'd died, but there was only so much Alayan was willing to explain to the locals. Instead, the three of them—the imam, Rafiq and Alayan—finished a ritual bathing of Kassim's body, then wrapped him in a plain white cotton *kafan* that reduced him to a vaguely human-shaped bundle reminiscent of a mummy. The rite had been strangely comforting; it allowed Alayan to say goodbye.

They lowered Kassim onto his right side in a hastily-dug grave at Mount Moriah cemetery beneath the gray shroud of a damp morning sky. The neglected and vandalized grounds mirrored the bleak emptiness inside Alayan. Kassim had deserved so much better than to spend eternity under this glorified pasture in a hostile and alien land.

Now Alayan had returned to the motel to find Gabir splayed on the blue-and-gray tile bathroom floor, shirt off, a dressing and bandage covering the hollow of his muscular right shoulder. Ziyad balanced on his left side in the bathtub, his trousers off, while Sohrab finished taping a dressing high on Ziyad's right outer thigh.

"Sohrab," Alayan choked, "get out here when you're done."

❖

When Sohrab's report reached the gun battle, Alayan's frustration and anger came to full boil. He bolted from his chair. "What part of this plan sounded like a good idea to you?" He leaned his face into Sohrab's. "Didn't you listen to anything I told you this morning? This isn't Damascus or Baghdad! People here *notice* when you have gunfights in train stations!"

Sohrab swallowed. "Yes, *sidi*."

"Whose idea was this?"

"It… well… we all agreed on it."

Alayan wrenched away from the now-trembling Persian and kicked the other armchair out of his way. Until that point, Sohrab had said the decisions were his. How convenient the greatest failure was decided by committee. "These police who were waiting for you. Who are they? How did they find you?"

"I don't know, *sidi*. The woman was in the car park yesterday. She was the one who shot at me in the van. They must have followed us."

"And you didn't notice them on your way?" Alayan growled. He wanted to put his fist through the window. All the plans, all their work… "I'd expect this of Gabir, I don't expect it of you. You realize what you've done, I hope?"

Sohrab shifted his feet nervously, re-squared his shoulders. "*Sidi?*"

Alayan advanced on Sohrab, fists balled at his side. "All our effort to avoid suspicion—wasted! In the rubbish!" He stomped to a halt directly in front of the Persian, his nose less than a hand's thickness from Sohrab's. "It's already on television! That means the police, the FBI, their spy agencies know who you are. This'll be headline news around the world! Do you understand what that means?" He paused to drag in a breath. "What happened to them? The Jews?"

Sohrab grimaced. "They escaped, *sidi*."

The slap echoed off the room's walls like a gunshot. Sohrab collapsed on the bed, stunned, holding his cheek. Alayan watched him try to shake off the shock, then commanded, "On your feet!" He waited for Sohrab to scramble back into parade rest. "You ruin this operation and you couldn't even kill these two miserable Jews?"

"They were warned, *sidi*. They knew we were there. The

woman had a gun. And they're not civilians, not like the others. They moved like soldiers."

"Of course they did! The Zionists are all trained soldiers, you idiot! That didn't stop us from killing the other nine. Why are these two special?"

"They were ready for us." Sohrab's left cheek was tomato red, his left eye watering, but the pain in his voice seemed to come from this thought, not the slap.

Alayan turned away, stalked back to the window, watched the mottled overcast flow across the sky. His head was too crowded to allow room for constructive thought. "Tend to the others," he snapped. "I have to figure out how to salvage this operation. You and I aren't finished."

But the team might be, Alayan brooded. So might the mission.

FIFTY

Gur trawled the half-full parking lot on the north side of the Macy's at Cherry Hill Mall until flashing headlights drew his attention to a blue Toyota with fogged windows sitting nose-out in a stall. He parked the Suburban two rows away, stepped into the chilly mid-morning air, and plodded to the Camry.

On the drive from Atlantic City, he'd listened with growing alarm to the radio news reports of the shootout at Philadelphia's train station. His gut had told him his team was in the middle of it. Kelila's phone call hadn't helped; all she'd told him was, "It's bad."

He slid into the center of the back seat. The doors locked behind him. Inside was close and humid from bodies and tension. "Where's David?" he asked.

Sasha—slouched in the front passenger's seat—grumbled, "She left him."

"What was I supposed to do?" Kelila snapped back. She'd burrowed into the driver's seat, her arms crossed so tight the veins popped on the back of her visible hand. "Pick him up and carry him?"

"I would have," Sasha said.

She twisted and bared her fangs at him. "Right. And then what? Let the covers get killed? Let the hostiles get away?"

Sasha swiveled his head and sneered at her. "They got away anyway."

"At least I shot mine. How'd yours do?"

"Enough, both of you." Gur leaned between the front seats and loomed over them. They broke off and drooped back into their seats, arms crossed, perfect mirror images. Gur realized he wouldn't

192

manage a real debriefing here, not with these two sniping at each other. Best for now to go for the bottom line. "What became of David?"

Kelila pressed her palms against the steering wheel, stared at the backs of her hands. "He didn't make it out. One of the Arabs shot him—that's what got the whole mess started. The last thing he said, the police were coming for him and he couldn't get away. I've already warned headquarters."

Truly mixed feelings: relief David was still alive, dread that the police had him. With any luck, they hadn't questioned him yet. Orgad would be furious. "Eldar and Schaffer?"

"They got out," Sasha said into the side window. "They took care of themselves pretty good for civilians."

"Good." And inconvenient. If Hezbollah couldn't find the covers, they might decide to cut their losses and escape back into whatever Lebanese sewer they crawled out of. Not a good exchange for losing half his team. "The Arabs?"

Kelila said, "Two wounded. I shot one, and I think Schaffer got the other."

"Schaffer? Where did she get a weapon?"

"I don't know, but she had one." Kelila paused, smirked at Sasha. "I recognized the third one from yesterday. Sasha lost that one in the tunnels."

"It was dark. The police were coming in. The same reason you let yours go."

Gur held up a warning hand to halt the imminent bickering. "Only three? You're sure?"

"Three was enough," Sasha said.

Where were the rest of them? What else were they up to? Was there another target? Gur would think about that in a while. "Are we blown? Is that why we're meeting here? Or are you going shopping?"

Kelila wrenched around to glare at Gur, face flushed, her mouth tight enough to snap a shekel coin in half. He'd seen machine-gun fire less intense than her eyes.

Gur held up his hands. "Sorry. A poor try at a joke."

Kelila thumped back into her seat, banged her head against the headrest, sighed. "We might be blown." The anger that had overwhelmed her voice just moments before was slipping away, revealing a frustration Gur recognized well from his own past. "We didn't want to go straight back to the hotel, just in case."

Sasha glanced at Kelila, then grumped, "I dumped the Pathfinder with a *sayan* and got this." His eyes gave Kelila a full dose of contempt. "Just in case."

"Good thinking." There would've been dozens of cameras in the station, hundreds of witnesses. The police had David and his false ID. The amateur videos were likely already on YouTube. *Good God, what a disaster.*

Gur fought to keep his face calm. He didn't need to tell these two how grim the situation was; they'd clearly had too much time to brood about it, never a good idea following a failed action. The *what ifs* and *could have beens* had piled up and turned septic. He'd seen teams wreck themselves this way. That was the biggest danger now, not the police or Hezbollah.

"Stop flogging yourself and each other." Gur wanted to sound brisk but not harsh. They didn't need a scolding. "There's no point. It's done, we have bigger problems. Give me your room keys." Sasha and Kelila dug out their plastic cards and reluctantly handed them over. "I'll go back to the hotel and look for police, see if anyone's been in your rooms. If it's clear, I'll ring you. Come back, check out, change your looks, then check in at the Crowne Plaza. Use your backup IDs. I'll follow in an hour or two. I'll want a full debrief from each of you, then we'll figure out how to go forward. Any questions?"

Kelila shook her head once, stared down at her hands in her lap. Sasha snorted, huddled tighter against the door, then mumbled "*Nyet.*"

"Good." Gur pushed open the left rear door. Before he climbed out, he turned to watch the remains of his team simmer. Their body language screamed "angry" and "frustrated" and "ashamed." He understood; he'd been where they were now. But they were also professionals, and they'd get past this. He hoped.

Gur lurched into the damp cold, then strode off to take his beating from Tel Aviv.

FIFTY-ONE

6 DECEMBER
CROWN HEIGHTS, BROOKLYN

Miriam peeked out through the hunter-green curtains of her new bedroom. Below her window lay hibernating flowerbeds flanking the concrete pad that passed for a back yard. A wooden fence with a swinging gate—both needing paint—then the alley, then the backs of the homes on the other side of the block. She knew she was somewhere in Brooklyn, but didn't know what the front of the place looked like, or even the street name.

A small, hard head knocked into her calf. She scooped Bastet into her arms without looking down. Bastet stared at her with resentful golden eyes, despite the cat's instant purring. "I'm sorry, sweetie," Miriam cooed as she scratched Bastet between the ears. "Today's been a bad day for all of us. I asked the nice policeman to get you some tuna."

Miriam plopped Bastet on the bed and made her way downstairs. In the kitchen, Jake looked up from the *Times* spread over the pickled-wood table to watch her cross to the cabinets flanking the stove. She couldn't read his expression. "Is something wrong?"

"No, sorry. Haven't seen you not wearing a suit or with your hair down, that's all."

She'd changed into her nicer black jeans and a tucked-in, long-sleeved cobalt mock turtle. Why was he so surprised to see her in jeans? He'd shed his jacket and tie and rolled up his sleeves, but otherwise still wore what he'd had on yesterday. All at once Miriam felt fortunate to have had a few minutes to pack. "Would you like some tea?"

"That'd be great."

She rummaged through the cabinets, found a brass kettle, checked the inside for dust, then filled it at the sink.

After a moment, he said, "Can you believe this place? It's like an '80s time capsule. My friend Danny Teischman in second grade, his folks did their house like this. Remember this?"

Miriam surveyed the kitchen—tan ceramic tile floor with brown grout, tile counters, white laminate cabinets with oak pull strips, fluorescent lights in a wood-and-plastic enclosure on the ceiling. "Not really. Decorating wasn't a priority at the kibbutz or in the barracks."

A gruff voice approached in the back yard, clomped up the steps along with its owner's feet. Miriam tensed, then eased out of flight mode immediately. The guard was outside smoking, no shots had been fired; it must be okay.

The back door burst open. A large man with a square head atop a square body rolled in, black wool overcoat open over a blue pinstriped suit. A badge flashed from his breast pocket. "Jake!" he called out.

"Gene!" Jake bounced from his chair and embraced his uncle in the middle of the kitchen with a lot of back pounding. They were physically so different that Miriam never would've guessed they were related. She lingered by the stove to let them have their reunion undisturbed. She couldn't help her flash of envy. How long since someone had hugged her when she came home?

Gene held Jake at arm's length. "Christ, kid, you need a shower or something."

"What I need is something else to wear. Thanks for putting this together."

"Thank JTTF, it's their show. I got your bag in the car." He broke free and turned to the back door. "Got something for you." He made a sweeping gesture toward the door. Nothing happened. Gene leaned toward the door and urged, "C'mon, Princess, you'll be safe here."

A little girl of about six in jeans and a pink fleece top edged into the opening. Her eyes filled her face, then she dashed across the room.

Jake fell to his knees, let her crash into his waiting arms. "Eve! Bunny! God, I missed you, I'm sorry I was gone so long, I didn't mean to..." They hugged each other so hard Miriam feared they might suffocate. Her throat knotted up when a tear rolled down Jake's face as he poured kisses over the girl's face. "I'm so sorry, Bunny, so sorry, I love you so much..."

Miriam turned away; this was too private. Gene stopped a couple feet from her, leaned back against the counter, hands in his coat pockets, smiling at Jake and Eve. After a moment, he gave Miriam a once-over. "You Schaffer?"

"I am." She held out her hand for him to shake. "You're Gene Eldar."

"Guilty. You've had a busy couple days."

"Yes, I have. We both have." She glanced toward the pair in the room's center. Jake stroked Eve's mop of black hair between hugs. The love on his face almost broke her heart. She felt a pull inside her, a sense of kinship in shared tragedy. "She still isn't talking?"

Gene folded his arms and shook his head. "You know, kid, you almost didn't get her back. Monica was redecorating the guest room. Lots of pink and Disney princesses."

Jake managed a half-smile and pushed a wisp of hair from Eve's forehead. "Were you a good girl for Aunt Monica?" Eve nodded. Jake kissed her forehead, stood, and led her by the hand toward the stove. "Eve, this is Miriam. She'll be staying here with us."

God, she was adorable. Even though her knee protested, Miriam knelt so she could look at Eve face-to-face. The girl's eyes were Jake's, but her heart-shaped face, her nose and mouth were straight out of that news photo of her mother. How did Jake feel when he looked at her? Miriam wondered how she'd have held up if she had a son who resembled Bill, reminding her day after day what she'd lost.

"Hi, Eve." Miriam held out her hand. After a moment of eyeing Miriam with undisguised suspicion, Eve slowly wrapped her delicate little hand around Miriam's fingers. "Your father's told me a lot about you. He's very proud of you." Eve took her hand back, but her bottomless brown eyes never shifted from Miriam's face. "Do you like cats?" Eve nodded. "I have a kitty here. Her name's Bastet. I'll bet she'll come see you when she gets done looking around. Would you like that?" Another nod. The girl's silence spooked Miriam; little kids were never this quiet. She wanted to tell Eve *I know you're hurting, I know how you feel, I've been there, too*, but didn't dare, not this soon. Not in front of Jake and his uncle. Instead, she gave the girl a smile and tapped her nose with a fingertip. Standing hurt every bit as much as Miriam expected.

Eve retreated to her father's side, grabbed a handful of the shirt spilling over his belt, and leaned against his leg.

"Well." Gene pushed away from the counter. "The Bureau'll come by in a couple hours, get started with you two. CSU's cleared the scene at your apartment. I'll give you the name of some people who clean up, they do good work. Oh, and here." He pulled a white card from his inside coat pocket, handed it to Jake. "Your ID. Came in yesterday."

"Thanks." Jake stared down at the card. "I guess I need to come back to work—"

"You already are. We detailed you to JTTF for this investigation. You're on the clock, kid." He bent over to look into Eve's eyes. "Chava, you take care of your daddy, okay? Keep him out of trouble." He straightened, looked back over his shoulder. "Ms. Schaffer."

"Good to meet you, Mr. Eldar."

"Call me Gene. If my crazy nephew here thinks you're worth getting almost killed for, you must be all right." He scrubbed the top of Eve's head with one of his big hands. "Help Chava here keep track of this nut, will you?"

Jake made a face. "Gene…"

"I will." Miriam stifled a smile. She was still trying to figure out Jake, but she liked his uncle the way she would a large, friendly neighborhood dog. "Thank you for everything."

Gene waved a hand in either *farewell* or *don't mention it* and lumbered out of the house.

FIFTY-TWO

Rafiq sat in the Gia Pronto coffeehouse at Market and 20th, staring at but not necessarily seeing the great twin gray slabs of Commerce Square on the opposite corner. Only two other people shared the place with him. He nipped at his still-too-hot cappuccino. Being in this place brought back all the good memories from his student days in Washington, memories he wished he had more time to savor.

He'd called Schaffer's law firm, Canby Matheson & Phelps, pretending to be a florist with a delivery for her. She wasn't there; no surprise. No car at the train station or at her apartment last night, either. She was hiding, probably with Eldar; exactly what Rafiq would do if he'd survived the couple of days they'd been through.

He should report to Alayan, but didn't feel like it. Car bombs filled his brain.

Last night, Alayan had told him about the deadline. "We have to be finished by midnight of the 22nd," he'd said on the drive back to the motel from Schaffer's apartment. "If we're not, the Council has a backup plan. Car bombs in all five of the countries involved, starting the 23rd."

Rafiq felt the flare of anger again. How could they be so stupid? They'd all seen the Zionists cause random death in their home towns; it was the brand of insanity they'd hoped the Party had left behind. How could they do this?

The Party would declare war on America. It had done that in 1983, of course, but it was one thing to kill Marines in Lebanon and quite another to attack New York or Washington. If the

Americans reacted even half as badly as they had in 2001, the result would make the last war with the Zionists look like a lovers' quarrel.

A pretty young woman bustled in, all in black except for a bright yellow scarf. Rafiq took no pleasure in watching her as she gave her order to the barista. Would she die in the bombing? How many others like her would be touched by this stupidity?

This lunatic plan wasn't the only thing that had soured his stomach since hearing the news. Alayan had kept the deadline from them. They had a right to know something this important. He'd always been open with them in the past, told them everything.

Or had he?

What else hadn't he told them? Was the Party already preparing its usual punishment for failure? If the team didn't kill Eldar and Schaffer, could they ever go home? Would they ever be safe again? What about their families?

Alayan had made Rafiq promise not to tell the others. If he kept that promise, he'd be just as guilty as Alayan. If he didn't, the secret could blast the team apart. They deserved to know. But could they handle it?

He imagined a car bomb going off in front of the skyscrapers across the street, the scattered body parts, the bloodied women and children and old people. Scenes he'd witnessed in Beirut and Baghdad. Images that had saddened him so on 9/11. And for what? Did he really want to be part of that?

For the first time since he'd returned home after university, he didn't know how far he was willing to follow the Party. He'd have to decide soon.

FIFTY-THREE

"Did you hear me?"

Al-Shami whispered "Fucking *finally*," then clicked off his microphone's mute. "Yes, I heard you. We'll leave on the tenth." He had no intention of leaving that early, but saying it would keep his handler off his back.

"Good." A tinny ringtone version of a Lebanese pop song squawked in the background at the other end of the Skype connection. Al-Shami's handler in Beirut muttered something profane; the music stopped. "Don't call your contact in the target area until you're ready to leave. He doesn't know about you yet, and he very likely won't be happy to hear from you. Let me know if he becomes a problem. Oh, and Majid? Don't get arrested like those fools in Hamburg. We can't afford to lose any more of you."

"Of course. It's definite? We're going to do this?"

The handler's pause gave al-Shami time to think dark thoughts about committees and indecision. "Nearly so. Your contact has a mission he very likely won't complete. If by some chance he does, then you stand down, but his time has almost run out."

"Fine. We'll be ready." Al-Shami disconnected before his handler could hedge any more.

Out in what the rental agent had called the "family room," Fayiz huddled over a tripod-mounted video camera while Haroun made his martyrdom declaration in English. He'd learned his faith in a Michigan prison, but not much of the faith's primary language. "Martyrdom is not death," he said, his black face both serious and serene. "Martyrs live in Paradise with Allah. We live forever because we've given everything to advance His will..."

201

And so on. This wasn't the first martyrdom video al-Shami had witnessed in the making, and *insha'Allah*, it wouldn't be the last. He stood a few feet behind Fayiz, arms crossed, letting the words float past. He wondered whether Haroun—the former Marlon Taylor Jackson—would fade into the black flag pinned to the wood paneling behind him, despite the twin studio lights aimed at him.

Haroun raised his fist and ended his declaration with "*Allahu akhbar!*" *Very nice*, al-Shami thought. *It'll play well on al-Manar.*

"Is good, Haroun," Fayiz said in English, not his best language. "You have passion, strength, is good. I make work on sound, put in pictures, is good video, yes." He jolted when al-Shami clapped a hand on his shoulder. "Yes, *sidi?*"

"We're going," al-Shami murmured in Arabic. "On the 19th. From now on, they don't leave the house."

"I'll tell them," Fayiz replied in Arabic. "I need to fix Mahir's video. He comes off flat and I can't liven it up with music. He's going to have to re-record."

Al-Shami shook his head in wonder. Fayiz used to shoot cheap music videos in Syria; now he was Martin Scorsese. "Whatever keeps them occupied. Feed them all the motivation you can, books, videos, whatever. I need them 100% ready when we leave here."

"Of course." Fayiz smiled. "Mahir and Haroun are good men. They'll make you proud."

"*Insha'Allah.* No matter what happens, they're not coming back alive."

FIFTY-FOUR

Gur glanced from the treadmill's digital display to Kelila. She glanced back. They'd done this for the past half-hour. Just as well they had the hotel's gym to themselves; the air between them sizzled like the summer sky just before a lightning storm.

She stood at the universal machine, hauling on a handle attached to a hefty stack of weights. Her black, second-skin calf-length tights and rust scoop-necked tank top showcased her figure. He'd seen her in trousers, skirts, dresses, fatigues, hiking shorts, *hijab*, skydiving gear, a wetsuit once (that was memorable) and ski clothes, but not until this mission had she worn anything this revealing. Strangely enough, that wasn't what kept his attention.

She could have died in the car park or the station. All through the two long days since the second attack, this thought had raced circles around Gur's mind until it wore ruts in his brain. Before the actions, he'd worried about making a misstep that would drive her away; now he understood a bullet could take her from him in an instant.

Kelila dropped the weight handle, dabbed at her face and throat with the hotel hand towel, then drifted to the front of Gur's treadmill. She watched him jog, folding her toned, golden arms atop the console, a serious expression shifting across her face. After the station disaster, she'd hacked off her lush bronze hair just above collar length and dyed it jet black. She'd never be identified as the woman whose face kept appearing on the television news, but it made her look older, harder. A future Kelila, if she didn't get out of this business.

After a few moments, she reached over the console and stabbed the "Stop" button. The treadmill moaned to a halt. Gur didn't object; he wanted to know what was on her mind.

"I've been thinking about Eldar and his wife," she said after a long pause. "I'll bet they thought they had forever, just like me and Yigal. We thought we had forever. We'd give Hasia a brother or sister and watch them grow up and have their own families. We'd grow old together." She sighed. "But we didn't get to. You and Varda, did you think you had forever?"

He swallowed the catch in his throat. They'd wanted to see the boys become men, retire together, travel, make up for all the time apart. "There is no forever."

"I know that now." She circled the console, stepped up on the treadmill to face Gur, close enough for her heat to curl around him. "With this job, we may not even have tomorrow." She placed her palm on his chest, fingers spread. "Look at poor Amzi."

Kelila's hand burned through his track-suit jacket into his breastbone; a blue-hot flame danced in her eyes. Gur's heart pounded harder than when he'd been running. He found himself bending toward her, her mouth now a whisper away from his, her breath quick and warm on his skin. The meadowy scent of her shampoo mingled with the tang of her sweat.

Last chance to stop, Gur's better judgment warned. But something even deeper inside him murmured, *she's right, she's right*. He'd wasted so much time fighting their attraction, and for what?

The instant their lips met she leaned into the kiss, flowing her body against him, pressing her hips against his when she felt his reaction. He wrapped his arms around her, caressed her strong, graceful back and firm rear. Her fingertips raked through his hair and down his back. The moment exploded in his head like a lightning flash.

When at last they surfaced, gasping for air, a twinge of regret shoved its way through the swirl of his emotions. "This isn't how I wanted it to happen," he whispered. He pulled back from her, checked the front door for spectators. "Not in the field, not with all this—"

"You wanted perfect," she shot back, also whispering. She hauled his body against hers again. "I don't need perfect anymore.

It doesn't last. You've got that lovely big bed, and that fancy bathtub and shower, and room service. That's plenty good enough for me. You too?"

Yes, more than enough. But... "You have to relieve Sasha—"

"In *four hours*." She stole a quick kiss, then leaned back. "You know what we could do in four hours?"

The possibilities flooded his mind. They kissed again, harder this time, more desperately. Gur forgot about everything except Kelila and this moment. His fingers found the strip of hot, damp skin below the hem of her top, slid up her bare back to the strap of her sports bra, down her flanks, over her hips. Her hands explored his body, torching everything she touched.

After a few false stops they broke the kiss, their chests heaving against each other. Gur tried to focus on her eyes. "We have. To be discreet. Around Sasha."

"Too late." Kelila shook her head. "The guys thought. We were sleeping together. In Mombasa last year."

They did? The absurdity pulled a trigger in him, and Gur started to laugh. After a moment, Kelila joined him. The laughter felt as good as her body did against his. After it died down, he bent to her ear and whispered, "It's too damned public here."

She kissed his throat, then smiled. "Yeah. Just think what we can do in the elevator."

He kissed her earlobe. "Let's find out."

FIFTY-FIVE

8 DECEMBER
CROWN HEIGHTS, BROOKLYN

Jake circled the edge of the stained concrete pad behind the house, hands deep in his coat pockets, sucking in great lungfuls of the damp, cold afternoon air. For the past six hours, three FBI and NYPD interrogators had dragged him face-down by the heels through the past two months—everything he'd done, where he'd gone, who he'd talked to. He'd looked at pictures of what must have been most of the male population of Lebanon. Another two cops did the same to Miriam in the kitchen. Yesterday they were at it fourteen hours straight. If this was how they treated people who'd come in voluntarily, he could just imagine what they did to suspects.

It had been a rough night. Eve had cried herself to sleep, and eventually so did Jake. He'd had Rinnah dreams—a couple good, then one featuring a dead but walking and angry Rinnah that ended when he bolted awake at four in a hot sweat.

Eve clutched at his coat. She looked nearly as tired as he felt. Would she ever smile or laugh again, or would she wear that solemn, wounded look forever? Even Jasmine seemed downcast as she peeked out of Eve's parka. Jake had hoped being together again might jog a few words out of his daughter, but no.

His cell phone started playing "All You Need is Love." Startled, he dug it from his pocket. "Hello?"

"Jake Eldar?"

"Speaking."

"This is Stuart Kaminsky. You called me several times."

Jake's brain burned some rubber as it tried to gain traction. Finally, the name emerged from the smoke and dust. "Oh, yeah, I

206

did. I almost forgot. Your office said you were travelling on business."

"What can I do for you, Mr. Eldar?" Kaminsky's accent was just thick enough to make Jake pay closer attention.

Jake glanced down; Eve's watchful eyes stared back. He switched to Hebrew. "You're on the list of people the Qataris released in September."

"Yes, I know. So?"

"So I am too. And so a Hezbollah team is trying to kill us all. That's why I called, to warn you."

Kaminsky made a clicking sound. "I see. How do you know this?"

"I've seen at least five of them so far. I'm with a woman who's also on the list. They tried to kill her twice in twelve hours on the fifth and sixth." Jake gave the man a quick rundown of the days since Rinnah's death.

"Such a story," Kaminsky said once Jake finished. "I'm very sorry for your loss. You say the NYPD has you now?"

"Yeah, we're in a safe house." And for the first time since Thursday, he did feel safe. Would Eve ever feel that way again?

A yank on Jake's coat caused him to switch his attention to Eve, who pointed toward the house. Miriam stood at the kitchen window, curtain pushed aside, holding up the kettle. He gave her a thumbs-up.

"Well, I'm glad you're protected. I'll do the same, in a way. My company owns flats around the city that we use for much the same thing."

Jake dredged up what he remembered of the website for Aluma Consultants, Kaminsky's company. The wording in the "Our Services" tab was artfully ambiguous, but he recalled the phrase "full-spectrum security." No kidding, if they ran their own safe houses. "Well, great, it sounds like you'll be okay, then."

"Yes, for now, at least. Mr. Eldar—"

"Call me Jake."

"Of course. I very much appreciate your call. This isn't the sort of thing one expects to happen. Thank you for taking the time to warn me, and for looking after Ms. Schaffer."

"Um... no problem. Take care."

"I will. Would you mind if I call again in a few days, to check up? We survivors need to stick together, to bear witness."

To *what?* The last time Jake had heard that phrase, it was a great aunt talking about Bergen-Belsen. Who was this guy? "Well, no, I guess not. Goodbye, Mr. Kaminsky."

Jake stared at the phone for several seconds. Kaminsky didn't sound surprised, or scared, or worried. Curious, maybe, but nothing more. Did that come from having a security company at his fingertips? Alarms, safe houses, big guys with guns? Well, Jake had done his duty and warned the man. If Kaminsky thought he could take care of himself, more power to him.

FIFTY-SIX

8 DECEMBER
CHERRY HILL

They didn't just vanish, Alayan told himself again, although it was getting harder to believe. He bolted from the cheap motel table to walk off some of his frustration. Fourteen days left to find and eliminate those two damned Jews.

Back at the table, Rafiq crossed off a name on his list of local hotels, took a swig of Deer Park bottled water, then tapped the next number into his cellphone. "Front desk, please... yes, hello, ma'am, this is Detective Turner with Philadelphia PD. We're looking for two people who may have checked into your hotel two days ago..."

He'd repeated this story forty-three times. Nobody had seen the targets or admitted to it.

"All right then, thanks for your help." Rafiq stabbed a button on his mobile and sighed loudly. "How many more do I call before we give up?"

Alayan had wondered that himself. "Until we run out of numbers."

"Right." Rafiq shuffled through the lists in front of him, shaking his head. "You're assuming they haven't gone to New York or Washington or Baltimore or—"

"I understand."

"I don't think you do. They could be staying with friends or relatives. They could've taken a train to Florida or Chicago or Canada, for that matter. That's what I'd do if I was Eldar—get as far from here as possible."

Alayan scowled at him. "Just keep calling."

While Rafiq made his forty-fourth call, Alayan tried to ignore the truth behind Rafiq's words. The targets could be anywhere in this vast country by now. Unless the team was impossibly lucky, they'd never see Eldar or Schaffer again. Alayan wilted onto the end of the bed in front of the television and dropped his head in his hands.

They'd failed. They'd been so close. Success was just a whisper beyond their fingertips. A black gloom billowed through his insides like octopus ink. Shame for all of them, a bullet for him, disgrace for their families, the Party's self-destruction. *All my fault.*

When he jerked his head away from this vision of doom, his eyes locked on the graphic on the television screen. He fumbled with the remote, turned up the volume on CNN.

> "...are reportedly in custody and cooperating with the investigation into the dramatic Tuesday-morning shootout in Philadelphia's 30th Street Station. Philadelphia police will not confirm the whereabouts of the pair, but a police spokesperson has said the unidentified man and woman are in a secure location and are providing valuable information concerning what law enforcement officials believe may have been a terrorist attack on America's rail network. We'll now go live to..."

"Did you hear that?" Alayan asked Rafiq.

"Yes, *sidi.*"

Alayan stood. The inky black gloom faded into something like gray overcast. They might still salvage this wreck. "See what else you can learn about this. Find them."

FIFTY-SEVEN

9 DECEMBER
CHERRY HILL

Gur stared at the man in the grainy black-and-white frame capture from a security camera at Rome's Fiumicino airport. Medium-light skin, shoulder bag, conservative Western casual clothes: this Fadi Alayan could be from any point along the Mediterranean coast. But he could also be Federico Alvarez from the white van outside Eldar's flat. "Perhaps. It could be the same facial structure, but it's hard to tell from this crap."

"That's the best Kaisarut could get from the State Police," Kelila said.

It felt so empty in the hotel room with just the three of them huddled around the little table, peering at Kelila's computer. Four days before, the team had filled a room psychically if not physically.

"We have nothing linking any of them to any operations?" Gur asked.

"Not so far, nothing solid. Research is still looking, but they're overwhelmed right now." Kelila brought up the three surveillance photos sent from Tel Aviv. Alayan, Kassim Haddad, Gabir Raad. Names to faces, at last.

Gur pointed to the picture of Raad, the big, dark Arab. "This one was with the Persian and the other Arab?"

Sasha said, "Yes, on the train." He looked shockingly young with his white-blond stubble and his hair buzzed to a recruit's 4mm brush.

"And Haddad was with that other man at the hotel."

Kelila nodded. "The really good-looking one, yes."

Gur did his best to ignore Kelila's remark. And her bare neck. So graceful, so soft, that little tender spot behind her ear... He forced himself back to work. "Six so far, then. And we think they're what, one down? Two?"

Kelila started stroking the laptop's touchpad. Gur's mind flashed back a few hours to his bedroom. He felt his neck flush.

"The Persian drove the van out of the car park in Philadelphia," Kelila said, "but Haddad was in the driver's seat when I first got into position. He left and I heard gunshots behind the van, so Eldar may have shot him. And there were two blood trails at the station, Raad's and the other Arab from the train."

So at best they were evenly matched, Gur calculated, the remains of their team against the remains of his. At worst, Hezbollah had men Gur's people hadn't seen yet.

Before he could pursue that thought, his secure mobile rang. He pulled it off his belt, saw "blocked number" on the screen. "Yes?"

"Good morning to you, Raffi," Orgad said. The encryption gave his voice a slight gargle.

"Chaim." Gur pushed away from the table and paced toward the window. "I'll assume since you're calling that there's been another disaster."

"No, nothing like that. The ambassador is working to get Holmeyer out of the hospital, so you may even be able to come home someday. The covers are still missing?"

"In a way. The news programs are saying the police have them, but we're still trying to find out which police. We're having no luck with the *sayanim*. Perhaps Kaisarut can help?"

"Forget Liaison." Orgad's desk chair squeaked in the background. "They're in New York City and being held in a safe house by the local police."

Gur nodded to his reflection in the glass. The phone number Kelila recovered when she'd searched Schaffer's flat belonged to Eldar's paternal uncle in the NYPD. "You know this how?"

"That's not something that concerns you right now."

A mole in the NYPD or FBI, perhaps, or a communications intercept. That explained why Orgad called instead of sending an email: no paper trail. "All right, we'll start following Eldar's uncle. This source of yours... is he going to have more information for us?"

212

"He might. Raffi, a word of advice. No one here is impressed by that operation in the train station. Four dead railroad cops, eight civilians wounded, and you managed to let the police arrest one of your people. Consider this your Lillehammer. You need to clean this up soon. Do you understand?"

"More than you know." During the hunt for Black September, a *Kidon* team killed an innocent man in the Norwegian town of Lillehammer. Six of the combatants were captured, five went to jail, and the aftershocks destroyed a huge swath of the Institute's operations in northern Europe. Gur knew the Director wouldn't do anything melodramatic like having him assassinated; they'd simply transfer him to field collection in south Lebanon and let Hezbollah do it for them.

"Good. Don't disappoint us again, Raffi." The connection squelched and died.

Gur stood watching the traffic go by. He tried not to agree too much with Orgad's verdict, but it was hard. Philadelphia had been a huge goat-fuck—twice—and no matter how misbegotten the mission, it was always the leader's fault if it didn't work.

"Sir?" Kelila asked. The one word carried a lot of worry.

"Be ready to leave by eleven. We're going north."

FIFTY-EIGHT

10 DECEMBER
CROWN HEIGHTS, BROOKLYN

Miriam shut her book on her finger, closed her eyes and eased her head against the plush armchair that took up a big chunk of her bedroom. Not that she minded its size; it was fine to have a cozy place to get away from all the people who wanted a piece of her.

A couple hours' break from the constant interrogation felt like sheer decadence. Since she and Jake arrived here, they'd been grilled by the NYPD, the FBI, Philadelphia PD, the Pennsylvania and New Jersey state police departments, the Amtrak Police and Immigration and Customs Enforcement. They'd looked at hundreds of pictures of Arabs, some mug shots, others surveillance photos. Jake was working with a police artist now, making changes to the passport photo of the woman who'd stopped him on the street last week claiming to be a tourist.

Who else would interrogate them? Foreign police? People from dark places like the CIA... or Mossad?

How did things like this happen?

She unmoored her thoughts and let them drift. After a bit, the current nudged them toward Jake.

Other than her fathers, Bill was the only man she'd ever lived with. It still seemed strange to share three meals a day with someone she barely knew. But Jake was nice, generally polite, cleaned up after himself, was protective of her and loved his daughter desperately. He was learning when to talk and when to leave her alone—something she'd worked hard to teach Bill. She could do worse for a housemate.

Then sometimes Jake's eyes would melt or his face would lose its shape, and he'd excuse himself to go to his room or out in the back yard. She knew why, and every time it twisted her heart. She'd done exactly the same thing for months after Bill died; she'd trip over a memory and all her strength would pour from her eyes, leaving behind a dark and heavy emptiness.

Last night, Jake had left off in the middle of washing the dinner dishes to flee out the back door. She'd almost followed him, but stopped before she could turn the doorknob. *He doesn't know you, and you don't know him*, she'd reminded herself. But she knew what he felt. And she knew how terrible it was to be alone with those feelings.

Someone was watching her. Miriam opened her eyes and looked warily toward the bedroom door.

Eve stood in the doorway, her big brown eyes staring at Miriam, wheels turning behind them. She had a book and her doll pressed against her chest, one in each hand.

"Hi, Eve."

The girl watched Miriam for a moment, then slid a half-step into the room. Her eyes searched for the tiger that would leap out and tear her apart.

"You can come in, sweetie, it's okay."

Eve took a full step this time, slow and cautious.

Miriam hadn't figured out Eve's doll. What made Jake and Rinnah think Harem Girl Barbie was a good toy for a little girl?

Eve stalled out at the foot of the bed. Her feet fiddled on the carpet.

Am I really that scary? "What book is that?" Eve slowly held the book out to Miriam: *Ramona the Pest.* "Is that a good book?" The girl nodded solemnly, saucer eyes watching her as if Miriam was a hungry hyena. "Um... would you like me to read to you?"

After some consideration, Eve nodded.

Miriam felt like she'd just aced an obstacle course.

Jake poked his head into Eve's room and found a cat but no girl. Bastet didn't bother to raise her head from her nest between the pillows; she just fixed Jake with an impolite stare.

Eve tended to stay in her room when strangers were in the

house. Jake stepped across the hall to his own bedroom, where she'd sometimes burrow under his blanket. No girl.

The first twinge of anxiety poked at his gut. *Where is she?*

He sprang for the bathroom door. Not there, either. Unease turned into fear. Did she get out? Where would she go? Would she try to go home?

Miriam's voice drifted from her open bedroom door. He followed the sound; maybe she'd know where Eve had gone.

Eve sat on the floor in the room's far corner, her back against a floral-print easy chair, Jasmine on her lap. Miriam sat beside her, a book open on her knees. ""No!' said Ramona, and stamped her foot. Beezus and Mary Jane might have fun, but she wouldn't. Nobody but a genuine grownup was going to take her to school...'"

Jake stepped back so he could just peek around the doorjamb. Perhaps two inches separated Miriam and his daughter. Eve's face showed not quite happiness, but something close to peace. Miriam's face, framed as it was with great swoops of her curry-brown hair, was softer and more open than he'd ever seen it. Her voice had a lift and a storyteller's pacing, and she gave Mrs. Quimby a personality with just a few words. She'd be perfect for Storytime at the Park Slope store.

Jake's breath stumbled in his throat. For a moment he saw Rinnah in Miriam's place, reading to Eve, stroking their daughter's hair. Sometimes Rinnah would slip in from somewhere just beyond his peripheral vision; suddenly she'd be there, a smidgen out of reach. A sucker punch from a ghost. Did that happen to Eve? Or was she moving on already, leaving him behind with his grief?

He watched the two of them for a few minutes. A complicated tangle of feelings wrestled inside him. Then he turned and carefully paced back to the stairs so he wouldn't disturb them, leaving his daughter with a woman who before this moment he thought he'd figured out.

FIFTY-NINE

"Montgomery and New York, northbound," Gur announced into his earpiece as he followed Eugene Eldar's black Crown Victoria through a left turn across the next intersection. He tightened the interval a couple car lengths; the north-south blocks were short.

"Montgomery and Norstrand," Kelila replied.

Gur, Kelila and Sasha had run a classic three-car tail on Eldar, switching off every three or four blocks as they dogged him from Staten Island to One Police Plaza in Manhattan to Brooklyn's Crown Heights. Now they passed through a neighborhood of turn-of-the-century brick townhouses, hedges lining small front gardens, graffiti on garage doors. Windows shone yellow in the twilight gloom.

This was a stab in the dark, Gur knew. Would Eldar really lead them to the safe house? Would he deliberately stay away—as he had the past two days—in case he was being followed? The driver had shown no signs he knew he had a tail, used none of the evasion tricks the Institute drilled into Gur's head. Was this complacency, or was Eldar baiting Gur's team?

Only one way to find out.

Eldar slowed to let the traffic signal turn green. Gur faded back, allowing another car to slip between them from a driveway. "New York and Crown, northbound."

The unmarked police car slowed dramatically once through the intersection, then swung right into a narrow alley between two 1920s brick apartment blocks.

Aha. Gur swooped into a no-parking spot just short of the

217

alley, pulled his pocket binoculars from the center console and watched the Crown Victoria flare to a stop at the top of a rise a few dozen meters away. Two dark man-shapes lurched from the car, one on either side, and dissolved through the shadow of a gate. Gur touched his earpiece. "Carroll Street, cross New York, south side, eight frontages east of the intersection."

"I'll get it," Kelila said. Her blue Toyota hissed past, then turned right at the next corner.

Sasha said, "I'll check from Crown."

Gur kept his binoculars locked on the car. It was still idling; steam rose from its exhaust, and its lights washed the dark alley with pale blue and stoplight red.

"Twelve-eighty," Kelila reported. "All the curtains are drawn in front."

Two men pushed out the now-invisible gate and piled into the car. Neither had Eugene Eldar's blocky shape. A good sign; he was staying for a while. The brake lights bloomed, then the car trundled away.

Gur said, "Alley's clear."

If he hadn't been watching for it, Gur wouldn't have seen the black silhouette slide along the charcoal blocks defining the alley's southern edge. A ghostly Sasha popped up on an invisible ledge, melted into the wall behind him. Nothing else moved in the alley, not even rats.

"Schaffer and Eldar in the kitchen," Sasha reported.

"The uncle," Gur asked, "or the nephew?"

"Nephew."

Gur allowed himself a whispered "Yes!" and a pump of a fist. "Good work. Return to base, both of you." He put aside his binoculars, thunked his gray Taurus into drive and lunged away from the curb. Three blocks later, he found a parking space.

How long would Hezbollah flail away at trying to find Eldar and Schaffer? Those Arab bastards had wiped out half his team and disgraced the rest; if they gave up and left America, they'd get away with it. Gur had been able to come up with only one solution—not an especially nice one, but to hell with that. Eldar and Schaffer had proved they could take care of themselves.

Orgad answered on the third ring. "Yes, Raffi."

"Hello to you, too. The covers are staying at 1280 Carroll in Brooklyn. We have visual confirmation."

"Very good. And Hezbollah?"

"I doubt they know about it yet." He hesitated, but only for a moment. One last quiver of conscience. "Chaim, pass that address to the Hezbollah desk. Have them feed it to their moles. We need Alayan's team to know where the covers are so they'll surface, otherwise we're done here."

Orgad breathed into the phone several times. "All right, I'll tell them. Make this count, Raffi. It's your last chance."

SIXTY

Five days since the shootout in the Philadelphia train station. Excruciating, endless days.

Alayan's haggard reflection in the dark window reminded him he was chewing himself up. Lately he'd done well to get three full hours of sleep a night. Fatigue shot a low fog through his brain; nerves put a slight tremor in his hands he'd worked hard to hide from the men. His stomach twisted and squeezed nearly nonstop now.

Rafiq had called a whole slate of police agencies while posing as a reporter for the Washington *Post,* trying to get one of them to admit to holding the two Jews. None did. They'd kept watch on Schaffer's flat in case she came home, but she never did. Two days ago, Rafiq went to Brooklyn to check Eldar's flat. A van from a crime-scene cleanup company was outside, but Eldar was nowhere to be seen.

He had to be missing something. There had to be something they could do, some way to salvage the situation. Alayan wished desperately for Kassim's advice, his patient, methodical mind. Why did he, of all the men, have to die?

Eleven days left.

The team's pictures filled the TV news and the newspapers. Disturbingly accurate police sketches and security-camera frame captures made Sohrab, Gabir and Ziyad as familiar as American movie stars. All three were prisoners in their rooms twenty-three hours a day, leaving only when the hotel maids drew near with their carts. Gabir and Ziyad were gradually recovering from their wounds, but like Sohrab were going mad from the inactivity.

Alayan's computer rang.

The sound jarred him out of his increasingly dark thoughts. He rushed to the fake-wood table that served as a desk, jammed the headset on his head, shoved the jacks into the side of his laptop, and clicked "answer".

"Majid," the voice said.

Alayan had been waiting for this call he'd hoped wouldn't come. His handler had told him who Majid was and what he'd do on the 23rd of December if Alayan failed to kill the Jews. Alayan swallowed. "Jabbar."

"I need two things. First, a safe place to put a vehicle. Second, a safe house for four men."

No pleasantries, no preamble. Straight to business, and Alayan was clearly just a clerk in this man's world. "How big a vehicle?"

"Larger than a saloon, smaller than a lorry."

Helpful. "When?"

"Tomorrow."

And so much time to work, too. "That's when you're arriving?"

"I didn't say that. I want it done then. I'll call tomorrow night. Any questions?"

The calling number was blocked. No way to get back to Majid. "No. I—" The line was already dead.

Alayan stared at the Skype screen, reminded himself it wasn't personal, it was just tradecraft, security. Still, the man was an ass. But Alayan couldn't afford to trip him up yet. He remembered his handler's words: "If you don't liquidate the remaining targets, the only way you can redeem yourself is to ensure Majid's mission succeeds."

Succeed or don't come home. Alayan didn't doubt this mysterious Majid would be happy to kill him and his entire team if given a reason.

Alayan reached for the room phone, punched a number. "Rafiq. I need you to do something for me tomorrow..."

SIXTY-ONE

13 DECEMBER
CROWN HEIGHTS, BROOKLYN

Jake pulled the back door closed behind him, flipped up his coat collar, and let his eyes adjust to the dying twilight. Scattered snowflake shards burned his face. Snow and low clouds dampened the constant rumble from the city beyond the fence.

Miriam stood in the middle of the yard, face tilted up. Jake had become pretty good at reading her; she'd get a distant look in her eyes and a flatness in her features that told him she was someplace else and wanted to stay there undisturbed. Now her back was to him. Risk it?

The slushy snow squeaked under his feet. He stepped slowly and heavily so Miriam could hear him coming. He didn't want to know what happened when someone crept up on her.

Snow burrowed into her hair and perched on the lashes of her closed eyes. "Got room here for someone else?" he asked.

Miriam peeked at him. "Yes." She closed her eyes again.

He stood beside her for a long few moments, judging her mood. "You okay? You've been awfully quiet this afternoon."

She took a deep breath. "I don't know." She blinked her eyes open and gazed into the falling snow. "I got fired today."

"Aw, shit. Those bastards. Why?"

"Unauthorized absence. I offered to take vacation, but I guess that wasn't the point."

"Are you going to fight it?"

Miriam shrugged. "How? I'm not stupid enough to sue a law firm. I could complain to the state, but on what grounds? I never got Dickinson's permission to have people try to kill me."

"Want the PD to help? Gene might be able to get the

Commissioner to call your boss."

"No, thank you. Really." She pressed her lips into what could have been a grim smile if the corners had turned up. "You sound more upset about this than I am."

"It's a shitty way to treat you. Incredibly unfair."

"Yes it is, not that that means anything anymore." She stood a little straighter. "I think maybe they did me a favor. I've hated the past year there, ever since my last boss retired and they gave me to that prick Dickinson. Maybe this is the push I need to find something new."

"On top of everything else?"

"I have a choice?" For the first time, she turned her head to look at him full-on. "What about you? You and Gene looked pretty tense just now."

"You didn't hear what he said?"

"I don't listen to your private conversations."

"Gotta be hard to tune out when Gene's talking." Worrying about Miriam's problems had briefly taken his mind off his own. Now they were back. "The medical examiner's released Rinnah. I asked Gene whether I could go to her funeral if we had one, and he said no."

She winced. "I'm sorry. What are you going to do?"

"Not much I can do." Jake looked away, through the solid planks of the nearby fence. "If a mortician picks her up, we'll need to have a funeral right away. So I have to leave her there, in a freezer, until this is over." Rinnah was supposed to watch with him as their children grew up. Just thinking about burying her churned up both deep anger and sorrow. He prayed the anger would keep the sadness from crushing him.

"I'm so sorry. If it helps at all… that's not really Rinnah in that freezer."

"Yeah, I know." He said it too fast, with too much of a bite.

Miriam turned her face away. "Sorry. That's what they told me when the Marines sent me a box full of Bill. It didn't work for me, either."

Jake sighed. "Sorry I snapped."

They stood together quietly, their shoulders just brushing. Jake wondered how Miriam had gotten through losing her husband.

Would he end up like her—a little distant, closed-off, hard to touch? What would that do to Eve? Would he take her over the edge with him?

After a while, he said, "Thanks for reading to Eve. Hope she isn't too much of a pest."

"Not at all. She's darling, and I enjoy reading to her."

Jake nodded. "That's great, I'm glad. Thanks." He pictured Miriam and Eve sitting close on Miriam's bedroom floor, wrapped in a story, warm and calm. Maybe he needed to read something other than police files. Maybe he should spend more time with his daughter. "I'll go. I don't want to bug you." He turned toward the back of the house.

Before he could take a step, she said, "Don't go."

He stopped, looked back at her. There had been something in her voice—not quite a plea but more than a simple request.

"Stay a while. We don't have to talk. Just... company."

He didn't ask why. Jake stepped beside her, his elbow pressed against hers. The contact felt strange but comforting. After a few moments, she looped her arm through his. Together they ignored the cold and watched the snow, the lights, and in the corners of their eyes, each other.

SIXTY-TWO

Gur leaned forward in the straight-backed wooden chair and peered through the tripod-mounted binoculars. Eldar and Schaffer stood together arm-in-arm in the paved back yard of the NYPD safe house, backlit by the kitchen windows, snowflakes gathering in their hair.

He sat back and wondered what—if anything—this meant. In the two days he'd watched them, this was the first time he'd seen them touch more than in passing. Perhaps they were turning to each other for comfort after all that had happened. He knew what that was like.

A *sayan* who sold real estate had put the team into an abused, foreclosed townhouse across the alley and three doors down from the safe house. This back bedroom had become their observation post, affording a sweeping view of the back of 1280 Carroll and much of the alley leading to the west. Sasha, on watch at ten, napped in the next bedroom; Kelila was still downstairs, trying to work.

Gur wondered what Kelila would think of him if she knew he'd handed Hezbollah the safe house. Was she cynical enough yet to appreciate the gambit? Would she consider it a betrayal? His heart recoiled at what this could do to their relationship. He'd done what was necessary for the mission. But at what cost?

No sign yet of Hezbollah, of course. It would take a few days for his message to wind its way through the multiple layers of cutouts between the Institute and the hit team's handlers. Had the hostiles already gone home? That would be a disaster, a clean escape after making his team look like fools. His Lillehammer, indeed.

He stole another look through the binoculars. The two of them were still there. Even now, nestled next to Eldar, Schaffer stood straight and squared-up; Gur recalled their service records and could easily imagine her in her green fatigues and web gear.

Miryam Gottesman—now Miriam Schaffer—and Jaakov Eldar. Two people screwed by the system, first in Israel, now in their adopted home.

And Gur had screwed them again. If his plan worked, the Hezbollah team would soon be heading this way to try once more to kill them. Should it work? In a just world, would it?

Gur stretched, scrubbed his face, sighed. *Who's the greater threat to them? Hezbollah? Or us?*

SIXTY-THREE

16 December
Cherry Hill

After hours of neither sleep nor rest, Alayan finally gave up and half-fell out of bed.

He lurched to the window in his underwear, peeked outside. The thick stream of cars heading west on Kaighns Avenue led with blue-white beams and trailed red dots. He scratched his head, yawned, drifted to his computer. Seven messages since one a.m. Four junk emails, two regular business (expense voucher overdue).

One from his handler in Beirut. "Targets are here: 1280 Carroll Street Brooklyn."

Alayan palmed the grit from his eyes and read again. *How did he find them?* He searched Google Maps for the address, dropped into Street View. His screen filled with a rank of brick-faced townhouses, each three window bays wide, stone trim and cornices, a full, red trash hauler partly blocking the view. He couldn't tell which house was 1280, but it didn't matter. His heart woke up, started trotting, then sprinting.

We can still do this.

Rafiq mumbled "Hum?" when he answered Alayan's call.

"Get the men together. We're going to Brooklyn. I know where Eldar and Schaffer are."

SIXTY-FOUR

16 DECEMBER
CROWN HEIGHTS, BROOKLYN

"'...and of course he couldn't say anything,'" Miriam read. "'But as Wilbur was being shoved into the crate, he looked up at Charlotte and gave her a wink. She knew he was saying goodbye in the only way—'"

Eve reached up and slapped the book closed. Miriam startled; Eve hadn't moved that fast since they'd met. After a moment, Miriam swept her surprise under her mental rug. "Don't you want me to finish? We're almost at the end of the chapter."

Eve sat close beside her without touching, little arms wrapped around little knees, big eyes staring at her lap. She shook her head.

Puzzled, Miriam cracked open the book and scanned the next two paragraphs. *The spider dies?* She slowly shut the cover and tucked the book out of sight behind her on the armchair's seat. As she moved, she felt something hard poke her left hip. Jasmine had fallen to the floor between them. Miriam picked up the doll and offered her to Eve. The gloomiest little-girl eyes Miriam had ever seen examined first the doll, then Miriam's face, then Eve took Jasmine in both her hands and nestled the doll against her thighs.

"Why did you want me to read that book?" Miriam asked. Eve fingered Jasmine's hands, hiding her eyes from Miriam. "Did your mother read it to you?"

Eve nodded, but didn't look up.

Miriam sighed. She remembered saving one of her father's shirts from the giveaway box as her mother emptied his wardrobe after he died. It didn't even smell like him, but it was his, and sometimes she'd curl up with it at night even though it always made her cry.

"You know, when I was just a little older than you are, I lost my father. I was so sad, I missed him so much. I thought I'd never stop hurting. Is that how you feel?"

Eve nodded again, hugged Jasmine against her chest.

Now what? Like the other teenaged *kibbutznik* girls, Miriam had been pressed into helping with the younger children, but that was more crowd management than nurturing. The past ten days had been the most prolonged contact she'd ever had with a child. Perhaps if she and Bill had been able to have kids she'd know what to say now. She knew she ought to say something, but what?

Miriam stumbled through a couple false starts before she finally said, "You know what my rabbi once told me? You know what a rabbi is, right?" Nod. "He said that as long as I remembered my father, he'd never leave me." To a ten-year-old girl feeling her heart shatter every day, it was great wisdom. This ancient, creaky platitude was all Miriam had to offer the grieving little girl beside her.

They sat together in silence, Miriam caressing Eve's shoulders and neck, Eve doing the same to Jasmine. Tension zinged through the girl's muscles like vibrating wires.

"Don't leave me."

At first, Miriam didn't realize what she'd heard. She huddled closer to Eve, searching her face. "Sweetie? Did you... say something?"

Eve peered up at Miriam through damp lashes. "Don't leave me and Daddy. Don't go away like Mommy did."

Miriam's mouth dropped open. *She's talking!* collided with *What do I say?* She scraped together some of her scattered wits, took Eve's cheeks in her hands. "Um... sweetie, I'm... I'm just staying here with you and your father for a while, not forever. He's trying to catch the bad men who hurt your mother so we'll all be safe. You know that, don't you?"

A tear perched on Eve's lower eyelid, quivered, then plunged down her cheek. "Please don't go! Everybody leaves me! Mommy's gone, Daddy went away..."

"But he came back!" Miriam caught her breath. "Your father loves you so much, he'd never leave you." If he had a choice. The Arabs might not give any of them a choice.

A couple more tears met their ends on Eve's face. She snuffled. "You're gonna go."

Miriam stammered, "Sweetie, I... it's...I have to—"

Eve's entire body jerked; her eyes dissolved the same way Jake's did. "You can't go away, you can't, not you too..." Her words trailed off into hiccupping sobs.

Miriam gathered Eve's little shaking body into her arms and squeezed as hard as she dared. She couldn't promise to stay forever. As powerless as she felt, she didn't have it in her to lie to Eve. She could kill a man at a hundred yards, beat information out of a prisoner, edit complicated legal documents, use power tools and change her car's oil, but she didn't know how to help this haunted little girl.

Jake knew.

She rocked Eve and patted her back with one hand while she fumbled her cell phone off the easy chair's arm with the other. "Shh, sweetie, it's okay, it's okay..." Miriam picked Jake's number out of her call log, stabbed out a text message—"eves talking"—then punched "send." Then she turned her full attention back to Eve.

Eve was so small, so heartbreakingly fragile.

"I know what it's like. When someone you love leaves you. You feel... I don't know, like you're standing in the middle of a desert where everything's dead. You feel like you'll be alone forever. But you won't, really."

Eve's face burrowed into her neck; hot tears trickled into the collar of her tee shirt.

"Shh, *motek*, it's okay, I've got you, hold onto me, that's right." Miriam held her tight, kissed her hair. "But... if you love someone, you're never really alone, they're never really gone. I know it's hard to believe, but trust me on this."

The great jolts that had run through Eve's little body were smaller now, the wails softer, the thin arms' grip around Miriam's neck a degree less desperate.

"You always... remember the love, the time you spent together. It keeps you warm. It keeps you company. Until... someone else comes along to... to fill the hole. Someone you can love, who'll love you, who'll make the hurt go away and help make you whole again."

"She doesn't understand Hebrew."

Miriam snapped her head up. Jake hovered a couple paces away at the foot of her bed, his face fighting his own emotions. "I was speaking Hebrew?" He nodded. "For how long?"

"Last three-four sentences. It's okay, I'm sure she got the message." He took a step closer, knelt in the beige carpet, stared at his daughter as if watching for a miracle.

"Eve?" Miriam gently untangled Eve's arms from her neck and turned her toward Jake. "Your father's here. Do you want to talk to him?"

Tear tracks and snot and wild hair covered Eve's face. Her chin trembled, her eyes scrunched into red slits. She snuffled, shook, hugged herself. "Don't leave me again, Daddy."

A tear coursed down Jake's cheek as he lifted Eve from Miriam's arms. "I'll always come back for you, Bunny." His voice stumbled. "Always."

Miriam swallowed, looked away. The love and sorrow and pain on their faces was so clear and vivid it could be painted there. A powerful urge hit her to throw her arms around them both and let them know their world would get brighter with time, that they'd survive the darkness.

Her hand began to reach for Jake, but she snatched it back. These two were skirting the edge of a huge emotional whirlpool, one she'd already fought too often. Getting any more involved would only drag her under. The last thing she needed in her life was to once again drown in grief.

SIXTY-FIVE

19 DECEMBER
NEAR WHEATLAND, PENNSYLVANIA

Al-Shami glanced away from the highway rolling beneath him toward the light-skinned Iraqi in the passenger seat. With his hair and eyebrows gone, Mahir resembled a mannequin come to life. He was the quieter of the two *shuhada*, the oldest by at least fifteen years, the one who'd needed the least convincing. A son dead in Ramadi, another in an Iraqi prison, a failed business, an absent wife, a body betraying him—he had quite enough reasons to take this step.

Mahir pulled the iPod earbuds out of his ears. "Have you known a lot of *shuhada?*"

"A few."

"What are they like, usually?"

"All kinds. They have different reasons, if that's what you mean. Some better, some worse."

Mahir nodded, turned his gaze out his window to the trees blurring past on Interstate 80. "Do they ever fail?"

Al-Shami stifled a sigh. This was why he tried to keep his distance from the people who used his products. "Never," he lied, "and neither will you." That part might actually be true. Mahir knew he'd die soon—instantly in four days, or slowly in agony over perhaps three months. He had no incentive to stretch it out.

"*Insha'Allah.*" Mahir paused. "Our target. Is it important? Will it make a difference?"

"Of course it is. Of course it will." In someone's fever dream, perhaps. Would it drive the Zionists into the sea, restore Palestine, bring justice to the Arab world? Of course not. That wasn't the point to it. But even he knew better than to pile this dose of reality

232

on Mahir. The man would be sacrificing his life, after all.

It would get the Americans' attention, though, make them angry so they'd lash out in stupid ways, the way they had in 2001. The more harm they did to themselves with their revenge, the more likely they'd face defeat in the end. *That* was the point, the long-term goal.

"How long before we reach New York?" Mahir asked.

Al-Shami pushed a button on the GPS unit resting on the front dash. "A little under eight hours. Then a four-day wait, and you'll enter Paradise." *And I'll be on a plane to Damascus*, he finished, *to do all this again.*

SIXTY-SIX

20 DECEMBER
CROWN HEIGHTS, BROOKLYN

Jake checked his watch when he heard Gene's rumbling voice outside the kitchen's back door. Almost seven; late for him. Next came his uncle's stomping-the-feet-clean ritual. The door burst open; Jake got one look at the thunderstorm in Gene's face and blurted, "What's wrong?"

"You're moving." Two plainclothes cops followed Gene through the door, closed it, planted themselves by the sink. "In an hour. Get packed."

"Can we finish dinner?" Miriam asked. Half her pasta still waited on her plate.

"If you can do that and pack in an hour, yeah." He leaned toward Eve. "How's my favorite princess?"

Eve twisted around until her knees balanced on her chair seat. "Hi, Unca Gene."

Gene popped her a gentle smile and ruffled her hair. Four days since she'd started talking again, and he still beamed at every word she said.

"Why are we moving?" Jake flicked his attention between Gene's face and a third cop just entering, this one hauling a large black duffel he dumped on the kitchen floor with a thud.

Gene's eyes shifted from Jake to Miriam and back, taking in the domestic scene at the little kitchen table. "The guys have seen activity. People walking, cars shuffling around, stuff that doesn't belong." Miriam squeezed Eve's shoulder. "Maybe it's nothing. But we got a place open in the Village, so just in case..." Gene shrugged.

Gene tried to sound casual, but Jake could see the worry in his

234

face. NYPD wouldn't move them unless there was good reason. *They found us.* Jake's heart stepped into double-time.

❖

Alayan watched from the dark shadow beside a garage as the two parked black sedans ticked away their warmth outside the gate into 1280 Carroll, ten meters away. Four men had gone through the gate with the authority that comes with a badge and a gun. Now one emerged hauling a black suitcase with wheels in one hand and a large duffel bag in the other. He heaved these into the lead car's boot, thunked closed the lid, disappeared back through the gate.

Suitcases? They're leaving? He chirped all four of the men. "They're moving, probably soon. Take your positions."

The team had to finish Eldar and Schaffer tonight. They couldn't fumble away this gift from Allah, this last chance to fulfill their duty. They had to save the Party from its own worst impulses... and save themselves at the same time.

❖

They gathered in the kitchen with five minutes to spare. Jake and Miriam each dropped a duffel next to Eve's *Princess and the Frog* roller bag at the kitchen door. Eve tucked Jasmine into her coat, and Bastet crouched in her blue carrier on the kitchen counter. Gene bent to look into the cat's golden eyes; they had a tense, silent standoff. "You can't bring it to the new place."

Miriam stiffened. "I'm not leaving her."

"You'll have to. Only two-legged animals where we're going." Gene stood straight in a clear attempt to assert his authority, but found himself an inch shorter than the now stone-faced Miriam. *Watch it,* Jake silently warned his uncle. *Don't mess with the cat.*

"Bastet goes with me." Every word left a blood trail. "If she stays, so do I."

"I want Bastet!" Eve wailed.

Bastet unleashed a summoning-the-dead yowl.

"Jesus," Gene muttered. He glanced toward Jake, who

shrugged. "All right, look. It can't go to the safe house. But tell you what, I'll take it home with me. Monica loves animals. The cat'll come back fat and spoiled, believe me."

Miriam braced her jaw, ready to protest. But then she caught Jake's eye. *Looking for support?* He cleared his throat. "We should live so good as she will at their place."

She considered the situation and the darkening in Gene's face. "She'll only eat this brand of food." She finger-stabbed the plastic grocery bag next to the carrier.

Gene held up his hands, palms out. "Fine, whatever."

"And she needs to be brushed once a day or she gets hairballs."

"Lady, my wife won't be able to keep her hands off the cat, it'll come back bald. Enough already." He jerked his chin toward the darker of the two cops blocking the doorway into the dining room. "Lou."

The cop circled behind Jake, unzipped the duffel and extracted a set of black body armor. He passed it to Gene, then produced a second set.

Gene held the body armor toward Miriam. "Here, put this on."

"You can't be serious."

"I'm serious. Put it on. You won't need it 'til you do, then you'll want it. You, too, kid."

Miriam looked again to Jake for support. He took the offered vest. "Go ahead, put it on, make him a happy man. At least they're warm."

Eve tugged on Gene's overcoat. "Where's mine, Unca Gene?"

Gene crouched in front of Eve and poked her belly through her parka. "Don't have one your size, Princess. Besides, your daddy'll protect you."

Eve craned around to peer up at Jake. "Is that true?"

"Yeah." Jake thumped his chest through the body armor. "Bullets bounce off me."

Sohrab kept the eight-power scope centered on the safe house's back door. He tried to ignore his wet front and freezing back. He'd been stretched out on the old brick apartment building's roof for over two hours, ever since the overcast afternoon had turned into a dark night.

His perch dominated the southwest corner of the block. A tangle of naked trees partly screened the safe house's door and the yard's west side, but not the gate. Seventy meters or so from his position through a narrow gap in the branches to that gate. Nothing like the firing range.

Sohrab wasn't a sniper. Kassim had been their sniper, but he was dead. This was Sohrab's chance to redeem himself for that disaster at the train station. When Alayan handed him the rifle, his eyes told Sohrab the contract terms: all would be forgiven if he killed the two Jews.

Still no movement.

He squeezed his eyes shut, waited for the red blob floating behind his eyelids to fade out, then fitted the scope to his right eye socket once again.

The door opened.

Jake stepped into the cold, damp night, a cop with the duffels ahead of him, Gene close behind. He couldn't help scanning the rooftops across the alley for movement. He snugged Eve against him with an arm around her shoulders; she had a death grip on his pea coat's pocket with one hand, the top half of Jasmine with the other.

Jake, Miriam and Eve were to go straight into the lead car's back seat and leave immediately. Gene and Lou (with Bastet) would enter the second car and follow. They'd take a roundabout route in case someone decided to follow them. Simple enough.

It was the thirty feet to the car that had Jake's animal brain on full alert.

Sohrab centered the T-shaped crosshairs on Eldar's chest. He wasn't interested in trying for an obscured head shot in bad light while the targets were moving. He had four rounds in the

237

magazine; he'd put the targets on the ground first, then finish them when they were still.

His finger squeezed the trigger.

❖

One moment, Jake was walking toward the gate half a dozen paces away.

The next, he was flat on his back, stunned, gasping, his breastbone screaming he'd been hit by a jackhammer.

Eve's high-pitched shriek filled the night. "Daddy! Noooo!"

Miriam's voice, from a long way away: "Jake? Jake!" Then a *thud*, the simultaneous *crack* of a rifle, and another howl from Eve.

❖

The *snap* of a very large stick being broken over an enormous knee echoed down the alley. Gur pulled his pistol and slid into the shadows. "Gunshot," he told his radio. "Move in."

He had no idea where the sniper was. If Hezbollah was using the Institute's playbook—as it seemed they had been all along—they'd have blockers on either side of the house to catch squirters. But where?

There in the shadow, five or six meters ahead of him: an indistinct shape. Cop or terrorist? Gur couldn't tell. He slid along the south fence to get a better look.

The cop by the vehicles opened fire.

❖

Gene bent over Jake, pistol in his hand. "Kid, you okay? Jake? Hear me?"

Jake couldn't get a full breath. The pain was like someone had cracked his chest open with a crowbar. Another cop charged past, gun drawn, aiming into the dark. Gunshots popped outside the fence. "Eve," he gasped.

"Shit." Gene's head swiveled fast, scanning the yard. "By the gate. She's okay." He waved. "Stay there, Chava! Stay there! Your daddy's okay, he just fell."

"Miriam."

"She's down, I haven't checked her yet. You—" Gene coughed out an "oof," then crumpled on his side next to Jake.

❖

Sohrab took stock. The police by the cars had started shooting at something, but he couldn't tell what. He steadied the SIG-Sauer in his arms, sighted on Eldar's head. One of the policemen—a broad-backed man in a dark overcoat—partly blocked the shot. *Don't you move...*

Sohrab's finger stopped at the trigger's first detent. He exhaled, squeezed.

The cop moved.

He collapsed on his side, his big shoulder blocking the line to Eldar's head. *Goh!* Sohrab tried to focus on the woman's head, but a dark mass of branches screened it from him. Her back was still clear. He aimed between the woman's shoulder blades, took his last shot, then rolled away from the roof's edge and dashed toward the fire escape.

❖

Sasha saw movement in a shadow across the alley, perhaps eight meters away. A man-like shape. It wasn't shooting at the rooftops; not a cop. Screw positive ID. Sasha aimed into the shadow's center, fired twice.

Fifteen meters away, the two cops behind the cars poured a waterfall of bullets on him.

Sasha dropped face-down, made himself as flat as he could. "I'm taking fire," he panted into the radio. "I have contact."

Gur's voice said, "Do you have a target?"

The sound of a straining engine bounced down the alley toward Sasha. He glanced over his shoulder just in time to see the back end of a white van barreling toward him. "Van coming! Block the end of the alley!"

The van squealed to a halt. Sasha didn't hesitate. He shot out both front tires, then used the cover of the van's bulk to climb upright, stepped to the passenger's window, and took aim.

He froze.

❖

No... not Gene...

Chaos. Gunfire. A voice yelling, "Officer down! Officer down! Send backup, ESU and EMS to..."

Jake managed to suck down enough of a breath to make the stars fade from his eyes. He rolled onto his side to face Gene—*Goddamnit, that hurt!*—grabbed his uncle's shoulder. "Gene! Where're you hit? Talk to me!"

"Fuck," Gene croaked. "Under my arm. Hard to breathe. Fuck. Fucking vests."

"Hang on. They're calling for help."

Eve's keening wail was gone; Jake could hear the gunfire again. He propped himself up on an elbow, searched the shadows for his daughter. He couldn't see her, but he couldn't see much through the pain-fuzz in his eyes. *She's okay. She's gotta be okay.*

He arranged Gene's left arm into a pillow for his big head. Panic crawled up his throat. "Don't you fucking die on me, you fat son-of-a-bitch."

"Take more than this. To kill me." Gene coughed; a loose, syrupy sound. "Kid. Get outta here."

"What?"

"We're blown. Someone leaked. Take Chava and Schaffer. Keep them safe."

"I'm not leaving you!"

"Go. Listen for once." Gene coughed again, pushed his pistol against Jake's chest. "Take this. Get lost. Before backup comes."

"Gene..."

"Go!" The shout broke loose a coughing jag that forced bloody froth past Gene's lips.

No, Gene, you can't die, I need you. But he knew he had to go. Jake took the gun.

The shooting moved east, away from the gate. No sign of Eve. Where was she? Was she hurt? Jake checked where Miriam lay; she struggled to sit up, unvarnished agony in her face.

Jake squeezed Gene's arm. "I love you, Gene. I wish you were my dad."

"I know. So do I. Maybe you'd listen." Gene made a weak sweeping motion with his right hand. "Fucking *go*."

❖

The van screeched forward, leaving Sasha completely exposed. He dropped, rolled into the darkest shadow he could find. Two cops advanced down the alley toward him, shooting at where he'd been moments before.

"I'm pinned," he whispered into the radio. "Two cops coming. I'm going to drop them."

"No!" Gur's voice hissed. "I'll draw their fire."

"You've got ten seconds, boss. Kelila, don't shoot the van. They have a hostage."

❖

Rafiq jammed his seat-belt buckle home. "What have you done?" he screamed. "What were you thinking?"

Alayan belted himself in while he fought the flat front tires to keep the van heading straight. "It just happened. Hold on."

A streetlight smeared yellow over a blue sedan parked across the mouth of the alley. Alayan punched on the headlights, switched to high beams to blind the driver. He glanced right: a brick railing ending just centimeters from the sedan's nose. Left: the stub of a concrete wall, maybe two meters clearance between it and the car's back end. Left, then.

The van smashed into the sedan's rear fender at nearly forty miles an hour, swatting away the blue car. The van's windshield cracked, the seat belt and shoulder harness bit into Alayan's body. He ignored the pain, Rafiq's swearing and the hostage's shrieking, skidded the van into the street, and stomped the gas.

❖

Jake crawled to Miriam, wrapped an arm around her shoulders. "You okay?"

"No, I'm not okay," she spat in Hebrew. Every move made her teeth clamp so hard, the points of her jaw shone bright in the back door's lightspill. She grabbed his coat lapel. "Don't worry about me. Eve ran out the gate. After Gene went down. You have to find her."

Another flurry of shots, this time to the west. *Oh God, Eve, no, not out in all that...* Jake gulped a couple breaths to tamp down the fear climbing up his throat. He lowered his voice so Lou—on one knee next to Gene, pistol sweeping the rooftops, Bastet's carrier behind him—wouldn't hear. "We both go. Gene said to get you out of here. Can you walk?"

She sat panting, staring at him through eyes that were barely slits. "We'll find out."

❖

Gabir pressed hard into the dark angle where a chain-link fence met a cinder-block garage, holding his breath while two policemen pelted after the man who'd shot him just moments before. Gabir thought the man was a cop, but if he was, why were cops chasing him?

He wiped the blood from his eyes with his sleeve. No cops in sight, but an entire chorus of sirens headed his way. He had to go, now. He chirped Ziyad's number. "Where are you?"

"Following the van. They're going to leave it in a bad area. Where are you?"

"In the alley, going east. Ring when you can come get me."

He'd scrambled past two houses when a movement near the police cars made him freeze mid-stride. Two figures stumbled out the gate and limped east, away from Gabir. Not police, not walking that way. The Jews? Still alive?

He followed them.

❖

Lou didn't try to stop them. "We gotta find Eve," Jake told him, neglecting to mention they weren't coming back. The cop grunted and stayed crouched over Gene.

They scooped up their abandoned duffels outside the gate and worked east, searching every nook and dark shadow. Miriam's Walther glinted in her hands, as steady as her breathing was ragged. Jake tugged Gene's pistol from his belt.

Eve had to be out there, scared, hiding. She had to be okay. The alternative was too awful for Jake's mind to process.

Walking was pure torture. Body armor was supposed to keep you alive, not unhurt. Jake wondered if it was possible to break a breastbone. Miriam had been hit twice; he'd seen the hole in her coat between her shoulder blades, just left of center. The way she was grimacing, she might have a busted rib. An inch over could have cracked a vertebra.

"How's your chest?" he whispered.

"Not too bad." She'd switched back to English, but her accent had taken over. "It hit right between my boobs, so there was a space. What about you?"

"Hurts like a son-of-a-bitch."

Lights shone in most of the back windows of the townhouses they passed. The alley rang with approaching sirens, a fire engine's air horn, the stutter tones of two or more ambulances.

Jake spotted something in a patch of weak light a few yards east of the still-idling unmarked police cars. He knelt by the object.

His heart withered.

"What is it?" Miriam asked.

"Jasmine." He picked the doll off the ground, brushed a leaf fragment from her hair. "Eve wouldn't leave her like this, not for anything." He choked on his next words. "They've got her."

SIXTY-SEVEN

20 DECEMBER
BROOKLYN

Rafiq rocked the little girl as best he could while strapped into the car's back seat. She pressed her face into his shoulder and sobbed, "Daddy! Daddy!"

"Shh, it's okay, Eve, I won't let anyone hurt you," Rafiq said in English. He pinned back Alayan's ears with a stare and hissed in Arabic, "You kidnapped a baby. I can't believe you'd do something that low."

Alayan looked out the window at the passing slums and the furtive shadows ghosting through them, jaundiced in the weak streetlights. The tires thudded over broken pavement. "She might be useful."

"Useful." Rafiq just managed to bottle his disgust. Abducting an enemy was one thing; he'd done that before without flinching. But a *child?* Beyond contemptible.

He hugged Eve tighter and stroked her thick black hair. He recalled her peeking around her mother's hips in the apartment, all shyness and big brown eyes. Now her mother was dead, and for all he knew, he was the only thing standing between her and the same fate.

"We can't harm her, *sidi*," Ziyad said, his voice unsteady. "The Quran says, 'Lost are those who slay their children.'"

"I'm aware of what the Quran says."

Sohrab said, "She's a Jew. It doesn't count."

Rafiq clamped a hand over Eve's ear. "She's a *child*. I didn't hear the 'except for Jews' part in that verse."

"What do we need her for, anyway?" Sohrab demanded. "The Jews are dead. I shot them both in the heart."

"Did you see blood?" Alayan asked.

Sohrab hesitated. "It was dark."

Alayan growled, "Until we hear that they're both dead, we keep the child so we can get to them again." He watched the girl for a few moments, his mouth working hard to keep something inside, then looked away.

Eve caught a second wind and wailed like a police siren. Rafiq whispered in English, "Hush, *sagirah*, you're safe with me."

"How many Palestinian kids have the Zionists murdered?" Sohrab sneered at both Eve and Rafiq.

Rafiq shot back, "So that's our standard now? We can be as bad as they are?"

Alayan clapped his hands once. "Enough! Ziyad, left at the next corner. Rafiq, you're in charge of the girl. Keep her fed and quiet. If she disappears, you'll pay, understand?"

He understood. He'd be happy to ensure nothing happened to Eve until Alayan came to his senses, even if it meant defying all of them. If he'd wanted to randomly slaughter women and children, he had plenty of Hezbollah teams to choose from; he'd gone with Alayan because he'd always chosen his victims carefully and kept collateral damage to an absolute minimum.

He prayed that hadn't changed. For Eve's sake—and for his own.

SIXTY-EIGHT

20 DECEMBER
BROOKLYN

At least none of the team died.

Not much of a victory, Gur thought. Still, it was better than they'd done lately. Kelila's car was wrecked; thank God she hadn't been in it. The *sayan* who'd rented the cars to them was probably already talking to the police.

"You're sure it was Eldar's child?" he asked Sasha.

"Yes, boss. She was half a meter from me, at most."

Kusemek! "Was she hurt?"

"I couldn't tell." The apprehension in his face made him seem almost vulnerable. "I looked in her eyes and... well, I couldn't..."

"I know." Gur wondered if he could have taken the shot. God knows he had before. He'd killed a Hamas man who held his sleeping infant son in his lap. On a bad night, he could still hear that baby crying. "Kelila, did you see her?"

"Yes, it was her. I only got a couple seconds' look, but I'm sure of it. Poor thing."

"The covers got away," Sasha said.

So had Hezbollah. "Yes, I know." Gur rubbed his eyes. "All right, take a few minutes to unpack. Make a sweep of this new neighborhood, see if we were followed. This is the last flat we'll get from this *sayan*, so let's not burn it unless we have to."

"We're going after the little girl, right?" Kelila's eyes filled with a mother's fear for a lost child, even one not her own.

"We're going after whoever we can find."

Sasha said, "When do we start, boss?"

"Soon. I have a hunch the covers are still in Brooklyn. I doubt they went to the local Hilton, so you know what that means."

246

"Hostels. Boarding houses."

"Yes, and cheap hotels. They'll use false names, so we'll have to go to each location with Eldar's and Schaffer's pictures. Kelila, work up a list for us. We'll start with Carroll Street as the center of our circle and work our way outwards. It's going to be a long night. Dress warm."

Once the others retreated to their bedrooms, Gur crossed to the tiny kitchen to splash water on his face. Eldar's child kidnapped; his fault. He'd become a menace to the people he was supposed to protect and to his own team—a hazard to everyone except Hezbollah.

It was time to quit. The Watch Center called his name. He'd teach at the Academy, live to see his grandchildren. Perhaps be with Kelila.

All he had to do was live through this damned mission.

SIXTY-NINE

21 DECEMBER
SUNSET PARK, BROOKLYN

Gabir slumped in the doorway of a commercial garage, its corrugated metal door cold against his back. There was nothing rich or fancy about this street—a Russian deli, a Chinese building-supply warehouse, a Hispanic food wholesaler, cheek-by-jowl in one low-slung, brick-faced, graffiti-scarred building after another. Trash, almost no streetlights, people he could hear but not see. It reminded him of Beirut.

The Jews had stayed on major streets all the way. He might have been able to kill them, but he'd never have escaped.

Blood dribbled into Gabir's eyes from the furrow the cop's bullet had carved across his forehead at the safe house. His shoulder wound seeped into his undershirt. He needed help, and soon. But he needed to do his job even more.

His hand trembled as it held the cellphone to his ear. By now, everything on him shook from the cold. Two rings, three. "Yes?" Alayan's voice.

"*Sidi*, it's me. I'm on 39th Street in Brooklyn." He focused on an old four-story brick hotel across the street, flanked by warehouses. A few windows were still lit. Two men sat on the front steps, passing a paper sack between them. "I followed them. I know where the targets are."

SEVENTY

Sunset Park, Brooklyn

"Miriam?"

She glanced away from the gap in the hotel room's plastic curtains toward Jake's voice. "Go to sleep. It's my watch until two."

"I can't. I close my eyes and all I see is Eve and Gene."

"I know." That's all she could see, too. She shifted on the squeaking wooden chair and flipped up her coat collar, willing away the cold. They'd shut off the heater to stop its clattering. "How's your chest feel?"

"Throbbing. How about your back?"

"The same. It's hard to get comfortable." She peeked out into the night again. The street and sidewalk were completely dead. Too bad the thumping, laughing, squealing party next door wasn't so quiet. Hezbollah's army could march down the hallway and she'd never hear them.

Jake asked, "Have you ever killed anyone?"

"Yes."

"Long-range or close-in?"

"Both."

"Doesn't sound like it bothers you much."

"It doesn't." She knew what she was about to say would make her sound hard and ruthless, but she didn't care. "Every one of those bastards I killed was like getting even for my father and all the other murdered people I know." No answer. She could hear him breathing, a surprisingly intimate sound. "Do you have a problem with that?"

"Not... really. I have to think about it, though."

"Have you?"

"What?"

"Killed anyone? Other than in the parking lot."

Silence, filled with thought. "Yeah. Couple times directly, with my rifle. A bunch of times with artillery."

"That doesn't count."

"It does if you're the one building the target packages."

"That's what you did?"

"Yeah, in *Yahmam*."

She dredged up what little she knew about the Target Field Intelligence unit in the Artillery Corps. They sent men behind the lines to find enemies to shell. It didn't seem like the kind of thing Jake would do... but he'd shot those two terrorists in the parking lot without hesitation. "You were a commando?"

"I guess. I was better with the intel than the field work, so they moved me to target development. I took the stuff the snake-eaters brought in and turned it into actionable targets. Mostly southern Lebanon."

Snake-eaters. She liked that; it said so much about those people. "You must've been good at it. You still are."

"Whatever." His bed creaked and the blanket crackled; he must have turned over. "Did you like the Border Police?"

A hard question; *like* had lots of meanings. Did he need to know about the power, the loss of privacy, the satisfaction of protecting Israel, the non-stop sexual harassment, winning citations for valor, being slapped with reprimands for doing what the men did? No, he wouldn't understand. "I suppose so. It's complicated."

"Yeah. Why'd you leave?"

"I wrecked my knee in a fight with a Hamas scout."

"How'd he come out?"

"Worse. Anyway, they transferred me into the command legal office. That's where I learned to do what I do now. With my experience, I should've been training recruits. If I was a man, I would've been, but a woman? They made me a secretary. It turns out the chief counsel liked having pretty girls in his office." It still rankled after all these years. She'd wanted to fight for her country, not type for it. "Then at the end of my enlistment, they forced me out because I was injured. Why did you leave the Army?"

"They told me to."

This, she hadn't expected. "Oh. Why?"

"Long story."

"Are you sleepy yet?"

"No."

"Well, help keep me awake, then."

"All right." He sighed. "There's this place called Yohmor, it's a village just north of the Litani. Hezbollah command center, plus they were running heroin through it for export. Northern Command was screaming for months to take the place out. So I finally worked up a package, sent it around for coordination, everyone gave us the thumbs-up. Except they never asked Mossad, or they didn't answer."

"They were watching it?"

"They were *running* it. They never said what they were doing, but their own people were in charge of the place. Well, we flattened it. Best pattern we'd laid down in months. For once we even managed to miss the school about a hundred meters from the compound."

Miriam was pretty sure she knew what was coming.

"Mossad went apeshit. We killed something like ten or twelve of theirs, both Israelis and Arabs. Mossad went at it with the Army, and everyone started looking for a scapegoat. Pretty soon all the fingers were pointing at me. I thought the Army would defend me, but they didn't. They threw me in an army prison for a few months, then court-martialed me for dereliction. They didn't convict me, though. I guess it would've raised too many questions. Anyway, they 'invited' me to resign, so I did."

It was like something the left-wing Israeli papers would print. Miriam had gone into the Border Police thinking the liberals were treasonous liars and came out wondering how they managed to miss so much of what went on in the country's sprawl of security agencies. "Do you think that's why they used your name in Qatar?"

"Wouldn't be surprised. I don't think they forgive and forget."

Miriam leaned back in the chair, thinking once again how incredibly unfair their situation was. Not that "fair" had been much a part of her life. But Jake's life? He didn't deserve this.

None of them had. But they deserved the chance to fight back. She looked forward to that.

SEVENTY-ONE

21 DECEMBER
SUNSET PARK, BROOKLYN

Jake watched the bustle around the Chinese construction-supply warehouse while he listened to Monica's phone ring. Trucks in and out, pickups double-parked, crews of men in the watery sunlight stocking up before the morning's jobs.

"Hello?" Monica's voice, tired.

"Hi, it's Jake. I tried to call again last night—"

"Jake! God, sorry I didn't call back. They made me turn off my phone in ICU and I forgot to turn it on again. They say he's going to be okay."

He sagged onto the edge of the bed in relief. All through the sleepless night, the only times he hadn't worried about Eve were the times he'd worried about Gene. "How is he?"

"Serious but stable. The doctor said if he wasn't such a big dumb ox, he might not do so good." Her voice broke. "Oh, Jake. I'm so scared. All these years on the job without a scratch, and now..."

"I know. He'll pull through. I'll be there when I can." She'd been a surrogate mother for him, and she was better at it than his real mother. He owed her more support than a phone call. "You got people with you?"

"Uh-huh. Louis, and Jean came down from Boston." Two of their three kids, the ones Jake had last seen at the birthday party a century ago. "Um, you know Reggie? Captain McLarty? He's here, he wants to talk to you."

"I don't want to talk to him, I—"

The voice on the other end had already changed. "Jake? Reg McLarty. Where are you, guy? We need to bring you in."

252

"Oh, no." Jake stood again, watched the controlled chaos in the street. "You got a leak. We're not coming in 'til you plug it."

"No way. We haven't lost a safe house in years."

"Well, you just did. It wasn't me and it wasn't Miriam, so it's on you guys. We're safer on our own right now, thanks."

"Come on, Jake, be—"

"No. Fix your problem, then we'll talk. There's things I have to take care of out here." He realized how harsh his voice had become. NYPD's screw-up had almost killed all three of them, but it wasn't McLarty's fault. "Look, I'm sorry, but we're done here. Take care of Gene and Monica. I'll be in touch." He disconnected before the exchange could deteriorate.

"How's Gene?" Miriam asked from behind him. She'd lost her accent again.

Jake looked back. She stood by the bathroom door, a towel in one hand, the ends of her hair still damp from the shower. He envied her the fresh clothes; he had his jeans and sportshirt and a bagful of underwear. The circles under her eyes told him she hadn't slept much either.

"Serious but stable. Doctors say he'll make it." He beckoned her to join him at the window.

"I'm glad." She drifted in his direction, worrying at her hair with the towel. "By the way, don't be shocked, but I hung my underthings on the shower rod to dry."

Which meant she wasn't wearing... no, that was the *last* thing he needed to think about. "I lived with a woman for almost ten years. There's nothing you can hang up in there that'll scare me." Even so, he'd avoid the bathroom for a while. "Wish you'd brought your other bag instead?"

"Yes." She peered through the dirty window into the grimy day. "The sun's almost shining."

"Yeah. Check that white Toyota down there, one in from the corner, across the street, with the guy in it."

"I see it."

"I'm pretty sure it was there last night, too."

"Same place?"

"No, over on the other corner."

"But the same car."

"Pretty sure. New tags."

"Perhaps it belongs here."

"It's too clean and new. And that guy's been in it for a while, now."

Miriam draped the towel over her shoulder and gripped the curtain. Her lips pressed flat. "Do you think it's them?"

"It's not the PD, or they'd have been up here already." Jake's heart perked up, stretched, started jogging. The combat edge was coming on.

She stared at the car for a full minute. "What do you want to do about it?"

"I have some ideas."

The street had been marginally more attractive at night than in the watery sunshine. Daylight revealed without pity the tired and dirty brick facades, battered awnings and faded signs.

Jake stopped for a moment on the sidewalk outside the hotel to adjust his coat, which didn't need adjustment. He checked the watcher's car: west thirty yards, across the street. A silver Impala had replaced the white Camry at ten. Miriam kept track of the watchers' shift length from her post at the window.

Jake trotted through a break in the traffic, pushed past the hardware store's water-spotted double glass doors. He met densely packed shelves, pyramids of paint cans, a wall of faucets and shower heads. He quickly filled his shopping list: duct tape, wire ties, a box cutter, a pair of two-foot-long crowbars, heavy rubber gloves.

Back outside, he headed west toward the bodega on the corner. Jake would pass right by the Impala, but he'd have only a couple seconds to check the driver without tipping him off.

One man sat in the car, broad-shouldered, round head. Side-view mirrors turned too far out so he could see what was happening behind him. As he passed the rear fender, Jake caught a glimpse of the man's profile: the big Arab again. He wasn't being paranoid after all.

While he bought toothpaste and a toothbrush for Miriam and chips and a couple sodas for them both, Jake pictured the Arab in the Impala. Would he try to shoot Jake here and now? Probably not; if that was the play, they'd have already stormed the hotel room. They were waiting for something. Nighttime? Reinforcements?

Jake had Gene's gun in his coat pocket; it would be so easy to step outside and put a couple rounds into the guy. But he needed one of these assholes alive if he was going to find Eve. Once he got her back, he'd settle with Hezbollah. If he survived.

❖

Almost midnight. No traffic, just the occasional dark ghost of a pedestrian. Jake and Miriam crouched behind a battered pickup sagging under a towering load of flattened cardboard boxes. The Camry sat gathering frost two cars ahead, the nearby signal casting red-amber-green lightwash on the roof.

"Can you see him?" Miriam whispered.

"Yeah. One guy, not the big one, thank God. He should be good and bored by now."

They'd gone out the hotel's back door into a narrow service alley, then circled the next block to the west to come up behind the Camry. As far as the watcher knew, they were still in their room. He wouldn't be looking in his mirrors so long as he believed that.

"Ready to make some noise?" Jake asked. Miriam nodded, hefted her crowbar. "Okay, let's go. Get it started when you're ready."

Heart thudding hard, Jake slipped around the pickup's left side, dropped, crawled on his elbows and knees toward the Toyota, holding his crowbar with both hands like a rifle at an obstacle course. The stiff body armor chafed his armpits and waistband. His coat and jeans softened the asphalt pebbles underneath him and muffled any stray noise as he passed the truck and the rusted-out Monte Carlo ahead of it. He paused at the Camry's back bumper, wiped his hands and tried not think how vulnerable he was down there. Moments later, Miriam slithered past on the other side. *Showtime.*

He'd just reached the rear door's leading edge when he heard Miriam shatter the safety glass on the other side. Jake shoved himself upright, gripped his crowbar like a baseball bat and hit a line drive through the driver's window. It imploded in a shower of glass cubes that caromed off the dash and passenger's seat. The driver had twisted to his right to see what had happened; Jake bounced the iron off the side of the man's skull. The shock rattled all the way up to his shoulders.

A few seconds' advantage, nothing more.

Jake wrenched open the driver's door, grabbed the man's hair and dumped him into the street. Jake buried his foot in the man's middle much harder than necessary, then ripped a pistol out of the man's waistband.

Miriam knelt behind the Arab, stuck a wire tie between her teeth, hauled his arms behind his back. He groaned but didn't fight. She expertly strapped his hands together, wrists crossed, then stood and covered him with her Walther.

"You've done that before," Jake said. She nodded. He used his foot to shove the man onto his back. "Recognize him?"

Her lips disappeared into a tight slit. "That's the bastard who tried to grab me in the parking lot." Miriam jerked her gun into line with his head.

"Whoa." Jake thrust his open hand in front of the muzzle. "We need him alive for now. We have to find out where Eve is so we can go get her."

She stared at him with eyes that reflected the red of the stoplight. He remembered the fire he'd seen in those eyes at the train station, when she was ready to take on Hezbollah with her bare hands. *Be smart*, he tried to tell her through telepathy. *Don't make me protect this worm.*

Finally, Miriam stepped back and aimed her pistol at the ground. "For now."

Jake blew out his held breath. "Search the car. I'll get him up to the room."

Miriam snarled in the Arab's direction. "Make sure he falls down the stairs on the way."

SEVENTY-TWO

22 DECEMBER
SUNSET PARK, BROOKLYN

Miriam stopped next to the bathroom in the hotel room's tiny entry hall and stared at the Arab.

The man's wrists and ankles were zip-tied to a ladder-back wooden chair in the small patch of open floor at the foot of the twin beds. A swatch of duct tape covered his mouth. Blood trickled down the back left edge of his jaw; little red nicks on his forehead and cheek showed where the glass had scoured him. The bruises from his broken nose had turned an evil shade of jaundiced yellow in the two weeks since he'd attacked her in that Philadelphia parking lot.

The Arab raised his drooping head at the sound of the door. His eyes widened a fraction, then set in a scorching glare.

"Remember me?" Miriam bared her teeth. "I remember you, *bala'a il a'air.*"

Miriam's hate bucked and strained against its leash. Hezbollah. Her father endured three days of agony before he'd died from the burns and wounds one of their rockets left behind. She'd vowed she'd pay them back for that. And now they had Eve.

Her fingers fondled the butt of the pistol in her coat pocket. It would take only an instant to empty the magazine into this insect, cut off his balls, then hang him by his heels from a street light. Just an instant. Almost not long enough to savor it.

Jake stepped between her and the Arab. He'd stripped off his body armor and sportshirt and stood facing her in a white V-necked undershirt and jeans. Thick black rubber gloves reached halfway to his elbows. "Find anything in the car?" he asked.

She took a deep breath, swallowed her fury. This was all about

Eve right now, not vengeance. Miriam stepped into the room and held up a black cell phone. "Just this."

"Great. We'll look at it later." He turned, yanked the duct tape from the Arab's mouth. "You understand English, right? What's your name?"

The Arab smirked at Jake, then turned his face away.

Miriam wanted to tear that smirk off his lips. Instead, she stalked toward the head of her bed, flung off her coat and ripped at the Velcro on her body armor. *Let Jake work*, she told herself. *You'll get your chance.* She plopped on the bed, one knee on the blanket, one foot on the floor, clamped her mouth tight, folded her arms and watched.

Jake hammered at the Arab, commanding, joshing, prodding, repeating variations of the same question over and over until Miriam wanted to scream. He stayed close to the man, less than a foot, always touching him, playing with the very compressed personal space typical of the Arabs. The man muttered Arabic curses and defied Jake with his eyes. Finally he spat, "Ziyad."

Miriam glanced at her watch. Twelve minutes to get the Arab's *name*. At this rate, she'd break long before the Arab would. She recognized what Jake was doing—following the old field interrogation manual page-by-page, insinuating himself, establishing a relationship—but that didn't make it any easier to sit through. She'd never been patient with prisoners.

"Okay, Ziyad, another easy one. Where are you from?"

Miriam kept her mouth shut for an interminable hour while Jake got very little useful from Ziyad. Jake's voice grew rougher, his face flushed, the veins popped on his forearms and temples from the strain. He started manhandling the Arab, yanking the man's hair to make him look up, twisting his already-broken nose, and slowly information dribbled out. Ziyad al-Amin was from the Bourj el-Barajneh refugee camp in southern Beirut. He boasted he was with Hezbollah. His team had been in the U.S. for a month. (A month! What happened to all that homeland security money?) One of the other vermin had followed Jake and Miriam from the safe house to this hotel.

And that was it.

She checked her watch for the nth time. Almost one-thirty;

Ziyad's relief would come at two. What would happen if he wasn't at his post? She needed to warn Jake, but didn't want the Arab to know what was going on. What other languages did that cockroach understand? "I'm going to shoot him, okay?" she said in Hebrew, keeping her voice as calm as she could, as if asking whether Jake wanted a Coke. No reaction from a grimacing Ziyad.

Jake, however, released the Arab's ear and stared at her. "What the fuck?" At least he answered in Hebrew.

"Their watch change is in half an hour. We need to know where Eve is. We won't have a lot of time once they know he's gone."

"Yeah." Jake pulled his wallet from his back pocket, flipped it open, shoved it under Ziyad's nose. "See that picture?" he growled in English. "The little girl? My daughter?"

Miriam knew the photo; he'd showed it to her at the safe house. Jake and Rinnah in summer clothes seated on a bench in a green, sunny place, a slightly-younger Eve on Jake's lap, smiles all around. Just thinking about it flared her anger.

"Got kids?" Jake snarled. "A little girl, maybe? How'd you feel if someone took her?"

Ziyad twisted away, but Jake grabbed the man's nose between his knuckles and forced his head to center. The Arab's face crumpled with pain. Jake thrust the picture into that face.

"Where is she, Ziyad? Where did you take her?"

Ziyad broke away, grinned through the blood from his nose. "We feed her to dogs!"

Jake seized Ziyad's throat. His face twisted and reddened. "Is she alive? Where is she? Where's my daughter?"

Miriam snapped in Hebrew, "He can't talk when you're strangling him."

Jake eased back a fraction. Ziyad coughed out, "You see her! Soon! In hell!"

Miriam didn't see the slap coming. Jake put his weight behind it, a roundhouse with his right hand and a big follow-through, gunshot loud. Ziyad's head snapped to his right; blood sprayed the dingy wallpaper. He sagged in the chair working his jaw, then pivoted his face fast and spit blood on Jake's chest. Jake backhanded him so hard Ziyad and the chair crashed sideways to the worn carpet.

"We kill her!" Ziyad choked out. Jake slammed his foot into Ziyad's chest; Miriam heard a rib crack. The Arab coughed, "We kill you!" Jake kicked him again, harder, then again and again, crimson-faced and absolutely silent. Ziyad half-screamed, half-laughed.

Miriam sprang off the bed. "Jake! Stop!"

Ziyad, gargling blood: "We kill all you! All!"

Suddenly Jake had the Glock in his trembling hand, aimed at Ziyad's head.

"No!" Miriam lunged toward him and thrust her hand in front of the pistol's muzzle, just as he had done to her two hours before. "Stop it!" she said in Hebrew. "We won't find Eve if you kill him!"

Jake sucked fast, deep breaths, as if preparing to dive underwater for a long time. He stared at Ziyad for an eternity before he shifted his focus to Miriam. White ringed his irises.

Miriam forced a deep breath down her throat, trying to tamp down her alarm at seeing Jake this way. "If we wanted him dead, I would've shot him two hours ago." She swallowed, ratcheted down the heat in her voice. The Arab might not understand her words, but he'd be able to read her tone. "We still don't know where they took Eve or how many of them there are. We won't find out anything if he's dead."

Jake's panting slowed, but his eyes were still blown. After a moment he spun, let out a strangled groan, and whacked his forehead against the wall. He stood with his back to her, trembling, head still bent, gun hand hanging at his side.

"We're running out of time, Jake, and you're out of control. He'll use that against you. I saw that in *Magav*. He wants you to kill him so he can be a martyr." She glanced down at the hacking, choking Arab. "Let me try. I've done this before, you haven't."

He turned and exchanged silent stares with her. She could tell Jake understood what she was offering. After a moment, he nodded.

She stole another peek at Ziyad, still strapped to his chair, groaning. It'd been years since she'd done this; could she now? The hate was still there. Was that enough? "Strip him and put him in the shower," she said in English.

"The shower?"

"It's easier to clean up."

Ziyad's bloody face whipped from Jake to Miriam and back. When he peered at Miriam again, she saw fear creep through his defiance. She gave him the nastiest smile she could dredge up. In her dreams, she'd felt triumph at this moment. Right here, right now, she was sick to her stomach.

Jake shoved his pistol into the back waistband of his jeans, crossed to the chair and dragged it upright using Ziyad's hair for a handle. He leaned his mouth next to the Arab's ear. "You should've talked to me when you had the chance, Ziyad."

❖

Jake left Ziyad strapped naked to the chair in the stall facing the shower head. Ziyad wasn't so cocky anymore; resignation shadowed the man's face.

The scarred brass floor lamp lay dissected on Miriam's bed, the shade tossed on a pillow, the cord coiled in her hands. She'd produced a small multitool from her purse. What else was in there? "What's that for?" he asked. "We've got lots of wire ties."

"You don't want to know." She stood, squared her shoulders, re-tied her hair behind her head. Her eyes were brown diamonds, bright and impenetrable. She stripped off her watch and earrings and tossed them on the ratty gold bedspread. "Lend me one of your undershirts."

"Why?"

"Because blood doesn't come out of silk."

Their Chinese take-out dinner lurched into the back of Jake's throat. He couldn't tell if he was crashing off his adrenaline high or reacting to the picture Miriam's words painted. He dug a clean undershirt out of his duffel and tossed it to her.

Miriam turned her back to him, her elbows wavering as she unbuttoned her gray long-sleeved blouse. Jake winced when she dropped her shirt on the bed; a malignant purple bruise the size of a bread plate sprawled across her spine just above her black bra strap, a near-match for the one on his breastbone. He knew how much his hurt.

She carefully slipped his t-shirt over her head, pulled it smooth and stood still for a moment, the hem in her fists. Her ribcage swelled and compressed with each slow, deep breath. When she opened her hands, they trembled slightly. Jake didn't dare say a word.

Miriam turned to face him, scooped up her blouse, the multitool and the lamp cord. "You should move his car." Her voice stretched tight enough to deflect bullets. "Those terrorist bastards should think he just disappeared."

"Yeah." He handed her the gloves, then reached for his coat. They couldn't meet each other's eyes. She was going in there to finish what he couldn't. Thank God she'd jumped in. If she hadn't, he'd have kicked that little shit to death—and maybe lost Eve forever.

"Jake?" He looked up. There was a lot going on in her face, none of it good. "Don't come into the bathroom unless I call you."

He heard the unstated *you don't need to see this.* "Okay."

Miriam stood rigid before the bathroom door for several seconds, her mouth working itself into knots. Jake watched her until the door banged shut behind her.

❖

Seventy-five minutes later, Miriam sleepwalked into the room.

Jake had tried to ignore the sounds coming from the bathroom: Miriam's low-pitched growls in English and Arabic; yelps and groans from Ziyad; and especially the ominous silences. Occasionally the lamp on the nightstand and the overhead light in the entry would dim for a second or two, accompanied by a strangled, muffled animal noise behind the closed door.

He muted the TV and waited for Miriam to speak.

She wore her gray blouse again and was far cleaner than he'd expected. She worried at her hands with a flimsy hotel towel; her eyes focused on a place somewhere on the other side of the ocean. "Eve is still alive. A man named Rafiq is taking care of her. There's five of them. They're in the Sleep Inn on 49th Street in Brooklyn. Do you know where that is?" He nodded. "The leader's name is Alayan. They killed all those people on the list. The one called

Gabir shot Rinnah. They're coming here at four. They'll use Eve to draw us out."

Miriam's voice was drained of all emotion, all energy, everything except her accent. Her skin crawled across her cheekbones and forehead. Jake tried to read her eyes, but the shades were drawn tight. He reluctantly glanced away long enough to check his watch. "Half an hour, if he's telling the truth." He watched her stare though the wall for a moment. "Is he still alive?"

She sagged onto the foot of her bed, fixed her gaze to the floor. Her ragged breathing rasped across the room. Finally, she gave her head one quick, sharp nod. "He probably wishes he wasn't."

Miriam's shoulders shivered. He hadn't expected this reaction; he'd figured she'd be amped, like she'd been at the train station. He slid off his bed, carefully sat beside her, and wrapped his fingers around her forearm. Close up, he noticed reddish-brown stains under her fingernails, at her hairline, and in the crinkles around her eyes. "You okay?"

The tremor in her hands became a rapid shake. "I've dreamed about getting one of these evil fucks in my hands," she whispered. "Ever since I was ten years old. Every time someone I knew was hurt... every time they were killed... because they were in the wrong place... I wanted it more." Her chin trembled for just a moment, then she squared it so hard the cords in her neck stretched tight. "When I met Bill, it was... it was like starting new. I started to... let it go. Then these shits blew him apart in Kandahar." Her voice slid into an animal growl. "And I wanted their blood. I wanted to tear them apart like they'd torn him apart. I wanted to make them suffer like they'd made my father suffer. I wanted it so much. It gave me a reason to go on." Miriam's entire body started to shake as if she was freezing, even though heat sheeted off her. "And tonight... tonight..."

Jake slid his fingers down her arm, grabbed her vibrating hand. She clamped her other hand over his so hard it hurt. "It's done," he whispered. "It's done."

She finally showed him her eyes. The brown diamonds from an hour ago had turned to shattered glass puddles. A drop crept out of the corner of her left eye, hung on her lashes, then slid down through the residue to become a tear of blood. Jake smeared it away with his thumb.

Miriam recoiled when she glimpsed the red stain on his thumb. The pain and horror in her face erupted out her pores. "I wanted it so much," she pleaded in Hebrew. "I wanted it so much, Jake. And now... now I just feel..." She tried one last time to get control, to suck down the sobs pulsing visibly in her throat, but her will broke with the grinding sound of the gears of her soul stripping under the strain.

Miriam began to weep.

Jake pressed her tight against him, her back arching in great spasms against his arms, her tears burning his neck. She clung to him as if he was the only thing keeping her demons from dragging her away. Seeing her like this was almost physically painful. She'd been so strong, so confident. He'd relied on that. He just held her and rocked her and tried to find something to say to comfort her, to give her back some of the strength he'd borrowed over the past couple weeks.

She finally settled into ragged sucked-in breaths, tiny hurt sounds deep in her throat and occasional shudders. Jake let her hang on, even though he was aware of the minutes ticking past. He knew from experience with Rinnah and Eve that rushing her would only make things worse. Just like them, she'd let go when she didn't need him anymore.

Eventually Miriam sat straight, turned away from him, snuffled, scrubbed her face with the towel. "I'm sorry," she said to the entry hall. She dropped her hands to her lap, twisted the towel in her fingers. "I hate sniveling like that."

Jake gently took her nearest hand and traced a circle on the back of it with the pad of his middle finger. "If all this didn't freak you out, I'd worry." She snorted, which turned into another snuffle. "You okay?"

Miriam glanced at him with bright red eyes. "Enough." She sat watching him for a few moments, sniffed occasionally, rubbed at her eyes or nose with the hand towel. Then she leaned forward, brushed his cheek with her lips, straightened again. "Thank you," she whispered.

Jake nodded. He tried to ignore the guilty burn her kiss left behind. "It's almost four. That phone rang three more times while you were... decompressing. They're looking for him."

With a parting squeeze of his hand, Miriam twisted and scooped her watch from the blanket. "They could be here already. They could be outside."

"I don't think so. I'll bet they're laying low, trying to figure out if he's been arrested. We may have some time."

"To do what?"

He stood, crossed to the nightstand, hefted Ziyad's phone. He thumbed on the screen; twelve missed calls. Jake held up the phone for Miriam to see. "We've got a direct pipe to them. We know who they are now. How many and where."

"So we go to their hotel?"

Jake shook his head. "Too public, and they'd be playing defense. We set up a trade on our home turf—their guy for Eve." He watched Miriam consider this, then nod. "I'm tired of reacting. It's time to take control."

265

SEVENTY-THREE

22 DECEMBER
BROOKLYN

Rafiq watched from the black high-backed hotel desk chair as the little girl twitched and rocked under the folded-over bedspread on the closer of the two double beds. Her broken whimpers were the only sounds in the room other than the whooshing of the wall-mounted heater. Every baby-bird noise, every jerk of her feet stabbed him deep in his soul.

When he was eleven, his younger sister Aishah contracted blood poisoning. He'd helped with the vigil, watching her fight her fever and chills each night. She'd made the same sounds Eve did, twitched the same way. Aishah survived. Would Eve?

Rafiq stretched, rubbed his gritty eyes. Two hours of sleep last night? Maybe three? None yet tonight. He'd spent most of the previous evening trying to calm the little girl before she eventually sobbed herself into a restless sleep. Did it help or hurt that she'd seen him as the Con Ed man just before Gabir killed her mother? At least he'd been able to tell her that her father was alive, not that it helped much.

Kidnapping a child. Had Alayan lost the last of his mind? He'd disintegrated over the past couple of weeks, both mentally and physically. It was a shock to see him now—bleary eyes, ragged hair, a hollowness in his face that spoke of missed meals and foregone sleep, a tremor in his hands he tried but failed to hide. The other men whispered about it, too. They'd never seen him like this.

Alayan had been irritable and snappish since Eldar killed Kassim. The closer the deadline came, the more prone he was to biting off the head of anyone who questioned anything. Desperate men don't think clearly, and Alayan was clearly desperate. That could mean nothing good for the rest of them.

Rafiq couldn't sit anymore. He lurched out of the chair, peeked out the tan curtains at the dark carpet of flat-roofed warehouses below him.

That damned deadline. Rafiq had rented the garage space and the rooms Alayan had asked for. He'd almost refused. He should have refused; who else would Alayan send, Gabir? Sohrab, who could barely speak English? So if the truck bomb exploded, Rafiq would be just as much to blame as whoever pushed the button.

He'd never been part of a martyrdom operation. He'd never wanted to. What had lured him from the Party's intelligence group into direct action was the style of operation Alayan advocated—focused, accurate, efficient, with a minimum of collateral damage. The very opposite of what was about to happen. The Party was abandoning its proud adulthood and regressing into its wild-eyed adolescence.

Rafiq shook his head for the hundredth time today. Could he go down this road?

True, he had reasons to be grateful to the Party. They'd chased those traitorous South Lebanon Army bastards off his family's land and thrown the Zionists out of southern Lebanon. Of course, they destroyed his childhood home and wrecked the orchards in the process, but for that he blamed the SLA. The Party built bunkers and a storage depot on the farm's edges, inviting periodic Zionist shelling that made recovery impossible. The Party considered his uncle politically unreliable for some reason, hobbling his trading business already crippled by the endless war in the south. Rafiq's once-wealthy family now scraped by in a pair of flats in Sour.

Was loyalty to the Party worth his soul?

It would be easy to call the police, tell them about suspicious people in the motel and the nearby garage on that industrial strip in North Bergen. He'd almost done it three times since last night. Each time he'd pulled back, afraid they'd somehow trace the call and he'd end up wearing an orange jumpsuit in that dungeon in Guantanamo for helping kill four Americans.

Two light raps on the door broke him out of his thoughts. He glanced toward Eve; still asleep. Rafiq hurried to the door, cupped his hand around the spyhole, peeled back the tape. Alayan stood outside, his head swiveling nervously left and right.

Rafiq undid the chain, eased open the door. "What is it? It's after two."

"And you're still awake."

Rafiq let him slip inside. Alayan stopped at the end of the little entry hall, peeked at the lump in the far bed's coverlet, then faced Rafiq. "Ziyad's missing," he whispered. "His car's gone, too."

More paranoia? "What do you mean 'missing'? Did you call him?"

"Of course I did," he snapped. "He doesn't answer. Gabir swept the area around the hotel but didn't see anything. I'm going out with Sohrab now to search."

Rafiq stopped to think. Did Ziyad just run off? No; he'd never choose to stay here. Did the police arrest him? Maybe; if so, they were all in immediate danger. Or did Eldar and Schaffer get him? A couple of weeks ago, he wouldn't have considered that possible, but they'd proved themselves far more capable than anyone could've foreseen.

"Are we still going into the hotel at four?" Rafiq asked.

Alayan's eyes filled with frustration. "No. We can't risk walking into a room full of policemen. We need to find out what happened to Ziyad first."

Rafiq felt more relief than he'd expected. "When do we leave this place?"

"We're not. Ziyad might try to come back here. You stay with the girl, I'll call with any news."

"But if the police have him—"

"It doesn't matter, we're not leaving. There's no need."

No need? Rafiq held up his hands in surrender; fighting with Alayan would just make the man erupt. Staying would give Rafiq more time to think.

Alayan took one more look at the far bed, then abruptly turned his back on it. "I won't make you kill her, if that's what you're worried about. I'll do it myself if it comes to that."

Rafiq stared at the floor, trying to hide his shock. The Alayan he'd known would never threaten such a thing. The man was falling apart. The operation was falling apart.

Rafiq had to decide where to be when it imploded.

268

SEVENTY-FOUR

22 DECEMBER
SUNSET PARK, BROOKLYN

Alayan yawned, rubbed his eyes, turned his attention back to the parked cars around them. Lots of Toyotas, some white, none the right one. *Where is that donkey?* He was too tired to be angry anymore. At this point, he just wanted to know what happened to Ziyad.

Sohrab braked for the light at 8th Avenue next to a forlorn Chinese grocery. The approaching sunrise faded the streetlight-yellow night sky to lavender and outlined the flat roofs of the frowsy two- and three-story brick buildings surrounding them.

Alayan's phone trilled twice before he realized it was ringing. He checked his screen and jolted wide awake. "Ziyad, you stupid son of a whore, where in hell are you? You idiot, you know that—"

"I'm not Ziyad."

An American voice. Police? FBI? Now he was wide awake with ice trickling down his neck. In English he said, "Who then? Who are you?"

"Jake Eldar."

Eldar? Alayan punched the mute button, snapped "Pull over" at Sohrab, tried to think what this meant. After a few moments of flailing, he turned off the mute. "Mr. Eldar, a good morning to you. Where is Ziyad, please?"

"I've got him. You Alayan?"

"Yes."

"You have my daughter."

How much did Ziyad tell Eldar? "I can talk to Ziyad, please?"

"Not until I get Eve back. Has your boy Rafiq done anything to her?"

How many of their names did the Jew know? What else did he know? Their hotel? Their plans? "No, he is making her okay, good." He hated trying to speak English for long stretches of time; it got all tangled up in his other languages. "*S'il vous plaît, parlez-vous français?*"

"*Atah medaber Ivrit?*"

Actually, Alayan did speak a smattering of Hebrew, but damned if he'd use it here. He signaled wildly to Sohrab for a pen and paper. "English, yes? You want what?"

"A trade. Your boy Ziyad for my daughter."

So obvious it was almost disappointing, but not a bad move anyway. Sohrab handed him a fast-food napkin and a pencil; Alayan scribbled "Call Gabir—Jews still in hotel?" and handed back the napkin. "If we come there, we just take him, yes?"

"You really think we'd hang around? We're not in the hotel anymore."

Not if Ziyad told them about the plan. *Damn that dog!* "If no deal, you are killing him?"

"Tempting, but no. He broke pretty easy, Alayan. I'll give him to NYPD, let them take him apart. I'll bet pretty soon he won't shut up. Bad news for you, huh?"

"Wait, please." Alayan stabbed the mute button and let fly a string of curses. He needed a few seconds to make sense of the situation, to try to grab some control.

Sohrab looked on, wide-eyed, hand over his cellphone's mouthpiece. "*Sidi?* What is it?"

"Not now. What did Gabir say?"

"He hasn't seen anyone leave except two whores, but there's no way to tell what happened after Ziyad left."

Alayan last spoke to Ziyad just before midnight. The Jews must have got him sometime in the following two hours, enough time to take his car and go almost anywhere.

How bad would it be to lose Ziyad to the police? If they could eliminate the two Jews, the rest of the team could leave the country immediately, and Ziyad would be of no use to the Americans except as a trophy. The child was worth a great deal more than Ziyad. A cold calculation, but that was his job. He un-muted. "Mr. Eldar? You can be keeping Ziyad, I think. I trade the child for another thing, yes?"

"What's that?"

"You, and the woman." Silence. *Didn't expect that, did you?* "The child, I do not want. Meet me, I make her go, we finish, you and the woman. Yes?"

Eldar breathed into the phone for a few moments. "Can't speak for Miriam. She's not here, we split up. We didn't want to make it easy for you."

True? Hard to tell. "We see her with you there. She is with you, yes?"

"No. It's just me. You want her, you find her."

This was a complication Alayan didn't need. He became aware of Sohrab frowning at him. Did he disapprove of giving up Ziyad? Too bad. "You not come? You both not come? No reason for the child, yes?"

He could hear Eldar thinking on the other end of their phone connection. Would he trade his life for his daughter's? What sort of man was he really?

"I'll come," Eldar said. "That's all I can give you."

So the Jew was willing to sacrifice himself. That was good to know; it meant he was more dangerous than they'd imagined. "You and the woman, or nothing."

"I can't speak for Miriam. Only she can do that."

"Good morning, Mr. Eldar." Alayan killed the call before either of them could say another word. It was the right place to stop, with the threat hanging over the child's head. Could Eldar convince the woman to give up her life too for the sake of the little girl?

"Go to the Jews' hotel," he ordered Sohrab. "Let's see if the man's a liar."

"What was that last part about?" Miriam asked.

Jake stopped pacing the asphalt Sunset Park footpath and watched the lights of Manhattan wink out as night became dawn. He and Rinnah had come here in the summer to swim and sit on the lawn and look at the view. Now the trees hunched gray and dormant, the shaggy grass limp and pale, as if someone had turned down the color gain on the picture. Winter? Or did this place miss Rinnah as much as he did? "He wants us both, or he'll kill Eve."

"He said he'd kill her?"

"Not in so many words. His English isn't great, but I got his meaning. He doesn't care if we give Ziyad to the PD. He must be getting desperate." His mind refused to connect *desperate killer* and *Eve* in the same sentence. He had to stomp down the fear so the anger could carry him through what was ahead.

Miriam's shoulders sagged. She looked toward a tanker lumbering across upper New York Bay but focused on something much farther away. "I guess he gets us both, then."

"No."

"No what?"

"I can't let you do that." Jake took Miriam's arm and turned her to face him. "She's my daughter. If I decide to do something stupid to save her, it's my business. I won't drag you—"

"You're not dragging me. I'm worried about her too. I can—"

"No. I may not come back, understand? I can't let you do this."

"*Let* me?" A flash of the pre-Ziyad Miriam of a few hours before returned. She drew herself up to her full height and squared her jaw. "It's not your decision, Jake. You're not my father, you're not my husband, you're—"

"Look, I—"

"Just shut up and let me talk. I make my own decisions, okay? First, this idea that you're going to walk in there and let them kill you is just..." she fished for words with her right hand "...macho army bullshit. Really, I thought you had more sense. Eve's already lost her mother—she can't lose her father, too. If you go there alone, they'll kill you, and then they'll kill Eve, and then they'll come after me. Besides, we're a team, or at least I thought we were."

This wasn't an argument he'd wanted to have, but knowing her the way he did now, he wasn't surprised it was happening. He sighed, looked into her eyes. They'd have been brown marble a couple weeks ago, but now they flashed with a mix of determination and concern.

"Yeah, we're a team." He squeezed her other arm just below

her shoulder. "They're not going to let us get away this time. They know what we can do."

"They didn't 'let us' get away before, but we did." She cupped his elbow with her left hand. "And even if we don't, at least Eve will be safe. I will *not* leave her with those animals, and I won't stand by and let her get killed. I just won't."

"Miriam... if anything happens to you, all this has been a waste. All of it."

She shook her head. "None of this has been a waste."

They stood face-to-face, less than a foot of air between them, for the better part of a minute before Jake said, "Any way I can change your mind?"

"I'm a sabra. We're born stubborn. Didn't Rinnah teach you anything?"

This was so wrong. Miriam was volunteering to die for him and Eve. If she was hurt or killed, he'd never be able to face himself again. But if anything happened to Eve, he'd walk in front of a bus. *What a choice.* The more he thought, the fewer options he could see. He released her arms, brushed her cheek with his fingertips. "Call him."

She gave him a brave smile. "Give me the number."

Jake read it off Ziyad's directory, then wandered a few yards away while Miriam placed the call. He couldn't listen to her volunteer to sacrifice herself. He considered Ziyad's phone for a moment, then pushed in the main number for JTTF and asked for the man who'd been his supervisor for the fourteen days in the safe house.

"Menotti."

"Hi, boss. Jake Eldar."

Pause. "Jake, where the hell are you? We're all over the place trying to find you."

"Never mind. I got time to say this once. First, there's a Hezbollah agent named Ziyad al-Amin in the trunk of a white Camry at 676 46th Street at 7th Av in Brooklyn. It's the only one with two windows busted out. He's yours if you get there right now. Can't guarantee how long he'll be there. He'll need a doctor."

"Hezbollah? Seriously?" Fingers rubbed the mouthpiece on the other end of the line, but didn't entirely block Menotti's urgent, muffled command to someone near him. "What's this—"

"Second. This number belongs to al-Amin's cell phone. Wherever he got it, there should be at least five others bought at the same time. Track it down."

"Damn good work." A couple blocks away, three police sirens exploded the quiet. "Where can we pick you up? You—"

"Not yet. Miriam and I have to stay out of sight for a while. I'll call later with more." He hesitated. "I'm sorry about all this, sir. I'll explain later. I'll make up the time."

Menotti coughed out a laugh. "Jesus, you keep handing us terrorists, you're on the clock, don't worry. But Jake—you gotta come in sometime, you know?"

"I know. I'll be in touch."

Miriam stood nearby, just out of earshot, her hands clasped in front of her hips. So calm, after what she'd just done. No matter what happened to them, he'd never forget this moment.

Jake slowly closed the distance, trying to read her face. It revealed nothing. "Well?"

"He'll call you with the arrangements." She flinched when another police siren cooked off nearby. "He's a smug bastard, isn't he?"

"He can afford to be. He's getting what he wants."

"Hm." Miriam continued to watch the Manhattan skyscrapers change color in the delicate, shifting light. "So what happens now?"

"Now we figure out how to save Eve. Then we finish these assholes."

SEVENTY-FIVE

22 DECEMBER
PARK SLOPE, BROOKLYN

"Mr. Kaminsky?"

"Mr. Eldar, is it?" Kaminsky switched to Hebrew. "Please, call me Stuart. Are you well? Were you involved in that police shooting in Brooklyn?"

"Yeah, that was us." Jake took a deep breath, checked the subway platform to see if anyone other than Miriam was close enough to hear. "Hezbollah's got my daughter."

"I'm very sorry to hear that. How can I help?"

"We need a sniper."

Gur unloaded three tall coffees on the black laminate table overlooking the street, then slumped into his chair. Kelila half-heartedly dragged away a cup; Sasha stared at his through eyes crimson with fatigue. "How many places so far?" Gur asked Kelila.

"Sixty-seven."

"A prime number," Sasha volunteered.

Gur glanced at him—*sleep-deficit dementia?*—then back to Kelila. The rings around her eyes could stand in for eyeshadow. "Where does that leave us?"

She took a long draw on her coffee, then wrestled with her folded-up street map of Brooklyn and the list of hotels. For a few moments, it looked as if the map would win. Little wonder; none of them had slept since the shootout at the NYPD safe house, and they'd covered most of the northern half of Brooklyn on foot or by taxi. "North and east are dead ends unless we go farther out on

275

Long Island. West is done. So that leaves us with south. There's three on 39th—Day's Inn, Kings and Hamilton—the Avenue Plaza on 47th and 13th Avenue, the Park House on 48th, the Sleep Inn on 49th. And a few others."

"Maybe they're gone," Sasha said. "Left the city."

"They're here somewhere," Gur said. He hoped volume would sound like confidence. "As long as Hezbollah has the child, the covers will stay close. Kelila, would you leave if someone took Hasia?"

"Absolutely not."

"Neither would I. They're here."

But where? Eldar and Schaffer weren't stupid enough to go to the obvious places—Eldar's flat, his uncle's hospital. Friends? A synagogue?

Gur nipped at his coffee and stared into the depths of the Park Slope Starbucks. Well-kept mothers with babies or toddlers surrounded them, chattering to each other, maneuvering tank-like prams past the busy tables. Oblivious to what was happening beyond the coffeehouse's walls. Not knowing—or caring—about the terrible things that happened to people just like them.

"Why are we always chasing these people?" Sasha grumped. "Why can't we get in front of them for a change?"

Kelila gave him a disgusted look. "If you have a plan, let's hear it."

"You like this shit? Looking like idiots?"

"Stop it," Gur snapped. It was hard enough to concentrate without the backchat.

How would the Arabs contact the covers? Alayan and his thugs couldn't hold the child for long. Would Hezbollah torture her for her father's mobile number? Would that even work? How could they use her as bait, unless…?

"Hezbollah knows where the covers are," Gur said before realizing he was about to say it. The other two squinted at him, perhaps looking for signs of delirium. "They must, otherwise taking the girl does them no good. They must have followed Eldar and Schaffer."

Kelila and Sasha exchanged is-the-old-man-crazy? looks. Then Kelila said, very carefully, "If that's true, this should be over already.

Alayan's people have no reason to wait."

She had a point, one he might have seen had his brain been working. He was too old for these all-night marathons. "If you're right, it would be in the news."

Kelila pulled her silver netbook from her shoulder bag, turned it on, plugged in a set of black earbuds. She looked so frayed, so drained. Gur wanted to cocoon her in his arms and sleep the day away with her, warm and safe, anyplace but here. No chance of that now, damn it.

After a moment, she leaned across the table toward him. "The Italians say they've rounded up a Hezbollah bomb team in Rome."

Another one? Gur swiveled the tiny notebook so he could read the three-line CNN "breaking news" bulletin. Then he thumbed a number into his secure mobile.

"Good morning to you, Raffi," Orgad said.

Gur growled, "We have to find out about Rome on CNN?"

"You could do worse. Our team in Italy—Lev Seitzman's the lead, you know him—they broke a six-man cell in Stazione. This was two days ago. This morning they turned over whatever was left to the Carabinieri. The Italians are very proud of themselves just now."

Gur knew that by "turned over," Orgad meant an anonymous call from a mobile that was on the bottom of the Tiber ten minutes later. "Two days ago? And you didn't tell us?"

"Without knowing exactly what we had? That's useful now, is it?"

"Yes, damn it. Anything's useful. We're grabbing at fog out here."

"And whose fault is that?" Gur heard a voice in the background, and Orgad's palm squished against his phone's mouthpiece. After a few moments, Orgad's voice replaced the scrubbing sounds. "Are you still in contact with the covers?"

Gur hesitated. The answer would only dig his hole deeper. "No. They've gone to ground again."

"Of course. They'll be at the main chapel in Green-Wood Cemetery in Brooklyn at six your time tonight. They plan to exchange themselves for the child, if you can believe that."

That made no sense at all. Gur snapped his fingers twice to

startle Kelila out of her trance, mouthed "Green-Wood Cemetery," then returned his attention to Orgad. "This is from your mystery source? How does he know this?"

"He spoke to Eldar."

Who's this source? Why does Eldar trust him? Gur sorted through the possibilities. The police? If Eldar trusted them, he wouldn't be running from them now. Eldar wouldn't tell his uncle; it would get back to the police. "Chaim... tell me Alayan isn't your source."

"He isn't. He'd be very useful, certainly, and if you get the chance, you should try to turn him before you kill him. But no, he isn't one of ours."

That left... "Kaminsky? He's the only other one I can imagine Eldar talking to. Is he a *sayan?*"

Orgad didn't answer for a few seconds. Then, parsing his words carefully, he said, "No, he is not a *sayan.*"

But he was the source, or Orgad would've denied it. The wheels in Gur's head ground and clashed, spat out a solution that was simply insane. "He's one of *us?*"

Again, Orgad let a few moments pass. "Yes."

"But not with the embassy station."

"No, not with them."

Kelila pivoted her netbook's screen to face Gur, displaying the website for the cemetery. He ignored it; the implications of Orgad's words filled his brain with an angry buzzing. "AL? He's with AL? And you didn't tell us?"

"You needn't be concerned with our America section—"

"Goddamnit, Chaim!" Nearby heads turned in Gur's direction. He throttled back his voice to a low snarl. "We needed those assets! You had replacements *right here* for Amzi and Natan and you didn't—"

"They weren't available. They have a higher-priority mission."

"Higher than a Hezbollah hit team in America? What, they're stealing American weapon designs again? We're chasing these fucking Arabs all over—"

"Enough, Raffi." Orgad's voice was calm but cold, as upset as he ever got. "Remember which side of my desk you sit on. AL is not yours to use or even think about. Understand?"

Gur understood. He pulled his phone away from his head and muttered curses that made Kelila's and Sasha's eyes pop. "What idiot decided to use his name for Natan's cover? That's—"

"He did. Some questions were being raised about his employment. He felt the quickest way to cement his credentials as a private citizen was for us to use his cover for the Doha operation. No one would believe we're stupid enough to burn one of our own. Brilliant, yes?"

"Wonderful." Gur knew he should admire the *chutzpah*, but instead he just felt like biting his coffee cup in half. "Any other surprises?"

"Nothing that concerns you. Forget Kaminsky. Make do with what you're given. You still haven't redeemed yourself for Philadelphia. Be sure you do this time. Ring me when you're done." The connection dropped into the usual post-call clunking and static.

Gur muttered a couple more particularly vile curses and scrubbed his face with his palms. That old son of a bitch! Playing his shitty little games even with innocent lives and this operation at stake. They had to go to the exchange; it might be their last chance to catch Alayan and his crew in the open. "Well," he finally said through his hands, "we can get some sleep now."

"You know where the covers are?" Kelila asked.

"Yes. Kaminsky's one of us, you probably heard. Try again to get the original ID photo from his passport. Sasha, do you still have David's rifle?"

"Yes, boss. Why?"

"Because you're going to need it."

SEVENTY-SIX

22 DECEMBER
GREEN-WOOD CEMETERY, BROOKLYN

Green-Wood Cemetery's gray Gothic fantasy of a main chapel emerged from the bony, leafless trees as Jake and Miriam approached from the south. A cupola and dome topped the central core; smaller domes capped each of the building's four corners, and a large, arched art-glass window faced them from beneath the roof's elaborately carved gable end. They stopped at the same instant.

"It's lovely," Miriam said. Her sad smile betrayed her mixed feelings. "I wish we weren't here for…"

"I know." Jake reached out, touched her coat sleeve with the backs of his fingers. "It'll be okay. We've got help this time. Come on."

He and Rinnah had often come to this beautiful green place. They'd played hide-and-seek with Eve on these rises, in these trees. He knew this place better than any other unpaved area in Brooklyn. That might just keep them alive tonight.

Inside the chapel, the great brass ring of the central chandelier blazed with light but couldn't take the chill out of the air. They dropped their bags; Jake slumped exhausted on one of the ranks of benches. He watched Miriam prowl the periphery, taking in the big stained-glass windows and stone carvings.

At five minutes to five, he ushered her into a janitor's closet. The smell of cleaners and damp mops surrounded them in the tiny, utterly black room. A groundskeeper called out "Closing!" The lights clacked off; the front door clunked shut, its lock ratcheted.

When not even echoes disturbed the still outside the closet, they slipped out into the semi-dark sanctuary. The fading sunset

280

straggled through the western windows, leaving just enough light for them to move without injury.

They sat side-by-side but not touching at the aisle end of the bench closest to the door. The chapel dimmed around them. Streetlights became glowing white balls behind the windows.

Sitting in the dark, he thought. *How appropriate.*

They'd spent all day cris-crossing New York City on one subway train after another, getting out at random stations, changing directions on a whim. They'd taken turns catnapping, one keeping watch while the other snatched a few minutes of restless oblivion. Jake could still feel Miriam's head on his shoulder, her hair brushing his cheek. Rinnah used to do that after a night at a film or the theater. Those Rinnah memories had ganged up on him under Harlem and he'd cried quietly into a McDonald's napkin while Miriam slept. He was glad she hadn't seen that; he didn't want to look weak in front of her, not now.

He didn't know whether he could protect Eve or if he'd even survive. He'd had all day to think about these next few minutes but could never see it all the way through. In every version, he saved Eve—perhaps not himself or Miriam, but Eve always got away. He hoped—prayed—that wasn't just wishful thinking.

Gene and Monica would take care of her if Jake didn't make it. The idea he might not get to see her grow up filled him with blackness more absolute than the dark surrounding him. It was leavened only by the knowledge she *would* grow up, have adventures, fall in love, get married, have children of her own. He hoped.

"Jake?"

"Yeah?"

Miriam's fingers found his coat sleeve, slid down his arm until they reached his hand. "Thank you."

The gentleness of her touch surprised him. Jake let the feeling linger for a moment. "For what?"

"For… for staying with me through all this. For reminding me what it feels like to be alive. For making me care about something other than me."

"You're welcome." He interlaced his fingers with hers. Those hands. So strong, but now so warm and soft. "Wish I could say I'd planned all this."

"We survived two weeks with a pack of killers on our tail. You did fine."

Would Rinnah think so? "I... well, I don't think I'd have made it without you around. You got Eve talking again. You and Eve gave me... I don't know, something to wake up for."

They sat holding hands until Jake's watch dial showed a glowing, straight-up-and-down line. He rose and pulled Miriam to her feet. They stood face-to-face for a moment, then fumbled into each other's arms, held each other as tight as their body armor allowed. Jake tried to borrow one last cup of strength from Miriam but sensed her stores were running low, too, so he simply took comfort in her warmth and nearness. "I'm glad you didn't throw me out of your office."

"So am I." Her sigh filled the chapel. "If I had, I'd be dead now. I can't ever repay you for that."

They let each other slip away. She was only a dark shape now. He wished he could read her eyes. "You don't have to. Just stay alive."

"You, too." Miriam touched her fingertips to his chest. "Let's go get Eve."

SEVENTY-SEVEN

22 December
Green-Wood Cemetery, Brooklyn

Sasha swept his rifle's night-vision scope across the dark tangle of trees on the other side of the chapel's car park, watching for movement or light. There was just enough ambient light from the streetlamps and the bounce off the overcast to wash out the picture. Night vision or no, there was still a lot he couldn't see.

His station behind the sober dark granite monument gave him a panoramic view of the entire arena—the chapel to his right, the car park in front with its oval of green shrubs, the wooded, tomb-flecked slope to the chapel's east and north, the access road to his left. He'd have an unobstructed line on Hezbollah wherever they were. All he had to do was not shoot the covers or the kid, and not get shot himself.

Movement to his right caught his eye. He swung the rifle toward the knot of gray trees just west of the chapel in time to see a figure drop to its face in the grass behind a large black headstone. Kelila. Once Sasha put Hezbollah on the ground, he'd cover her while she moved in for the *coups de grace*. The boss would patrol the woods north of the chapel for squirters.

It was time to make those bastards pay for Amzi and Natan and David.

Sohrab pressed himself flat against the roof of a tomb halfway up the steep slope northeast of the chapel. He slid the SIG-Sauer rifle from its sheath, uncapped the scope, and checked his sightlines. His scrubby new beard scratched against the stock.

Everything south and west of him was clear. Excellent.

He'd spent the past half-hour slipping through the trees, checking positions, looking for enemies. A few times he thought he wasn't alone—a sensation, a half-heard sound, the unexplained twitch of a branch. He never saw anyone, but that didn't mean anything.

Sohrab settled his rifle onto the granite, fished the night-vision monocular from the scabbard, switched it on. The lens coated the world with a couple dozen different shades of green. He scanned 270 degrees clockwise, alert for the yellow-green bloom of body heat.

Headlights flared in the monocular. Sohrab shut it off, took up his rifle. A few moments later, the van's familiar blocky shape trundled down the narrow road. He checked his watch: 6:07. They were late.

Did it matter? Just an extra few minutes of life for Eldar and the woman. He was less than seventy clear meters from the chapel's front doors, and the Jews would be standing still the moment Rafiq brought out the brat. Now he knew they had body armor, he'd go for head shots. They wouldn't get away this time.

Miriam edged Jake aside to peek past the chapel's heavy wood door into the night.

A van slowly circled the landscaped oval in the center of the tiny parking lot, its headlights blaring off random tree trunks and monuments. It squeaked to a halt alongside the walkway leading to the chapel's steps.

I should be scared. Every time she'd walked into a firefight in Israel, she'd felt the icy drizzle of fear in her brain and gut. Not this time. Had she become used to being a target?

Adrenaline trickled into her system, making her aware of the pulse in her ears, the extra sharpness creeping into her vision. Her body was hiding the fear from her, distracting her with a flood of input. Well, that was okay. She'd rather be hyped than scared, even if the rush made her stupid. She'd survived stupid before.

She reviewed their plan again. Jake would step outside first, finish the negotiations with Alayan. The Arabs would demand to see her before they let Eve go. Miriam would drift to her left, staying in shadow as much as possible. When they released Eve, Miriam would dash twenty or so feet to the building's northwest corner, lay down covering fire for Jake while he collected Eve and bolted for the chapel. *Covering fire like hell—I'm going to shoot these animals.* Kaminsky's sniper would keep Hezbollah busy and maybe pick off one or two of them while Miriam faded into the night.

That was the plan. Would any of it work?

It had to. They had to rescue Eve. There was no other way.

"Two of them just got out," she murmured. "One of them looks like the big Arab from the station. He's got a bandage on his forehead."

"The other must be Alayan." Jake shifted his pistol into his right coat pocket. "It's showtime."

Alayan stepped from the driver's seat to the asphalt, his boot soles crunching tiny fragments of pavement. He left the van's door open; they'd need every extra second to get away after they finished the Jews. The engine chugged and the headlights threw a dazzling white-blue patch on the road. Eldar and the woman would have to look into the light, while it would be at Alayan's back. Every little advantage counted.

They'd come to the end. In a few minutes, their mission would finally be complete. Eldar and Schaffer would try to fight the way they had before, but they were alone and up against himself and Gabir, while Sohrab commanded the entire arena with his rifle and scope. They wouldn't slither away this time.

He joined Gabir on the sidewalk. They stationed themselves at the outside corners of the bottom step, Gabir to his right, with a good eight meters between them. A clear field of fire for each of them; a spread target for the Jews.

A dark shape squeezed around one of the cracked-open front doors, took a step forward. "Alayan?" Eldar's voice.

"I am," Alayan said in English, just loud enough to carry the five or six meters between them. Sohrab should be lining up his shot now.

"We kept our part of the deal." Eldar sidestepped to his right, propped a foot atop the boxy half-wall flanking the top four stairs. "We're here. Where's my daughter?"

"The woman. She is here? I see her where?"

"Not until I see my daughter. Bring her out."

Alayan nodded to Gabir, who dropped back a few steps, slapped the van's side twice. Gabir advanced a pace and brought his pistol out in front of him, aimed at the concrete.

One of the van's back doors thunked open. Adult feet hit the road, then a murmur of what could be comfort, then Rafiq's voice: "That's a good girl." Rafiq stepped up on the sidewalk, the child in his arms, his eyes firmly aimed toward the chapel.

"Your daughter, Mr. Eldar," Alayan said with a sweep of his hand. "Now, the woman, please?"

Sasha anchored the scope's crosshairs to the chest of the beefy Arab standing near the van. Fifty meters and a big target; an easy shot. He'd already rehearsed the sequence: two rounds in the big bastard, a couple degrees swivel, two in the smaller one. Three, four seconds, and with his suppressor, the Arabs wouldn't know where the shots were coming from. Kelila could deal with the one who'd just scooped the kid out of the van.

He forced his breathing to slow. He had to wait until the Arabs either released the child or started shooting. Any moment, now.

Sasha caressed the trigger.

Sohrab had the Jew's head locked in the T-shaped crosshairs of his scope. An easy shot.

He had to hold his fire until the woman was in the clear. Where was she? Had she even come?

The door inched open. Another dark, human shape appeared in the doorway's shadow.

Sohrab's fingertip brushed the trigger.

❖

"Here she is." Jake notched his head back toward the sound of Miriam's feet scraping stone. "Now let Eve go. And, Alayan?"

"Yes, Mr. Eldar?"

Jake couldn't take his eyes off Eve as she clung to the third Arab standing at the foot of the stairs. His soul ached for her. *So close...* "The business between us has nothing to do with my daughter. I want your word you'll let her get out of the way before we finish this."

"Our deal is made, yes? Why I agree to this?"

"Because you think you're a soldier and not a thug," he hoped out loud. "Soldiers don't shoot children. Thugs do."

Was that a smile? "You tell this maybe to the Zionist army?"

Miriam snapped, "You first. Tell those bastards of yours to stop firing rockets at farmers."

"As the Zionist army shoots artillery at Lebanese women and children?"

"Sure, after some Hezbollah *zayin* kills Israeli women and children."

"That's enough," Jake growled. Miriam muttered a Hebrew curse. "Come on, Alayan, it doesn't cost you anything. Let her go, let her get to safety, then it's just you boys and us." He was glad he had his hands in his pockets; he could sop up the sweat on his palms. He and Miriam were helpless so long as the Arabs had Eve. He wouldn't put his daughter in the crossfire, no matter what it cost.

Alayan pursed his lips and seemed to consider Jake's request. After a moment, he nodded. "We are soldiers. Okay." He then motioned to the man holding Eve.

❖

Just another two steps, Sohrab urged the woman. *Just a bit more, then you're mine.*

He noticed movement at the edge of his scope's field of view.

He nudged the rifle's muzzle to the right.

Rafiq climbed the stairs toward Eldar and the woman. He held the brat in his arms.

What? Did the plan change? What's he doing? He was supposed to just let her go.

Sohrab snapped his aim back to Eldar. Rafiq's head was in the way now.

Sohrab would finish his job. Too bad for that weakling Rafiq if he got in the way.

❖

Jake watched the Arab approach, every nerve ending in his body on red alert. Was this the Rafiq guy Ziyad had mentioned? Was he going to get in a close-range shot, using Eve for cover? Jake wrapped his hand around the Glock's grip. If that's how they were going to play it, he'd make sure he took someone with him.

He glanced at Alayan. The man's eyebrows bunched together, his mouth crushed tight. Who was running this show?

The Arab stopped on the top step, even with Jake. He supported Eve's weight with one arm, wrapped the other around the back of her head, pressing her face into his neck. Eve's little body shuddered in his grip.

Jake and the Arab exchanged stares for a moment. Then the Arab made a gesture with the first two fingers of the hand behind Eve's head, pointing twice to the landing. He very slowly, carefully knelt.

Jake squatted warily, keeping his grip on the pistol, trying to figure out the plan.

The Arab gingerly set Eve on her feet, pulled her arms from his neck, and turned her to face Jake. Tear tracks glimmered in the lamplight below eyes that went huge when she saw him. The strip of duct tape across her mouth muffled her whimpers as she squirmed in the Arab's grip. "Please listen," he whispered. "I kept Eve away from the others. She's scared, but she's fine."

This must be Rafiq. His English had no accent; he could be the Channel 5 weatherman. "Um... thanks." Eve reached to Jake with both arms, but Rafiq held her back. Jake held out his left hand for her to grab. "It's going to be okay, Bunny," he murmured to her.

"There isn't much time," Rafiq continued. "There's a man in the trees behind us. Don't go that way."

"Why are you telling me this?" Jake hissed. "Who are you?"

Rafiq's eyes sagged. "I used to be a soldier. Now I kidnap children." He guided Eve into Jake's embrace. Even trembling and snuffling, she felt so good. "Send her into the chapel. When I step away, they're going to shoot. I'm sorry."

Both the Arabs on the sidewalk had their weapons ready. This Rafiq wasn't joking.

Jake kissed Eve's forehead, her cheeks, the side of her head, and stroked her hair. He wanted to hold her tight and never let go, to rip the tape from her mouth and hear her voice. But there was no time. He had to focus on staying alive and keeping her safe. Safe wasn't with him.

He nudged her away, then took her face in his hands, kissed her nose and whispered, "Bunny, I need you to listen and do exactly what I say. This is very important, understand?" She nodded. "Remember at the house a couple days ago, when you ran away from the bad guys?"

She nodded hard, hurt in her eyes.

"I need you to do that again, when—"

Her "No!" was clear, even through the duct tape. Eve yanked his coat collar with both hands.

"It's just for a few—"

"NO! NO!" came out "Nnnn! Nnnn!"

Jake held up a warning finger. "Listen to me." The fright in Eve's eyes turned into stubborn. She was just like her mother. "When I say 'go,' you run as fast as you can through that big door, okay?" She glared at him. "Jasmine's in my bag, under the bench. You need to get her and hide and keep her safe. It's just for a few minutes. You can take the tape off inside. Okay?"

Anger and fear fought in her big eyes. Her little fists tortured his collar. Finally, she nodded.

Jake pulled Eve against him, held her tight. "I love you so much, Bunny," he whispered in her ear. "I always, always will. And I'll always look out for you, even if I'm not around." *I will see her again*, he told himself. *I will. Somehow.*

With an exchanged nod, Jake and Rafiq stood simultaneously, their eyes locked. Eve clamped her arms around Jake's hips and buried her face in his stomach.

"I'm sorry about your wife," Rafiq said. "That was a mistake."

"No shit. Is that bastard Gabir here?"

"The man to your left, with the dressing. I see you already know he did it."

Jake flashed a glare at Gabir, who had his pistol trained on Miriam. Anger shot lava up his throat. Jake slid the Glock out of his pocket. *You're going down, asshole.*

Eve jerked on the front of his coat. She stared pop-eyed up at him. He tried to blank his face so he wouldn't scare her any more than she already was. "Remember what I said, Bunny?"

She peeked at Rafiq, then back to Jake, then nodded.

He took one last, hard look at Rafiq. "Go."

SEVENTY-EIGHT

22 DECEMBER
GREEN-WOOD CEMETERY, BROOKLYN

Alayan's anxiety spiked higher than the chapel dome. What was Rafiq doing? What was he saying to Eldar? Was he betraying them all? He steadied his aim on the back of Rafiq's head, now blocking Eldar's face as the two of them stood. *If that dog turns with a gun in his hand...*

The woman crouched in the doorway's shadow, aiming a pistol at Gabir, who aimed his at her.

The child scrambled through the chapel door.

A thunderbolt rammed through Alayan's body.

Time turned to rubber cement for Jake. His senses were impressions, snapshots.

Alayan crumpling to the sidewalk. Falling slow, as if through water. The *crack* of the sniper's shot echoing for hours.

Jake on one knee, Glock trained on Gabir, three white dots lined up on his sights. One shot, two. Holes in the Arab's billowing coat. The man's slow grunts rippling out like waves. The ping of spent casings on stone.

Gabir shooting at Miriam one-handed as she flung herself to the ground. The hollow *thump* of a hammer hitting a body. A gasp from Miriam.

Miriam on her side, grimacing, weapon held straight out in both hands. Twin muzzle blasts like lightning. The clank of bullet on metal, a spray of blood on the van's white paint. Gabir stumbling over the curb, toppling behind the van.

Rafiq in mid-stride dashing down the stairs. One bloody hole in his back, then a second. No weapons sounds, just his cry of surprise. Sprawling forward, hands out, head back.

Another crack, lower-pitched this time. A tug on his ear, the buzz of a huge, angry bee.

Time returned to normal speed.

"Miriam! Sniper! Theirs!"

❖

Miriam crawled over the half-wall, dropped to her hands and knees on the steps just as a second bullet sprayed her with more shards of stone. She huddled below the wall, took stock. A mule with giant steel hooves had kicked her in the gut. No blood, though; the vest had saved her again. This sniper would hit her before she got another three steps. Now what?

The rifle sounded again. She croaked out to Jake, "Are you okay?"

"Yeah. He's too damn close."

Another shot. She braced for the *zing* of lead striking stone at nine hundred miles per hour, but realized that should have already happened. Kaminsky's sniper? The echoes died away enough for her to hear the first police sirens in the distance. She and Jake had survived so far; just a few more minutes. "Now what?"

"I—where the hell is Alayan?"

❖

Sohrab let off his fourth round, then flattened to switch magazines and get his bearings. Someone had shot at him from his left, not from the direction of the chapel. Police? Would they have a sniper here? Was this a trap?

Alayan, Gabir and Rafiq were all down. Sohrab had heard the shot that hit Alayan, but not the one that got Rafiq, which meant someone had a silencer. *A second sniper?* He snatched up his night-vision monocular, probed the darkness. He couldn't see either of the Jews, but he knew where they were. Alayan's prone form inched past the van's nose. Gabir was behind the van. As

292

Sohrab watched, Rafiq's arm draped itself over his chest.

Something shrieked into the stone a foot away from his head, pelting him with fragments. The sniper with the silencer must also have a night-vision scope. *Madar sag! Hunt or escape?*

The splat of a bullet smashing into granite was loud in his ear, louder than the rifle shot he heard an instant later. He brushed the splinters from his face and let his anger guide him. *Forget the Jews. Time to hunt.*

❖

Alayan panted face-down on the asphalt immediately below the driver's door. Crawling twenty feet had drained his strength more than running twenty miles. The sniper's bullet had exploded inside him, and now every inhalation was like drowning and every exhalation forced blood into his mouth.

Snipers. Not one, but two, at least. How had Eldar managed it? It wasn't the police; they'd be swarming the area by now. This was something else.

It was over. His team was gone. He'd failed, and because he'd failed, the Party would fling itself off a cliff. He deserved to die here with his men.

He coughed hard, each spasm grinding his rib cage. Alayan spit out a mouthful of blood, then let his head sag onto his crooked left arm. He could stay here, rest, let the blackness now fuzzing the edges of his vision engulf him. So easy. So hard to move.

A thought staggered through the thickening fog in his brain: *you can't let them take you.* Not alive, not to be paraded on television, not to be the toy of every policeman and spy in America. That would be the ultimate humiliation. He'd lost his weapon somewhere by the chapel. He had to get away, to die someplace hidden, anonymous, to spare what was left of his family the curse of his captivity.

Get away.

The left side of his chest sloshed when he pushed himself onto his side. Reaching for the open door's sill was nearly as hard as grasping the nearby treetops. He gasped when he hauled himself semi-upright, clutching the steering wheel and the door's armrest.

The blood from the hole in his chest streamed down into his waistband.

Somehow he managed to lever himself into the driver's seat. He sagged against the wheel, trying to scrape up enough strength to close the door. A drumbeat echoed in the back of his head: *failure, failure, failure.*

Alayan jammed the gearshift into "drive" and wedged his foot on the gas.

❖

Gur slithered through a stand of trees, sliding his feet through the grass to keep from snapping any fallen twigs. The nearest rifle shot had come from just ten meters or so ahead.

He rounded a thick tree trunk, leading with his Beretta. A rank of tombs curved along the face of the rise until the gloom swallowed them, every one a great hiding place. Damn Eldar for choosing this place, if he did.

A shadow peeled away from the top of one of the tombs and scrambled toward the ornate mausoleum a few meters upslope at the crest of the ridge. Gur automatically fired at the ghost, who snapped a quick shot behind him with the rifle Gur had heard a few seconds before. The ghost dissolved into the darkness.

Gur flopped against the sheltering side of a tree trunk. The man he'd been stalking now held the high ground; Gur wasn't young enough or dumb enough to chase after him in the open.

He heard a shot farther along the slope, a smaller sound than the Hezbollah shooter's. Another sniper, but whose? Sasha had said someone else took out Alayan. If there was another sniper, then Gur and his team would have to avoid becoming targets themselves.

Three hostiles down including the leader, according to Sasha. One on the run. Both covers and the child still alive. A good few minutes' work. But now sirens approached from the north and west, and a supernova flash in the western sky told him a helicopter was on its way.

He keyed his radio. "Pull out. We're done here."

Sasha's voice squawked, "What about their sniper?"

"Let the other party take care of him."

"Alayan's heading your way!" Kelila barked.

Gur checked the car park. The van jerked away from the curb and rolled toward the road.

❖

Kelila had watched the covers and the two friendly snipers do their work the way she would a television program. It had been so fast and clean, it hadn't seemed real. But then the Hezbollah guy in the trees pinned her down, and now he was gone, Schaffer sheltered on her side in full view of Kelila's hide, gun at ready. Would Schaffer shoot her by mistake?

The van shuddered forward.

No! No escapes! This ends here! Schaffer or not, Kelila had to do something.

She bounded out from behind the big headstone, Beretta in her left hand, and fired twice into the blackness of the open back door. Kelila charged across the grass toward the retreating van, hurdled the big Arab's body, held up her right hand toward the steps. She yelled "Friend! Friend!" in English, hoping that was enough.

Movement snagged the corner of her eye. She glanced toward the steps. Eldar and Schaffer both tracked her with their weapons, but didn't shoot.

Kelila poured on the speed, sprinted toward the van now rapidly pulling away from the curb. *Get inside. Finish him.*

The van swerved onto the road leading to the front gate. It veered and overcorrected, slowed and lunged forward unpredictably, helping her close the distance.

The driver oversteered and took down an ornamental streetlight. The bulb's pop-flash seemed to freeze him for a moment—enough for her to catch up. The engine revved just as she leaped through the void and slammed into the hard, ridged metal floor inside. The van lurched beneath her, helped her roll to her knees.

Alayan hunched over the wheel, breathing hard, his head wobbling from side to side as he hauled the van away from a row of monuments. Kelila leveled her pistol. She could—should—kill him right now. At this speed, she'd survive the crash. She hadn't had any qualms about shooting these Hezbollah assholes since one of them killed her husband in the 2006 war. But she was a professional. Alayan's information had value, even if his miserable life didn't.

"Stop now!" she barked in Arabic.

Alayan looked back over his shoulder, almost lazy, like he had nothing but time. Blood coated his face from his nose down. "Or you'll shoot me?" he choked. "Please do."

She shot him in the right thigh.

The van swerved right and smashed into the hillside.

Sohrab crouched behind triple white headstones and waited. He'd been able to retreat to a hillock just overlooking the gingerbread-Gothic front gate without getting killed by either of the other snipers or the man with the pistol, whoever he was. Once he'd figured out they were tracking the sound of his rifle, he stopped shooting. He had a better weapon.

He peeked his monocular between the grave markers. The vivid lime-green form of his closest tracker darted past the monuments on the other side of the road, rapidly growing closer. This one had slung his rifle across his back and now constantly painted a wide arc with the pistol he gripped in both hands.

Sohrab unclipped his black, collapsible steel baton from his belt, pressed the release button, and silently extended it to its full two-thirds of a meter. That first time they'd tried to kill the Jew woman in Philadelphia, he'd used it to put down that muscle-bound cop with two strokes. This new enemy wouldn't be any harder.

He could hear the man's footfalls now, even over the growing chaos of sirens. A light tread, but not light enough. Sohrab tensed, masked his breathing, bounced on the balls of his feet to keep his knees and ankles limber.

A pistol and a pair of small black-gloved hands slid past the monument into his sight.

He brought the baton down hard on the man's wrists, felt the bones give but couldn't hear the crunch over the reflexive pistol shot. Sohrab popped up, aimed a vicious backswing at the man's throat. The gunman fell to his knees as if he'd been dropped from a great height. He tried to clutch his throat, then toppled onto his side. His pistol tumbled out of his useless hands.

Sohrab bent over the choking, gasping man and knocked the black baseball cap off his head. A knot of light-colored hair spilled out. The hands, the fine-featured face, the hair... a *woman?* Another damned *woman* had been hunting him? This wasn't the one from the train station. Where did they all come from? They belonged at home with their children.

The clank of metal crashing into an immovable object caused Sohrab to twist to his left. The van's nose was jammed into the steep slope at the base of the hill; a bit of steam already escaped from under the hood. Alayan hadn't got far.

Sohrab looked down at the gasping blonde at his feet. He could just let her suffocate, but she was a woman, so he decided to be merciful. He snapped her neck with the baton, then charged downslope toward a line of headstones to see what was happening with Alayan.

Jake could still hear occasional shots, but they didn't seem to have anything to do with him anymore. He stood straight, squared his shoulders. Nothing. "I think we're clear."

Miriam swayed to her feet, pistol ready, and pivoted through a visual search of the area. "Who was that woman?"

"Maybe the Mossad chick. You okay?"

"Okay enough."

Jake watched Gabir drag himself through his own blood toward his pistol, a few feet away on the drive. When the Arab was almost within reach, Jake strode to the gun and kicked it into the landscaped oval. Gabir wheezed in defeat, looked up though eyes brimming with pain.

Jake said, "You're the asshole who killed my wife."

The man's eyes shifted from pain to resignation. He opened his mouth twice to speak, but couldn't or changed his mind. He finally nodded, coughed, winced.

Jake closed his eyes. This son-of-a-bitch took away the best thing in his life—by *mistake.* That part was unbearable. Rinnah died because of a mistake. *God damn him.*

He glanced behind him. Miriam stood a few feet away, her left arm clutched around her stomach. She stared back at him, her face partly lit by the glow of a streetlight but not enough for him to read her expression.

Jake looked down at Gabir—at the blood dribbling from the man's mouth, the seeping holes in his chest—and felt triumph surge through him. He hadn't until this moment heard his primal brain scream for revenge since the day Rinnah died. The civilized part he'd spent the past decade nurturing was horrified by his reaction, but it was smothered by a pulsating cloud of red-hot hate.

He saw Rinnah's dead face, the black hole above her eyes. Her tear of blood.

He raised the gun, aimed at Gabir's forehead, and pulled the trigger.

He didn't know how long he stood there. Probably only a few seconds. The next thing Jake was truly aware of was Miriam's voice. "You had to."

Jake had fired all his hate into Gabir along with the bullet. Now a familiar gray void took its place. He realized he was still aiming at the man's ruined head and let his hand fall to his side.

"If you didn't, it would've haunted you for the rest of your life. Believe me, I know."

He looked up from the dead man to find Miriam standing on the other side of the body, her face set hard against the pain in her midriff.

"You're bleeding," she said. "Your ear."

He reached up to touch the hot, tingling spot on his right ear. His fingers came away with blood. The sniper had missed by a whisper. He swallowed hard, took in a ragged breath.

They flinched in unison when another shot sounded from the trees. Recovering, Miriam asked, "What did that other man say to you? The one with Eve? I couldn't hear."

"He told me about this piece of shit." Jake motioned toward the body.

298

Sirens echoed through the trees and tombs. Miriam scanned the access road. "Let's get Eve. We should go."

"Is it done? Did we get them all?" Jake tried to believe it, but the threat he'd lived under for a month wouldn't let loose of him that easily. He turned to stare at the man sprawled on the sidewalk at the foot of the steps. "I'll bet he knows, if he's still alive."

They paced to Rafiq's side. Jake knelt by him and gently rolled the man onto his back. More blood, more coughing. Rafiq whistled when he breathed.

What should Jake say to the terrorist assassin who took care of his daughter and possibly saved her life? Thanks? His tongue was so confused it couldn't get a coherent word out.

"Eve?" Rafiq whispered.

"Inside. She's okay."

"Good."

"Are there more of you? Are we still in danger?"

Rafiq gulped in a dollop of air. "Another group. Not us." Gasp, cough. "Truck bomb. In the city." He squeezed his eyes shut, rolled his head forward. The pain and effort marched across his face. "Super 8. North Bergen." He let his head fall back, began panting fast and shallow.

Jake realized his mouth had fallen open. A truck bomb? Here? He felt Miriam's hand on his shoulder, looked up into her stunned face. "You heard that, right?"

She nodded. "Where?" she asked Rafiq. "When do they attack?"

Rafiq turned unfocused eyes on Miriam's face. "Tomorrow. Don't know target."

Tomorrow? Jake shook his head into gear, tried to ignore the craziness of the situation. "How many? What do they look like? Who are they?"

"Truck in. Global Storage. Under..." Rafiq's hand spasmed into a fist. "Under Alvarez. From the twelfth."

Oh, fuck. This can't be real! The blood slowly creeping across the sidewalk told Jake that Rafiq was dying, though he realized it with none of the joy he'd felt at Gabir's pain. This man didn't need to make up stories; he no longer had a use for lies.

A helicopter shredded the sky overhead, carved a tight orbit over the chapel no more than a hundred feet up. The spotlight pinned all three of them in a painfully bright, jittering circle of white-blue light. "NYPD," a voice boomed over the loudspeaker. "Lay down your weapons and put your hands in the air. Do not try to escape."

"Better do it," Jake told Miriam. "Put your gun on the sidewalk, raise your hands. These guys don't have a sense of humor."

She peered up through the glare at the chopper, then placed her Walther next to Rafiq's foot. "What about you?"

"In a minute." He leaned in to Rafiq, wrapped his hand around the Arab's clenched fist. "Anything else? How do we find these guys?"

Rafiq had screwed his eyes shut when the light flipped on. He shook his head. "Don't know. Don't talk to us." The effort he'd put into those few words launched him into coughs that jolted his upper body off the ground. Blood splattered from his mouth, down his cheek.

"Hang in there, Rafiq." A part of Jake asked *what are you saying to this animal?* "The cops are here, they'll fix you up."

"Too late," Rafiq gasped, barely audible above the helicopter's scream. "Too late."

A few moments later, he was gone.

SEVENTY-NINE

22 DECEMBER
GREEN-WOOD CEMETERY, BROOKLYN

Gur wrenched open the wrecked van's passenger door, thrust his Beretta inside and said in Arabic, "Keep your hands where I can see them."

Alayan, slumped in his seat, cranked his head to look in Gur's direction. The blood stink from him nearly turned Gur's stomach, and Gur had smelled a lot of blood in his time. Alayan coughed out what might have been a laugh. "Just shoot me. Your girl won't."

Girl? Gur glanced into the back and saw Kelila's face reflecting the dim street light, a paper napkin pressed to her nose. What was she doing in the van? "Are you all right?"

She nodded. "I hit my nose on the headrest when we crashed."

Gur slid into the passenger's seat. A helicopter roared overhead, its spotlight momentarily turning the evening into high noon. The harsh light showcased the blood covering Alayan from nose to knees. The Arab didn't have long to live. "Alayan? Or should I say, 'Mr. Alvarez?'" He caught the twitch in Alayan's face. "Oh, yes, I know. I saw you at Eldar's flat. I called the police. Too bad we didn't finish our business there."

"It's okay," Alayan croaked. "I had work."

"I know." Gur leaned in, breathing through his mouth to cut down the butcher-shop smell. "The police will be here in a minute. If they take you, they'll keep you alive on machines and tubes. They'll put your picture on every newspaper and television with the title 'failed terrorist.' Do you want that?"

Alayan hacked twice. His entire body shook from the effort. "Would you?"

"No. Tell me what I want to know and I guarantee they won't

301

arrest you. Understand?" No answer, just distant, dark eyes. "How many on your team?"

After a moment of fighting to breathe, Alayan whispered, "Fuck you. Shoot me now."

Stubborn Arab idiot. "Your man in the trees, the sniper. Who is he?"

Silence, except for the man's rasping. Flashing blue lights reflected off the main gate's stone spires. The helicopter rumbled through a tight circle behind them.

None of them had much time. Gur switched to Hebrew. "Kelila, get out of here. Meet up with Sasha as we planned. I'll be along in a minute."

"I'm not leaving you alone with that insect."

She had a let-me-help glint in her eyes. But any moment the police would come crashing in, and he couldn't bear the thought of her being caught and interrogated, perhaps going to prison. "I've been alone with much more dangerous insects. Please. We have to split up to avoid the police anyway. I won't be far behind you."

She frowned, shot a worried glance between him and Alayan. "Is that an order?"

"It is."

Kelila nodded. "Be careful."

She disappeared out the back door without another look behind her.

Sohrab focused the monocular on the van's windshield. Two men. The one behind the wheel draped the seat rather than sitting in it: Alayan. The other man-shaped blob faced Alayan from the passenger's side, leaning forward, talking.

Police? Perhaps. At least five police cars blocked the front gate, just a few dozen meters to Sohrab's right, their strobing lights casting bizarre shadows all around him. The helicopter droned over the chapel, its searchlight a perfect white cone underneath its belly. Still more sirens screamed down the streets.

If the police had Alayan, he could tell them far more than they should ever hear. But there was only one man with him; the others huddled behind their cars, guns drawn, waiting. Sohrab could still salvage the situation. He'd get only one shot, though; too many police were too close to risk more.

He steadied the rifle's barrel on a headstone.

❖

Alayan's view out the windscreen dimmed with each agonizing breath. Blue lights, orange clouds, black shapes of buildings and monuments, all out of focus. His mind drifted like a toy boat caught in the surf at Khalde beach. He loved going to that beach as a child. He could see the sky all around him there, not just a slot of blue between the high-rises.

"Who's your handler? Who do you report to?"

Damned Zionist, still asking questions. But even as he felt the last of his life trickle down his chest, Alayan wouldn't betray his team or the Party.

"You beat me," he rasped. "But you lost."

"What do you mean?"

Alayan licked his lips. "The Party. Always has. Another plan."

"A bomb team?" The Jew's voice crackled. "Like Hamburg and Rome?"

The bomb. He'd driven himself and his men to the limit to stop this "other plan," but now his failure guaranteed it would go forward. But tell this thug? "Why should. I help you? You killed my wife. Mother. Father. Bombed my city. Go to hell."

"Your people murdered my wife." The Zionist's voice was diamond-hard. "Everyone on your team, everyone on mine, we've all lost someone, we've all been wronged."

Alayan rolled his head back to center, fixed his gaze on the police lights a few dozen meters away. Instead he saw his wife and parents, one moment alive and happy, the next dead, burned, mangled. *We've all been wronged.*

The Zionist leaned close enough for Alayan to feel his heat. "Tell me about the bomb. If you help, we can stop the next wrong. We can save others from what's happened to us."

The vision of his dead family dissolved into a nightmare of scattered, bloody bodies of strangers, women, children, burning wreckage and dust and broken glass and sirens. Like so many bombings he'd seen growing up in Beirut.

Alayan willed his mind to drift back to the beach, the sun, the blue sky of home, but the Jew's words snagged him like a rock in the water. *Stop the next wrong.* Stop the bombs? Alayan had devoted these last years of his life to show the Party another way. He'd failed.

He could save the Party from its own stupidity, but it meant betraying the Party. To this gangster? Maybe Allah had given Alayan this Zionist as one last test.

Samirah, what do I do?

He couldn't see or hear his martyred wife anymore.

He panted like a winded horse but still couldn't get enough air. It was so hard to swallow. If only he had water, anything to wash the bitter, coppery muck from his mouth.

Stop the next wrong?

The world outside the van grew dimmer still. Alayan gulped down enough breath to whisper one word. "Majid."

"What's Majid? A name? The operation?"

Out in the night, straight ahead, Alayan saw a white flash. A star? A burst of light, all its brilliance spent in one great moment of life.

When the flash died, so did Alayan's world.

EIGHTY

"You *knew?*"

"Of course we knew." If Orgad objected to the acid in Gur's tone, the phone connection masked it. "The moment the Germans broke the Hamburg cell, we assumed Hezbollah would have teams in the other four nations. That's why we had no replacements for Amzi and Natan."

"And you didn't think to tell me?"

"Really, Raffi. I'm surprised you're surprised. It was inevitable that someday they'd do something like this. You've just confirmed that someday is now."

Gur halted his pacing at the edge of the bright trapezoid spilling onto the sidewalk through the all-night kebab store's dirty window. He kicked the wall in frustration. "There was a third sniper there besides the Arab and Sasha, a friendly. Was he Kaminsky's?"

Orgad's chair creaked in the background. "As it turns out, yes. He wasn't authorized to engage, not that he bothered to tell us he was going to. We've recalled him and he's gone dark. The Director is very unhappy with him since one of his people turned up dead in a public firefight. So now it's down to you."

Of course. The moment Alayan told him about the "other plans," Gur began to hear Orgad's voice in his head ordering him to find this Majid, whoever or whatever it was. He'd hoped to get a few hours sleep first, though. "How do I get to Kaminsky?"

"You don't. If he happens to contact you, grab him and drag him home by his ears. We'll send you what we've given him. Now that your original mission is done, you need something to do, and you're already there."

"I'm always glad to save the Institute from spending money."

"Don't be that way, Raffi. You redeemed yourself tonight. Consider this a reward. A Hezbollah bomb in America may be the most important event this decade. Of course, if you don't find it…" Gur could almost hear the shrug over the phone.

Inside the store, Gur slid onto a one-piece laminate bench next to Kelila. The bored clerk at the counter didn't look up from his Turkish music magazine. Three people in black fatigues eating dinner and no one notices; only in New York. Gur surveyed the robust shawarma Sasha attacked on the other side of the table. "How can you eat that thing so late?"

"It's not even midnight," Sasha mumbled through a mouthful. "I have to eat sometime."

Kelila slid her paper plate of four falafel balls to a place Gur could reach. He broke one in half, dragged it through the paper ramekin of tahini and popped the golden-brown snack into his mouth. Not bad, but not up to Falafel Hakosem in central Tel Aviv. The taste of chickpea and sesame and the random memory of home it sparked left him even wearier than before. He sighed. "We have a new mission."

"Majid?" Kelila asked. Gur nodded. "Can we get some more sleep first?"

"Probably not. We have to play catch-up." Gur pushed the other half of his falafel around its corner of the plate. He never was hungry after an action. Once again he watched Alayan die in front of him, a third eye drilled in his forehead. Kaminsky's sniper? Or Alayan's own? "Eldar and Schaffer had some time with Raad and the other Arab, didn't they?"

"They might have," Kelila said. "They were on the steps when I went after the van, but after that I can't say. I don't know if the Arabs were still alive then."

"Eldar talked to one of them," Sasha said. "The one carrying the child, before the shooting started. They were at it for a minute or so."

"Really? Kelila, did you—"

"No, I couldn't hear them. I heard Alayan and Eldar talking, but they were pretty loud. They didn't say anything about Majid."

That would have been too easy. Gur let his gaze wander to the window but didn't register anything except darkness. "Desperate times," he muttered to himself.

"We have less than a day," Kelila pointed out. "Do we have anything we can work with?"

"We have a deadline. Where would the police take Eldar and Schaffer?"

"The local station, I guess. My computer's in the flat or I'd look up which one. Why?"

Why indeed? They were less than fifteen minutes into this new operation, and already he was grasping at straws. "All through this, Eldar's been a step or two ahead of us. We should find out if he knows anything more."

Sasha exchanged a dubious glance with Kelila. "You want us to pick them up, boss?"

Gur considered this a moment—the many possible ways it could go bad, the few ways it could pay off. Unfortunately, the latter outweighed the former. "Kelila, I want you to bring them both in." He focused on her. "When we get back to the flat, figure out where they might be. Then change into your nicest clothes and wait for them. It may take a while. Eldar might not react well if I'm there, but you may be able to bring him around. You can also work on Schaffer and see if she'll help convince Eldar. She wasn't screwed quite as badly back home as he was."

"How far do I take it if they won't come?"

"Do what you need to." *Force?* He hoped it wouldn't come to that, but it was always an option. "Sasha, reserve suites at the Brooklyn Sheraton for them and us. Stock their bar and get room service on standby. By the time the police are done with them, they're going to be tired and hungry. A little kindness might go a long way."

"As we kindly kidnap them," Kelila mumbled.

"Right. Finish your food, both of you. This is our only lead. Let's not let it slip away."

EIGHTY-ONE

23 DECEMBER
BROOKLYN

Jake rested his head on his folded forearms but no longer tried to get any sleep. His closed eyelids glowed orange from the bright strip lights in the interview room. He was too tired to sleep, too wrung out from the past couple of days—hell, the past five weeks—and too intent on Rafiq's last words.

Six hours of interrogation so far with no end in sight. A revolving cast of 72nd Precinct detectives had kept at him since the moment the patrol officers brought him in, grilling him as if *he* was a terrorist. Just procedure, he knew. Except for one: Tatum, forties and going to seed fast, who'd come in with an attitude and kept it going strong. "Two weeks on the job and you're bucking for Commissioner, huh?" he'd sneered. Later, it was, "Ready for your medal, Rambo?"

The union lawyer next to Jake didn't say anything, his default setting. Jake said, "Is there a problem?"

"Yeah, showboat, there's a problem." Tatum threw down his pen. "You do your army-of-one thing and go chase bad guys and you're a fucking *analyst*. This far from little people." He held his thumb and forefinger an inch apart, right in Jake's face. "You get in our shit and leave us to clean up. Hope you have a good time on TV."

Jealous? This asshole was *jealous?* Jake ignored the red mist in his vision and got in the detective's face. "You want it?" Jake growled at him. "You want the 'glory'? You want the medal? Great. Bring back my wife and fix my daughter so she won't have nightmares for the rest of her life and you can have it. *All of it.* It's yours."

308

That was an hour ago. They'd left him alone ever since.

The door clacked open. He looked up to see a short, thick-chested man step inside and close the door behind him. Rumpled blue suit shirt, loose tie, shoulders that come from weightlifting.

"Hello, sir," Jake sighed. "Long day for you, too."

"Uh-huh." Menotti spun the other padded chrome chair around, straddled it, passed his palm over his wavy black hair going grey at the temples. "You've been asking for me. What don't you want to say to the detectives, and why?"

Jake sat up, stretched his arms behind him until his joints stopped popping. He then glanced at the camera in the far corner of the room, near the ceiling. "You saw the tapes?"

"Uh-huh. That's a hell of a story, even if it's only half a story. What's the rest? Al-Amin and one of the stiffs at Green-Wood were at Philly station, right?" Again, Jake eyed the camera. "It's off. So's the mike. It's just you and me, Jake. What's the problem?"

"Someone blew the safe house, you know that. I don't know who I can trust. So…"

Menotti pulled a cell phone, thumbed in a number, listened, then said, "Put him on." He handed the phone to Jake.

"Hello?"

"Hey, kid." Gene's voice, tired and weak, but a wonderful sound.

"Gene! Thank God. I wanted to come by, but…"

"I know, you've been busy. Sal told me. Monica said you called." Jake winced when Gene grunted and let out a muffled "augh." "Sorry, kid. Can't get comfortable in this damn bed. Fucking doctors keep giving me this stuff, makes it like there's fuzz on everything."

"You have no idea how good it is to hear you swear."

"Yeah, yeah. Look, Sal's good people, we go way back. Trust him like you trust me. No, better than that. Listen for once. Play straight, he'll back you up. Got it?"

Jake couldn't help smiling. "Okay, Gene. You get better. I'll be by soon."

Menotti took back his phone, dropped it in his shirt pocket, folded his arms on the chair back. "Talk. Start at the safe house, work up to now. Go slow, I'm tired."

"Wait. Where's Eve?"

"With ACS in the break room. Half the precinct's in love with her by now, so if you end up on Rikers, there's plenty of fosters for her."

Fosters? Like hell he'd let that happen. "How's Miriam?"

"Fine. She's next door. She's holding out, too." He glared at Jake. "Talk."

Jake talked for nearly ninety minutes, detailing everything he and Miriam had done from the moment they fled the Crown Heights safe house to the instant the police snapped handcuffs on them at the chapel. Menotti asked a few questions but otherwise just listened, letting his eyebrows and hand gestures make his comments for him. At the end, Jake slumped in his chair, drained, and focused on the now-empty liter bottle of water on the table before him.

Menotti sighed, shook his head with a worrying amount of solemnity. Finally he said, "Do you know how many felonies you just confessed to?"

Oh, shit. "A few?"

"More than that. The really impressive part is, you did it in less than two days. On the other hand, you took down five terrorists."

"I got one, sir."

Menotti fired a flamethrower look at Jake. "You took down *five* terrorists. Maybe—just maybe—we can get a Jack Bauer exemption for you." He pushed out of the chair and headed for the door. "I have to talk to the Commissioner and the Feds. Stay here and don't say anything to anyone, understand?"

Jake couldn't believe they weren't going to hang him out to dry. Or maybe they were.

If he didn't end up in prison, what then? At the safe house, Google had given him over a million hits on "coping with grief." Several had talked about finding a "new normal." He still couldn't imagine a normal featuring that huge hole where Rinnah should be.

Once he was out of here, he needed to hold onto Eve and not let go, let her know he had enough love to make up for Rinnah's missing share, show her he wouldn't leave her again, that she was safe. To hell with this special-ops bullshit; from here out he needed to be the best dad ever. He had no idea how he'd pull that off, but knowing he had to was scarier than being shot at.

What about Miriam? Where does she fit in?

Good question. Eve liked her. Jake had come to like her, too, although it still felt like cheating on Rinnah. But she had her life in Philadelphia—work, home, friends, probably a boyfriend—and she'd want to go back to it, forget all this insanity... and him, and Eve.

That thought hurt far more than he'd expected.

Menotti returned two hours later, his shirt more rumpled, his tie completely gone. He thunked a new liter bottle of water in front of Jake and straddled his chair again. "All right, here's the play. We're going to turn on the camera and you're going to tell your story again, from the top. Only, it was all you. You used 'enhanced interrogation techniques' on al-Amin, ones you learned in the Israeli Army. When you called me yesterday, I authorized you to continue the investigation. You shot the three at the chapel in self-defense. You tracked the gal on the hill and killed—"

Jake perked up. "Gal?"

"Uh-huh. The one on the hill, with the sniper rifle. Busted arms, busted neck, crushed windpipe."

"She's not Hezbollah. They wouldn't use a woman." Jake had a vision of the Mossad woman at the chapel. "What color was her hair?"

"Blond. Long, down past her shoulders."

The female agent who chased Alayan's van had short, pitch-black hair. "She's Kaminsky's. Which means Hezbollah's sniper killed her and got away." *One's still out there*, he realized. This part wasn't over after all. He ran the Hezbollah team's lineup through his increasingly foggy brain. "It's the Persian kid. You already have a sketch of him. Miriam and I both saw him at 30th Street Station."

"Aw, hell." Menotti ran his hand over his hair, left it wrapped around the back of his head for a moment. "Whatever. Mention him. We'll pin Alayan on him, which is probably the way it was anyway. But the woman's Hezbollah and you did her hand-to-hand before all the rest went down. Otherwise we have to explain who she really was."

Are you insane? "But—"

Menotti shot his palm straight out at Jake. "Listen, don't talk. The Bureau's taken charge of the bodies. They'll do the post at Quantico, they'll make sure they come up with the right answers. That's how this plays. No Kaminsky, no Mossad. Your girlfriend was just—"

"She's not my girlfriend."

"If she did all the things you said, *and* she's covering for you, she damn well ought to be. Like I said, she was along for the ride. If it's you, we can work out an LOD determination for this mess. If it's her, she'll be looking at a few years upstate."

"But this is so far outside my line of duty—"

"Your job is to catch terrorists. You caught terrorists. We'll work it. Right now, we have to explain a live scumbag in custody, one on the loose, four dead bodies and a lot of shooting at Green-Wood. We'll make the story simple. Besides, it's already going out to the *Times*."

"Miriam gets away clean?"

"Uh-huh."

"What about the bomber? There's less than a day left."

"Already working it. FBI's getting warrants now."

Jake propped his elbows on the table and rested his eye sockets on his upturned palms. The "simple story" meant everything got pinned on him. They probably were going to try to make him some kind of hero, for God's sake. If it fell apart, he'd be burnt toast. But Miriam would go free and he might survive to watch Eve grow up. A good enough trade? It was the only one he'd get, so it had to be.

He ignored the sour taste of doom in the back of his mouth and looked up at Menotti. "Okay, sir, I'll make the statement. Let's do this."

EIGHTY-TWO

23 DECEMBER, 6:45 AM
NORTH BERGEN, NEW JERSEY

Al-Shami leaned a shoulder against the warehouse's brown concrete wall, lit a cigarette, drew deep, blew the smoke over his right shoulder. In his flannel and watch cap, he was just another worker waiting for the doors to open. He'd left the binoculars in his car. A man smoking isn't suspicious; a man with binoculars is.

The Super 8 motel hunched on the other side of traffic-choked Highway 495. Squat, white, two floors stretching back from the highway, each side lined with half-full parking. The early-morning gloom sucked the color out of everything, making this desolate commercial area even more barren and depressing.

The first police cars had arrived thirty minutes earlier, just as he'd expected. Now the driveways into the motel were blocked by a collection of marked and unmarked cars—North Bergen, Hudson County, New Jersey State Police, a lone NYPD car, black four-wheel-drive vehicles, an ambulance—stretched along the access road west of the motel. SWAT had just scrambled along the edge of the car park on the low bluff overlooking the building's east side.

The police formed up into their groups on either end of the motel. Al-Shami pinched out his cigarette, stuck the butt in his pocket, and waited for the show.

At precisely seven, the police charged up the outside stairwells and poured down the walkway toward four rooms in the middle of the motel's east-facing side. Men in tactical gear, helmets and assault rifles led the uniformed and plainclothes police with their shotguns and pistols. They ducked beneath the four rooms' windows, took up position outside each room. Yes, there were the two men flanking each door. Yes, now the pipe-like door rams.

313

Police around the world must follow the same manual.

Doors smashed in, men raced inside. Al-Shami smiled as he pictured the shouting and waving of guns. And just about now...

Black smoke poured out each doorway. After a few moments, the smoke turned gray as the motor oil he'd pooled on the sheets gave way to the burning bedding. One by one, police tumbled from the rooms, coughing and waving their arms.

"That'll keep them busy," al-Shami said to himself. He turned and walked toward his rental car a block away.

Today's headlines on the New York *Times* front page had made him glad he and his team hadn't stayed in these rooms Jabbar had rented. They'd checked in, of course, and he and Fayiz had come back to leave their little gift for the police. But he'd never actually use travel arrangements anyone else had made, not if he wanted to stay alive.

On his way through the morning damp to the car, he considered the new problem from his handler Altair. The last surviving member of Jabbar's team had asked Beirut for instructions. Could al-Shami use him, then extract him?

Normally, al-Shami hated working with people he didn't know. Altair had hinted at the "political considerations" around this one, which usually meant the damned Iranians were involved. Not that al-Shami cared, but Hezbollah would soil themselves trying to keep their sponsors happy. And they were the clients, after all.

He reached his dark green Chevrolet sedan, checked the underside and wheel wells for unwanted presents, then backed off and unlocked it with the remote. No explosion; good. He looked back toward the motel, chuckled at the plume of smoke.

Take this new man or not? This Sohrab had survived that battle in the graveyard, so he was either capable or a coward, and it was unlikely he was a coward. Fayiz was increasingly miserable with a stomach bug he'd picked up on the road. The heightened security around the target made an extra man desirable.

Very well, then. He'd call Altair and make the contact. They didn't have much time. In twelve hours, they'd either be victorious or dead. Or, perhaps, both.

314

EIGHTY-THREE

23 DECEMBER, 3:00 PM CET

Over seventy tourists waited in a line that stretched from the museum entrance across the Westermarkt's brick pavers, then east along the neat brick wall of the café Werck. The saw-toothed wind off Amsterdam's Prinsengracht canal tore at their winter coats and pinked their faces.

The Westerkirk's hour bell bonged three times.

A sudden rush of visitors spewed out the museum's exits. Two women and a man wearing museum ID tags shouted, "Please move back! Please!" repeating the same words in Dutch and English as they shooed the evacuees and the queue away from the museum's glass walls. A fire-alarm klaxon ratcheted through the open doors.

Two police cars followed the blare of their sirens into the opposite end of Westermarkt. They swerved into a vee formation across the street, blocking it. Around the corner from the museum, a white police VW Golf slid to a halt just shy of the Werck, closing the road along the canal. More sirens wailed in the distance, grew louder.

In the confusion, almost no one noticed a white Mercedes van slip behind two police vans as they charged onto the short stub of Westermarkt from the Keizersgracht. No one except the driver of the second police van, Anje Rogier, a short, blond female cop four days on the job.

Rogier checked the mirror again. The vehicle behind her didn't have a light bar or the familiar red-and-blue stripes on the side and nose, and its driver was a dark-skinned civilian. It showed no sign of stopping. She took in the swirling crowd rapidly filling her windscreen.

How could someone attack the Anne Frank House?

She acted before she could think. Rogier stomped her brakes and slewed across the intruder's path.

The intruder plowed into her van's left side, blasting glass and air-bag powder through its cabin. Tires shrieked across the brick pavement.

The last thing Anje Rogier saw was the bloody-faced driver of the third van slamming his palm against his dashboard as he broke into a triumphant grin.

❖

The grinding racket of the fire alarm drowned out the well-lubricated buzz of five hundred Crédit Industriel de l'Orient managers and executives mingling, gossiping and flirting in the two-story nave of Paris' Palais Brongniart. Until this moment, the Champagne flowed as relentlessly as the Seine and the *hors d'oeuvres* piled up like the bank's gaudy profits. The only nod toward politically prudent modesty was the unfashionably early hour, meant to limit the extravagance (no orchestra, no pop-star entertainment, and no "+1" guests) and the drinking.

The event manager tapped the microphone on the dais. "*Mesdames! Messieurs!* Our apologies. Please leave the building through the main entrance. There is no danger." The ushers and serving help echoed their boss' instructions as they herded the still-festive group through the main doors into the grand colonnaded portico and the plaza beyond.

Guillaume Berton hung back, matching his companion's progress step-for-step. Celeste was a sleek brunette new to the bank's compliance department, and from the moment they'd both grabbed for the same flute of Champagne forty minutes before, they'd wrapped their conversation around themselves like insulation against their colleagues. She had quick eyes, lips that bore much watching and an ivory knit dress that was both demure and ravishingly provocative. A ring, but no mention of a husband to go with it. Two years after Thérèse had disappeared into a Parisian autumn, Berton allowed himself to hope he'd not spend another Christmas alone.

Sirens greeted them when they stepped outside: the familiar

two-tone shrill of police cars, the lower-pitched blare of fire engines. Berton and Celeste paused next to one of the portico's giant granite columns to watch the show.

Car horns, squealing tires. A white van slalomed through traffic on Rue Vivienne, cutting off oncoming cars on Rue du 4 Septembre. A police Renault, blue light strobing and siren wailing, followed just seconds behind.

The van swerved past the green news kiosk on the corner, jounced over the curb, and plunged into the midst of nearly five hundred people milling in the forecourt between the Palais and Rue Vivienne.

"*Baise!*" Berton gasped.

The van slammed into a man in a black suit, sent him flying into the now-screaming crowd, then plowed over a woman already on the ground. People scattered like gazelle from a cheetah. Those closest to the Palais stampeded toward the grand staircase.

Berton clamped his arms around Celeste's waist, then flung them both to the floor behind the column's base.

A flash. A thunderclap.

Every pane in every window behind them turned to dust and daggers. Then a hail of tiny projectiles smashed against the columns and walls—the sound a "snick" times a thousand—spraying stone chips and steel throughout the portico. Berton covered a sobbing Celeste's head and face as best he could, caught something sharp in his elbow, felt a slice across his cheek. The bloody, riddled body of an usher collapsed next to him. Shrieks drowned the crackle of fire.

Berton glanced down at the marble floor beneath him. A silver ball bearing, chipped on one side, lay just beside Celeste's trembling shoulder. He flicked it away.

Just beyond the column, a battlefield stretched to the street.

EIGHTY-FOUR

23 DECEMBER, 9:40 AM
WILLIAMSBURG, BROOKLYN

Gur checked the number on his mobile's screen, then thumbed the "answer" button. "Kelila?"

"Where are you?"

He squinted through the windshield at the street signs across the road from his parking place. "Kent and Hooper in Brooklyn, by one of the ugliest temples I've ever seen. It's like an aircraft hangar but with less style." Still, according to the list of potential targets he'd received from headquarters, Kehilas Yetev Lev was one of the largest Haredi synagogues in the world, capable of seating up to 4,300 people.

"When are you coming back?"

Gur finally caught the anxiety in her voice. "What's wrong?"

She joggled her phone, sucked in a breath. "About ten minutes ago, another bomb went off outside the Palais Brongniart in Paris. There—"

"What's that?"

"It used to be the Paris Bourse. There was some kind of Christmas party there. The news is saying 'dozens dead,' but there's nothing concrete so far."

"How does that fit the pattern?"

"It doesn't!" Kelila's frustration blasted through the tinny connection. "It's the old Exchange, Jews in finance, *I don't know*, it just happened."

Gur sagged against the Taurus' driver's seat, stared at the beige-and-brown slab of a temple without seeing it. This, and the Anne Frank House? It made no sense at all. "All right, check it out. Have the police released Eldar and Schaffer yet?"

"No. Sasha's getting nervous, he's afraid he'll be spotted." She sighed. "Raffi, they've probably told the police everything they know by now."

"Are you willing to risk having the locals botch another raid?" he snapped. "That they'd miss something we might see? We need to talk to them."

"We're wasting time!" she spat back. "It's going on ten. Sasha's fighting to stay awake, and I'm useless here in the hotel. We need a plan, not whatever this mess is."

Gur knew he deserved the rebuke. They all were tired; he needed to be more focused. "Sorry. You're right. Go keep Sasha awake. The minute Eldar and Schaffer leave the precinct, bring them in. Don't let them say 'no.' I'll be back soon."

Once Kelila cut the connection, Gur squeezed his gritty eyes closed. Kelila was right: they were wasting time, and they needed a plan. He considered the next temple on his list, Shaare Zion, a Syrian congregation; damned unlikely Hezbollah would dare touch that, given how deep they were into Syria's pocket. He certainly wasn't going to drive all the way out to that crazy *shtetl* in the exurbs to look at what supposedly was the largest—and most obscure—temple in America. Given Amsterdam and Paris, were synagogues even on the agenda anymore?

They needed more information. A break. More time. Anything but this shitty hand Orgad dealt them.

He checked his watch. Nine hours before sunset. Nine hours to stop a disaster.

EIGHTY-FIVE

23 DECEMBER, 10:40 AM

Four men stared up at the imposing building across the street.

"The pictures don't do it justice, do they?" Al-Shami had looked at so many photos of this place, being here felt strange. His first face-to-face confrontation with the target always felt surreal.

Mahir calmly looked around them, at the hurrying cars and tall buildings, the milky sky and the colorful banners hanging from the lamp posts. "That's the entry?"

Al-Shami noticed the dullness in the man's drooping eyes. He was on his pain medication again. "Yes. Once you're inside, pick the right time to detonate. Remember, your goal is to frighten, not kill. We need the people to panic and leave the building quickly. Haroun will take care of them once they're outside."

Mahir nodded slowly. If the plan caused him difficulty, he didn't show it. Then again, he'd had plenty of time to become used to the reality of dying.

"What do you want me to do, *sidi?*"

Al-Shami took another measure of Sohrab. Young, slight, his black leather bomber jacket vaguely too rugged for the rest of him, his patchy beard somehow making him look younger rather than older. But he had a zealous glint in his eyes that reminded al-Shami of men he'd met in prison and in the bomb factories, men who embraced killing as a calling, not a job. "You protect Mahir from outside the blast range. Make sure no one interferes with him. Eliminate anyone who gets in his way. He needs only a second to trigger his weapon, and you may need to buy him that second. Understand?"

Sohrab nodded, a little smile creeping onto his lips. "Perfectly, *sidi.*"

EIGHTY-SIX

Miriam had tweaked her bad knee at the cemetery; now gravel scraped between the bones as she limped through the squad-room chaos until she reached the precinct's break room. Her stomach throbbed from Gabir's bullet hit. Her internal clock had gone haywire from stress and lack of sleep. What she'd seen in the ladies' room mirror had been scarier than being shot.

But she was alive and free. Thanks to Jake.

He sprawled on the break room's worn gold-beige sofa, tilted slightly to his left, his head thrown back against the wall, mouth half-open. Tape and gauze shrouded his right ear. Eve curled sound asleep in his lap, her face buried in his chest, her feet twitching. Jake's arms wrapped around her like a cocoon.

Miriam drifted to the table, fumbled into a well-used chrome-rod-and-plastic chair, and watched them sleep. She tried to convince herself she'd known them less than three weeks, not forever, but her overloaded brain would accept only so much.

Eve whimpered, shifted, tucked a little fist under her chin. *You'll have dreams, sweetie*, Miriam wanted to warn her. *Some you won't want to end. Some you'll be afraid will never end.*

What would these two be like after all this? There was no way a child and parent could ever be the same after living through all this fear and violence and death. It helped that Jake and Eve seemed to love each other intensely, something Miriam would never be able to say about her mother and herself. What little relationship they'd had died when Hezbollah killed her father. Maybe he was all they'd ever had in common.

Starting over was so hard. Perhaps having each other would

help them through the bad days. Eve would give Jake—what was his phrase?—a reason to wake up. Jake would give Eve someone to hold when the shadows got too dark. She envied them both. When Bill died, all she'd had were a few well-meaning friends who didn't get it and a Navy chaplain (Pentecostal! Not even a rabbi!) who was more concerned about her soul than her heart.

On the subway, she'd jolted out of a catnap to hear him quietly weeping; she'd pretended to be asleep until he was done. Jake was a nice man, a good man. He didn't deserve to hurt so much. She'd been where he was going, and it could be a hard, lonely place.

But it didn't need to be. If only she could help them through this...

What's got into you? she chided herself. He probably wouldn't want to see her again after this. She'd only remind him and Eve of this nightmare.

Maybe he'd have the same effect on her.

Maybe not.

People talked and phones rang a long way away. Cops wandered in, got their coffee, glanced at the three of them and left quietly.

She didn't want to wake him, but she wished they could talk now they were safe. Jake eventually solved her problem. He rolled his head forward, pinched the sleep from his bloodshot, unfocused eyes, then shook his head hard and squinted at her. "Hi."

"Hi."

He yawned, grimaced, rubbed his neck. "Time's it?"

She checked her watch. "Just past eleven."

Jake kissed the top of Eve's head, stroked her hair, then readjusted his focus on Miriam. "How you doing?"

"I don't know. I'm numb."

"Yeah." He yawned again. "How long have I been out?"

"Not too long." Enough to thoroughly confuse herself. "How's Eve?"

Jake glanced down again at his daughter, gave her a little squeeze. "Tired. Confused. Getting over being scared. Told her the man who hurt Rinnah won't hurt anyone ever again."

Miriam's mind flashed a replay of Jake executing the big Arab. Would she have done anything different? She might have started with the bastard's knees and worked her way up. At least, the her from two days ago might have. "Did she believe you?"

"She's six. You always believe daddy when you're six." He watched Eve for a moment, chewed on his upper lip. "What scares me? She hits sixteen and asks me how I know he's gone."

Miriam reached out to caress Eve's skinny thigh through her jeans. Eve squirmed deeper into her father's arms. "Maybe she'll be ready then."

"Sure." Jake's face was more awake now. "Anyway, you're off the hook."

"Your Captain Menotti told me. Thank you. It sounds like you're going to be a hero."

"Yeah, or get fired." He brushed the back of her hand. "I won't let you go to jail."

His tone made those words a vow. After all he'd sacrificed, she truly hoped he wouldn't lose his job—or freedom—for keeping her safe. "What happens now? They said I can go."

"Yeah, me too. Guess they're done with us for now. I'm on administrative leave until the hearing, three-four weeks or so. Don't know what they've got planned for you."

She'd asked, but all Menotti said was, "Don't leave the country." Her life was on hold again, and she had no idea when it would re-start. "What are you going to do?"

Jake's eyes went distant, then he finally shook his head. "Don't know. I really don't. Can't go back to the apartment yet." He glanced down at Eve. "I can't take her back to that, not so soon. There's Gene and Monica, I guess. We can put all the casualties in one place."

When he looked up at her, Miriam read the hopelessness in his eyes. Perhaps he'd just noticed the horizon in front of him was blank. She remembered that from right after her father's funeral, and Bill's. "Maybe they'll want your help."

"Maybe." Again they exchanged bedraggled gazes. "You going home?"

What does he see in me? A friend? A fighter? A woman? Damaged goods? "I... I don't know. There's nothing there. I need to get Bastet back before she forgets me. But..."

"Well, Menotti sent our bags over from the safe house." Jake gave her a tired smile. "Wherever you go, you'll have clean underwear."

"And you'll have a change of clothes. Which you *really* need." *And we'll be on our own again.* She'd forgotten what it was like to have someone share life's little moments. The past two weeks had reminded her. She wasn't ready yet to go back to living alone, inside her own head.

"I could ask Monica if..." Jake searched the room for the right words. "They've got the room. If you'd like that. Until you're, you know... ready to go home."

Now she had to look away. She'd like that, more than she cared to admit to herself. Wanting it—wanting anything—both buoyed her heart and dropped a brick in her gut. Having something meant having something to lose. She'd lost too much in her life.

But not having anything wasn't living—it was hiding.

"Are you hungry?" she asked after a pause.

"Starving. Let's get lunch."

EIGHTY-SEVEN

23 DECEMBER, 11:10 AM
BROOKLYN

The gloomy sky ladled an extra helping of drab on the run-down neighborhood's low-rise clutter. Miriam clutched her coat collar against the cold. "You take me to all the best places."

Jake frowned. "Sorry there's no IHOP around here."

"We're not going home, are we?" Eve—puffy-faced, slit-eyed, hair gone mad—yanked at Jake's hand. Even Miriam could tell the whine in her voice promised more and louder to come.

"Not yet. We're going to White Castle. It's just down on the corner. See? Hamburgers and fries. Yum, huh?"

"Mommy says hamburgers clog up your insides."

He fixed his eyes straight ahead. "Yeah, she said that."

Jake steered them past the cars—police and civilian—half-blocking the sidewalk behind the precinct's long driveway cutout. Miriam tried her best not to limp; Jake would try to help her, and she didn't want to be babied.

Eve whimpered, "I don't like this place. I want Mommy. I wanna go home."

"I know, Bunny. So do I. In a little while."

"You always say that, *always*, and it takes *forever!*"

Jake sighed, squatted next to Eve. "Please, Bunny, not now. First we'll eat and go see Uncle Gene and Aunt Monica. We'll go home later, okay?"

Eve stomped her foot. Miriam didn't know kids actually did that. "No more *later!* You always say *later!* I don't want hamburgers, I wanna go home. Now!"

A soft throat-clearing drew Miriam's attention away from Eve's impending meltdown. A middle-aged man wearing a black wool overcoat stood a couple paces away, his collar turned up to frame his rugged face and windblown amber hair. The strap of a black computer bag cut across his chest. His gaze shifted from Eve to Jake to Miriam and back. "Good morning, Mr. Eldar."

Jake slowly rose, unwound his body, squared his shoulders. He pushed Eve behind him. "Who are you?"

"Are you a policeman?" Eve demanded. She peeked around Jake's side, her face twisted with anger and frustration. "I don't wanna talk to no more policemen."

"No, Eve, a policeman I am not." The man scanned Miriam top to toe. A small smile crossed his face. "Your photo does you no justice, Mrs. Schaffer." He had an accent, but Miriam hadn't heard enough to place it.

She exchanged a wary glance with Jake. "How do you know us? Who are you?"

He shrugged deeper into his coat, rubbed at the stubble on his chin. "My name is Stuart Kaminsky."

Jake choked out, "*You're* Kaminsky?"

Miriam rocked back a step. The third survivor from the Doha Twelve, the man who'd lent them the sniper at the cemetery. What was he doing here? How had he found them?

Kaminsky shifted into Hebrew. "I assume your daughter doesn't speak Hebrew, Mr. Eldar. Correct?"

"Right."

Kaminsky nodded. "Good. There are things children shouldn't hear. Across the street, at the corner of 29th Street, there's a black Impala with two people inside, a man and a woman. They were here when I arrived, some while ago. Do you see it?"

Miriam dragged her compact from her purse and used the mirror to sight along the row of parked cars. "I see it."

Jake said, "So?"

"I believe they're here for you. As long as you're with me, they won't approach you, I think."

"Who are they?" Jake demanded. "What do they want? Why are you here?"

Kaminsky opened his mouth to reply, but a noise behind them caused his eyes to turn hawk-like. Miriam glanced back; two civilians taking a smoke break at the precinct's front door.

"As things are now, Mr. Eldar, I'd prefer to not talk to you in front of a police station. You were on your way to White Castle, yes? To eat? Perhaps I can come with you. You can eat and we can talk."

Eve yanked Jake's hand. "Daddy, let's go! This is boring!"

"Shhh. Hold on."

Miriam watched Jake think this through. He gazed down at Eve, stroked her hair.

"I'd prefer to not mention that you owe this to me, Mr. Eldar, but I will if I must."

"No, that's okay." Jake looked over his shoulder to check the black car again. "Let's go."

EIGHTY-EIGHT

23 DECEMBER, 11:20 AM
BROOKLYN

They crowded into a tiny booth overlooking the parking lot, the blue laminate table covered by blue plastic trays scattered with wrapped miniature hamburgers. The place smelled of hot oil, seared meat, and disinfectant. Jake sat next to Eve; across the table, Miriam perched on the aisle end of the bench next to Kaminsky. The lunch rush swirled around them, but Jake figured none of the mostly black and Latino customers would understand Hebrew.

Jake asked, "Who's in the car?"

Kaminsky leaned back, smiled a little. "You may have seen the woman. Now she has short black hair, a proud nose, quite a nice suntan—"

"Elena?"

"Yes, that's one of her names. I prefer 'Sandrine,' the name she used in Paris. A very special girl. She had such lovely hair back then." He laid his fingertips on the back of Miriam's wrist. *Hands off,* Jake thought. "Though not as attractive as you, Mrs. Schaffer. I may call you Miriam?"

Miriam swept her hand away to unwrap her second chicken-breast sandwich. "'Ms. Schaffer' is fine. Who's the man with Elena?"

"I don't know him. Perhaps his name but not his face. Blond, cut very short."

"The Russian from the train station," Miriam reminded Jake.

"What are you talking about?" Eve hunched behind her tray, arms folded, face dark.

"Grown-up stuff," Jake said, temporarily back to English. He tried to put his arm around Eve but she jerked away, as Rinnah

328

would when she was mad. He sighed and switched back to Kaminsky and Hebrew. "How do you know these people?"

Kaminsky rocked forward and said gently in English, "What upsets you, Eve? Why angry with your papa?"

Eve peered at him, then dropped her focus to her tray. She murmured, "I wanna go home."

"Of course." He scrunched down further to look into her eyes. "May I tell you a secret, Eve? I too want to go home. I know what you feel, very much. You should be good to your papa, I think. He loves you and wants you to be safe."

Jake watched this exchange without quite catching what Kaminsky was up to, other than avoiding his question. The man's voice and expression had become kindly Uncle Stuart in an instant, and the tension and anger in Eve's face drained away as Kaminsky smiled at her. She glanced up at Jake, mouth puckered in thought, then silently went to work on her next slider.

"Your daughter is a beautiful girl," Kaminsky said to Jake, still in English. Then he switched to Hebrew. "I see so many children in this city, and it gives me such hope for the future. As a father, I'm sure it is the same for you. That's why I hope you and—" he held out his hand toward Miriam "—the lovely Mrs. Schaffer, of course, will help me protect the beautiful children of New York City such as Eve, and their parents. The innocents. May I explain, please?"

He'd said all this while switching his focus regularly between Jake and Miriam, fixing all his attention on each in turn. Jake's brain took a moment to catch up. "Help you with what?" he finally asked.

Kaminsky leaned forward on his elbows and lowered his voice. "You know a team of homicide bombers is here, in your city, yes?"

Jake and Miriam exchanged startled looks, then edged closer to Kaminsky to hear him better. "How do you know about that?" Miriam said. "We just told the police."

Kaminsky smiled. "I have information about them. Who they are, what they look like, their vehicles." His eyebrows lifted into an unspoken *are you interested now?*

Had a small earthquake cooked off underneath him, Jake couldn't have been more surprised. If it was true, all that intel needed to get to NYPD sooner than instantly. "How did you get this? Who have you told? That's got—"

Kaminsky raised a cautioning hand, leaned back to look out the window, nodded, then resumed his place nearly shoulder-to-shoulder with Miriam. "It doesn't matter where I got it. I have it, and with you, Mr. Eldar—" he tapped Jake's forearm "—a trained intelligence analyst, and you, Mrs. Schaffer—" his fingertips hovered a few fractions of an inch above her hand without touching "—and Mr. Eldar assures me you are a very capable woman as well as being extremely attractive—"

"What did you tell him?" Miriam hissed at Jake.

"All very good, very impressive things," Kaminsky answered. "This pack of mad dogs intends to attack today, just as they have in Amsterdam and Paris. The three of us together, we can stop a mass murder of your neighbors, your friends, little children such as your beautiful daughter. I *know* we can do this."

Kaminsky's hands were mobile and expressive even though his elbows were planted on the table. Jake made the mistake of watching those hands; their fluid and near-constant movement was hypnotic, especially as tired as Jake was. He tore his attention away long enough to notice Miriam had locked on Kaminsky's intense eyes, the color of an overcast blue sky. He nudged her foot with his own. Miriam snapped back her head as if he'd flicked ice water in her face. Jake would have to keep an eye on her; neither of them was tracking too well.

"What do you want from us, Mr. Kaminsky?" she asked.

Eve broke in, yanking at Jake's sleeve. "Daddy, can I have a pencil? I wanna draw."

Jake patted his pockets. Kaminsky produced a pen seemingly from out of thin air and extended it to Eve. "Please use this, Eve," he said in English, "and draw a nice picture, yes?"

Eve eyed the pen carefully, then slid it from his fingers. She flipped the tray liner on its face and started drawing vigorously.

"What do you say, Bunny?" Jake asked.

"Thank you, mister."

"You are very welcome, Eve." Kaminsky stared out the window again for several seconds.

"What are you looking at?" Jake asked, returning to Hebrew.

330

"I'm confirming our friends outside haven't decided to join us."

"Would they?" Miriam asked.

Kaminsky pursed his lips for a moment. "I think not. There are many people around us, this would not suit them. Mr. Eldar, you ask where I get my information. I imagine you've already deduced that Aluma Consultants is not my only employment. I learned of these terrorists the same way I learned of three other groups in the Detroit area with attachments to Hamas or Hezbollah. Those other groups are no longer with us, and good riddance, yes? Of course, I know you would agree. I now must send this fourth group to Paradise to rejoin their colleagues, and for this I want... I need... I implore your help." He held his palm just a whisper away from Miriam's shoulder. "And why *you*, you ask, Mrs. Schaffer? We are all survivors, the only three of the twelve still alive, which makes us like brothers and sisters, we who can bear witness together, yes? You and Mr. Eldar have taken this threat from my shoulders, Mrs. Schaffer, for which I'm grateful." Kaminsky offered both hands to Jake, as if pleading. "And now we must act one more time, together." He peered outside again.

Jake wished Kaminsky would just get to the point. He checked Eve's drawing: a house, rocky ground, a couple penguins, some rain clouds or something, nothing too unusual. He whispered to her in English, "Whatcha got there, Bunny?"

Eve didn't look up. "Stuff." At least she wasn't so mad anymore.

Jake leaned back and sighed. The many loose threads of Kaminsky's story began to weave themselves together in Jake's mind. Detroit, the terminated Arabs, the intel on the bombers, the sniper... "You're Mossad, aren't you?"

Kaminsky's eyes stared back at him, calm and still. Then a bright smile broke over his face. "I knew you'd be a perceptive man, Mr. Eldar, my compliments. Yes, I'm with Mossad."

"Mossad isn't supposed to operate in America."

"Do you still believe that?"

Jake groaned. "Shit. Can't you knuckleheads follow rules?"

"We wouldn't be so successful if we did."

Miriam pointed out the window. "You're with those people out there?"

"Ah. No." He laid both hands palms-down on the table, carefully, as if touching something priceless. "We are, you might say, from the same village—ours is a very small service, we all know one another—but not the same neighborhood. Also, I have to admit to you that I am not the most favored in the village because of the help I provided to you. You've seen these people before, yes? Yet they did not protect you. They don't care about you. I lent to you someone very dear to me to help rescue your beautiful daughter from those assassins and this person—a very warm, very committed young woman—did not survive. And because of this, the Institute considers me an embarrassment and a threat." Again he spread his hands. "I *of course* don't blame you for this, it *of course* is not your fault."

Each time Kaminsky said "this isn't your fault," Jake felt the guilt dig a little deeper into his chest. Guilt had bought Kaminsky a hearing until now, but Jake was tired of the barrage. "What exactly do you want us to do?"

Kaminsky smiled and leaned forward again, wrapping the three of them in a cloak of intimacy. "I wouldn't ask you to do anything dangerous, not after everything that's happened—"

"Kaminsky. Answer the question."

His smile had a dent in it. He pulled back, flicked his gaze between Jake and Miriam. "Of course. I'm not an analyst like you, Mr. Eldar. I know who these bombers are and what they're going to do, but not where. I need you to work out the target. And Mrs. Schaffer—" again he came within a finger's breadth of touching her wrist "—if we find the target we have to go help end this, and for that we'll need your special talents."

"Why don't you just give this information to those people out there?" Miriam asked.

Kaminsky turned a full dose of eyes and smile on her. "We sent everything to Tel Aviv. Our friends outside may have it already, but two of them wait for you, so do they have another agenda? I have my suspicions, which I won't burden you with. Since Elena is here, I know who's leading their team. We'll call him 'Ephraim.' A good man once, but a bit of a prig."

"If you know him, can't you talk to him?" Miriam asked.

"I said I know him. I didn't say I like him, or that he likes me.

Please remember I'm not in favor with the Institute because I gave you the help they refused to you. Very simply, I'm certain Ephraim and his people have orders to detain me, and knowing Ephraim, he'd be happy to shoot me or bless me with a heart attack."

"They'd kill you?" she asked, unconvinced.

"Is there anything you know about the Institute that makes you doubt that?"

The concept of Mossad eating its own didn't surprise Jake. "Give me your intel and I'll get it to people who can run with it."

"The police, you mean?" Jake nodded. "Of course, I understand perfectly. However, it's all highly classified and I need to sanitize it, otherwise Tel Aviv will know who let it go and things will not go well for me or anyone with me. Which includes you now, I'm sorry to say."

Figures. Jake tried to scrub the weariness from his eyes. "Where is it?"

"Here." Kaminsky patted the computer case on the bench beside him. "It's far too valuable to leave unguarded. It's my analyst's—"

"Let me see it."

"It would be so much better if we could go to my hotel—"

"*Now.*"

Again, the dented smile. Kaminsky rested his palms against the edge of the table, watched Jake carefully. He then turned to Miriam. "Mrs. Schaffer, surely you understand—"

She fixed him with her granite stare. "Mr. Kaminsky, I think it's time you showed us some proof."

The smile faded. "Yes, of course." He hauled out a battered black laptop, flipped it open, fiddled it to life, then swiveled it on his food tray to face the aisle end of the table. Dozens of folder icons with Hebrew names blanketed the dark-blue screen. "Here, see the proof I have. See my treasure."

Jake slipped off his bench to squat at the table's end, angling the computer so Miriam could see better. He opened folders with names that interested him, skimming the contents to get a flavor for what Kaminsky had. Each new file set off slot-machine jackpot bells in his head. Maps, photos, transcripts, diagrams, briefing slides, cable traffic, all priceless in the right hands.

Eventually he stopped, took a deep breath, looked up. Kaminsky might be playing them, but he had the goods. Miriam raised a questioning eyebrow. He nodded. This material had to get to NYPD and JTTF. Whatever snake oil Kaminsky was selling, Jake would buy it if he could move this intel.

Miriam slid off the bench and gestured toward the narrow corridor leading to the restrooms. "Mr. Kaminsky, could you give us a moment?"

Kaminsky's eyes questioned her, then Jake. He flashed a dimmer-than-usual smile. "Of course, I understand perfectly, this is a decision you want to make carefully." He quickly packed up the laptop. "I hope you'll see how important this is, and how important you are to me. I mean to find these murderers and put them down. You too should want this, after all they did to you." He stood, laid his hand on Jake's shoulder; Jake resisted the urge to shake it off. "Please help me." He turned to Miriam, warmed his smile. "We'll be the perfect team."

Once he walked away, Miriam growled, "Now I've got a headache."

Jake returned to his bench. "Same here. The man can shovel it out."

She watched Kaminsky disappear into the men's room, then settled back onto her bench. "Do you trust him?"

"No. Do you?"

"No. Do you believe him?"

Jake blew out a long breath. "Enough to want to get that stuff to the PD. It's insane they don't have it already. If we have to put up with Kaminsky a while to get it, well, it's worth it." He hooked a thumb toward the window. "Besides, I trust those people out there even less."

"How do you know there even *is* anyone out there?"

"He described two of the ones we've seen. That's not random. If we're going to end up with Mossad, I like the odds better when there's two of us and only one of them." He leaned forward, wrapped his fingers around her wrist without thinking about it. "What do you think?"

Miriam glanced down at his hand, then began stroking his knuckles. "If he's telling the truth, then we have to tell the police so they can stop the bomber. I don't understand why he doesn't go to his own people, but if he won't and he won't go to the police…"

"He probably really is in deep shit with Mossad." Jake sighed. "We owe him, you know. We got one of his people killed and blew up his operation. He's in this jam because of us."

"I know, he kept reminding us. I've got enough guilt now, thanks."

Kaminsky reappeared in the narrow restroom corridor. Jake gave Miriam's wrist a final squeeze, then sat back. "I don't like it, but I think we have to play along."

Miriam heaved out a sigh. "Fine, but don't be surprised if I gag him." She glanced toward Eve, frowned, then tapped the table in front of Jake.

Jake realized he'd focused so hard on Kaminsky that he'd lost track of his daughter. He followed Miriam's nod toward Eve's picture. The penguins were now shooting at each other, dead stick figures littered the rocky ground and thunderbolts and fire trailed from the rain clouds. Seeing what lived in Eve's head twisted his gut into a complicated braid.

"What does she normally draw?" Miriam asked, still in Hebrew.

"Penguins, dogs, cats. She got on a zebra kick a while ago, don't know where that came from. But this." *Oh, God.* "This looks like the first-grade version of *Guernica.*"

Eve sat, arms folded, staring at her nightmare. Jake carefully wrapped an arm around her and pulled her into his side. She resisted, but not hard. After a moment, he heard a tiny sniff and saw a tear dribble down her cheek. A new, fresh stake drilled through his heart.

"This insanity has got to stop," Jake finally told Miriam. "I've got to put our lives back together again. If I can."

Miriam nodded, watching Eve with stricken eyes. She slid the picture off Eve's tray, examined it, then shook her head. "It's the 23rd. If Rafiq was right—if Kaminsky is—this will all be over tomorrow." She swallowed. "One way or another."

EIGHTY-NINE

"Here they come," Sasha said.

Kelila whirled in her seat and switched on the camera. Sasha dropped the left rear window without waiting to be asked. She focused the monster lens on Eldar and his daughter in the lead, then slid the view back to Schaffer. Finally, the mystery man whose face she couldn't see on the way in.

Anger lit her face on fire.

He'd aged in the past few years. Deep lines crossed his strong forehead and spidered out from the corners of his gray-blue eyes. His hair was still that deli-mustard yellow, with less gray than he should have by now. Still, she could see in his face the deceptive gentleness that had drawn her to him in those hard, cold months after Yigal died in Lebanon. That womanizing pig.

"Something wrong?" Sasha asked.

"No. Yes." She clicked off a series of pictures, stopping only when the three targets disappeared behind the police station's bulk. With every frame, her mind chanted *bastard, bastard, bastard.* No wonder he'd seemed familiar.

Once they were gone, she thumped back into her seat. "They're back on 30th. Don't lose them."

Sasha cranked the engine to life. "What's got your knickers in a wad?"

"Just drive." She punched her speed-dial button for Raffi.

"Yes?"

"Where are you now?" she demanded.

"On a bridge, coming back into Manhattan. What's happened? Another bomb?"

That would almost be easier. Kelila grabbed the dash as Sasha launched them into a squealing U-turn across six lanes of traffic. "Guess who's with Eldar and Schaffer."

"I'm too tired to play guessing games. Who?"

"Avidor Grossman."

Sasha burst out laughing. "Really? He's still alive? I thought he'd be dead from screwing every woman in the Institute."

Kelila slugged his shoulder hard, leading with the knuckle of her middle finger. He yelped and started muttering Russian curses, all of which she understood.

Raffi spat, "*Ben zonah.*"

The more she thought about it, the angrier Kelila became. The man was a walking security risk as well as a threat to women everywhere. "I have a sick feeling he's Kaminsky."

"I wouldn't be surprised. Follow him. Let me know where you end up so I can meet you. And Kelila? Don't do anything stupid. You're entitled, but don't, all right?"

"Fine." Not fine; she'd love to cut off that shit's balls. "I'm worried about Schaffer now."

"Schaffer against Grossman?" Raffi chuckled. "I'd like to see that. Stay on him. This could be our big break."

NINETY

Gur managed to find a semi-legal stopping point next to the low-slung brick Essex Street Market. He had no good idea where his GPS had taken him and his fingers already hurt from squeezing his phone so hard. He couldn't drive and deal with Orgad at the same time, not in this mess. "Grossman is Kaminsky? Do you think you could've told me that sooner?"

"You didn't need to know," Orgad said. Other than a certain roughness in his voice, Gur's boss sounded as stolid as ever. "You have more important things to worry about."

"I'm not so sure. Just so I know: if I drag him in, do I end up in Lebanon? Whose ass is his nose buried in to get a sensitive position like AL?"

"You don't need to know that, either. If it makes you feel better, his *sus* isn't any use to him anymore. This blunder is too public, he's been disowned. Concentrate on your mission."

"Yes, about that. We have Grossman's intel on dead terrorists but not on the live ones. Can we use his people? We need help."

"He has no people anymore. They're leaving the country. Make do."

"Damn it!" Gur slammed the steering wheel with his palm. "I need more information. Anything from Paris or Amsterdam, I don't care how small, I want it immediately. I hope Kaisarut is finally talking to the Americans."

"They have... contact. We have to protect our sources, of course."

"Fuck that! Stop playing these idiotic games. Give them everything you know, *now*. If we're going to stop this, we need

338

every policeman on this island looking for these people. If Kaisarut doesn't start sharing information, so help me I'll go straight to their FBI and give them what I know. *All* of it. Am I clear?"

The phone overflowed with dead air. Then Orgad said, very carefully, "That would be unwise. We'd make certain you spend a great deal of time in an American prison. It would hurt to do that, Raffi, but I'd do it to protect the Institute, please believe me." Gur believed him; he'd seen it happen. "Liaison is doing what it's authorized to do. There are issues you're not privileged to know, at the highest levels."

Meaning the Prime Minister's office. Meaning withholding information about this from the Americans had become a matter of state policy. Meaning... "You want Hezbollah to succeed. You want the bomb to go off."

Static hiss stretched on far too long.

Gur's rushed lunch fought its way back up his throat. The Institute had manipulated events in America before, he knew, but *this*... "So should we stop? Let it happen?"

"Of course not. Do what you can. If you stop it, they'll owe us a great debt. Not all things are possible, though." If this last thought gave Orgad any heartburn, it didn't reflect in his voice.

"So why send us here at all? What's the point? What did Amzi die for?"

"We had to eliminate the assassination team. If they survived, we'd see them in Israel, we couldn't have that. This is different." Orgad cleared his throat. "Good luck, Raffi. Please try to stay alive. It would be a shame to lose you for no reason." Before Gur could say anything, Orgad broke the connection.

Gur sagged into his seat, rubbed the throbbing between his eyes. All these busy shoppers rushing past. How many would die tonight?

He wasn't naïve. He understood the Institute—and by extension, Israel—looked out for its own interests above anyone else's. But withholding information from the Americans, and allowing the deaths of dozens if not hundreds of innocents, just to goad Israel's only real ally into attacking Hezbollah...

The idea didn't shock him. Twenty years of taking out his country's garbage had left him so jaded that he had no trouble believing Israel could be this cavalier about friends, supporters, fellow Jews. *Is there no outrage left in me?* Gloomy storm clouds hid the sun from what remained of his soul. *Can I let this happen and still call myself a man?*

No. He had to act. His team could act. They must. And if the Institute didn't like that he'd wrecked their twisted little plot, he'd hold his head high as they marched him off to prison.

He checked his watch. Past noon local time. Sunset at six-thirty. So little time.

Grossman was key. He had the information Tel Aviv had buried. He had Eldar and Schaffer, too, and whatever they'd learned from the terrorists. Gur didn't know what that bastard was up to, but knowing Grossman, he was trying to cover his seriously overexposed ass... which meant shifting the blame to someone else, such as Gur. If he did, he could survive to screw someone else on his scramble up the ladder to the Director's chair.

Unless Gur and his team could find the bombers first.

NINETY-ONE

No one noticed the FedEx Ground panel van parked in the red outside the Commerce Bank at Broadway and Wall, flashers promising a quick return. Few paid attention to Haroun in the FedEx uniform. How else could a black man walk down Wall Street and not stand out?

The private security guard stomping his feet under the black-topped metal shelter outside the Bank of New York Mellon just nodded as Haroun passed. The New York Stock Exchange cop at the Exchange's entrance yanked the door open for him. "Don't drop it," the cop said, nodding toward the carton in Haroun's hands.

That wasn't an option.

He slid the box onto the receiving counter, shook the blood back into his hands. The package wasn't big, but it had grown heavy after carrying it a block. The "Fragile" stamps were a nice touch. A pot-bellied Puerto Rican guy at the desk behind the counter looked up over his glasses, frowned. "Vlad was just here half an hour ago. He forget something?"

Haroun's mind flashed on Vlad, dead under a tarp in the back of his van, strangled so no blood would get on his uniform. Haroun spread his hands. "What can I say, man? Sign here."

He'd never dreamed he'd stick it to the white man *and* the infidel at the same time. He'd enjoy coming back in a couple hours, driving that other van no one would see until too late.

Before prison, before he'd found his new faith, being here in the middle of the financial world's viper den would have made him furious; he would've wanted to butcher every passing white man in

341

a tie. Now with his path and his destiny set, he didn't feel angry or tense or anxious. He felt free, weightless. Everything seemed just a little brighter and sharper, the girls a little prettier, the air a little crisper. He'd have these pictures to take with him to paradise.

Haroun nodded at the NYPD Emergency Services truck making its way through the vehicle barriers at the mouth of Wall Street. The cops passed without even looking at him. Asleep, just like the rest of them. He smiled to himself.

In a couple of hours, he'd wake them up. He wouldn't be invisible anymore.

NINETY-TWO

23 DECEMBER, 3:10 PM
MIDTOWN MANHATTAN

This is useless, Jake told himself for the hundredth time. They'd never find anything in this mess. Shoppers, hawkers, workers, security guards and street sweepers jammed the sidewalks of 47th Street's midrise brick-and-stone canyon. The usual Friday mid-afternoon wall-to-wall filled the street cutting through the heart of New York's Diamond District. Armored cars lined the north curb, loading or unloading gold and cash.

But no extra cops. One patrol unit held down the corner with Fifth Avenue across from Chabad's twelve-foot-high aluminum menorah, and another sat by the intersection with Sixth. Where was the PD? The sooner the cavalry got here, the sooner Jake and Miriam could ditch Kaminsky and leave this mess forever.

The sooner he could get back to Eve. He flashed back almost three hours to when he'd faced down Monica in front of Kings County Hospital, where Gene lay recovering. "She needs to be with you," Monica had scolded him, fists on her formidable hips. "You need to stop running around saving the world."

Eve's "Daddy, don't go!" still echoed in his ears. *What kind of father am I?*

Jake trotted across the street through stalled traffic toward the garish neon "47 Diamond Exchange" sign. He turned a full 360 looking for Lieutenant Fitcham, Menotti's deputy, who was supposed to meet him here.

He felt muzzy and unfocused even after a shower, shave and change of clothes at Kaminsky's hotel suite. He wished Miriam was with him; she had good eyes and good instincts, and he wouldn't feel so alone.

This had been his idea. Kaminsky was all hot about Wall Street, but Jake had shot him down; the area around the Stock Exchange had been locked down after 9/11 and was much too hard a target. Now he began to wonder. So far today, Hezbollah had targeted two synagogues, the Anne Frank House and a Christmas party at a conference center in Paris. The strike here could come anywhere. Did Hezbollah even know about this place?

Jake checked the oncoming pedestrians and drivers against the faces of the four bombers running on an endless loop through his head, wishing he'd *find* one already. The news said the Paris bombers embedded ball bearings in the explosives; that van had been a huge Claymore mine. A hundred ten dead so far. If it happened on this street, that would be just the start.

❖

Miriam huddled against the cold under a scaffold blocking the front of the huge half-completed International Gem Tower, halfway between Fifth and Sixth Avenues on 47th Street. She propped Kaminsky's computer against a scaffold pier and waited for it to connect to the unsecured WiFi signal she'd found.

It had taken some badgering on Jake's part to get Kaminsky to leave his laptop with her. "You need to be free for action, right?" he'd said. It was "action" that finally won the argument; Kaminsky seemed to swell each time Jake brought it up. With any luck, "action" would keep him away from her for the rest of the day.

She didn't mind being sidelined. Standing still would save her knee. More than that, she'd felt stupid and useless at the hotel for not being able to help find the target. Now she could take a few minutes to look at the data, try to make sense of what had happened so far today.

A nearly unbroken line of traffic streamed westbound in front of her. She'd counted a dozen white vans growling by in the past ten minutes. While none had the Eastside Electric logo, Miriam knew how easy it would have been to switch registration plates or graphics in the two weeks since Kaminsky had last seen the thing. For all they knew, the van could be black by now... like the one parked illegally a few feet from her.

Miriam shivered, not from the chill.

❖

A midnight-blue Crown Victoria squeaked to a stop next to the gray plumber's van shielding Jake from the street. A man with hair the color of a new penny unwound from the passenger's seat; when he stood straight, he towered over the car's roof. Fitcham.

Jake raised his arm. Fitcham nodded, waved the car into the intersection, then circled the van to reach the sidewalk. They shook hands. "Alright, Jake, where'd you get that intel?"

If nothing else, Jake had managed to send Kaminsky's files to JTTF. "Later. You see the pictures?"

"I saw. We got copies going out to patrols and the Feds, and a BOLO on the van." As they walked, Fitcham cased the street and crowd, his tan raincoat flapping at his knees. His handheld police radio squawked from time to time. "How sure are you they're coming here?"

"Not bet-my-life, but it makes sense. It's the largest unsecured Jewish target in the city. Wide open at both ends, no barriers anywhere. Drive the van through, pull the pin and you're guaranteed three figures' worth of casualties." Jake sighed, glanced around. "It just feels right. It's like, you look up 'soft target' in Wikipedia, a picture of this place comes up."

Fitcham looked unconvinced. "The Feds like Wall Street. So does the boss."

"It's a fortress. Why work that hard?"

"Just sayin'. Captain wants me to check this out before he sends anyone else up here." Fitcham stopped abruptly, cocked his head like an Irish setter. "You hear that ringing?"

Jake concentrated for a moment. "Fire alarm."

Across the street, people streamed through the five glass doors of number 55, a glass-and-granite frontage that proclaimed itself in giant aluminum letters to be the "World's Largest Jewelry Exchange." Workers in shirtsleeves, Haredim in full suits and hats, shopgirls and customers all spilled out onto the sidewalk, most with phones pressed to their ears, many wearing bewildered faces.

"Just like in Amsterdam and Paris," Jake said. "They called in bomb threats to flush people outside. It's happening."

"Great," Fitcham grumbled. He stepped off into the street, holding up his shield to stop the traffic. People filled the sidewalk in front of number 55, sloshed into the street. Fitcham began barking commands into his radio.

"Believe me now?" Jake called after him.

"Shit." Fitcham, now halfway across the street, shot his hand in the air to stop an oncoming armored car. "Yes, West 47th at Fifth!" he yelled into his radio. "10-85 for a roadblock ASAP!"

"Lieutenant! What do you want me to do?"

Fitcham jabbed a finger eastbound. "Take Schaffer and get the hell out of here."

"What about all this?"

"Captain's orders. You, Schaffer and your little girl, on a plane to Miami tonight." Fitcham stepped backwards while he waved his radio at Jake. "Drink rum, lay on the beach. He doesn't want to even smell you until the hearing. Understand?" He gave Jake a *getouttahere* wave and disappeared into the crowd of evacuees.

Jake shrugged, dropped back to the sidewalk and continued on his way to Miriam. Flashing blue lights marked the east end of the block, and sirens approached down Sixth Avenue. He'd turned over the scene to NYPD; he and Miriam could leave with clear consciences.

But there were still all these white vans here. *Not my problem*, he told himself.

Dozens—hundreds—of people packed both sidewalks. *Let the PD deal with it.*

He stopped to peek through a white delivery van's window. Off-white mesh blocked the view behind the front seats. Kaminsky's photos hadn't shown a cargo cage. *Keep going.*

Another white van—from a plumbing company—rolled past. The driver's face didn't line up with the pictures in Jake's head. Two cars behind it was another white van—boiler repair—and the driver… he looked a little like that Fayiz guy, didn't he? Maybe a bit older, more gray in his shaggy black hair. They could've changed the signs on the van by now, stuck on new plates.

The traffic lanes thinned out after Jake had covered a few more yards; the roadblock must have kicked in. But the momentary flash of relief turned to dust when he noticed a dozen or more white vans parked along the small stretches of curb he could see. Where were the uniforms? Why wasn't anyone checking the drivers?

Over there, in front of the Ross Exchange's blue awning, next to the growing lake of evacuees: a parked white van, flashers on, "Empire Electric" on the sides, a black guy head-down behind the wheel. Texting? Filling out forms?

Praying before he sent himself to Paradise?

The driver looked a lot like that Haroun Sahabi character: thirties perhaps, dark skin, almost no hair, a blue cloth coat. Jake checked the street; the nearest cops were too far away. The evacuees eddied around the van, oblivious.

A hand grabbed Jake's elbow. "Come with me," a man growled in Hebrew.

Jake tried to wrench away, but the man's fingers cranked down on the nerves in his elbow and wouldn't let go. "But that van—that guy—"

"Just shut up and come with me." The man flashed an open leather ID case at him. A bad photo, a blue Shield of David inside a wreath, a name and police rank in Hebrew between them. An Israeli cop?

Jake tried to make sense of this as they marched down the sidewalk. *JTTF?* Dozens of agencies were part of it; maybe the *Mishteret* was, too. But somehow the man knew Jake understood Hebrew. "Who are you?"

The man pushed him forward. "Call me Ephraim."

Ephraim? Jake recalled Kaminsky's words at the White Castle. He broke Ephraim's hold when the man answered his phone and swiveled to take a good, straight look at him.

Mid-forties, triangular face, broken nose, straight black hair, Mediterranean olive skin. The photo on the Red Notice: *Alias Eldar, Alias Jacob.* Only the moustache was missing.

Jake's bubbling lava pit of anger sent up a geyser. "You son-of-a-bitch!"

❖

Miriam frowned to herself. She'd read everything she could

find on the computer about the four European targets. Jake was right, the few common threads were very generic: no meaningful security, direct access to crowds, lots of Jews. Now she'd had time to look at the data, though, the tickle of an idea played hide-and-seek in the back of her mind, just out of reach.

She woke up her dormant border-cop brain, the one that usually had had good instincts before she started second-guessing them and ended up with a thrashed knee and an aborted career. She turned off the facts and tried to connect with something more elemental—how did the targets make her feel?

Kaminsky materialized next to her. Sweat beaded his forehead despite the cold. "The others are here. Elena was watching you a few minutes ago. She's not even trying to hide."

Miriam didn't feel threatened. She'd put up with Kaminsky; how much worse could the other Mossad agents be? At least the female one had been trying to help. "What are you going to do?" she finally asked.

He checked both ways, bounced on the balls of his feet. "She may not have seen me. I'll find an observation point. Please, Mrs. Schaffer, don't be alarmed if you don't see me."

I'll be delighted, she almost said.

He took a step backward and froze.

"Hello, Avi." A woman's voice, low and steady, speaking Hebrew. "Before you ask, that's a pistol in your spine. If I shoot, your prick'll never work again. Please let me shoot you."

Kaminsky swallowed so hard, Miriam could hear it. "Sandrine! What a lovely surprise." His voice climbed a full octave.

"Not for me. Mrs. Schaffer, we've met, but we haven't, if that makes any sense."

Miriam turned to find a familiar face peering at her over Kaminsky's shoulder: Jake had called her "Elena," Kaminsky used "Sandrine." "You were at the station and the cemetery. I guess I should say 'thank you.'" She tried to read the woman's eyes, but got back a cool distance. "Are you here for him or for me?"

"Both. I'm glad you've survived, I've had my fingers crossed for you." She did something that made Kaminsky wince. "Avi, just because you don't feel this anymore doesn't mean I can't shoot you."

348

Miriam watched a gloved hand slide around Kaminsky's waist, first on his left then his right, then feel under each arm and disappear into his coat pockets. A plastic card—the hotel room key—whisked out of the left pocket. The hand slipped a pistol butt out of his right pocket.

"Take this for me, Mrs. Schaffer."

A gun could be useful. Miriam put down the computer, then edged to her left to block the crowd's view. She took the Beretta from Kaminsky's pocket and slid it into her own.

Kaminsky suddenly pivoted, rammed an elbow into Elena's side, then sprang for the curb. Elena stumbled backward, swearing. Miriam managed to grab the middle two fingers of his right hand, used his own momentum to wrench the hand up between his shoulder blades, the way she used to do on the border. When he tried to twist out of it, she clawed the fingers of her free hand into his hair—he squawked in pain—then charged him head-first into the aluminum scaffold pier. His skull rang like a church bell.

It wasn't until he crashed to his knees that Miriam noticed the staring faces all around her. "Police business!" she called out, from old habit. "Move along, please." Then she realized she needed to repeat the command in English. To her surprise, most everyone obeyed, although a couple took cell-phone pictures before leaving.

"Good job, Mrs. Schaffer." Elena, face red and eyes blazing, dug a white zip-tie from her chunky black nylon shoulder bag and presented it to Miriam. "Make it real tight."

"Sandrine, listen to me," Kaminsky croaked while Miriam bound his wrists. Blood dribbled down his forehead. "The bombers are coming here! Let me help you stop them! Let me clear my name, please!"

"In your dreams, you bastard," Elena growled. "I hope they send you to Lebanon."

❖

Jake ignored Ephraim's raised hand, his urgent murmurings into his phone. "Who are you? What do you want? How'd you find me?"

Ephraim pressed his phone to his chest. "We followed you

349

from the hotel, but never mind all that now. Tell me what you're looking for."

Jake closed on him, fighting the urge to beat the man senseless. "Why?"

Ephraim stiffened as Jake approached, maybe reading Jake's mind. "There's a bomb on Wall Street. Please, what did you see back there?"

"Oh, shit." Was it the NYSE after all? Had he screwed up? Jake took in the spreading pool of evacuees across the street. "White Ford Econoline, 'Eastside Electric' on the sides, New York tags 49612YR two weeks ago. There may be a black guy driving it." He pointed to the still-hemorrhaging building. "But what's with all this…?"

Ephraim repeated the information into his phone, then shoved it into an inside pocket. He grabbed Jake's elbow and set off toward Miriam. "It's possible they're both targets, or neither is. I need to talk to you and Mrs. Schaffer—*now*."

Kelila couldn't take her eyes off the computer Schaffer hugged against her chest. What had Grossman managed to keep to himself? "This is really the target? You're sure?"

Schaffer said, "Jake thinks so. You must, too, I mean, you're here. Do you know something different?"

"We're here because you are. Ephraim thinks the target's Wall Street. What's your intel?"

Schaffer hesitated, then passed the computer to her. "If it means anything, I've looked it over and I'm not so sure, now."

Kelila opened the lid and brought up the desktop. As she read the names on the dozens of folders, her face began to burn. This was everything they'd needed, and far more. "You bastard," Kelila hissed. "You sat on all this?"

"No!" Grossman's eyes popped. "We sent everything to Tel Aviv! Everything!"

"Snake." Both her hands trembled. After all these years, she still reacted this way to the thought of him. To break her heart was one thing; it was already missing pieces when they'd met. But to break a three-year-old girl's heart, too? For that alone he should burn in Hell.

Kelila glanced right to see two squads of NYPD officers in tactical gear approaching from Fifth Avenue on either side of the street. A cop would stop at each parked car, nod into the radio handset on his or her shoulder and say a few words. Trucks and cars and vans headed out the roadblock one by one. The locals were finally clearing the place; about time.

She balanced the computer with one hand and pulled off her black cashmere scarf with the other. "Mrs. Schaffer, cover his hands with this. The police are here."

Schaffer twisted the scarf in her hands. "Is that an order?"

Attitude was the last thing Kelila needed now. She forced a smile. "Please."

Grossman gazed out at the cops for a moment, then watched Schaffer wrap the scarf around his wrists to hide the zip-tie. His sagging shoulders and drooping head told Kelila the spirit had gone out of him.

Then he bolted.

He was in the street before Kelila could shove the computer at Schaffer and pull her weapon free. He angled toward the cops on the other side of the road. "I surrender!" he cried in English. "You look for me! I surrender!"

"Don't you dare!" Kelila spat. She couldn't let him go to the locals; he knew far too much. She tried to snap off a shot, but Schaffer pushed her arms down.

"They're too close," she said into Kelila's ear. "Let the police have him."

"It's not that simple!" Kelila spat back.

Half a dozen police voices began yelling, "Put your hands up! Hands up! Halt! Stop!"

Grossman swung his bound hands upward, the tail of Kelila's scarf flapping. "Please! I surrender!"

"Gun! Gun! Gun!"

The gunshots sounded like midnight of Chinese New Year. Kelila stood stunned as four assault rifles and two pistols unloaded into Grossman. The crowd screamed and dived for the sidewalk or behind parked cars, but she couldn't move.

Hands grabbed Kelila's arms, dragged her behind a nearby black panel van. She twisted to break free until she saw Raffi bending over her. "What happened?" he demanded.

"He just... ran." She felt like a stupid rookie. He'd looked so defeated. She'd forgotten what a good actor he was. Then she realized: *Grossman's dead.* She'd fantasized about that for years, but this wasn't at all what she'd had in mind. "I'm sorry. I didn't think—"

"Never mind," Raffi said. "We have to leave. Now. The police will lock this place down. We're all at risk now. You, too, Mrs. Schaffer, Mr. Eldar."

Schaffer watched the cops approach Grossman's prone, bloody body, a hand over her mouth. "What about the bombers?"

"If they haven't made their move by now, they won't," Eldar said. "I screwed up."

Raffi said, "Perhaps not. Let's go, we have a lot to talk about."

NINETY-THREE

Jake stalked into the suite's bedroom a few paces behind Ephraim, or whatever his name was. He'd just been able to hold himself together while the four of them marched back to the now-late Kaminsky's suite, but no more. "I have a message from my wife," he growled.

Ephraim stopped next to the bed and turned, scowling. "What are you—"

Jake crashed a right uppercut into the man's jaw. Ephraim staggered back a step, then the bed caught him behind his knees. He toppled backward, bouncing when he landed.

Jake waited for him to struggle up on his elbows before he said, "She's dead because of you. Our baby's dead because of you. My daughter's head is broken because of you. Tell me why I shouldn't put you through that window."

A pistol's hammer cranked behind him, cutting through his words. "Is there a problem, Mr. Eldar?" Elena's voice was loud and hard.

Then another pistol hammer cocked. Miriam's voice cooed, "Is there a problem, Elena?"

Jake looked over his shoulder. Miriam pressed the muzzle of a Beretta against the back of Elena's skull. Elena stood rooted, her pistol aimed at Jake's head, self-disgust all over her face.

Ephraim barked, "Both of you, stand down. Mr. Eldar and I have things to talk about. Leave us to it."

After a moment, Kelila raised her pistol beside her head, decocked, and let it dangle by the trigger guard from her index finger. Miriam slowly lowered her weapon and stepped aside. She swept an after-you hand toward the table outside the door.

"You've made your point, Mr. Eldar," Ephraim said once the two women left. He rolled into a sitting position, massaging his chin. "Hit me again and I'll break your arm."

Jake could barely see through the red haze in his eyes. "Now what?"

Ephraim dabbed his fingertips on his tongue, examined the wash of blood, then rubbed his hands clean. "Believe it or not, I know what you're feeling. I am not your enemy."

"*You* know what *I'm* feeling." Jake let out a sharp, bitter laugh. "You assholes got me thrown into prison, then court-martialed me and kicked me out of the army. Then you steal my name and get my daughter kidnapped and my wife killed." His voice had climbed from a growl to a roar, then broke on his last word. He gulped down a knot of air. "You're not my enemy...?" He stalked toward the window, his hands wrapped around the back of his neck.

Ephraim stood, shook out his shoulders. "I understand, Mr. Eldar, and I can't blame you for being angry. You were used shamefully. But everyone in this suite has also been wronged—Elena, Mrs. Schaffer, even myself. A larger wrong is about to happen and we're running out of time. Right now, you and Mrs. Schaffer are the two most valuable assets the Institute has."

"We're not your assets."

"Yes, you are. You know what Kaminsky has on that computer, you've had time to look it over. I need to know why you went to the Diamond District." They both glanced toward the sound of the TV switching on in the sitting room. "I know you hate me and the Institute and quite frankly, I would too. Forget it for now. You're an analyst, a good one according to your record. Report your findings."

This didn't make any sense. Enough of the red fog cleared away so that Jake could try to think. "Are you saying you don't have this intel? Kaminsky said he'd sent it to Mossad."

"We have some, but not what you have if you know about a vehicle and suspects." Ephraim held up both hands. "I can't explain what's going on. All I know is that you and I and the women and my other man are on the same side for now. When this is over, you can beat me bloody if you want, I won't resist. I need your help

354

now. Do you understand?"

Shit. Jake turned to stare out the window past the Chrysler Building a few blocks away. He'd so hoped he'd get the target right, that the PD would roll up the bombers and he could finally bail on this and go home to Eve. But that didn't happen. His frustration exploded when Eve's drawing filled his head again. He slammed his palm against the wall over and over until he couldn't feel it anymore, roaring to drown out the banging of his hand and in his head.

Help this Mossad asshole? Jake would sooner stuff him down the nearest trash chute. But it sounded like Mossad was playing this Ephraim guy, too, which was just twisted enough to be true. "I don't get it. Doesn't Mossad want you to find these guys?"

"I don't know." Ephraim rustled behind him. "Oh, to hell with it, yes I do. They won't mind if we find them, but they also won't mind if we don't. They win either way."

Figures. "So you're off the reservation."

"If by that you mean we're exceeding our brief, then yes." Ephraim joined Jake at the window, hands in his pants pockets, his face grim. "Would you like to help me screw the Institute, Mr. Eldar?"

Jake rewound and replayed that in his mind to make sure he'd heard right. "Seriously?"

"Seriously."

Put that way, Jake didn't have to think twice. "What do you want to know?"

Kelila plucked two Stoli miniatures from the back of the minibar. She resumed her seat at the computer and watched Schaffer scribble lists of places on a portable dry-erase board, her movements quick and confident. "Would you really have shot me?"

Schaffer, scattering notes beside the place names, didn't even turn around. "Yes."

Kelila didn't doubt it. The past three weeks had showed her Schaffer was a hard woman. "I'm glad you didn't." She drained one of the vodka bottles in one long swallow, then debated downing the second one. The burn took her mind off Grossman's execution and her disappointment she hadn't killed him herself.

She'd powered her way through the folders Schaffer pointed out and a couple others that looked promising but would have to wait. If she'd had this stuff yesterday, they might have been able to figure out what was going on and stop it before now.

"Where are those lists coming from?"

"Jake built them when we were with Kaminsky. I'm trying to think if I've forgotten anything." Schaffer spanked her palm with a marker. "I can still remember lists pretty well. I guess it's from memorizing license plates on the border."

"Oh, God, they did that to us at the Academy, too." Kelila leaned back into her chair. "I've seen the way Eldar is with you. I've got to ask. Are you two sleeping together?"

"No!" Schaffer wheeled on Kelila, horrified. "How can you—"

"He's a good-looking guy. You've been through a lot together. You're both single—"

"His wife died three weeks ago! He hasn't even been able to bury her yet. He's just..." She hesitated, clearly searching for a word. "He's just... a friend."

"You threatened to kill me for a 'just friend' you met three weeks ago?" Schaffer opened her mouth for a counterattack; Kelila raised her hand. "Okay, if you say so." *Let her kid herself.* Kelila watched Schaffer for a few more moments, then played a hunch about the woman's character. She pulled her pistol from her coat hanging on the chair back, dropped the magazine, locked back the slide and placed it at the far edge of the table.

Schaffer turned to watch the whole process. They read each other's eyes. Then she drew the Beretta from her waistband at the small of her back and repeated what Kelila had done.

Kelila held up the surviving tiny vodka bottle and smiled. "You told me you had a theory about the targets. Come walk me through it."

❖

Gur followed Eldar out the bedroom door to find the women sitting shoulder-to-shoulder at the small, round table, talking with their heads together like best friends. He noted the empty pistols and liquor bottles and shook his head in wonder. Less than an hour ago, Schaffer had threatened to blow Kelila's head off. How do women manage these things?

Eldar had briefed him on the Hezbollah team and the targets in Europe. Gur now understood why he'd picked the Diamond District. Tension still hummed between them. Gur recalled how angry he'd been after Varda was murdered; had their situations been reversed, Gur would still be looking for a chance to slit Eldar's throat. Détente was all he could hope for now.

Gur stepped to the table. "Elena, do you have anything for us?"

Kelila leaned back and smiled at him. "Yes, *Raffi*, we do. First, I told Miriam our names. With what we've put them through, they deserve to know."

Gur stifled a growl. So much for cover. "And?"

"Miriam has a theory about the target." Kelila turned to Schaffer. "Go ahead, tell them."

Schaffer turned her chair so she could talk directly to Gur and Eldar, who idled near the minibar with a bottle of beer. "Look, I know I'm not a spy or an analyst or anything." She steepled her hands in front of her lips. "But I was a cop. I learned to look at a situation and figure it out quickly so I wouldn't get myself killed." She pointed to the whiteboard. "The only special thing those four places have in common is the pictures they paint."

"Pictures?" Eldar sounded bewildered.

This was what Gur had wanted to avoid: amateur "theories." "Really, Mrs. Schaffer—"

"Just let me show you." She reached in front of Kelila to click on one of the computer's browser tabs. "Jake couldn't understand why they picked the target they did in Berlin. Well, this is the Rykestrasse temple in Berlin, the biggest one in Germany. It's a brick wall."

Gur moved closer to the screen. She was right; an attractive brick wall, perhaps, but a wall nonetheless. He knew it screened a courtyard with the sanctuary behind that. "So?"

She clicked on the next tab. "Now here's the target, the Oranienburger Strasse temple. It's gorgeous." The picture featured a huge central onion dome with gilded ribs, flanked by two smaller companions atop towers. She stepped through more photos showing the intricate stonework, arched windows and ornate tripled front doors. "Now imagine this with burning cars and dead people. It's even more horrible because it's so pretty there. That's why they'd attack a congregation of two hundred instead of the one with two thousand."

"These savages don't think that way," Gur said. "You can't–"

"Let me finish," Miriam snapped. She popped up the next picture, a striking white Art Nouveau building with a squarish silver dome. "This is the Tempio Maggiore in Rome. Did you know it's not the largest in Italy? The largest is in Trieste, but it's just a big gray box. Look how pretty this is. This is the view the news cameras would have. Imagine dead and wounded people all over this little plaza. Obscene, isn't it? It's another picture of beauty and evil."

"Um, Miriam—" Eldar ventured.

"Jake! Just wait!" She brought up the Anne Frank House, no longer visible behind the modernist façade screening it. "Here the neighborhood's pretty. All these little brick townhouses, the canal, the trees. Here's the Westerkirk, isn't that steeple great? With the red clock? It's all so Dutch. Now put dead burned people all over the street and floating in the canal."

She burst off her chair, hurried to the TV and thrust a finger at the picture. "Paris. Does this building look familiar? There's something like it in every Western country. The columns, the stairs, the statues—it's like our Capitol, or the Supreme Court, or the British Museum. It's pretty, it's impressive, it says 'power.' How many Christmas parties do you think are going on in Paris tonight? Why attack this one? Maybe because of how it looks."

Gur sighed. Superficially, she had a point. But everything he knew contradicted that superficial notion. "Mr. Eldar," he began carefully, "can you remember Hezbollah ever choosing a target because of how it looks?"

"Never. They choose targets by what they mean."

"They also assassinate people with bombs." Schaffer held her hand out to Eldar. "Remember three weeks ago? We had this same talk, except I was the one who kept saying 'they don't work that way.' Well, I was wrong, they do, so maybe they also do this."

Gur probed the seed of a headache between his eyebrows. He'd hoped for something serious. They didn't have time for this. "Kelila, do you believe... this?"

Kelila flipped through the photos on the computer, her lips flat. "I can see why Eldar picked the Diamond District. If I was Hezbollah, I'd have a go at it, too." She raised her hands palms-up. "But it isn't there or Wall Street. Miriam's idea explains the European targets better than anything I can work up. Sometimes we can know our enemy too well, we can't see when he changes."

"Like Alayan and his people," Schaffer said.

"Exactly." Kelila stared into the screen for a few more moments, then shook her head. "I don't have any better ideas. Do you?"

He didn't, but that didn't convince him. "Then why the package bomb at the Stock Exchange? Why the threat in the Diamond District? How does that fit?"

Eldar said, "Well... it fits with al-Shami's shtick. He's into deception. He pulled a job in Yüksekova last year for PKK. He planted five different decoy bombs to keep the Turks busy, then killed a Turkish general with a sixth. Maybe he's laying smoke."

That at least sounded sensible. "What else do we know about this al-Shami?"

Kelila took over the computer and stabbed at a list of files. She turned the screen back toward Gur. "Adad al-Shami, Syrian, around forty. He learned his business in the Syrian special forces in the early '90s, mostly in Lebanon. Since then he's been for hire, and he doesn't play favorites. He's done jobs for Iran and Iraq, both sides in Syria and three factions in Yemen."

Gur studied the photo on the screen. A long, weathered face, stubble hair in full retreat up his forehead, dark eyes, large ears. He looked like a killer as much as Orgad did—that is, not at all. But killers looked the part in films, not always in real life. "Mr. Eldar, is this possible?"

Again Eldar exchanged silent words with Schaffer, who'd drifted back to the table. He drained his beer, set the bottle on the minibar, then scrubbed his face with his hands. "They've got their own TV channel. They make video press releases now. Hell, they've got a theme park. I guess it's not nuts to think they've discovered how to use images." He shrugged. "They haven't moved on the two most obvious targets here, so I'm tapped out. Miriam's idea is the best thing we've got going." He looked to Schaffer. "Mind if I guess where you think they're going?"

She turned up the corners of her mouth. "Go ahead."

"Emanu-El?"

Schaffer nodded. "Kelila, bring up the picture."

Gur's first reaction was, *that's a cathedral, not a temple.* But he had to admit there was a power to the place that most temples lacked, a solidity and grandness that he imagined Hezbollah's mad dogs would love to defile. "Why here?"

"It's the most obviously Jewish place in the city that actually looks like something," Schaffer said.

"It's the largest Reform temple in the world," Eldar said. "If they were just after body count, I'd say they'd hit that big one out in Williamsburg, but that looks like a damn warehouse. Also, that one's Orthodox. Hezbollah's gotta know by now Americans don't care about foreigners. Hasids look foreign even if they're fourth-generation New York. Hell, most people here can't tell the difference between a *shmata* and *hijab.*"

Gur watched over Kelila's shoulder as she flipped through the pages of Emanu-El's website. He had to admit, the place was impressive. "What's the congregation like?"

"Big," Eldar said. "Two grand or so."

"Twenty-five hundred," Kelila said without looking up.

"Whatever. Rich. The whole neighborhood's expensive. A lot of Upper East Side Jews, some of the city's Jewish power elite. The Mayor goes there, we saw him once."

Which meant the dead bodies would wear suits and dresses. The survivors on television would be prosperous and probably good-looking in a Western way. There'd be at least one cute little blond boy or girl with some hideous injury. It would drive the Americans into a frenzy.

Gur cursed and paced to the window. The sky was twilight-dark under a quilt of bruised clouds. He glanced at his watch: nearly five-thirty. Sasha's last text said he was on his way north from Wall Street, and where should he go? Good question.

This was their last chance to stop the bombers. If he forgot everything he knew about Hezbollah operations, Schaffer's theory made some crazy kind of sense, as did the proposed target. He'd acted on hunches before, but they'd been *his* hunches, not a civilian's.

"Raffi?" Kelila's voice cut through his thoughts. "Look at the television."

Gur saw an African newsreader in front of a "NYC Terror Siege" graphic. Someone turned up the sound with the remote. "...so far: CNN sources have identified nine areas throughout New York City currently locked down due to anonymous bomb threats..."

A list replaced the newsreader's face. City Hall. Diamond District. LaGuardia. Lincoln Center. New York Stock Exchange. Penn Station. Rockefeller Center. Times Square. United Nations. *Good God*, he thought. *How many of these are real?*

Eldar said, "Those places are scattered all over the island. The PD's probably stretched damn thin right now. And, notice anything missing? There's nothing near the temple."

Kelila said, "Whoever's doing this wants people looking everyplace but there."

No more dithering. It was time for Gur to do what he was paid for. "All right, we'll go to Emanu-El. Mrs. Schaffer, are you with us?"

"Yes," Schaffer said without hesitation. "I'll help."

"Mr. Eldar?"

The two civilians exchanged worried looks. Schaffer's eyebrows arched. Eldar shut his eyes and leaned his head back.

I'm sorry to ask so much, Gur thought, *after costing you so much.*

Eldar opened his eyes and looked straight at Gur. "I'm in."

NINETY-FOUR

The five of them stood in a row on the west side of Fifth Avenue at 65th Street, their backs to a dark, winter-dormant Central Park, necks craned upwards.

"My God, it's huge," Kelila whispered, her jaw hanging open. "I had no idea."

"We've got a Temple Emanu-El in Cherry Hill," Miriam said, "but it's nothing like this."

Refael shook his head. "What a target."

Jake said nothing. When he returned to America with Rinnah, they'd attended their first American Yom Kippur worship here. Rinnah's face had worn Kelila's same wonder-struck expression when she first looked up at the buff limestone façade towering more than a hundred feet over them, the huge rose window glowing like a giant jewel under its massive central arch.

He remembered the excitement in Rinnah's eyes. He recalled her dress, the first one she'd bought in New York—velvet the green of moss deep in the forest. He felt her hand in his. Tasted the roasted chestnuts they'd bought from a street vendor a block away before the service. It was yesterday, it was years ago, and he ached to pull her close, to feel her warmth again.

Someone touched his sleeve. "Jake?"

"Yeah." He fake-smiled to Miriam beside him. In her charcoal pantsuit and slate-blue blouse, she looked just like the Miriam he first met a thousand years ago. "Just thinking."

❖

They stood quietly, watching the parade of cars drop worshippers into the thickening stew of people sloshing around the temple's three pairs of bronze main doors. A flutter came and went in Miriam's stomach. One of them could be a suicide bomber. Would these people live to see a second candle lit?

"Because this is a temple," Refael said, "we have to assume they'll follow the pattern they'd planned in Berlin and Rome. That means a *shahid* in the congregation, probably near the front. Sasha?"

The Russian took a swallow from his coffee cup. "No metal detectors, but security on the doors. They wanded some people who looked maybe too big. They also search big bags."

"So no backpacks and probably not a vest," Jake said. "If he has a bomb, it'll be small."

A small bomb, Miriam thought. *How comforting.*

"Yes, meant to force everyone outside," Refael said. "Just to make things more complicated, our U.S. and U.N. ambassadors will be at worship tonight." He turned toward Jake. "Watch for anyone suspicious. If you see someone, don't approach him. Tell the security detail."

"How will we know them?" Miriam asked.

"They'll look like these guys in suits," Jake said. "With wires in their ears."

Refael nodded. "Near enough. The rest of us will be outside looking for the vehicle, if there still is one. Mr. Eldar, did you contact the police?"

"Yeah." His shoulders drooped. "My captain told me they have too many 'real threats' to go chasing another theory. Thanks and get lost, basically."

"It's down to us, then." Refael signaled to Sasha, who circled around Refael and Kelila and stopped before Miriam. He dipped into the gym bag dangling from his shoulder and brought out two bundles the size and shape of cigarette packs, handing one each to Jake and Miriam along with wedge-shaped earpieces. "Your radios. We share one channel, don't fuck with it. Tell us what you see."

Miriam pulled the pins on her bun and shook down her hair to camouflage the little black pod now growing from her ear, then checked her work in her compact mirror. Jake, sharp once again in his gray suit, nudged her and tried to smile. Her return smile felt as shaky as his.

Sasha tapped Miriam's arm. When she looked up, he offered her a pistol. "No, thanks. I have one already." He shrugged, gave it to Jake and returned to the other end of the line. Miriam rearranged her purse to fit the radio and Kaminsky's Beretta. Did spies carry bigger purses?

"Don't shoot unless you absolutely have to," Refael warned. "Gunshots will panic the crowd. They'll try to leave the building, and the last place we want them is outside. Also, the ambassador's security detail will kill anyone with a weapon."

All this should have been exciting but wasn't, just strange and a little unreal, as if Miriam was living a movie. She understood straight-out combat but not this secret-agent charade. She felt unprepared, off her edge, which worried her. She knew what she could do when she was at her best. She wasn't now, not even close. She hoped it wouldn't kill her, or Jake.

Refael stepped before Miriam and Jake, looking gravely at each in turn. "If they have an inside man, he'll have a weapon. Do what you can. I'll let you know if we stop the bomber before worship is over. Otherwise, don't be the first ones out the door, understand?"

Another flutter, this one longer. *Let the others take the blast.* Logical, practical, and utterly cynical. This had become all too real, all too quickly.

Refael shook her hand, then after some silent eye contact, shook Jake's. He gestured toward the temple. "Good luck. Go with God."

NINETY-FIVE

23 DECEMBER, 6:10 PM
CENTRAL PARK EAST

Al-Shami helped Mahir out of the sedan's back seat on 65th just past the corner with Fifth Avenue. The entry to the synagogue was already packed with well-dressed Jews jostling to get inside to talk to their god. Mahir would be just one more.

Mahir leaned back against the sedan's fender, straightened his somber black suit, waited for al-Shami to wrestle the false oxygen cylinder from the back. Al-Shami connected the clear plastic cannula's trailing end to the oxygen valve, then placed the cart's handle in Mahir's hand. The wispy, graying wig and false eyebrows transformed Mahir into the older man he'd never become. He looked utterly convincing; no one would suspect. "Try to be near the front," he told Mahir one last time. "Remember, you have to close the valve all the way to trigger the charge."

"Yes, yes." Mahir held out his hand. "*Ma'a salaama, sidi.*"

The gravity, the peace in Mahir's eyes briefly touched something inside al-Shami. He usually didn't think of his *shuhada* as anything but vehicles. Their zeal and bombast tired him. But this man, with his calm confidence and quiet acceptance of his destiny, was more human, more of a man than anyone al-Shami had met in a long time.

He gripped Mahir's hand for the last time with both of his own. "*Ma'a salaama, sadiqi.*"

Jake watched Miriam's face as they passed from the temple's sumptuous Art Deco marble foyer into the sanctuary. Wide eyes, check; dropped jaw, check; sucked-in breath, check.

Five massive arches on each side marched down the length of half a football field to the great central arch, which towered over the *bimah* and the pale-marble ark. Soft lights transformed the buff wall tiles into flowing amber. A geometric riot of color and gold leaf glinted from the twilight of the rafters and pitched ceiling a hundred feet above them. Organ music wafted from behind pastel marble columns above the ark, hymns Jake half-remembered, the Muzak of God's house.

Jake had come here five or six times with Rinnah, and each time she'd glowed like the candelabra. Jake gulped down the swell of longing and loss in his throat. *Not now*, yakiri, *not now.* "Ever seen anything like this?"

"In Europe, in cathedrals." Miriam's head swiveled this way and that, trying to take in everything. "Never in a temple before. I hope I'm wrong about this being the target."

He started noticing the crowd, which until then had been a shifting blur. Prosperous, well-kept, dark suits and nice dresses. Lots of handshakes, embraces, air-kisses. The children were turned out in their Hanukkah-at-Bubbe's outfits—pint-sized slacks and suit shirts for the boys, skirts and bows for the girls. While not everyone here was rich, Jake still felt out of his league, even in his good medium-gray suit and burgundy tie.

He pointed toward the sprawling group of people at the far end of the sanctuary, near the north pulpit. "That'll be the ambassadors up there, with their security goons and the rabbi."

"Should we introduce ourselves?"

A gaunt, thin-haired man in a black suit two sizes too large labored by, towing beside him a green-topped stainless-steel oxygen tank on wheels. Miriam grimaced. "Poor man. Bill's father ended up like that, from emphysema."

As he watched the man shuffle up the aisle, Jake couldn't shake the feeling that he'd seen the guy before. Where, he couldn't place.

Jake steered Miriam up the aisle. They both scanned the crowd, touching each other's sleeves and nodding toward people who stood out: a darkish young man with pale skin where a beard used to be; a barrel-shaped young woman wrapped in a heavy jacket; a South Asian man with nervous eyes. None of al-Shami's people crossed their paths, but there were so many faces to check and so little time.

Miriam said, "I don't like it, but I think we'll need to split up if we're going to keep a good watch."

"I think you're right. I'll sit up there, you back here. Let me know if someone's coming, I'll tell you if something's going down in front. Okay?"

She raised a skeptical eyebrow. "Still protecting me?"

"You bet."

Miriam sighed and shook her head, but the little upturn at the corners of her mouth didn't go away, so Jake figured she couldn't be too annoyed. Then her eyes went all business, checking sightlines, searching for exits and hiding places. "Okay. But if you have to be a hero, at least give me time to come help."

"If there's a vehicle, it's nearby, and the driver will be in it or by it," Gur told the others as the long-threatened snow's first drizzle started. Traffic noise easily drowned out their conversation should anyone try to eavesdrop. "They're going to need to respond in a minute or two, no more. Kelila, search the six blocks north of here. Sasha, the six blocks south. Don't bother going much more than two or three blocks east. The service will be 45 or 50 minutes. If you see anything suspicious, let me know, then run it down."

Kelila nodded. Sasha said, "Can we engage?"

"As long as you know what you're engaging. Our rally point will be in front of that building." He tipped his head toward the Arsenal's brooding shadow behind them. "I'll keep watch here and along these two blocks. Stay warm."

Sasha snorted. "You think this is cold?" He ambled off, shaking his head.

Kelila turned to go, but Gur snagged her hand and reeled her in. After a check to ensure Sasha was gone, Gur kissed her, their first time in public. They let it linger, drawing out every second. She settled easily into his arms, a warm, wonderful feeling Gur had missed so much.

When they finally drew back, Kelila unleashed a big, dreamy

smile. "That was nice."

"Yes, it was." He held her close, brushed the snowflakes from her hair. "When we're done, we should go somewhere, just the two of us. Have you been to the Seychelles?"

"No," she murmured. "They're beautiful, I hear."

"They are. Let's go."

"Love to." She pulled away just enough to look up into his face. "Are you okay?"

He gave her the best smile he could. "I suppose I want to know we have a future. Going into an action like this—"

"Shh. We do." She stretched up to kiss him again. "This'll be over soon. Then we'll have lots of time."

Gur wished he could believe her.

Mahir watched the pews around him fill with well-dressed Jews. So many in one place. Only a handful of Jews remained in Iraq, and they stayed out of sight. He'd never met a Jew until coming to this country; now they surrounded him.

He knew he stood out, but not in a way that would make anyone suspicious. The people who edged past him couldn't mask the pity in their eyes. They'd never believe why he was really here, or that someone so obviously frail could do such a thing. He hoped he'd have the strength when the time came. Sitting on this cushion, leaning into the end corner of the polished wood pew, was very comfortable. Leaving would take some will.

"Excuse me, sir. Sorry to disturb you. Are those seats taken?"

She was young—perhaps in her early thirties—her open, pretty face still unlined, her black hair still thick and shiny. A perfect miniature of herself held her hand. The little girl's big brown eyes stared at his face. It was the tube, he knew; children always noticed that first. He tried on a smile. "No, no. Please. Sit."

"Thanks." She returned his smile, shooed the little girl past his feet, then edged by facing forward, giving him a fine view of slender hips in a cadet-blue pleated skirt. Then a young man stepped in, towing a boy of perhaps six or seven. The boy thumped onto the cushion next to Mahir, wiggled to get settled, then craned his neck to take in everything there was to see.

Mahir turned away to watch the last few stragglers dart into their places. A few moments later, a little voice peeped, "What's that in your nose?"

He looked down at the puzzled green eyes staring back at him. Diya's eyes had been green until he was almost six, when they'd turned amber. So long ago. "It helps me breathe."

"Are you sick?"

Sick? Yes, his body was sick, enough to kill him soon. But his spirit was sick, too. Sick of what the Americans had done to his country, sick of living with the memory of a slaughtered wife and son, sick of being just another broken man with splintered dreams.

"Brandon, that's not nice," the father chided his son, saving Mahir from answering. He was also young, fresh and unlined as his bride. He and his son wore matching dark hair, blue jumpers and gray trousers. "Don't bother the man."

"No, is okay." He'd come to kill these people; how could they show him such consideration? "He is... like my sons, asking the questions always."

The young man nodded. "You know how kids are. Want me to trade places with him?"

"No, no. Is no problem." Diya and Rashad showered him with *why* when they were little, before they'd learned the danger of asking questions in Saddam's Iraq. When the Americans came, his sons started again with questions, but it was still dangerous. Little Brandon could ask anything he wanted and risk nothing more than a scolding. What would his sons have become if they'd had that luxury? Would Diya be alive? Would Rashad be free?

Mahir settled back and let the organ music wash over him. That was all done, all in the past, beyond reach. He needed to savor the next few minutes. His last few minutes.

Brandon fidgeted next to him the way Diya had at the mosque so long ago. Mahir watched the boy and wondered if there were such things as ghosts.

NINETY-SIX

The organ segued into the almost Anglican "Maoz Tzur." The crowd buzz died away with the first major chords; only the sharp squeaking of a few small children broke the sudden hush.

Jake made a slow scan of the sanctuary with his eyes. The pews were nearly full except in the far back, but the gallery was empty. Two thousand, maybe? A little less? The two ambassadors sat under their yarmulkes with their wives and entourages in the center section's first two pews. Dark-suited security men lurked in the side aisles.

"Maoz Tzur" gave way to the choir singing "O Chanukah" from its loft above the ark, accompanied by the piano. Jake's childhood in Hebrew school stirred inside him. While part of him watched the crowd, another part sang along silently with the choir, in Hebrew to their English.

The guy with the oxygen tank sat across the aisle and one pew up. He, too, looked all around, his eyes amazed. Jake had picked a seat near him to see if he could figure out why the man seemed so familiar. The oxygen tank rested outside the pew's side panel; a clear plastic tube snaked over the man's shoulder to his nostrils. Their eyes met. The man bobbed his head, either as a greeting or in embarrassment, Jake couldn't tell which.

"O Chanukah" became "S'vivon." The women in the choir made a sound like the wind whistling around a corner while the men chanted the words. The minor chords and Oriental melodies reached out to something elemental inside Jake. He wasn't devout; his parents hadn't been, either. Still, more than anything else, the music linked him to the hundreds of generations before him, spoke

370

to him of roots and tradition. He prayed he wouldn't let them down tonight.

After the final flourish of "Ocho Kandelikas," the graying, balding rabbi in a black robe raised his arms in greeting from the north pulpit. "Good friends, good *shabbas!* Happy Hanukkah to you all! This is truly a joyous Hanukkah celebration this evening in our congregation, as we welcome to our temple and into our hearts two very special, surprise guests. With us tonight is His Excellency, the Ambassador of the State of Israel to the United States, Avraham Steinitz..." a murmur bubbled through the crowd "...and His Excellency, the Ambassador of the State of Israel to the United Nations, Lev Avital." The rumble grew louder for a moment until the rabbi raised his hands again. "These two esteemed gentlemen honor us with their presence and together will light the first Hanukkah candle. Your Excellencies, to you we say *baruch ata b'shai modunai;* blessed are you who cometh in the name of the Lord."

Jake glanced at a movement across the aisle. The guy with the oxygen tank leaned forward, eyes wide, mouth cracked open, as if he'd just discovered his favorite movie stars were a few feet away. *Whatever turns you on*, Jake thought. He opened the leather-bound *siddur* to the page the rabbi called for, kept one eye on the prayer book and the other on the crowd.

Ambassadors! Mahir couldn't believe his luck. Al-Shami never mentioned this. Had he even known?

It didn't matter. Mahir's timing had just been decided for him. He'd strike when the two Zionists rose to light the candle. He'd make what little was left of his life count.

Kelila marched westbound on 67th Street, blinking away the snowflakes. Windows glowed from the stone apartment blocks and co-ops all up and down the street, making even this paved canyon feel homey. Colored Christmas lights twinkled around window frames; elaborate evergreen wreaths hung on several doors. Not that she had a lot of time to appreciate the décor.

She tapped her earpiece. "Sasha, find anything?"

"No. A lot of the right kind of vehicles, but nobody in them."

"Same here." She checked her watch. The worship had already started. "Keep looking. It's got to be here somewhere."

❖

This Jewish place didn't impress Sohrab. His father had taken him to the Goharshad mosque in the Imm Ridh shrine back home, a 15th-Century imperial Persian riot of blue tile and massive arches. This synagogue was almost understated by comparison. These snooty Jews all around him with their expensive clothes and squawking dress-up-doll children were nothing like the boiling mass of humanity at Goharshad, either. Twenty million pilgrims went there every year, the old and young, the rich and poor, a cross-section of the Shia world.

The Jews who really held his attention were the security men standing under the balconies on either side of the hall. If anyone would try to stop Mahir, it would be those thugs.

When the choir launched into yet another song (so much singing!), Sohrab slowly scanned the audience again. A few young men, none of them remarkable; women, children, old people, fat people. No threats he could see.

Wait. Twelve or fifteen rows behind him, other side of the aisle. *Is that...?*

The Schaffer woman.

Dark suit, blue shirt. She looked different with her hair down—not as old, not as hard. But it was her, no doubt.

An! Eldar must be here, too. The last thing he needed was their interference again. They knew what he looked like. They could call down the thugs on him.

He snapped his face forward and shrank in his seat. Now he couldn't look behind him. He couldn't pick out Eldar in the crowd, but he had to be there somewhere, waiting. He felt trapped, unable to find the enemy, vulnerable. He needed a secure observation post, someplace where he could see everything and act immediately if he found a threat to him or Mahir.

Sohrab's eyes zoomed to the empty galleries just below the large stained-glass windows.

❖

Something was off with the sick guy.

Jake's eyes kept creeping back to the man. He was always late to stand or sit, and when the congregation recited a passage the man's jaw didn't move. He'd wiped his forehead with a pale green handkerchief several times since the worship had begun. Maybe that was from his meds or his disease; it wasn't all that warm in the sanctuary.

Jake murmured along with the others, "It is He who redeemed us from the path of the oppressors, and revived our spirits when our own strength failed us." Again, the sick guy's mouth didn't move.

The rabbi called out, "His works and wonders surpass our understanding; His gifts and blessings are without number."

"We rejoice in His sovereign heart. We praise and give thanks unto His name."

While the cantor and choir sang again, Jake kept coming back to the oxygen tank. Sixteenish inches tall, four or so in diameter, on four-inch wheels. Maybe his time in *Yahmam* had warped him, but the thing reminded him of a small artillery shell.

Paranoid? Maybe the guy was a foreigner, here for the big show. Maybe he couldn't read English. Maybe he was sicker than he looked and couldn't move quickly.

Still, someone could pack a lot of ugliness in that tank.

Jake ducked his head away from the grandmother sitting to his left, tapped his earpiece. "Can you get the security guys on the radio?" he whispered in English.

Refael's voice came back instantly, in Hebrew. "Is there trouble?"

"Maybe. There's this guy, something's off." The grandmother shushed him; Jake held up a hand and tried an apologetic smile.

"No, I'd have to go through the embassy. Approach them yourself, or check the subject."

Sure, and get thrown out. Or shot.

"Jake?" Miriam's voice, tight, barely audible. "The Persian boy from the station is here, about ten rows behind you. I just saw him."

Shit. This was really the target. The bomb was here, maybe just ten feet away. Jake switched to Hebrew and hissed, "Refael, call the cops, now!"

A pause. Then Refael said, "When a policeman walks into the temple, the man with the bomb will explode. Find the bomber, neutralize him. Then we'll get the police involved."

❖

Gur checked his watch again while he plodded north into the shrinking tunnel of visibility along Fifth Avenue. No parked cars to shelter behind, remarkably few people, narrow tree trunks. He was so exposed out here. Not even the thickening snowfall offered cover.

He stopped halfway down the block, watched the three-lane parade of cars rolling by. It would be a miracle if he saw anything, much less stopped it. He could just visualize the van exploding in Times Square, bodies and blood and fire everywhere while he stood blocks away.

No, Alayan's Persian was here. It was the first *shabbat* of Hanukkah. They'd had their chance at dozens of secular targets today. It had to be here.

A man not much older than himself trundled past in a northbound wheelchair, a thick blanket shrouding his dead legs. A shiver skittered up Gur's spine. A prison on wheels, a life sentence with no parole. *Kill me if you must, God, but don't do that.*

The snow turned the middle distance into a gray Impressionist watercolor. Beyond the wheelchair, Gur could just make out the dark shape of a man at the next corner. He'd been there for at least fifteen minutes. Unlike the rest of the steadily dwindling number of passers-by, he stood rooted in place.

Gur's internal anomaly detector began to ping softly. He slipped his hand around the pistol grip in his coat pocket and padded toward the end of the block.

Kelila's feet and face had become cold, dead wood. Not even Paris had been this cold. She huddled under the antique iron-and-glass portico between Cartier and the Marina Rinaldi boutique, stomped some blood back into her feet, beat the clinging snow from her coat and hat. She stole a quick glance into Cartier's windows: only disappointingly empty display stands.

Across the street, in front of a brick-fronted townhouse, a white van idled at the curb.

She snugged her cap over her ears and jogged to the other side, then strode past the van, absorbing the license number as she went. Steam from the exhaust, melting snow on the roof, a dark-skinned man tapping the fingers of his right hand on the steering wheel's rim. Was he al-Shami's African? She couldn't tell.

Kelila yanked her mobile out of her pocket as if it had just rung and pressed it against her radio earpiece's switch. "I need info on a registration plate."

Raffi's voice barked in her ear. "Did you find the van?"

"Not sure yet. White van, 'Newtown Electric', engine on, a man with dark skin inside." She ducked down a concrete staircase thirty meters west of the van, next to the green awning over the entrance to a tan-stone apartment block, and put her phone away. "I'm on 69th between Fifth and Madison. New York registration, five naught one nine three Vingeyt Sefer."

"Hold a minute."

Kelila snatched a peek over the stone railing along the stairs. The van hadn't moved; the driver was still behind the wheel. Her heart banged away, ready for action. While she waited, she checked her pistol, already rehearsing her next moves. She removed her watch and zipped it into one of her shoulder bag's many pockets. "Come on, Raffi," she mumbled to herself. "Come on, before he leaves..."

Miriam just caught the rabbi's "Be Thou a shield about us, protecting us from hate and war" when the Persian rose, stepped past the person to his right into the aisle, then hurried toward the back of the sanctuary. His body bent slightly forward as if fighting a headwind.

Their eyes met as he passed.

He knows we're here. She felt the familiar jolt of adrenaline dumping into her system. "Jake, the Persian boy just left. He saw me." She swung out of her seat. "I'm going after him."

"No! Wait for me!" Jake's voice hissed.

"Watch the other one. If I need help, I'll call." If she got the chance.

"Be careful."

She burst through the doors into the foyer just in time to hear footsteps slapping up the stairway to her right. Upstairs, into the empty gallery. Miriam sucked in a breath and some courage, slung her purse strap over her head and left shoulder, and rushed toward the stairs.

Jake's anxiety level hit the rafters a hundred feet up. *Damn it, why can't she wait?* Was she seriously going to take on that guy with her gimpy knee and no backup?

The music stopped. A moment went by filled with the rustling and scattered coughs of two thousand people waiting for the next event. Then the rabbi announced, "For a special Hanukkah prayer, turn now to the bottom of page 89 as we call upon all the young people and their parents in the congregation to join us on the *bimah* for the lighting of the menorah."

The piano began to play. Brandon's father stood, leaned over his son and murmured to Mahir, "Excuse me, sir. Sorry to disturb you."

Mahir reached over the pew's arm, twisted the knob on the phony oxygen valve through two full turns. Another quarter turn would close the valve completely and trigger the bomb.

Now?

Mahir labored out of his seat, stood in the aisle, watched the young family file toward the raised platform at the front of the nave. The two ambassadors were already stationed behind the tall, eight-armed brass candelabrum. All around Mahir, children and their parents streamed toward the front.

The children. Dozens of them, scrubbed and wide-eyed and beaming with excitement.

Something other than his familiar nausea gnawed at him. *Allah, is this really your will?*

The sick guy's hand dropped to the tank, drawing Jake's attention. The guy covered the black knob at the top, twisted counter-clockwise twice. Shutting off his oxygen?

A mother and her twin sons edged their way down the pew toward Jake. He used their approach as an excuse to stand in the aisle and do a full sweep of the sanctuary. The sick guy lurched upright and shuffled into his side of the aisle, grabbed the handle on his tank for support.

Chattering, excited children everywhere, filtering toward the *bimah*. Jake's mind flashed him a vision—or a nightmare: an explosion, dozens of tiny burned bodies, screaming that wouldn't end. He fought back the bile scraping up his throat. *Stop this. Even if you gotta throw yourself on the damn bomb, don't let it happen.*

The young family who'd sat next to the sick guy was gone now, but he still stood. The man took a hesitant step forward.

Don't let this happen!

Jake crossed the aisle with two quick strides, took the man's elbow as if to help him. "Who are you?" he whispered into the man's ear. "And what's in the tank?"

The stairs led to a stone-walled vestibule with two exits, an arched one in front of Miriam, a square one to her right. The space wasn't any larger than her apartment's bedroom and bathroom put together. Ranks of empty pews stretched out from each, leading to other arches.

The Persian boy stood in the arch before her, perhaps ten feet away, an arrogant tilt to his head. His shadowed eyes examined her as if he was thinking of buying her. A thin, black sectioned tube stretched from his right hand, the tip tapping against his calf.

Miriam gulped. Whatever that thing was in his hand, she didn't want any part of it. She had a gun but didn't dare use it; the shot would send the congregation stampeding for the exits, straight into the truck bomb. *Don't let him know you're afraid.* She scraped together all the grit she could find and said in Arabic, "Put that away and we can settle this man-to-man."

The Persian snorted out a couple notes of a laugh. "There's only one man here," he said in Arabic. It took Miriam a few seconds to decipher his thick accent.

"I'll pretend you're one, then."

His face clouded over. The black tube clacked when it slapped against his leg. "I should have shot you at the train station when I had the chance."

"You tried, but you failed." She swallowed the knot in her throat, raised her hand, beckoning him. "Come closer. You're not afraid of me, are you?"

When he moved he moved fast, the tube a blur. She ducked it just in time, the whir loud in her ear, then lashed out with her good leg and buried her foot in his crotch. He squeaked, bent double, crashed down on one knee. Miriam recovered, dropped back a pace, shot a kick at his throat, but the Persian rolled under it and swept her left foot out from under her.

The impact of the marble floor knocked a cough out of her. Her head snapped back when she hit and dinged off the tile, filling her eyes with static. Miriam fought to catch her breath and stop the spinning in her brain.

The Persian was back on his feet, grimacing but mobile. He lunged, driving the tube's end down toward her outstretched leg. She jammed her right elbow into the floor, ignoring the burst of pain, and flipped herself over just as the tip of the tube dug into the marble with a metallic *clunk.* Sharp chips of stone sprayed her hand.

Okay, Plan B time. She levered herself off the floor using the back wall for support, heard rather than saw the tube hurtle toward her, and let herself fall back against the brass railing. The tube caromed off the wall close enough for her to see what it was—a collapsible steel baton. *Magav* had been looking at those when she left the service. They'd learned it was too easy to kill someone with one of those things.

The Persian wound up another swing. Miriam lunged off the railing and drove her right fist into his temple. He staggered, half-turned to face her. She smashed the heel of her left hand straight into his nose. The crack of cartilage filled the vestibule. As he staggered back, he got off a sloppy swing that almost missed, clipping her forearm. More stars in her eyes.

They retreated to their corners, steadied themselves, panted in some air. The Persian's eyes glowed with pain and hate even as blood poured down his upper lip and chin. Miriam leaned back against the wall next to the arch, shook her head to clear it, then reached for her earpiece. Gone. It lay near the railing, crushed. No time to dig the radio out of her purse. No Jake, no backup.

The Persian twisted his face into a snarl, raised his baton, then leaped at her.

Hurry up, Raffi. How long does this take?

Kelila peeked around the stone wall again, seemingly the thousandth time in what felt like a year but was perhaps five minutes. The driver was still in shadow, just a shape.

"I've got it," Raffi's voice rasped. "Black Chevrolet Express registered to Ernest d'Avila of Nyack, New York."

"No, no and no. It's white and a Ford and right in front of me." *It's him, it's the bomb...*

"Take care of it," Raffi said. "Be careful."

Kelila stepped back into the little alcove sheltering the door to the basement flat, knocked the snow off herself, rehearsed the next few moments one last time. Then a quick prayer, for Hasia, for herself, for Raffi. *Please let us have a future.*

She squared her shoulders and stepped out onto the sidewalk.

Kelila then turned in the van's direction and strode forward with both hands in her coat pockets, right hand curled around the butt of her pistol. *Let's end this.*

❖

People nearby were starting to look at them curiously. Standing together in the aisle without the company of children made them the most conspicuous adults in the temple.

"Police?" the sick guy asked Jake in heavily-accented English.

Jake shot a glance toward the nearest security guy, who was apparently paying attention to the scene on the *bimah.* "I'm Jake. You're...?" He stared at the man who squinted back at him. Then he saw it; the face in front of him morphed into the half-fuzzy picture of the Iraqi *shahid.* Jake had been looking for a bald guy. "You're Mahir, right? What's in that tank?"

The Rabbi started the Hanukkah payer. "Rock of Israel, father of all men, we are stirred by the sacred memories of Thy wondrous help..."

Mahir licked his cracked lips. His eyes darted to the crowd on the *bimah,* to Jake, to the side aisles. Sweat beaded on his forehead. "Please," he whispered. "Please, I must do my duty."

"What duty?" Jake's heart beat so fast it felt like one continuous throb. He balled his hands into fists to keep them from shaking. "Show me your hands."

Kelila's voice in his ear. "White van, engine on, a man with dark skin inside." A flash of hope lit Jake's brain. Did they find the other bomb?

"When violent men rose up against Thee to desecrate their sanctuary, to demolish its altar..."

Mahir frowned, but turned up his palms so Jake could see. No switch, no wires; wherever the trigger was, it wasn't there. Jake had to find the trigger. If he didn't, Mahir could set off the bomb any moment, before Jake could figure out what was going on.

"You don't want to do this." Jake tried to ignore the sweat running down his own sides and make his voice comforting despite the vise wrapped around his lungs. "It's kids. Look at them, Mahir. They haven't done anything to you, to anyone. Please don't do it."

Mahir licked his lips again, focused on the crowd of children. His eyes and lips saddened.

Jake felt a tiny buzz of success; he'd touched something inside the bomber. "You got kids, Mahir?"

After a long moment, Mahir nodded once.

"I have a little girl. She's six. She just lost her mom, she needs me. Your kids need you."

Mahir turned on him with an expression that shot a bolt of panic through Jake's body. "Americans kill Diya!" he snapped, a bit too loud. More people looked their way; the nearest edged away on their pews. "Americans put Rashad in the prison. I am now nothing to them."

Shit! Jake backpedaled out of this man's bulls-eye of pain. "I'm sorry. But those kids up there aren't your enemy. They don't deserve to die, any more than your son did." He swallowed, hoped he wasn't about to step off a cliff. "Don't do to their parents what got done to you."

"Grant, oh God, that the heroic example of the martyrs of old may inspire us with renewed devotion..."

Mahir's head swiveled to stare at the side aisle. Jake followed his look; the nearest security guy had noticed them. The man touched his ear, moved his lips. His cohorts focused on Jake and Mahir, began to slide out of the wings.

"You kill those kids, you hurt your own people," Jake told Mahir. "You hurt Lebanon and Palestine more than you can ever help. Let it go. Let it go."

Mahir's eyes softened as he took another look at the mass of children on the *bimah*. He stiffened his jaw to stop it from trembling.

All around them, the congregation recited, "...may the light of Thy presence and Thy truth shine forth to dispel all darkness and lead all men unto Thee. *Amen.*"

"Is the trigger on the tank?" Mahir hesitated, then nodded once. "Let me take the tank."

Mahir yanked the tank next to him like a straying child. "Stay away."

Jake glanced from Mahir's face to his white and trembling knuckles on the tank's vinyl handle. No way he was going to just give it up. Jake fought to keep his dinner down, to keep from turning and running.

Kelila in his ear again: "No, no and no. It's white and a Ford and right in front of me."

Refael: "Take care of it."

They found it? For real? Jake allowed himself an instant of hope. "Listen, Mahir. Your friends outside? We got them. It's over." He swallowed and extended a shaking hand toward Mahir, palm up. "Let me help you."

Mahir swept a dull steel-blue pistol out from under his suit jacket. A woman screamed. A man yelled, "He's got a gun!" People nearby cowered or stood up, ready to flee.

Tears trailed from Mahir's eyes, down his yellowed cheeks. "I cannot fail." Then he aimed at Jake's face.

❖

Gur paced steadily toward the man standing on the corner at 66th Street. While he tried to look as if he was on a casual stroll, he felt the familiar tingling rush of imminent action. He drew his weapon, held it behind his back. He had no backup. If this was the bomber, Gur knew he'd likely have just one chance to end this cleanly.

The man materialized out of the murk, a dusting of white on the shoulders of his dark car coat and brimmed hat. The streetlight on the northwest corner backlit the falling snowflakes and partly silhouetted him. Gur glanced at the banner under the light—an abstract blue dreidel, "Celebrate Chanukah!" *After tonight, perhaps.*

Gur closed to within two meters of the man, who now watched him curiously. He was roughly Gur's height but appeared stockier, although that might have been the winter clothes—or a bomb vest. The hat brim shadowed the man's eyes, but Gur could make out the long face, large ears and close-cropped hair.

"Pardon," Gur asked in English, "what is the time, please?"

The man pulled his left hand from its coat pocket—it held a cell phone—and nudged back his cuff. The streetlight glimmered on silver around his wrist. "Seven hours, ten minutes." His heavy accent was from someplace in the Levant.

Gur flipped his pistol's safety. "Are you Adad al-Shami?" he asked in Arabic.

The man cocked his head, as if he didn't understand. He shifted slightly, twisting his body toward Gur without moving his feet.

The shot caught Gur by surprise.

He sensed rather than heard the muffled *thud*. A red-hot arrow of pain drilled through his gut. Gur staggered backward a step, collapsed on one knee into the snow. He wrenched his Beretta out from behind his back, fired three rounds into al-Shami's blocky torso before the bomber freed his pistol from his coat pocket. Al-Shami rocked backward, grunted.

Gur lined up a head shot. His finger tightened on the trigger.

Al-Shami fired twice.

The baton's tip plowed a furrow in the stone just above Miriam's head, spraying rock shrapnel in her ear. Already bent over, she launched off the wall and drove her shoulder into the Persian's stomach, carrying them both into a heap in the middle of the floor with her on top. She grabbed his ears, slammed his head into the marble. He grunted, tried to buck her off, but she used her weight advantage to stay on and bounce his head off the floor again.

Suddenly, she found herself flat on her back with fireworks bursting inside her head. Everything she saw was fuzzy and doubled. Miriam struggled up on her elbows, blinked away the whirlies, then tried to find the Persian.

He used the back wall for leverage, struggling to his feet while keeping his eyes locked on Miriam. The Art Deco chandelier above them picked out a shiny wet spot on his hair; his eyes didn't focus correctly. But he still held that damned baton.

Miriam lurched upright. Her momentum carried her to the nearest doorway. She had to get that baton away from him. Until she did, he could hurt her a lot more than she could him.

She noticed the brass stanchion and plush scarlet rope blocking the door. In a moment, she'd unhooked the rope and hefted the post into her arms. It was a meter long, heavy, about the same weight as the loaded Negev light machine gun she'd sometimes packed in *Magav*, but not as well balanced. It'd have to do.

They pushed off their walls at the same time, the Persian's baton poised at the back of its next swing. Miriam led with the stanchion's base. When he was just over a pace away, she feinted a jab at his chest. He slapped the post with the baton, trying for her hand but only smacking the base. The *clang* echoed louder than any gunshot. While he winced and shook out his hand, Miriam drove the base into the side of his head.

The Persian fell like a sack of rice. Miriam took a step closer, raised the stanchion high. The next one would smash his skull.

His arm moved faster than she could register. The baton crashed into her left knee.

Her entire leg exploded.

Once again she was on the ground. The stanchion slammed against her ribs. The pain in her knee drilled directly into the middle of her brain, passing through her stomach just long enough to put it through a blender.

She squeezed away involuntary tears, searched for the Persian. He'd crawled a few feet away, out of reach, and while she watched, he forced himself onto his hands and knees. Blood trickled from his temple into the mess on his chin. His unfocused eyes searched for hers.

Miriam tried to sit up, but the blowtorch in her leg scorched more of her nerve endings. The pain burned off what little adrenaline she had left. She gasped out a string of Hebrew curses, fell back. The radio or gun in her purse dug into her kidney.

The Persian used the other stanchion and the arch to haul himself to his feet. He collapsed back onto one knee. Through it all, he never let go of that damned baton.

Miriam realized she couldn't hear the rabbi anymore, or the singing or the piano, just the little mewling noises from the crowd downstairs. Why was it so quiet? Where was Jake?

A gunshot echoed through the massive cavern of the sanctuary. Then screams. Then the unmistakable sound of masses of people moving fast all at the same time.

Oh, no. God, no. Jake? Was that Jake?

She caught the Persian's eye again. His face reflected the thought screaming in her head: *fuck this, no point holding back now.*

They both scrabbled for their guns. He drew his first.

NINETY-SEVEN

Kelila approached the van, trying to look casual as her mind crunched through all the possibilities. Someone in the back. Bomb vest on the driver. Deadman's switch. No, that would be too dangerous for someone who had to drive. He'd have a traditional detonator, something requiring thought, even if not much thought.

Just do it.

As she approached the van's nose, she pulled her hands free of her pockets, pushed up the cuff of her left sleeve and pretended to discover she'd forgotten her watch. She stopped, stamped her foot, looked back over her shoulder as if deciding whether to go back. When she turned toward the van, the driver looked her way.

Now. Do it now. She smiled, stepped up to the driver's window, held up her bare left wrist and tapped it, the universal got-the-time gesture. She slid her right hand into her coat pocket, gripped the pistol.

The driver's window whirred down. A black face peered out at her. *His* face. The face of the African *shahid.* "Yeah?"

Every muscle in Kelila's body clenched. "Excuse, what is the time?"

The driver looked down at his watch.

Kelila drew her weapon, thrust it toward the man's head, and fired three times before he had a chance to look up. The *pop pop pop* barely escaped the van's cab. Three red blotches bloomed in a tight group over his left ear. He slumped in his seat harness, his right hand thumping against the center console. Then, silence.

The van didn't explode. *I'm still alive.*

Kelila pulled her red Mini Maglite from her bag and checked

the interior through the window, careful not to touch the van. No stacks of dynamite or barrels of ANFO, just metal shelves full of cardboard boxes. No blood in the passenger seat; all three bullets were still inside the man's skull. A hand-operated detonator was clamped to the center console, gray with a T-handle, one of the German ones scattered all over the Mideast. *Right van*, she thought.

Four cars had passed since she'd shot the driver. It was long past time to go. Kelila yanked the keys from the ignition, dropped them in her pocket, stowed her flashlight, then sauntered west toward Fifth Avenue. "It's done," she told her earpiece. "Someone needs to secure the van."

No answer.

Two sharp *thumps*. They could have been backfires. Kelila knew they weren't.

"Raffi? Are you okay?"

"Come on, Mahir. There's no point. Put that away."

Mahir edged backward, dragging the tank along. His pistol muzzle shuddered more than just a little. Jake hoped the man wouldn't shoot him by accident.

Two security men edged down the aisle behind Mahir, guns aimed and ready. The congregation melted away from them row by row; Jake could hear the shuffle of feet scurrying down the side aisles. Four security men swept the ambassadors off the *bimah*, and the now-crying children burrowed into their parents' bodies. The rabbi stood frozen in the pulpit, face turned to plastic. All around him, sobs and squeaks and inhaled gasps of "ah!" "oh!".

Jake couldn't move even if he wanted. His legs and feet simply wouldn't answer his brain. Everything inside him had collapsed into a tiny, self-protecting ball. He could barely breathe, but he knew he had to keep talking. Talking might keep him alive.

"Put that thing down," he whispered. "How about you and me, we both live tonight?"

Mahir's mouth twitched into a grimace, full of pain and a hint of regret. "I die in months, I die now here. My life you cannot save."

The security men stopped, perhaps fifteen feet away. Both had their weapons locked on Mahir. The one behind him stepped up on a pew. If either of them missed, they'd drill Jake.

Jake stifled a sigh of frustration. How could he reach a man who had absolutely nothing to lose? "Don't go out like a monster," he said, without realizing he'd been thinking the words. "Don't kill those kids. That's not Allah's will. Make peace with our God." Mahir's brows wrinkled. "We have the same God, Mahir. We're both people of the Book."

Mahir swallowed hard. His shoulders began to shake with suppressed sobs. Slowly the trembling hand aiming the pistol at Jake's face drifted downward. "I must..." he rasped in Arabic. "I can't... forgive me..."

"It's okay," Jake said just above a whisper, the way he'd comfort Eve when she was upset. "It's gonna be okay." Jake slid forward, reached for the gun.

The shot echoed like a cannon through the sanctuary.

The bodyguard on the pew nailed Mahir's head on a downward angle, spraying Jake with blood and bone. The bomber's body collapsed like week-old broccoli. Jake lunged forward to catch the tank before it hit the ground. No explosion. *Goddamnit! He was giving up!*

The security men were on Mahir in an instant, but it was too late to stop the stampede. People poured screaming out of every pew, clutching each other, their coats, their children, racing down the aisles toward the exit. Jake watched a middle-aged woman tumble to the aisle's red carpet and nearly get trampled by the people behind her.

"Who are you? Who are you?"

Jake yanked himself away from staring at the oxygen tank to focus on the dark-faced security man braced before him, gun aimed at Jake's chest. "NYPD!" Jake blurted. "This tank... this tank's probably a bomb. Don't let anybody mess with it."

He was going to say *don't let anybody leave*, but he was too late. The front pews were empty. Knots of people huddled in the more distant pews, eyes the size of hubcaps. Behind him stood a mass of people crowded close together, watching now, their cries caroming off the tiled walls. He didn't want to imagine what the street looked like, or whether the truck bomb was dead or on its way. Had he failed? Had he succeeded?

"Show me ID!" the security man demanded.

Jake steadied the tank, held up his right hand, reached behind himself to pull his wallet with his left. He slowly brought it out, let it fall open, held it in front of him.

The man peered at the picture, then lowered his gun. "Okay. This is a bomb?" He nodded toward Mahir's oxygen tank.

"I think so. Call the cops. There might be another one outside."

Behind him, an echoing *clang* and a flurry of gunshots. He spun, looked automatically up and to the right, to the gallery's back corner.

Miriam. The Persian kid.

The crowd at the back of the sanctuary broke screaming for the exits. Jake charged down a pew's seat cushion for the side aisle. "Miriam!" he yelled into the earpiece. "Are you okay?" *No, this isn't fair, she can't die, not after everything...* "What happened? Answer me!"

❖

The Persian swung his pistol toward Miriam, his finger tightening on the trigger.

Miriam's instincts took over. She hurled the stanchion at him, ignoring the supernova of pain the move caused.

The base caught him in his upper chest, rocked him back just as he loosed off a shot that pinged off the stone walls. The metal-on-marble racket set her ears ringing. He tumbled backwards into the second stanchion, took it down. His gun popped out of his hand and slid a couple feet away.

Miriam bit down so hard her teeth threatened to turn to powder. She rocked forward, yanked her purse out from under her, dumped it out on the floor. The pain fuzzed her eyes with tears, but she could see well enough to pluck the Beretta from the mess, swat the safety, and find the Persian just eight feet away. He struggled up on one shoulder, reaching for his gun.

She put four shots into his chest, the *pop-pop* sound like a child's cap pistol. The Persian shuddered, looked down, gasped, but didn't fall. His shaking hand stabbed at his pistol.

Goddamned wimpy gun! Miriam palmed her eyes clear, aimed one-handed at his forehead, fired.

The Persian's head jerked. He flopped onto his back, arms spread wide.

Miriam aimed at his temple, pulled the trigger again, just in case. Blood spattered the floor. Then she fell onto her back, laid her head against the cool marble, and let out a strangled scream of agony.

"Miriam! Are you okay?" Jake's voice scratched out of the radio next to her. *Thank God he's alive!* "What happened? Answer me!"

She fumbled the radio out from the jumble next to her, found the "transmit" button. "I got him! I got him. Where are you?"

"I'm coming. Hang in there."

An interminable minute later, two sets of running footsteps clattered up the stairwell. Jake's face appeared over her, his eyes huge with worry and relief. "Are you okay?" He knelt, seized her hand. "What did he do to you?"

She didn't want to talk, just lie there, hold Jake's hand, let his voice cover her in a warm, safe blanket. "My leg. He got my knee. I can't walk." She noticed the streaks of blood on his face and shirt. "Are you hurt? There's blood all over you!"

"Security shot the guy with the tank." He looked over his shoulder, snapped, "Call an ambulance, now! Call several, we're gonna need them."

Miriam tilted her head up enough to see one of the ambassador's security men holding two fingers to the Persian's throat. He let go, pulled a cell phone from his pocket.

Jake slid closer to her, brushed hair from her face. "You scared the hell out of me."

Since the safe house she'd wondered how he felt about her. Now his eyes and his gentle voice told her everything she needed to know. She touched his cheek. "You, too. I heard the shot and I thought…"

"I'm okay." He squeezed her hand. "They're fighting each other to get out down there, but I think Refael's guys found the truck bomb. It's over."

❖

Kelila pounded down Fifth Avenue, dodging the scattering of other people on the sidewalk, trying not to slip on the thickening crust of snow. The facades of towering apartment blocks blurred by. She kept replaying the sound of the gunshots. They'd been too throaty for Raffi's Beretta; the Institute's issue weapon was a .22, meant for close-in work, designed to make minimal noise.

At 66th she caught a break at the light, raced across Fifth Avenue, dodged a cab accelerating into Central Park. A dark shape sprawled in the snow on the southwest corner.

"Raffi! Oh God!"

He lay on his back, his legs turned in unlikely ways, pistol still clutched in his right hand. Kelila dropped on her knees next to him, took his face in both her hands. "Raffi! Are you shot? Where are you hurt?"

Raffi flopped his left hand onto her nearest arm. "Listen," he panted. "It's al-Shami. He was here. Watching. I shot him, two or three rounds. He went north."

Kelila tried to stuff down the panic rising in her throat. *Think!* she screamed at her brain. *He needs you to think!* "The van's north of here."

"Yes." He coughed, a phlegmy sound. "Is it secure?"

"I have the keys. The driver's dead. I checked it for a second man, but didn't touch anything. You'll be okay, we'll get you out of here." She slapped the button on her earpiece. "Sasha, get the car! Raffi's been shot!"

"*Chyert podyeri!* Where?"

"Fifth Avenue at 66th, park side. Call Tel Aviv, find a *sayan* who's a doctor. Hurry!"

Raffi tried to squeeze her forearm, but there was no strength behind it. "Kelila. Stop him. Before he gets to the van."

She leaned closer, brushed the snowflakes from his face. "I'm not leaving you."

Down at the corner of 65th, a stream of people scattered from Emanu-El, moving fast, squealing and shouting. *It's happening!*

No, not now, not with al-Shami out there, no…

"Stop him!" Raffi's voice broke. "Finish the job!"

❖

"Jake!" Kelila's screech drilled straight through Jake's head. "We need help! Raffi's been shot, and al-Shami's heading for the van!"

No! It should be over! Jake slapped his earpiece. "I can't. Miriam's hurt."

"Go on." Miriam brushed his free hand. "If the people downstairs are going outside—"

"I'm not leaving—"

"Jake!" Her voice was far stronger than he expected. "I'm safer here than anyplace else. Go. We've got to stop him."

He could feel the pain he saw in her now-soft brown eyes. He wished he could say something, do something to help her, but he couldn't do anything more here. Jake muttered "shit" under his breath, then barked, "Where?"

"Fourteen East 69th." Kelila's voice was on the verge of cracking wide open. "A white van with 'Newtown Electric' on the sides. The driver's window is down. Hurry!"

Jake squeezed Miriam's hand one more time, then laid it carefully on her stomach and sprung to his feet. The security man was already moving toward the stairs. "Where the fuck are you going?" Jake demanded.

The other man stopped on the top step. "To the ambassador."

"Bullshit! You're staying with her. Nobody gets to her except EMS, understand?" Before the man could answer, Jake plunged down the stairs.

❖

Al-Shami stumbled across 68th Street, slipped on the slick curb, nearly fell. When he pulled his hand from his midsection, it came away bloody. The waistband of his trousers was soggy and warm in front and in back. Whoever that man had been, he'd done some damage.

Winded, al-Shami sagged against a tree trunk just past the traffic light. One more block. Haroun hadn't answered his call, which meant he was dead or arrested or fled. With Jews escaping the synagogue like rats, now would be the perfect time for the van to drive to that corner and detonate, but it needed a driver.

Me?

Sirens approached from at least two different directions. This wasn't ever how he'd planned to die, but his chances of escaping alive were very slim now. A cloud of anger boiled up inside him. He wouldn't allow himself to be arrested or to be cornered like some pathetic animal. He'd control his death the same way he'd controlled his life.

Al-Shami pushed away from the tree and staggered toward the next set of traffic lights, red halos in the falling snow. Pain pulsed from his midsection to every inch of his body.

Flashing blue lights and an ear-punishing siren raced toward him. He readied his weapon, holding it tight against his stomach, and waited for his last gunfight. The police car filled his vision and his brain. Headlights stabbed his eyes. Then it charged past. A second police car followed moments later.

They'd block the street, he figured. Nothing would get close to the synagogue. Well, he may not be able to kill Jews tonight, but he could still deliver Hezbollah's message to the world. If he had to die, he certainly wasn't going alone.

He reached 69th, grabbed the traffic-signal pole, took a second to gather his breath. His head echoed; his eyes blurred, breaking the lights into rings of colors. Blood loss? No matter.

Al-Shami shuffled unsteadily across Fifth Avenue. A couple of taxis steered around him. He missed the curb with his first step, paused, then lurched onto the sidewalk. The van was halfway down this street. He could make it on his hands and knees.

The street grew longer with every step. When he reached the green awning at number eight, though, he spied the van in a pool of streetlight ahead. Almost there. Just beyond he heard female laughter. Four gabbling girls in coats, skirts and knee-high boots approached from Madison Avenue. No threat.

He'd just reached the glowing twin carriage lights at number twelve when he heard the unmistakable ratchet of a pistol's hammer cranking back. A man's voice said, "Freeze."

❖

Gur stared up into the snowflakes falling sharp against his forehead. Melted snow and cooling blood chilled the back of his head and shoulders. Something in the left side of his chest reminded him of a child twisting a stick in an ant hole.

Below his rib cage, he felt nothing. He told his legs to move, but the command vanished. He tried to shift his hips, but his hips weren't there anymore. He knew what this meant.

Kelila knelt over him, anxiety and fear twisting her face. The streetlights glimmered in the tears hanging on her bottom eyelids. She'd ripped off her gloves, and her bare hands stroked his hair and chest and face. Her skin felt so lovely against his. *If only...*

"You hang on," she urged him, softly, fiercely. "We'll get you home. Sasha's coming with the car. We'll get you fixed."

He shook his head. "This can't be fixed."

"No!" She grabbed his coat lapels, leaned down until their noses nearly touched. Her face radiated heat. "No! You can't die! I won't let you!"

Such fire, such strength. It shouldn't be wasted on a cripple. He wrapped a hand around her wrist. "It's not up to you, *yakiri*. I can't live as half a man. And I can't be arrested. The shame, the scandal—"

"No! You don't have my permission to die." She swallowed, blinked. "We haven't had enough time."

They hadn't, and wouldn't. One last regret to pile on all the rest. The approaching sirens told him they had at most a few more seconds. "Get out of here. Don't let the police get you—"

"No!"

"Kelila, yes. Go. Now. I'm done." He knew she'd stay until they dragged her off to prison, that she'd fight, she'd get hurt. And if they saved him for whatever reason, she'd stay with him, in his wheelchair or hospital bed or whatever hell he'd be consigned to. She'd be ruined along with him, disowned by the Institute, abandoned. Her loyalty would destroy her. He couldn't have that. "Go. Please, do this one last thing for me."

Her tears dripped onto his cheeks, warm against the gathering cold. Kelila struggled to keep her jaw firm, to keep from sniffling, to be strong. Her face threatened to shatter. Then she thrust her mouth on his and kissed him with a fury that eclipsed even the first time they'd made love. He let the passion and sadness and anger and fear wash over him, warm him, and he tried to give her what little courage he had left to help her on her way.

The sirens were very close. She drew back, the streetlight shining in the tears now pouring down her face. She glanced down the street, then back to him. "Raffi..."

Gur's heart ripped itself to shreds. "Go, *yakiri*. My dear one. Go home to Hasia. Live."

After one last look, she stood, squared her shoulders, held up her head. She marched away like a mechanical soldier.

He waited until he could no longer hear her footsteps, until the police lights flashed against the walls and trees. While he waited, he whispered the Kaddish.

...May He who makes peace in His high places grant, in His mercy, peace upon us...

Gur pressed his pistol to his temple and closed his eyes.

...and upon all His nation Israel...

He pictured Kelila's face in his bed in the morning light, the life they might have had together. Then he saw Varda on their wedding day.

...and say Amen.

Then he pulled the trigger.

❖

The face Jake had studied on Kaminsky's computer now stared at him, the man's eyes tight with pain. The streetlight behind him threw a shadow from his hat over his face, but the bounce from the snow-covered sidewalk picked out the lines, the nose, the large ears. Dark, wet stains marred the front of his hip-length coat. Something metallic glinted against his stomach.

Jake aimed the Beretta between al-Shami's eyes. He was still breathing hard from the four-block sprint; keeping the sights steady was a chore. He knew he could just shoot the man and be perfectly justified, but he also knew someone like al-Shami would be worth his weight in diamonds alive and talking to the FBI. "Drop the gun. Now. It's over." He noticed the chattering girls approaching al-Shami from behind. "Stay back!" he shouted. "Get away from here!"

The four girls—teenagers?—halted a couple feet behind al-Shami, just ahead of the van. Dressed for a night out: short skirts and high-heeled boots in a snowstorm. One giggled, but her friends shushed her. They looked among themselves, confused.

Goddamn fearless New York girls... "This man is dangerous! Cross the street now, get away!"

Jake almost didn't see al-Shami's right arm twitch away from his stomach. He swirled to his left, fired blind into al-Shami's center of mass, just as the gun in al-Shami's hand blasted once way too close and something hard and hot slammed through the left side of Jake's chest. He stumbled, ended up on his butt in the street between two parked cars.

The teenagers screamed and scattered. Al-Shami swiveled, grabbed the nearest one by the hair and reeled her against him, one arm across her throat, the pistol in her ear. She shrieked, struggled, but he held her tighter, forced her chin in the air.

Shit! Jake heaved himself to his feet. He couldn't breathe right. A rib floated free on his left side, stabbing something tender under the skin. He coughed, staggered forward a step to face al-Shami, panted in a couple breaths, then leveled his gun at the bomber's head.

Al-Shami lurched a step closer to the van. Another two or three steps and he'd be at the driver's door. Jake could see the dead man slumped behind the wheel. He wouldn't let al-Shami get there.

"You kill her, you're done," Jake said. "You're not the martyr kind, are you? Not like your boy in the temple."

Al-Shami dragged the girl back another step. She gripped his forearm with white-knuckled hands. Her tears ran her too-heavy mascara down her cheeks. "Please don't please don't please please *please* don't kill me I don't wanna die pleeeeease!" she whimpered.

God, twice in one night. Jake's insides were still the size of a baseball and about as hard. Even in the cold, sweat poured down his sides, stinging his wound, mixing with the blood on his belly. In the temple, it had been just his life he'd pleaded for; now it was this girl's life, too.

Blue-and-white lights bounced off the buildings lining 69th ahead of him. The cops rolled out, took cover behind their car doors. A loudspeaker grated on. "Drop your weapon!"

"NYPD!" Jake bellowed. "Hold your fire! He has a hostage!" Thank God he'd watched all those police shows. He turned back to face al-Shami. "Now you're fucked. You hurt that girl, you're dead before she hits the ground. Let her go, you survive this."

Al-Shami glanced over his shoulder, then back at Jake. Jake couldn't see enough of the man's face to tell what he was thinking. *What do I say? How do I reach him?*

How do I not kill the girl?

"Sir, put your hands where we can see them!" The loudspeaker again. Jake heard a car pull up behind him, saw the lights strobe in the van's windshield. "We have this under control!"

"You don't have shit under control!" Jake yelled back. The effort kicked off a hacking jag. "That white van is a bomb. Call ESU and the Bomb Squad. This guy doesn't get to the van."

Police radios buzzed furiously in stereo. More sirens faded in from all around. A helicopter hammered overhead, then swooped off to the south. The girl had run out of words and just wailed like another siren. Windows lit up all along 69th.

Al-Shami stood stock-still, his one visible eye locked on Jake's face. He then jammed his gun under the girl's chin, disengaged his left arm, and pulled a cell phone from his coat pocket.

A phone?

The bomber shifted to peek around the left side of the girl's head. The phone screen's blue light washed the side of his face. His eyes flicked from Jake to the phone and back. He stabbed his thumb on one of the phone's buttons.

In a flash, Jake knew what al-Shami was doing. The phone was a trigger, like in Iraq and Lebanon. Dial a number, set off the bomb.

The blast would shred the buildings, blow out windows, light fires. But that wouldn't end it. Stone lined either side of the street in both directions. Al-Shami, the girl, the cops, people on

Madison—and Jake—were all inside even a "small" bomb's lethal radius, and Jake bet this one wasn't small. *Shit!* "Don't do it, al-Shami. It buys you nothing."

Al-Shami thumbed another key. Two digits of the eleven he'd need. He'd stopped paying attention to Jake. His face had drifted out from behind the girl's bobbing, shaking head.

Take the shot.

I can't, I'll hit her, I can't take that chance.

Take the shot!

Al-Shami's trembling thumb beeped across the keypad. Three digits. Four, five, six...

Jake adjusted his grip on the Beretta. His vision was clouding, his head starting to pound. He sighted on al-Shami's left eye, squeezed just enough to feel the trigger move. *Do it do it do it no no no what if I kill her I can't I can't...*

Eight, nine...

He took the shot.

Al-Shami fell back as if in slow motion. His arms spread wide when his body hit the snowy sidewalk. A dead snow angel.

The girl stood silent, shocked. Then she screamed, a wail that let out her fear and horror.

Jake tottered forward, took her in his arms in equal parts to comfort her and to not fall over. She clung to him, sobbing, the way she would a life ring in a flood. He leaned on her as his own fear and tension and hypervigilance flushed out of his system. She was alive. He was alive. Miriam was alive. None of their lives would ever be the same. But they'd awakened from the nightmare at last.

NINETY-EIGHT

The cemetery was hushed, as cemeteries usually are, as if even nature held its breath passing by. Airliners leaving LaGuardia or landing at JFK whispered as they flew overhead.

Miriam let Jake lead her up the rise through the thicket of monuments, the wind nibbling at their stocking caps and the hems of their winter coats. Eve held onto the flap of Jake's coat pocket. Solid, upright granite markers, Stars of David, Hebrew lettering, lions, tablets, menorahs. The few inches of snow frosting the ground was pockmarked and crunchy from too many freeze/thaw cycles since the last storm, but still slick enough to be a struggle on crutches. Winter was a bad, bad time to be a gimp, and after a month she dearly hated the things.

Jake moved stiffly. She knew the cold bothered his still-wrapped, not-quite-healed wound, but he hadn't wanted to talk about it. They hadn't said much past "Good morning" today. It wasn't the sort of day, or occasion, to invite conversation.

"We're here," he said just loud enough so she could hear. Miriam drew up next to him, leaned on her crutches, checked his face. He looked lost. She knew that expression; she'd seen it in the mirror two years before.

Miriam wanted to reach out to lend him some strength, but it didn't seem right. Not in front of his wife. "Do you want some time alone?"

"No. Please stay."

A low wooden marker poked its head through the snow about eight feet in front of them. If he followed the traditions, the permanent monument wouldn't come until December, around

399

Yahrzeit. She wondered if he'd wait. Would she have, if Bill had been Jewish? It had been a comfort in a way, not to have to choose.

"Daddy?" Eve looked up at Jake with confusion all over her face. "Where's Mommy?"

He stroked her head through the hood of her purple fleece jacket. "Right here, Bunny. Part of her's here."

Jake carefully stepped toward the marker with Eve in tow, bent, brushed away the snow, revealing a white tag covered with plastic sheet. He knelt, hands in his lap, staring at the ground with eyes that didn't see anything in this world. Eve stood next to him, leaning against his shoulder, looking around for a missing someone.

"Hi," he eventually murmured. His voice just barely climbed above the shushing wind. "It's me. I guess you know that, I…" He glanced up at the horizon, swallowed, then rested his gaze on the snow in front of the marker. "Sorry I haven't come sooner. It's been crazy. Hearings, investigations… It'll be over soon. The men who did this… they won't hurt anyone else again."

He reached out, touched the ground with one gloved hand. A tear rolled down his cheek, dropped onto his sleeve. "I miss you. So much. I hear your voice, I feel you… feel your touch. Maybe you're trying to take care of me, I don't know. Like I should've taken care of you."

Oh God, stop. Miriam felt a squeeze in her chest that wasn't from her coat and sweater. *Don't do this to yourself. It doesn't help. I know.*

"I… want to hope we'll see each other again someday. I…" His voice broke.

Miriam saw the quiver in his shoulders, heard the ratcheting sounds in his throat. She blinked to clear her eyes, drew herself up a little taller. This was where she needed to say something; she hoped she'd get the words right. "May His great name be exalted and sanctified in the world which will be renewed," she said in a voice that grew stronger and clearer with each word, "and where He will give life to the dead and raise them to eternal life."

Jake watched her through eyes shimmering in the tears that sheeted down his cheeks. "Amen," he rasped.

"It helped. When Bill died. It really helped."

He nodded, snuffled, dropped his gaze to the ground again. "This is Miriam. She's one of us, one of the people whose names were stolen. We helped each other stay alive. She's a good person. I wanted you to meet her." Jake patted the ground. "I'll be back soon, we can talk. I love you."

"Is Mommy talking back?"

Jake turned to face Eve. Sitting on his heels, they were almost the same height. He brushed her cheek with his fingertips. His mouth opened to answer, but only little breaking sounds came out.

"Eve?" Miriam hobbled forward, held out her hand toward the girl. "Come here, sweetie." She exchanged looks with Jake as Eve drifted to her side. He pushed himself upright, stumbled a few yards away, shoulders hunched and shaking.

Eve looked up at her, bewildered. "Why's Daddy crying?"

"Because he misses your mommy." Miriam wrapped an arm around Eve's shoulder, pressed the girl against her good leg. "Just like you do sometimes."

"Can Daddy see Mommy?" Eve asked. "I can't. I wish I could."

Miriam hugged Eve one-handed. "Close your eyes." Eve closed her eyes. "Now think of your mommy. Can you see her?" Eve nodded. "That's where she is. Inside you. You can see her anytime you want."

Eve opened her eyes, sniffed, looked to her father. Miriam braced with a crutch, bent and kissed the top of Eve's head. "Go take care of your daddy." Eve edged past Rinnah's grave, then trotted to Jake's side and wrapped her arms around his hips.

Miriam felt a little twinge as she watched them. She and Jake spoke on the phone nearly every day now. At first they'd just been checking up. But then they'd started opening up to each other, talking about the nightmares, the residual anxieties, the physical therapy after her knee replacement—courtesy of the City of New York—and her lingering fear of being alone, Jake's visions of the people he'd killed and sudden breakdowns when Rinnah's ghost intruded on his sleep. They also talked about his work with the police, her job hunt, movies they'd seen, Gene's slow recovery, Eve's school. She'd been there for some of what he called "the hero stuff"—his commendation, the photo op with the mayor, a TV appearance on *Good Day New York*. He and Eve had visited Cherry Hill once; this weekend was her first chance to see their new apartment, a few blocks from the haunted one where Rinnah had died.

She considered the finger marks he'd left on Rinnah's grave. "Um, Rinnah... this is a little strange for me. Jake's told me so much about you, I feel like I know you, at least a little. I wish we could've really met." She looked up to check on Jake and Eve. "Your husband's a good man, a very brave man, like my husband was. He protected me. He saved my life. You should be proud of him." Miriam swallowed, thought about her next words. "If you don't mind, I'd like to keep an eye on him for you. He needs someone to talk to. I do, too. I'm not trying to take him away, but... well, I don't want to lose him, either." She fumbled a pebble from her pocket, rolled it in her fingers. "That's all." She placed the rock on the marker, then stood and waited for Jake.

He and Eve eventually paced back to the grave, subdued but back in control. He pulled off his right glove, dug a small white stone from his coat pocket, and carefully laid it atop the marker next to Miriam's. "Bunny? You have your rock?"

"Uh-huh." Eve pulled from her jeans pocket a pyramidal gray stone the size of a quarter. "What's this for?"

"It's a present for Mommy. It means, 'I remember.' Put it next to ours."

While Eve skipped ahead, Jake and Miriam drifted back toward the car, each tied up in their own thoughts. In all of their talking, she and Jake had skirted the big question—what was next for them? Would they remain just good friends, or would there be more? She'd meant what she'd said to Rinnah, about watching out for Jake. What did he want? She thought she knew, but still wasn't quite sure.

When they reached her car, Jake touched her elbow. "Thanks."

She nodded. "Are you okay?"

He shrugged. His eyes were red but almost dry again. "You going back tonight?"

"I don't know. It's not like I have to go to work tomorrow. I think Philadelphia lawyers have a blacklist."

"Figures. Well, I'm still good on the couch if you want to stay."

Jake turned his head toward the distant whistling of JFK. "There's a lot of law firms up here, you know."

"I know. This city kind of scares me, though. It's so big."

Jake looked into her eyes. He tried to smile. "It's... not so bad if you know someone."

"Maybe I should give it a chance, then."

"Maybe you should."

Perhaps it was time to leave New Jersey behind, start fresh. She reached out to touch his forearm through his sleeve. "Hungry?"

"Starving."

Miriam smiled. "Where can we get some lunch around here?"

"I got a couple ideas." Now he managed a real smile, his first for a long time. It looked good on him. "Come on, let's eat."

About the Author

Lance Charnes has been an Air Force intelligence officer, information technology manager, computer-game artist, set designer, *Jeopardy!* contestant, and now an emergency management specialist. He's had training in architectural rendering, terrorist incident response and maritime archaeology, but not all at the same time. Lance's Facebook author page features spies, archaeology and art crime.

Like What You Read?

Share your experience with friends! **Leave a review** on your favorite online bookselling site, on a readers' social network (such as Goodreads), or just on your blog or Facebook wall. Someone told you about this book; please pass on the favor.

Want to Know More?

There are lots of ways to keep tabs on Lance and his novels, and to find additional material, reading group guides, deleted scenes and more.

Official Website
http://www.wombatgroup.com
Sign up for Lance's newsletter! Be the first to find out about new books, special deals, and the occasional giveaway.

Facebook Author Page
http://www.facebook.com/Lance.Charnes.Author

Goodreads
http://www.goodreads.com/lcharnes

Twitter
http://www.twitter.com/lcharnes

More Thrills from Lance Charnes

Luis Ojeda owes his life to the Pacifico Norte cartel. Literally. Now it's time to pay.

Luis led escaping American Muslims out of the U.S. during the ten years following a 2019 terrorist attack on Chicago. He retired after nearly being killed by a border guard. But now in 2032, the Nortes give Luis a choice: pay back the fortune they spent saving his life, or take on a special job.

The job: Nora Khaled – FBI agent, wife, mother of two, and Muslim. She claims her husband will be exiled to one of the nation's remote prison camps to rot with over 400,000 other Muslim Americans. Faced with her family's destruction, she's forced to turn to Luis – the kind of man she's spent her career bringing to justice.

But when the FBI publicly accuses Nora of terrorism, Luis learns Nora's real motive for heading south: she has proof that the nation's recent history is based on a lie – a lie that reaches to the government's highest levels.

Torn between self-preservation and the last shreds of his idealism, Luis guides Nora and her family toward refuge in civil war-wracked Mexico. The FBI, a dogged ICE agent, killer drones, bandits, and the fearsome Zeta cartel all plan to stop him. Success might free Luis from the Nortes… but failure means disappearing into a black-site prison, or a gruesome death for them all.

> "*South* is a compelling futuristic thriller, as convincing a cautionary novel as Margaret Atwood's The Handmaid's Tale was in its day..." – *CriminalElement.com*

> "*South* is a riveting work of action/adventure suspense that is a real page-turner… Lance Charnes demonstrates a truly impressive knack for deftly creating a complex and thoroughly engaging story…" – *Midwest Book Review*

International Crime – The DeWitt Agency Files

Allyson DeWitt is the president of The DeWitt Agency. Its headquarters is a brass plate outside a discreet Luxembourgeois lawyer's office door. Its corporate treasury is in Vanuatu. Its directors are strangely untraceable. Its only other full-time employee is Olivia, who's able to arrange for the damnedest things when an Agency associate needs help.

Matt Friedrich is the Agency's newest employee. He has a certain useful set of skills that he learned while working in a crooked L.A. art gallery, and other knowledge that he gained while hanging out in federal prison with Wall Street types who had bad lawyers. He's out on supervised release and working for $10 an hour at Starbucks to pay off over half a million in debts.

When one of Allyson's clients has a need to fill that involves art in whatever form, Matt gets the project. He can knock down a chunk of his debt with each payoff... so long as he stays alive and out of jail. Sometimes he's paired with Carson, a disgraced Toronto cop who has her own debts, problems, and useful skills. Together they make a pretty good team – if they don't kill each other first.

Follow Matt as Allyson's projects drag him around the world, where he sees new places, meets new friends, avoids new enemies, and discovers (or pulls off) new scams. If he plays his cards right, he can make a lot of money, pay off his debts, and build a new life. All he has to do is not screw up... which is much harder than it sounds.

The DeWitt Agency Files series

Four years ago, what Matt Friedrich learned at work put him in prison. Yesterday, it earned him a job. Tomorrow, it may kill him.

Matt learned all the angles at his old Los Angeles gallery: how to sell stolen art, how to "enhance" a painting's history, how to help buyers hide their purchases from their spouses or the IRS. He made a load of money doing it – money he poured into the lawyer who worked a plea deal with the U.S. Attorney. Matt's out on parole and hopelessly in debt with no way out... until a shadowy woman from his past recruits him to find a cache of stolen art that could be worth millions.

Now Matt's in Milan, impersonating a rich collector looking for deals. He has twenty days to track down something that may not exist for a boss who knows a lot more than she's telling. He's saddled with a tough-talking partner who may be out to screw him and up against a shady gallerist whom Matt tried to send to prison. His parole officer doesn't know he's left the U.S. Worse yet, what Matt's looking for may belong to the Calabrian mafia.

Matt's always been good at being bad. If he's good enough now, he gets a big payday with the promise of more to come. But one slip in his cover, one wrong word from any of the sketchy characters surrounding him, could hand Matt a return trip to jail... or a long sleep in a shallow grave.

"The mystery has enough twists and turns – with the characters keeping plenty of secrets – to keep the reader guessing until the very end... A charming start to what promises to be an intriguing series." – *The BookLife Prize*

"*The Collection* is a breezy read in the way the very early Leslie Charteris' Saint novels were breezy: entertaining with an underlining of grit below the surface..." – *Criminal Element*

Dorotea DeVillardi is ninety-one years old, gorgeous, and worth a fortune. Matt Friedrich's going to steal her.

The Nazis seized Dorotea's portrait from her Viennese family, then the Soviets stole it from the Nazis. Now it's in the hands of a Russian oligarch. Dorotea's corporate-CEO grandson played by the legal rules to get her portrait back, but he struck out. He's hired the DeWitt Agency to get it for him – and he doesn't care how they do it.

Now Matt and his ex-cop partner Carson have to steal Dorotea's portrait from a museum in a way that nobody knows it's gone, and somehow launder its history so the client doesn't have to hide it forever. The client's saddled them with a babysitter: Dorotea's granddaughter Julie, who may have designs on Matt as well as the painting. As if this wasn't hard enough, it looks like someone else is gunning for the same museum – and he may know more about Matt and Carson's plans than he should.

Matt went to prison for the bad things he did at his L.A. art gallery. Now he has a chance to right an old wrong by doing a bad thing for the best of reasons. All he has to do is stay out of jail long enough to pull it off.

"Interlacing storylines give this series its charm...It's nice to have some modern *It Takes a Thief* escapism to slip away to in this world gone awry. Suffice it to say, I can't wait for The DeWitt Agency Files #3." – *Criminal Element*

"A brilliant heist story filled with fascinating art history reminiscent of Dan Brown or Steve Berry. Only better." – *Seeley James, author of the Sabel Security thriller series*

43099387R00234

Made in the USA
Middletown, DE
19 April 2019